OMEN UNRAVELED

OMEN UNRAVELED

THE SILVER CURSE BOOK 2

ANNA ORR

To my beloved husband, Jerry. I could go on about all of the blood, sweat, and tears it took to get here, but this dedication is supposed to be about you, not me. Thank you for embracing my weirdness.

PS: Any similarities between you and a certain lovable side character are purely coincidental. I definitely didn't write you into this series knowing you'll never read it . . .

Cover design by Edward Bettison

ISBN: 978-1-0394-5770-6

Published in 2024 by Podium Publishing
www.podiumaudio.com

OMEN
UNRAVELED

CHAPTER ONE

Rising Waters

Veins of yellow light pulsed through the trembling rock, weaving across the walls of the cramped storeroom and out into the passage beyond, like shimmering streams branching from a river. A deafening rumble tore through the cavern seconds before the ground jolted beneath Oralia's feet with such force it nearly threw her off balance. She steadied herself, straining to listen over the rampant beat of her own heart as another section of the pass gave way farther down. Rasp's magic was the only thing keeping the rest of the cavern intact. Judging from the way the yellow light pouring from his body flickered and waned, it would not hold for long.

Oralia's gaze dropped to Faris. The faun was crouched on the ground beside Rasp, doing whatever he could to ensure the witch's concentration did not slip. Oralia had stayed back with the pair to see that they were not left behind once the rest of the party had gotten through. It was a mistake she would not likely live to regret.

"We have waited long enough," Oralia said. "Anyone who is getting through the pass already has. We are leaving *now*."

"You hear that, Dingle? Time to go." Faris threaded his arm under Rasp's shoulder and attempted to heave him upright.

"Don't touch me!" Rasp snapped, shrugging Faris off as he kept his palms planted against the floor.

"We have to go," Faris insisted.

"You have to go! I can't." There was a waver in Rasp's already strained voice. It was a sad, undulating note that felt unrelated to the fact he was holding up a mountain pass through sheer willpower and determination alone. "It's slipping, Faris. I can't hold my magic and run. Go without me."

"But—"

"Go!"

Faris swiveled his head in Oralia's direction. His pale eyes were wide with terror and pleading for something he dared not ask aloud. "Then let someone else do the running for you. We're not leaving you."

How generous of Faris to volunteer her. As the faun did not appear to possess the ability to carry a full-grown human on his own, Oralia suspected the honor would be left to her.

To the seventh realm of chaos with it! With the mountain coming down over the top of them, she didn't have time to argue. Oralia crossed the buckling storeroom in two short strides and stooped to throw the stubborn witch over her shoulder, when a second shockwave tore through the chamber, jerking her footing out from under her and knocking her to the ground.

The storeroom rattled as a hairline crack split open across the ceiling, raining loose pebbles and debris over them. Oralia rolled onto all fours, coughing the dust from her lungs as her gaze followed the pulsing yellow light back to its source. Rasp was still bent against the ground, eyes screwed shut as he poured the last of his strength into keeping the storeroom from collapsing over them.

Oralia reached for him a second time. Rasp sensed her nearing presence and bared his teeth threateningly. "Don't even think about it. Try to move me and you'll sever my connection."

Her hands froze midair, inches from his glowing body as the weight of his statement settled in her gut.

"Take Faris and get the fuck out of here already!" Rasp snapped.

She knew well enough not to argue. Doing so would only waste time and Rasp's dwindling strength. Rolling to her feet, Oralia seized Faris by the elbow and dragged him toward the entrance. The faun fought, thrashing to escape her iron grip, but his physical prowess was pitiful compared to hers.

Faris's hooves scraped futilely against the stone floor, attempting to slow their progress. "We can't leave him!"

It was not often that Oralia agreed with Rasp over anything, but for once the boy was talking sense. She pulled Faris along as she broke into a trot. "I cannot move him, Faris. It will bring the entire cavern down if I try. At least do him the courtesy of making his sacrifice mean something."

She was almost to the doorway when a dark shape came bounding through. "No time for that, swabbies. Get back!" Rali's voice rang out over the growing clamor. "She's coming down!"

Rali was barely inside when the passage gave out behind her. The earth rumbled and roared as the ancient supports finally gave way to the pressure.

The insides of the mountain spilled forth, filling the empty passage as it caved in on itself. Oralia pulled Rali to her as the surrounding walls shook so fiercely, it rattled her clenched teeth together. There was no place to run, nowhere to hide. All Oralia could do was cover her head and wait for what she hoped would be a swift end.

Splintered slabs of rock fell from the ceiling and struck the ground in bursts of razor-edged shrapnel. The shaking continued, and yet, the worst of it never reached them. Confused, Oralia tentatively slit her eyes open. A dull yellow light lit the gloom, highlighting the falling debris and shifting clouds of dust. Oralia found herself crouched at the center of the storeroom with Rali huddled into her and Faris balled at their feet. Rasp had moved from his original position and now knelt beside the trio with his hands braced against the buckled floor, screaming.

Waves of dancing yellow light poured from his body and weaved into a tight, protective shell overhead, shielding them from the falling debris. The cavern chamber shook and shuddered in protest, but the magic, as stubborn as its wielder, held strong against the onslaught. Minutes passed before the mountain yielded. The quaking gradually died away until the only sound left was the hiss of falling dirt from the cracked ceiling above.

With an agonized whimper, Rasp's arms gave out beneath him and he collapsed against the upturned ground. The yellow light dimmed as the tendrils of magic dissipated into dark nothingness.

Oralia blinked as her eyes slowly adjusted to the gloom. Dust kicked up by the cave-in clouded the air. She pulled her tunic over her mouth and nose to keep from breathing in the worst of it. Unable to see more than a few inches from her face, Oralia groped the area around her for familiar bearings.

"Ow." A pained voice came from the floor. "Those are my fingers you're stepping on."

"Sorry, Faris." Oralia lifted her boot, grateful that at the very least that the faun was alive and hadn't succumbed to shock. "Can you reach Rasp? Is he alive?"

"I'm not so sure I'm alive, to be honest."

"You are speaking to me, Faris. I assure you, you are very much alive." For how long, however, remained to be seen. Oralia kept that particular thought to herself. She left him to check on Rasp as she turned her attention to the other member of the party currently huddled against her. "Ralizak?"

Rali's fingers were dug so deeply into Oralia's waist, she could already feel the muscle bruising. The dwarf didn't reply. She only held on tighter, trembling.

Oralia rested her hand lightly on Rali's head, unsure of what she could possibly say to comfort her. "Rali, are you hurt?"

"I can hear them," Rali whimpered with her face pressed into Oralia's flank. "They're screaming and I can't reach them."

Apart from the occasional shift of rock, Oralia heard nothing. "Who?"

"Udduc and Henog. I can't hear Fraegar anymore. She's gone quiet."

Oh gods. The collapse, of course. She should have known to send Rali ahead with the others.

Oralia drew her arm over Rali, feeling the dwarf's shoulders rise and fall with each shaky sob. Rali wasn't in the present time. She was stuck years in the past, thousands of miles away, reliving the worst moment of her life. Red Rock, the famous breach—how Quartz Ralizak first earned her notoriety—was not the glorious tale of heroism the realm painted it to be.

"I am here with you, Rali. You are not alone." Slowly, Oralia eased them to the floor.

"They're all going quiet. Henog's crying but I can't hear Udduc anymore." Rali pressed closer, sobbing, "Make it stop, make it stop, make it stop!"

Rali was working as lead tunneler on the southwest shaft when the enemy broke through. She brought the shaft down to stop the invasion, with her and her crew still inside. Rali spent three days underground, listening to her friends die before the rescue team dug her out. She was the only survivor.

Red Rock was the reason Ralizak refused to go back underground, why she awoke in the night screaming and turned to the bottle to get through the next day. It was the reason the other dwarfs hated her. The realm pretended the reassignment was a promotion, that serving under Oralia was some form of reward for Rali's bravery. In truth, it was the only option she had. No one else, especially not the dwarfs, would tolerate a glorified killer.

Oralia gently pried one of Rali's hands from her side and searched her fingers. "Where is your ring?"

Tears streamed from the lieutenant's tightly closed eyes, leaving streaks on her dirt-caked face. "I'm sorry. I'm so sorry, Henog. I had to."

Faris's voice cut through the dark. "She traded it for a handle of booze."

Oralia whipped her head at him, tusks bared. Her ferocity, alas, was wasted upon the faun, who could see no further than his own nose in the gloom. "That was her grounding ring," Oralia said, fighting to keep her voice calm for Rali's sake. "She uses it for flashbacks."

"Well nobody told me!"

She and the young Belfast were going to have a serious talk about dealing contraband to an addict when they were through. Provided they got through. Oralia removed the pendant from her neck and cupped it in Rali's trembling hands. "Open your eyes, Rali. What do you see?"

The dwarf's reply came between fast, panicked gasps for air. "A necklace."

"Take a slow breath with me. Hold it." They repeated the exercise three times, until Rali's breathing was less irregular. Oralia kept her voice calm yet firm, as if this was a perfectly ordinary exercise and they weren't trapped gods knew how far underground without any hope for rescue. "Describe the necklace to me."

"White gold chain," Rali sniffled, brushing the tears from her eyes with the back of her hand. The effort left dark streaks across her dirtied face. "Amorphous mineraloid gemstone."

Even in the midst of a flashback, a dwarf was still a dwarf. Oralia prompted her further. "And to a layman you would call it . . . ?"

"A blue fire opal." Rali turned the stone over in her dirt-smudged fingers. Her breathing was still unnaturally quick, but coming down. "It's a good size, but the color's clouded. Usually you see a lot more blue and some green or violet. This one looks like it's turning gray."

That wasn't right. The stone was normally a bright sapphire blue. Oralia tilted her head to get a better view of the pendant held in Rali's hands as a new series of panicked thoughts rampaged through her head. Something was amiss. Was Whisper's magic thinner here? The Iron Ridge was named for its rich, mineral-laden rock. Was it possible that the iron was interfering with the power stored in the stone?

There was another possibility as well. One she did not dare consider given their already bleak circumstances.

"I—I know this necklace. My friend . . . she wears it." Rali placed the opal into her palm and tapped it. When the stone stayed the same dreary color, she repeated the action several times more to no avail. "I feel like something should be happening. Like someone should be shouting at me. Is this thing broken?"

Oralia breathed a quiet sigh of relief. Rali was starting to come out of it. The severity of the attacks had lessened over the years. In the beginning, they'd lasted hours. Now, with time and practice, Rali had found ways to bring herself around much faster. The issue of Whisper's fading magic, however, was an entirely different matter. Something that would have to wait until later, after their rescue.

The rescue that Oralia was not so certain was coming.

"Uh, Protector?"

Oralia lifted her eyes to look at Faris. With Rali recovering, she could at last focus her attention on the other downed member of the group. "Please tell me Rasp is alive."

"He's in and out of it, but he's still breathing at least. That's not the problem." Faris posed his concerns as a question, as if hoping it was simply a figment of his imagination and not reality. "Does the floor feel wetter to you?"

Oralia felt the ground and winced, realizing that the buckled stone indeed felt wetter than it had mere moments before. The first rule of a cave-in was to stay where you were and await help. This, alas, did not apply to flooding. Through the shifting gloom, she could see the doorway was still intact. She only hoped the stairwell to the surface was in similar condition.

Oralia jumped upright, her knees screaming, and pulled Rali with her. "Up, Ralizak. We need to get to higher ground."

"Hm?" Rali gazed up at Oralia with a far-off look in her eyes, as if caught in a dream.

Oralia's stomach dropped another rung lower. Although she was aware of her surroundings, Rali was still not processing the danger around her. Such inattentiveness did not bode well for an emergency evacuation.

The dwarf lifted one boot curiously. "Why are my feet wet?"

"There is a slight flooding issue." There was no sense in making Rali panic. Faris was already doing enough of that for the both of them. "We need to go up the stairs and find the exit. Can you walk, Ralizak?"

"I'd rather sit."

"No." Oralia yanked her upright again. "Do not do that."

"Oralia," Faris said, his voice wavering, "I can't get Rasp to come around."

Perhaps it was a small blessing that the faun possessed horrible night vision, otherwise he would have seen the absolute despair etched across her face. *Calm*, Oralia told herself. *You have to stay calm. At least on the outside, else everything will go to shit.*

Not that everything wasn't already shit. What was worse than shit? Oh yes, drowning. Definitely drowning.

"I will carry Rasp," Oralia said. "We are going to move single file. I hold your hand, Faris, and you hold Rali's. Do not let her sit."

"Or we won't get her up again. And dammit, I can't carry two bodies!" was the part Oralia kindly left unsaid. Gods, she wished she had some rope.

She'd sent her pack on up with the rest of the supplies. A lot of good it did her now.

Faris stood and shook the water from his left hoof. "Is this a good time to point out the water's getting higher? We're at ankle height here."

"I noticed. Thank you for your astute observation." Oralia heaved Rasp's limp body by the arm and ducked low, slinging him over her shoulder. She reached for Faris and he squeezed her fingers so tightly she nearly snapped her tusks at him.

No time for that, go!

Water splashed underfoot as she sprinted through the narrow doorway and out the other side, pulling the others with her. The mouth of the cavern was completely caved in. She could hear the fast trickle of water worming its way through the rubble. This, she realized, was the source of the flooding.

The foot of the stairwell was only partially obstructed. Oralia wedged herself between the fallen slabs of ceiling and led the others through. She bounded up the stone steps, grimacing as the muscles in her legs and lower back competed for the title of most abused. Faris kept pace. So much so, he kept accidentally nicking her in the back of her calves with his sharp hooves.

Trouble up ahead caused Oralia to skid to a stop. Faris didn't react nearly as quickly and slammed into her. With his face firmly pressed into her lower back, Faris emitted a muffled "Maybe warn me we're stopping next time?"

She caught the wall and steadied herself, grateful the faun hadn't thrown her completely off balance. Oralia crouched lower and examined the break in the stairway. Even equipped with night vision, she was unable to see past a few yards of darkness, leaving her with the grizzly conclusion that the bottom was a very, very long way down. "Some of the steps have fallen. The other side appears stable, but I cannot cross with all of you. You are going to have to jump, Faris."

"What?"

The sound of churning water below told her there wasn't time to consider an alternative course. "You cross first and I will throw the others to you."

"I don't like this plan."

"Would you rather I throw you?" As much as Oralia tried to make it sound like a genuine offer, it still came across as mildly threatening.

"Not really."

"You are a faun, Faris. You were born to do this. Take three steps back for a running start. Lift your feet high so you do not trip. Full speed. When I say jump, you jump."

Reluctantly, Faris let go of Rali and did as instructed. "I hate you, I hate you, I hate you!" He screamed as he broke into a run.

"Jump!"

The faun's hooves scraped against the rock one last time before he sprang high over her head and sailed across the gap. He struck the other side and slipped, coming to a grinding halt inches from the drop-off. To Oralia's relief, the staircase held beneath him.

With Faris safely on the other side, Oralia turned her attention to the next person to brave the crossing. "Ralizak, can you hear me?"

The dwarf lifted her head, still oblivious to the danger. "Huh?"

Oralia draped Rasp's limp form over the stairs and checked to make sure her feet were firmly planted with her knees bent. She'd left most of the heavy lifting to Curly since his enlistment. Gods, she hoped she didn't break her back attempting this. "I am going to throw you across the pit to Faris, alright? If you get to the other side and start to slip, try to grab onto something. Preferably not Faris."

"Wait, what?" Rali snapped from her daze too late.

Oralia heaved with all her might and threw the dwarf, perhaps too force-fully, into the awaiting arms of Faris. Faris didn't catch Rali so much as he cushioned her landing. They were both shouting incoherently at her by the time the pair had recovered enough to stand, but Oralia wasn't listening. She repositioned Rasp securely over both shoulders before skirting several steps back in preparation for her own running start.

Her voice reverberated off the surrounding rock. "I would advise getting out of the way."

"Oh shit, she's coming in hot!" Rali scrambled up the stairs, hauling Faris by the elbow with her.

Move, Oralia commanded, and her leaden legs obeyed. She pounded up the stone steps and pushed off, keeping her sights focused on her landing and not the dark, gaping chasm below. She came down on the other side with both feet planted below her, knees bent to absorb the impact. The staircase shuddered and groaned beneath her. Already, she could feel the fractured stone beginning to slide.

Oralia forced one throbbing foot in front of the other. "Go!"

CHAPTER TWO

Memory Ever After

Fresh out of the mind fog, Rali grabbed Faris by the hand and led the procession up the stairs at a bounding sprint. "Come on, bucko! Lift those knees or she's going to plow right over us."

Behind her, Oralia heard a rumbling crack as the lower portion of the stone steps broke away and fell into the rift below, bouncing against the sides until the clatter was swallowed by distance altogether. She didn't dare look back to see how much of the staircase was still intact. She kept her gaze straight forward and her concentration focused on lifting her feet high enough not to catch on the uneven steps as she hurtled upward. Rasp hung slack over her shoulder. His body was unnaturally hot, causing her to perspire more than the situation already demanded. Still, she would take a little sweat over kicking and screaming, and was relieved she did not have to make the death-defying escape with Rasp's running commentary in her ear.

With the exception of a few dislodged boulders and the occasional shattered step, the rest of the climb went quickly. It wasn't until they turned the corner, where the doorway to the surface should have been, that death mocked them.

"Shit," Rali panted as she slowed to a halt.

"What?" Faris whipped his shaggy head from side to side, attempting, unsuccessfully, to see what they were seeing. His nostrils flared in and out as he tested the air. "What is it? I can smell fresh air. We're close, aren't we?"

"Well, technically, yes," the dwarf said grimly. "Unfortunately, the doorway is about thirty feet above us. This part of the stairwell must have collapsed during the cave-in."

"The lower stairs gave out just after we crossed." Oralia sucked in lungfuls of dusty cavern air between ragged sentences. Her legs felt like thick jelly and the inside of her chest burned. Speaking only exacerbated the hot, smoldering sensation within her lungs, but she persisted in the unlikely event Rali or Faris panicked and tried to turn back. "We cannot go back the way we came."

"Take a breather, boss. I'll see if I can find us an alternate way out."

Unable to muster a verbal reply, Oralia merely nodded, watching as her lieutenant carefully picked her way across what remained of the damaged stairwell. Tapped for the foreseeable future, Oralia supposed it was as good of a time as any to lose the dead weight hanging from her shoulders. She bent and arranged Rasp onto the steps, ensuring any sudden movement wouldn't send him careening back down them. Finished, she stood straight and flexed her aching shoulder blades until they popped.

Her gaze moved out across the gloomy destruction. The steps ended a few feet from where they stood, butting up against a mound of broken rubble, which stretched for ten yards or so before hitting a solid rock wall. Above them, a small length of the original staircase was still intact. It jutted out over the destruction like a tantalizing prize, just out of reach. Even if by some miracle they could access it, the exit beyond was blocked. Oralia could see small shafts of sunlight filtering in between the cracks from the other side.

Rali returned from her search a short while later, delivering the grim report Oralia had already reached on her own. "We can't go up and we can't go back down. Looks like we're stuck here for the meantime."

Faris stood beside Oralia, wringing his hands. He had his head tilted upward at the ceiling. "The exit's just on the other side, isn't it?"

"What used to be the exit is just up yonder, yes," Rali replied grimly. "Doesn't appear to have held during all the shaking, though. Even if by some miracle we were able to get up there, we'd have to tunnel our way out."

"My point is, everyone who did get through is just on the other side, right? Wouldn't the logical thing be to call for help? Let them handle the tunneling part, maybe?" Before either Rali or Oralia could explain why this plan was less than ideal, Faris cupped his hands to his mouth and shouted, "Help! Can anybody h—"

Rali lunged forward and clamped her hands securely over his mouth, muffling the scream. "Not a good idea, bucko," she hissed. She tilted her head, scanning the surrounding walls for any signs of disturbance. The crumbling passage, fortunately, appeared unaffected by Faris's distress call. "No loud noises from here on out. The vibrations of your voice are liable to trigger a second collapse. Let's avoid making Rali a dwarf pancake, alright?"

"But . . ." Faris pushed her hands away as his mind raced to come up with a viable solution. "But . . . but how do we . . ."

Oralia examined the nearest wall as she stretched her legs. The sides of the stairwell were smooth and shot straight up. Her sharp eyes scoured the stone siding for crags or footholds and found none. Even with the proper equipment, the walls would be near impossible to climb. "We wait and hope someone on the other side of the doorway is working to dig us out."

"Oh my gods." Faris sank down, pulling his knees to his chest. "We're dead. That's what you're saying, isn't it?"

"Chin up, Faris. We've got an ace up our sleeve, remember?" Rali's feet clomped lightly against the stone, echoing from one end of the cavern to the next as she moved to Rasp's side. With some effort, the dwarf sat him against the wall and jabbed her forefinger into his chest. "Hey, you, bucko. Nap time's over. How's about you rebuild the steps or try lifting us to that platform up yonder, yeah?"

Rasp's eyes flickered open briefly before his entire body slumped back onto the steps like the world's most dramatic puddle.

Rali was having none of it. With stubborn determination, she seized him by the wrists and clapped his palms together. "Come on, spark. Don't just sit there. Do something."

Curling his upper lip, Rasp awarded her a faceful of spit for her efforts.

"Leave him be, Rali." Oralia grimaced as she kneaded the stiffness from her arms. The likelihood of someone coming to their rescue before the water reached them was slim. Still, it wouldn't hurt to be a little more limber for whatever obstacle awaited them next. She severely hoped it didn't involve swimming. "He has overextended himself. Upset him now and he is liable to bring the rest of the cavern down on top of us."

Magic was a give and take. Every time a witch accessed their power, there was a letdown period immediately after. The severity of the crash depended on the amount of energy expended. In Rasp's case, it was a small wonder the boy was still breathing. Not only had he held the pass aloft, but his magic had extended beyond the cave, lifting the boulders along the cliffside into the air as well. It was an amateur mistake, exerting one's power beyond the area of focus, but that didn't make it any less impressive. Oralia had seen more practiced witches drop dead from less.

It was a shame his survival instincts were still holding strong. A sudden death from overexertion would have been a mercy compared to drowning.

From below, accentuated by the cavernous quiet, the steady sounds of gushing water crept ever closer.

Dread hung thick in the air like a swarming cloud of gnats over a swamp. Without light, Oralia was forced to rely on the encroaching waterline to gauge time's passing. It had been too long, she feared, watching the dark, lapping line as it climbed steadily higher. Help would not be coming. They would have heard something by now if it were.

The others seemed to sense their impending doom as well. They sat arranged along the upper steps, waiting in silence for the flood to claim them.

Rasp stirred below. Having spent most of their stay drifting in and out of consciousness, he was finally coming around on his own. The man's lips curled into a grimace as he explored the area around him with his fingertips. ". . . Where am I?"

Faris's head was buried in his arms. He didn't bother to lift it, offering only a grim reply. "Dead."

"If that were true, you and I would not be in the same place."

"The cave-in collapsed the exit. We are trapped in what used to be the upper stairwell," Oralia answered, knowing he wasn't going to get much of an answer from the other two.

"Oh, you're here." Rasp frowned. "I guess this *is* the bad place."

Oralia resisted the urge to kick him. "I just carried your carcass up half a mile of stairs."

"And I held up a cave-in long enough for your people to get through. I think that makes us even."

"A cave-in you triggered!" She froze, realizing she'd said that louder than she'd meant to. Her voice echoed along the cavernous stone walls, growing fainter in the distance before the eerie quiet returned. Oralia released her bated breath, relieved that the splintered ceiling had remained in place above them.

Faris lifted his head from his trembling arms, mouth flared into a snarl as he glared in Rasp's general direction. "Speaking of which, I'm still mad at you for that, by the way. I knew you were planning to ditch us, but would it have killed you to have pulled me aside for an actual goodbye? And not just an 'I hate you, Faris, name the dog after me?' Shameful!"

"What?" Oralia's brow furrowed at his heated admission

Faris, realizing this was perhaps the wrong thing to say in her presence, shrank back down, stammering, "I mean, how dare you. I had no idea whatsoever. Bad Rasp."

Of course Faris knew Rasp had been planning to attempt something stupid.

Not the time, Oralia decided. If she was going to die in the next hour, she wanted to do it with the least amount of bickering possible. Preferably no bickering at all. Was it too much to ask to simply drown in peace?

"Look, I didn't know about the swamplanders, alright? That wasn't part of the plan. I tried to hold the pass long enough for all of you to get through." Rasp seemed to be directing this at Faris and possibly Rali, as Oralia doubted he truly cared what happened to her. "I didn't mean for you to get stuck down here with me."

Faris narrowed his eyes, which naturally had no effect as Rasp had no way of knowing. "You knew you were going to get stuck, didn't you? You were practically begging us to leave you."

"It was either you or me. I chose you. I can't help it that you three were stupid enough to try and pull me out afterward!"

"Stupid?" Rali balled her hand into a tight fist and drew back for maximum impact. "Oh, that's it. I'm going to cave your face in, you ungrateful shit!"

"Ralizak, no." Oralia reached out and caught her lieutenant by the wrist. She suspected it was an empty threat, but the extent of Rali's recklessness had a funny way of surprising her. The last thing they needed was for the boy to accidentally finish what he had started. "Hitting him solves nothing."

Rali wrenched free, massaging her hand as she grumbled, "That's not true. It would definitely make me feel better. Who knows, maybe the little pervert would enjoy it as much as I would."

A glare from Oralia was all that was necessary to convince her lieutenant to drop the subject. Rali crossed her stubby arms with a *harrumph*. "Can't fault me for trying to make it a little more exciting, you know. This isn't how I pictured it."

"Pictured what?"

"Dying," Rali said. "I always imagined it would happen in battle. Blades swinging, blood gushing, the stuff they sing songs about. One moment I'm on my feet, and the next, everything's growing fuzzy as my friends gather around me, telling me it's not my time yet. Suddenly, the warm and fuzzies set in and, as the world goes dark for the final time, the last words I hear are how great I am. How no one will ever be the same without me."

Her graphic imagery must have stirred something back to life in Faris. He shook his head at her, both ears flicking in irritation. "Who in their right mind pictures their death? Much less like *that*?"

Wordlessly, Rasp raised his hand.

"It's not that unheard of, bucko. Some of us just prefer to go out with flair is all." Rali's gaze traveled the damaged stairwell as she spoke, eliciting a silent shudder that worked down her shoulders. "Not in some quiet, dark tomb underground where no one can hear you."

Faris glared up at the ceiling with a sigh. "Unfortunately, some of us *can* still hear you."

Dread must have been getting to her, because Rali refused to give in to the silence. Whether the others appreciated it or not, she remained bent on lifting the mood. That, or at least keeping the peace and quiet at bay for as long as possible. "You know, being that it's the end and all and we're already on the subject, I suppose it's appropriate to ask if any of you believe in memory ever after?"

No one responded. It was of no matter to Rali, who carried on without missing a beat anyway. "Memory ever after is the orc equivalent of the afterlife, in case you didn't know. Except, instead of going into some magical beyond, you exist in a part of your own past. Essentially, right before you die, you think of your happiest memory. After you've breathed your last breath, you wake up there and you get to relive it forever."

"Does sound kind of nice," Faris admitted.

"I thought so, too. Do you believe in it, Oralia?"

"No," Oralia answered before realizing perhaps the truth wasn't necessary.

"Alright, well we're going to pretend for however long we've got left that you all do. Think of your best memory. I want details, people. Paint me a picture so I feel like I'm there."

There was a general grumble of reluctance, but no one refused outright.

Rali demonstrated by volunteering her version of the afterlife first. "I want to go back to the time Mika Strongborn and I ran away and spent three days together, alone, in a cottage in the woods. It was pouring buckets outside, but inside the fire was roaring and we fell asleep each night listening to the rain." Rali closed her eyes, smiling. "Mika was my first love. He was young and dumb, but sweet. And his beard was so soft. I could bury my face in it forever."

Faris gawked at her, surprise written across his dirt-speckled face. "I did not realize you were such a romantic."

"Granted, that was before his mother kicked down the door and sent him off to work in his uncle's mine halfway across the territory," Rali said absentmindedly. "What about you, Faris? Where are you going to spend eternity? Fleecing someone? Rolling in a giant pile of money?"

"End of the week supper. The one right before the realm came knocking at our door. Back when things were simpler." By the warm look on his face, he was there now, reliving it. "The end of the workweek was the cook's days off and Mum always insisted we make one of the evening meals together as a family. Father and I had been fighting something fierce that week. But the rule was, no matter how bad the quarreling got, our differences were put aside until afterward.

"I got up early that day to help mum make the bread. Dinglehead was being as helpful as usual, so we stuck him on the opposite counter out of the way. Father came in a little later to start the stew. Mum kept distracting him with questions and every time he'd go back to chopping, half of his diced vegetables would be gone. He got through an entire bunch of carrots before Father realized Rasp was tossing handfuls out the window whenever his back was turned. Mum laughed so hard she cried. Which got me going too, and before long everyone was on the floor 'cause no one could stand. Father eventually composed himself and made a big show of banishing them to the parlor. It was only me and him after that. We spent the rest of the afternoon just us two in the kitchen. I can't for the life of me remember what we talked about, but for the first time in weeks, it didn't feel like there was an invisible weight hanging over us."

"Your best memory is making dinner?" Rasp's muffled voice came from below. The Stoneclaw was stretched on his back across one of the lower steps, with his arms tucked behind his head, staring upward at nothing. "Not even the best part, where you get to eat it. No, you want to live forever *making* it."

"Some of us had a decent homelife, alright? And yes, I enjoyed spending time with my family," Faris snapped. "Now tell me yours so I can judge it just as harshly."

"Don't have to. I'm going to come back as a warbear and haunt the shit out of my brothers."

"Oh come on, Rasp," Rali said. "You've got to have a happy memory in there somewhere. How do you want to spend eternity? Are you raiding a village? Doing despicable things to your penis?"

"Fine, what are the rules? Do I die knowing everything I know now? Or only what I knew in that moment?"

"You return as you were in the memory," Rali answered. "No knowledge of the future or the fact that you're dead."

The boy was quiet for some time, as though actually considering his answer. At last, in a far-off voice, Rasp replied, "Holding my son for the first time."

CHAPTER THREE

Winter Solstice Eve

Faris's ears twitched as he sat up with a start. "You have a child?"

Rasp, lost in the memory, spoke with an unusually peaceful expression on his scarred face. "He's perfect. Tiny, with a little tuft of hair and the biggest brown eyes you ever saw. It's the middle of the night and we're in the rocking chair by the window, watching the snow fall. His mother's asleep in the bed across from us. She had a difficult birth, but she's okay now. My brothers have all tiptoed in to say hello. Even Father comes by and tells me I finally did something right. For the next few weeks, life is the best it's ever been."

"You have a child?" Faris said again, this time louder. "He's probably up at the Stoneclaw village right now and you're just content to lie here and die? Why aren't you fighting to get back to him?"

"I visit with him often enough."

"How?"

"Mother brings him with the rest of the flock sometimes."

". . . Oh." Faris sank back down as the stiffness in his shoulders wilted. "Oh muck, I'm sorry."

"He didn't make it to spring. 'Failure to thrive' is what the healer called it. His mother couldn't stand to look at me afterward. Said it was the curse that did it. She picked up and moved right after." Rasp's normally grating voice was as soft as a whisper. "He doesn't remember who I am anymore. That's the problem with coming back as a raven when you die so young. Having not been in your body long enough, the human part won't stick. Probably for the best, really. One less person to disappoint."

"Oh my gods, will you stop?" Rali said, wiping her grubby hands hastily under her eyes. "Even your happiest memory is horribly depressing."

Rasp only shrugged. "You're the one who asked."

"Oralia, I know you don't believe in happily ever after, but you're going to have to give me something," Rali said, still sniffling. "Make it up for all I care, but gods dammit, don't mention any dead babies!"

Oralia was seated on the topmost step above Rali and Faris. Below, through the creeping dark and scattered rubble, she could see the black water was already halfway up the stairway and rising. Rather than draw attention to it, she reached under her chainmail and withdrew a tarnished flask from the hidden pocket sewn into her tunic. Ignoring the teary-eyed look of indignation from Rali, Oralia took a swig, wincing as the bite of peppercorn brandy worked through her sinuses. She slumped lower, sighing, "Sharing an eternity in a warm bed with Sascha sounds lovely about now."

"Wait, hold up!" Rasp sat upright, pointing vaguely in her direction. "First of all, I smell booze. Give it here. We're sharing. Secondly, you and the mountain are a thing? How is that possible? He's so nice! And you, well you're, ah . . . you."

"Sascha tied you to a log," Faris reminded him.

"Exactly! Had I shanked anyone else with a potato peeler, they would've kicked my skull in."

Rali intercepted the flask on its way to Rasp and took a swig. With her pale face scrunched into a bitter grimace, she snarled, "Gods, this stuff is the worst! This is why you drink it, isn't it? 'Cause you know even I'm not desperate enough to swipe it from you!" She took another fast slug with the same results as the first. Finished forcing the swallow down, she narrowed her red-rimmed eyes at Oralia accusingly. "Now, let's circle back to that important bit. Are you finally admitting feelings for the fuckmate?"

"I said lovely, not in love."

Rali fended off Rasp's grabbing hands only to have her prize snatched from her clutches by Faris. Wiping the last of the moisture from her grime-coated cheeks, the dwarf turned back to Oralia and crossed her arms challengingly. "I say this as your friend who loves you. You've got to get over this personal hang-up of yours. Denying the existence of feelings does not make a person strong. True strength is acknowledging your emotions in spite of the possibility of rejection."

"Gods, Rali," Faris said. "That's actually kind of insightful."

"Well, obviously. I'm not just all drunk and disorderly. I have layers too, you know!"

Oralia tilted her head back and gazed up at the darkness that seemed to stretch endlessly overhead. It was not so much for the view as it was to avoid Rali's withering glare. "Still not in love."

"And you're sticking with that?"

"Until the day I die." Which, judging from the level of the steadily rising water, was not too far off.

"Fine, then your answer doesn't count. You don't get to settle for some mediocre afterlife just because it's quiet. Try again. I want to hear your best memory. And you better make it a good one, or I'll just annoy you until I can't speak anymore on account of the water filling my lungs."

"You said I could make it u—"

Rali clapped her hands to drown out Oralia's protests. "I don't care what I said before! I changed my mind. No made-up fantasies about warm beds and blankets and people you may or may not love. I want the real deal."

Alas, from her lieutenant's fixed expression, Oralia knew it would be pointless to argue. If this was their last moment together, she may as well make it worthwhile. "Winter Solstice Eve." She plucked the flask from Rasp and threw her head back, finishing it in a single slug. It burned like liquid fire the whole way down. "That first year Curly joined the four."

They'd gotten snowed-in in a remote village north of Sunstorn and had to spend the holiday trapped in a tiny cottage together. Curly, missing his family, was in the pits and could barely be roused out of bed. With nowhere to go, Oralia announced they would take the day off to celebrate.

Ellisar slipped out through one of the top windows of the cottage and came back lugging the top of a spruce down the stairs with her. The decorations were left to Oralia, who regrettably could not recall the steps required to fold the paper lanterns. In the end, most of them resembled crumpled snot tissues more closely than lanterns, but it was the thought that counted, surely. While Oralia cursed over bits of paper, Snag and Rali scrounged the pantry for whatever ingredients they could throw together for a last-minute feast. If she remembered correctly, the menu included such oddities as reconstituted pork strips with a side of apricot preserve, mushroom-and-pickle turnovers, and a host of intricate hors d'oeuvres that looked far prettier than they tasted.

A cough from Rali drew Oralia back to the present, reminding her that she was supposed to be saying all of this out loud. "The food was barely edible and my attempt to decorate was even worse. The only thing I remember being good was the apple cider. I was three cups in before I realized Snaglebrag spiked it." After that, their quiet, awkward evening took a turn for the unexpected. Snag, to this day, declared his innocence, insisting it was one of the others who tampered with his cider. No one, naturally, ever came forward to claim responsibility.

"Gods, that was the only time any of us ever saw you absolutely smashed. You were so fun," Rali laughed. "I convinced you to sing sea shanties with me, remember? You knew the harmony, but not the words, so we just made them up as we went."

"And then you had us falling out of our chairs with your impressions." Oralia had particularly enjoyed Rali's impression of her, which involved a very thorough run-through of Oralia's many facial expressions. The more memorable titles included 'someone shut this idiot up,' 'I don't care who designed the bodice, I'm not wearing it,' and Oralia's personal favorite, 'for the love of gods, Ellisar, stop stealing the silverware.'

"Oh, and the presents! El gave us all presents. Do you remember that?"

"Yes. All items she had stolen from us over the years, returned and wrapped with sprigs of holly." Oralia covered her face, surprised by her unexpected smile. "I got the key to my apartment. What did you get?"

"All the pages she'd ripped out of my books over the years. They were all the naughty bits, too. Story's not the same without all those, you know." Rali rolled her head back, groaning, "Oh my gods, the pipe. She gave Snag his pipe back and he played that wretched thing all night."

Oralia peeked at Rali through her fingers. The smile on the dwarf's rosy face was real, just like her own. "How did we get him to stop? I do not recall."

"You plucked him from his chair, determined to teach him to dance. When Snag eventually escaped into the rafters, Ellisar cut in and the two of you waltzed for hours. I got Curly to twirl with me a few times, but we kept tripping over each other's feet and ended up on the floor. Somehow it turned into a wrestling match."

Outside the cottage was dark, but inside, by the light of the hearth, spirits were high. The smell of cinnamon and fresh spruce permeated the air. Oralia remembered the sounds of laughter, lots of slurred cursing, and filthy jokes, accentuated by the soft squeal of Snag's pipe in the background. For the first time in many years, home felt a little closer. They'd done it for Curly. But now, sitting in the dark of a collapsed cavern with water steadily rising below, Oralia realized she'd needed it just as much as he had. There had never been time for family. And the game she played was too dangerous for friends. Her faithful four had somehow filled the void. She would be lucky to spend eternity with them.

"Is it too late to change my answer?" Rali said, lifting her head hopefully. "I mean, if you don't mind sharing it with me?"

"You are going to give up Mika Strongborn for us?"

"Eh, it was young love. Before I realized a full beard and shiny helm didn't make up for a milquetoast personality."

"Happy to have you, as always."

"Gods almighty!" Rasp gagged. "Faris, is the water high enough for me to jump in yet? I'd rather get it over with than to listen to this heartfelt crap."

"Will you shut up?" Faris said.

"I forget, you're a sap for this cutesy family stuff, aren't you?"

"No, I mean actually shut up. I think I hear something coming from the other side." Faris jumped upright and signaled for the others to remain quiet. His next words seemed directed at Rali. "Permission to yell now? Or are you still concerned about spending the afterlife as a pancake?"

"Just try not to bring the whole mountain down."

Faris cupped his hands to his mouth and shouted, "Here! We're in here!"

Oralia craned her head and listened. The digging grew louder until a significant clump of dirt and rubble fell away, allowing a shaft of light through. There was some muttered cursing as part of the hole caved back in. After a few more minutes of furious digging, the opening was large enough for a lithe figure to wriggle through. Dropping to his belly, their rescuer slid out onto the remaining strip of platform and peeked his head tentatively over the side.

CHAPTER FOUR

The Trouble with Being a Goody

Oralia could barely make out the pair of yellow, glistening eyes staring back at her. The warmth of hope swelled in her chest and spread to her face like the first sip of aged absinthe. "Snaglebrag, I could kiss you."

"Got hit on the head with a rock, did you?" His gravelly voice reverberated down from above. "What about the rest of you? Anyone else injured?"

"Rasp doesn't have his land legs, but the rest of us are shipshape," Rali replied, glancing hurriedly over her shoulder at the dark water creeping up the broken stairwell paces below them. The sight caused her to shift her weight from one foot to the other. "We do have a bit of a flooding problem, so speed is of the essence here."

"Oh, so now would be a good time to discuss my salary then?" Snag, cackling to himself, scuttled back through the opening before anyone could yell at him. He reemerged moments later, hauling a length of cord coiled over one slender shoulder. The goblin kicked it over the side of the platform and, after wrapping his hands in protective cloth, slid down the rope and landed gently on top of the rubble pile.

Snag wasted no time with heartfelt reunions. He scrambled down the rest of the way, already looping the end of the rope in anticipation for a makeshift harness. "The dwarfs did what they could to reinforce the passage, but it's not going to last. We've got a team of muscle topside ready to pull. I'll be sending you one at a time, lightest to heaviest to minimize the strain. Maggot, you're up first."

Rasp remained stretched across the lower steps, unbothered by the water lapping mere inches from his body. "Pass."

"We do not have time for one of your tantrums." Oralia was already halfway to Rasp, limping on stiff legs. She lifted him from the ground, allowing

Snag to secure the harness over his body. Rasp didn't protest. He hung in the air limp like a rag doll.

"He's not even calling me *pet*," Snag remarked, tightening the sheet bend knot until it was to his liking. "Did you finally break him, Protector?"

"He overextended his magic."

"Ah, did it to himself then. That's the trouble with being a goody, maggot. It's a slippery slope. It starts with one or two, and the next thing you know, you're running yourself ragged trying to save everyone." Snag yanked the rope twice and yelled upward, "Ready!"

Seconds later, Rasp was gradually lifted to the remnant of the broken staircase. A pair of hands reached over and pulled him the rest of the way. Snag made the mistake of looking at Oralia's face and flinched. "What?"

"You just dug through a landslide to save us. That makes you a goody too, does it not?"

Snag was already trotting toward Faris, waving his clawed hand in the air above his head dismissively. "What? Can't hear you, sorry."

The others ascended with less fuss. First Faris, followed by Rali. When the rope dropped back down the fourth time, water had started to pool around Oralia's ankles. She offered the lifeline to Snag. "If that platform is coming down, it will be under my weight. You go first."

He gazed back at her, mildly offended. "I was planning to jump onto your shoulders and shout 'yeehaw,' actually."

"I will cut the line if you try. Go." In case this was the last chance she would get to say it, she added, "And thank you."

With a swift salute—which may or may not have been sarcastic—the goblin scurried above her, utilizing both hands and feet to grip the braided rope. Oralia wished a more majestic animal came to mind, but all she could envision in that moment was a wharf rat, racing up the dock line onto the awaiting ship.

Oralia waited until Snag was over the lip, and then waited some more for good measure before hooking her boot into the bottom loop and hoisting herself higher. The rope creaked under her weight, stretched taut. She lifted, slowly, as the rope began to twist, disorientating her view of the stairwell. She closed her eyes. Not for fear of falling, but to fight the sudden dizziness.

Of all the things she hated, being airborne ranked third on the list. Right below tight spaces and attending public events in full ceremonial dress. The situation would have been more tolerable had Oralia been in control of the rope or, at the very least, could have braced her legs against the sides of the cavern to alleviate some of the horrible twisting. Alas, neither was possible and she was forced to cling uselessly to the rope, entirely reliant on whoever was heaving the other end.

Above her, the voices in the distance grew louder until she could almost make out individual words. Oralia eased one eye open and was blinded by the flood of light cascading from the makeshift tunnel. The diameter of the shaft had grown significantly larger since its initial creation, enough so that she might actually fit through it before the ledge came down underneath her.

She was nearing the platform now. Through the dust mote–laden light, she could see someone's feet dangling nonchalantly over the side. "Settle the issue for me, Protector," Ellisar said, kicking her heels. "Killing is a full point while maiming is only half. Curly nicked someone's arm off moments before I dropped them with an arrow. I say the point is mine. He says we split it."

"She keeps shooting my kills to bolster her numbers!" Curly's strained voice roared from the tunnel beyond Ellisar.

"I was protecting you," Ellisar corrected, looking down her slender nose at Oralia unconcerned. "You're the official referee on these things. Verdict?"

"Why are you here?"

"That's a very philosophical question, Protector. You could say it is a result of poor choices, bad timing, and general apathy. For many centuries I drifted aimlessly on the plane of life, bringing mayhem and destruction wherever—"

"Why are you on the ledge, Ellisar? The one, specifically, that is about to fall!"

"They needed someone of the featherweight variety to make sure the rope didn't catch. Strangely, none of the other elves volunteered to dangle precariously over the giant rock pit. Bunch of cream puffs."

They traded expressions for a single, unnerving second, Ellisar's purposely blank stare for Oralia's toothy grimace. "So," the elf ventured, unaffected by Oralia's visible outrage, "about that verdict?"

"I will say whatever you want me to say, just move so I can pull myself over!"

The start of a smile threatened to cross Ellisar's expressionless lips. Clicking her heels, the elf leapt upright and disappeared out of sight, calling, "Suck it, Baby Face! The point's mine. Oh, and in case they're her last words, Mumsy says she loves you very much and please don't drop the rope."

Hand over fist, Oralia pulled herself across the lip of the broken staircase. Lying flat against the rock to distribute her weight, she clambered across it with a speed not normally associated with orcs. The platform trembled precariously beneath her. Oralia glanced up through a clump of sweat-soaked hair, realizing the damn elf was pressed against the wall, watching her. "What are you still doing here?"

"Someone has to put an arrow through you if you fall. You want to die on the first shot, don't you?"

"Go!"

Obediently, Ellisar ducked through the mouth of the tunnel. Knowing there wasn't time to second-guess, Oralia leapt to her feet and sprinted after her. The slab steps splintered from the wall with a thunderous *crack*, teetered for a heartbeat, and then dropped. With her arms stretched out before her, Oralia dove into the opening, clawing her blunt fingertips into the dirt and rubble for traction. She fought her way upward. Debris spilled from the sides in choking sheets of dust and rock as the makeshift walls gave way, collapsing around her.

Ahead of her, Ellisar sprang clear as a pair of large hands darted into the crumbling shaft. Strong fingers caught Oralia around the wrist and lifted her clear of the rubble. For a moment, blinded by the unrelenting sunlight, with her head swimming, Oralia could not see. A pair of burly arms drew her into a crushing embrace. The familiar scents of garlic and cloves engulfed her as she buried her face into Sascha's heaving chest. From the rapid drum of his heartbeat, she dared not raise her head to look at his expression—fearful of what she might find.

"Sascha?" she managed weakly.

"Hm?" his deep voice rumbled in his chest next to her ear.

"Put my feet on the ground, please."

"Not until you look at me."

Easing her eyes open, Oralia peered up at him reluctantly. Past his razor tusks and the deep worry lines of his mouth, she saw an amalgamation of her worst fears: terror, anger, relief, and a fat helping of unrequited love. Guilt gnawed at her stomach and she suddenly found herself yearning to jump back into the collapsed stairwell. It was bad enough Rali had already given her grief over the matter. Was it necessary to face this head-on right now? After everything she'd already been through?

Sascha must have seen the terror on her face and misinterpreted it for something more heartfelt. His sable eyes softened around the edges. Unlike his grip, which remained as strong and steadfast as iron. "I will put you down only if you promise not to run back into another collapsing mountain. Or go after another dragon. Or—"

"The moment we reach Sunstorn, I am handing in my resignation and leaving to travel to the parts of this world I have not seen. And I want to do it with you." The words that sprang from her mouth caught even her by surprise. Dear gods, near-death trauma was making her sentimental.

Whatever he was expecting, it wasn't that. His mouth hung slack as a warm, violet flush washed over his nose and cheeks.

Oh gods, no. She knew that look. It was hope. *No, no, no, take it back! Quickly, before he gets ideas!*

Sascha's voice was dangerously soft. "You mean that?"

No. Absolutely not. Maybe. A little. Regardless of what she felt, now was not the time to be making hasty, life-altering decisions. Unfortunately, her mouth seemed to be disconnected from her panicked thoughts. ". . . I think so."

"Are you drunk?"

"Possibly."

"Then I have one condition."

Oralia dared not say anything lest her tongue betray the fear rampaging on the inside. She only stared, wide-eyed and helpless, wishing the uncomfortable vise in her chest would lessen its grip on her lungs.

He threw his head back, simultaneously pulling her tighter. "No more climbing fucking mountains!"

"Agreed," Oralia gasped, finding it impossible to breathe around his crushing embrace. This wasn't real, was it? Could it be a dream? A demented form of the afterlife, perhaps? She wasn't capable of these feelings. She'd squashed them down so many times before, they'd eventually learned to stay buried. What was wrong with her? This was worse than sentimental. She was teetering dangerously on the cusp of senile. This wasn't her. Oralia Dawnsight did not make proclamations of love, especially not in front of this many people.

Beaming like a lovestruck fool, Sascha set her feet back onto solid ground. The moment Oralia took a grateful step backward, a second hulking shape took up his place. Despite Curly's smaller size, his grip was twice as strong. He buried his face against her shoulder, muttering, "I'm still mad at you."

Her response came without thinking. "And I am still discharging you from military service."

Tilting her head, Oralia could make out the three distinct shapes lingering on the edge of her peripheral vision. Slowly, like the steady trickle of sap from the spile of a maple tree, clarity crept over her. There was a reason she'd never mourned the loss of a family. As she stood there, held awkwardly in the arms of a child not her own, surrounded by the strangest company she had ever had the pleasure of keeping, she realized she had more than enough family already.

Her startled gaze darted back to Sascha and something inside her stirred. No, not enough. Surely there was room for one more.

With her breath caught in her throat, Oralia hugged Curly back, the intensity of which elicited an unsuspecting flinch from him. "But I was wrong about your place in court," she whispered. "Find what makes you happy. And I expect you to tell me all about it every year at the winter solstice."

He pulled away just far enough for their eyes to meet, his black to her gray. A line of confusion wrinkled across his broad forehead.

"We may not always be a team," Oralia said, "but we are forever a family. I will never abandon you. I promise."

CHAPTER FIVE

The Endless Dark

He's gone?"

Captain Monk knelt in front of Daana, taking her trembling hand in his own. His voice was a gentle murmur. "I am so sorry, my dear. Will fought bravely. I tried—"

"Willem," she snapped.

"Pardon?"

"His name was Willem." Was? Daana sank back onto the blanketed ground as her mind refused to come to terms with this revelation. Her chest felt simultaneously heavy and hollow. Hot tears sprang from her eyes unbidden. "He hated it when people called him Will. It made him sound more approachable."

"I tried to reach him in time, but that bloody dragon, it . . ." Captain Monk's voice trailed as he averted his gaze. "I failed you, Emissary Lazuli. I swore I would bring back your man, and I didn't."

She said nothing, because there was nothing to say. Willem was gone. Not gone, dead. Dead, dead, dead . . .

Musty darkness stretched around her, held at bay by the single, low-burning oil lamp flickering in the far corner. From the other side of Captain Monk's canvas pavilion, Daana could hear the muffled bustle of the weary soldiers pitching their own tents. She couldn't remember why she was here. Only that, after a brief stint in the chaotic infirmary, a pair of soldiers had brought her to the captain. She winced, trying to recall his initial words. Something . . . something about making room for the injured? Gods, she was too exhausted to remember. And the sorrow weighing her down made it easy to no longer care.

A droning sound, closer than the ruckus emitting from outside, made Daana vaguely aware that the captain was speaking again. "I want you to know that I saw him through to the end. Willem said that it was a joy to serve alongside you. He asked that I look after you. That I keep you safe and ensure your eventual return to Sunstorn."

In the rolling darkness that spread across her mind, a faint light flickered against the gloom. *A joy to serve? Joy?*

Willem didn't serve her. They were partners. That didn't sound like something he would say. In fact, none of it did. Willem would have cursed the Division of Divination for sending him out into the wilderness to die. He would have used his final breath to tell Captain Monk exactly what he thought of him. Which, knowing Willem, didn't amount to much. Maybe he had. Maybe the captain was fabricating Willem's last words to bring her comfort.

Wordlessly, Daana rose on leaden legs and started for the entryway. The rectangular canvas door was framed by a crack of sunlight spilling in from the outside. She managed two shaky steps before stumbling. A choking sob caught in her throat as she crumpled to the ground. *No, no, no. Not now. Anywhere but here. Keep it together, Daana. Just for a few seconds longer.*

Captain Monk's arm wrapped around her waist and lifted her from the floor. His normally spiced scent smelled like burnt ash. It singed the inside of Daana's nose and she turned, trying to free herself of his grasp. His grip tightened. "My lady, I really must insist you stay. You're in shock. It would be irresponsible of me to leave you unattended in a state like this."

Daana stared longingly at the blurred doorway until it faded from her vision entirely. Captain Monk's muffled voice melded into a continuous drone around her. A fog moved in and hung heavy in her mind. The few times she attempted to lift above it, the hurt in her chest weighed her back down. She slipped below the surface of consciousness. The crushing ache dulled to numbness as the fog gave way to the endless dark. Daana sank lower, lower, lower.

Above her, faint in the distance, a voice whispered to her, "No."

Daana shrouded herself deeper in the sinking dark. It was safe here. The pain couldn't reach her. She could exist without feeling, endlessly, until she forgot why she was here in the first place.

The voice called again, "I don't want this."

Her eyes snapped open, annoyed. There was that dim light again. Like a sky lantern, bobbing above the still surface of her deep, dark pool of nothingness. Why wouldn't it go away? Couldn't it just leave her alone? She was safe. Nothing could touch her. Not the pain, not the guilt, not the crushing realization that the closest person she had to a friend was dead and—

"I said no!"

The voice, Daana realized, was her own. Her consciousness shot for the surface, clawing at the dark as she fought to reach the dimming light. *I'm almost there,* she told herself. *Hold on just a little longer. I'm coming. Wait for me. Wait for me!*

She surfaced in a gasping fit of rage and tears. She was seated on the blanketed floor and no matter how she pulled, she couldn't seem to get away. Daana glared at her hands. And then to the person grasping them. A growl rattled deep in her chest. "Release me."

Her words startled Captain Monk into loosening his grip. Daana yanked free and stood, catching her balance as her stiff legs threatened to give out beneath her. She willed one protesting foot in front of the other as she staggered for the doorway.

Captain Monk leapt after her. His hand brushed against the curve of her back as he fell into step at her side. "Daana, don't leave. It's alright."

"Don't touch me!"

"My dear, you are not well. I was only trying to comfort—"

A bright blue wave of energy pulsed from her palm and slammed into him, sending the captain reeling across the ground. Daana's startled gaze jumped from him to her hand. Had that come from her? She hadn't uttered a spell. And even if she had, the spell shouldn't have worked. She'd spent the last of her magic on the wyrm.

Daana's stare shifted to her armlets, realizing the stones on each band were glowing a brilliant sapphire blue. Her heart lurched. *Willem?*

"You're going to regret that."

Captain Monk was back on his feet and marching toward her with his upper lip curled. The tent flap ripped back without warning and a channel of sunlight filled the space, temporarily blinding them. A scruffy shape barreled inside, shouldering its way between Daana and Monk with an ungentle shove. "Emissary Lazuli, there you are!" Briony sent Captain Monk sprawling with a forceful slam of her hip. "Thank you for finding her, Captain. I'll take it from here."

Captain Monk regained his balance, stammering, "That won't be necessary. Her ladyship is staying here tonight. I have taken her under my protection."

Briony's fierce eyes were rimmed in white as she stared at him with varying degrees of murder written across her flared lips. "Curly," she said calmly, refusing to break eye contact with Captain Monk. "Will you assist Daana to the infirmary for me, please? I need to have a private word with the captain."

Daana looked behind her. Curly stood at the entrance, his broad shoulders taking up most of the doorway. She could hear his tusks grinding against his upper teeth. "Are you sure there's not some other way I could help?" he said, venturing a daring step inside. "I have a few suggestions."

Blinking away hot tears, Daana rushed to the safety of his arms. She buried her wet face in his shirt, ignoring the overpowering stench of sweat and musk that brought fresh tears to her eyes. There was a time she might have recoiled from the smell. But in that moment, with his arms wrapped securely around her heaving shoulders, feeling safe for the first time since the falls, she vowed to hold on for as long as she could.

Curly's voice emitted above her head in the form of a low growl. "Did he hurt you?"

The surrounding light was suddenly brighter than before. Lifting her head, Daana realized Curly had moved her outside. They were standing paces from the doorway, the canvas flap billowing gently in the breeze behind them. "No," she managed, weakly. "He didn't get the chance."

"Good. I'll only break his arms then." Curly caught her stare and allowed a teasing smile to chase some of the fire from his dark eyes. "Don't look at me like that. You know I'll let you help. You can snap the left and I'll shatter the right."

"I don't want to be anywhere near here."

With a final snap of his tusks, Curly locked his jaw and led her away. From the way he walked, with his shoulders held high and stiff, Daana suspected it was taking most of his self-control to leave without causing a scene. Behind them, beyond the fluttering doorway, Briony's voice raised to a muffled roar.

"Wait!" Daana ground her heels into the dirt, realizing the direction he was taking her. "Not the infirmary, please. Not there." Captain Monk had already removed her from its premises once. There was no sense in returning to the first place he would go looking for her. Her heart raced as panic gripped at the base of her throat. No one had bothered to stop him the first time. Would his soldiers simply stand back and let him have his way if he found her again?

"I'm taking you to Oralia," Curly said. "There's less paperwork if she's the one doing the arm breaking."

"No! I mean, yes, of course. Just not yet. I need to lie down somewhere first, get my head straight." While she felt safe with Curly, said trust did not extend to the protector. Daana knew she would have to summon the courage eventually. Just not right now. Not with her thoughts spinning so violently she could barely string together cohesive sentences. "I can't go back to my tent, though. I—I don't even know where it is. Oh gods." She covered her face as heat rushed to her ear tips. "I think I dropped it during the ambush. My pack, too. It had all of my things in it and—"

Oh no.

Daana stopped and searched her pockets with sudden urgency. After a few seconds of desperate patting, she realized they were empty. The little green spellbook she kept tucked in the front pocket of her trousers was gone. A fresh swell of crippling pain crashed over her. *Oh gods. No, no, no, no . . .*

"My tent's empty. I'm supposed to share it with Snag, but he's got his hands full with the whole medic thing. I don't think I'll be seeing head nor tail of him for a while." Curly took her hand and squeezed. "I could sit and keep watch outside if you wanted me to."

Daana bit her lip to hold back the sobs and nodded. She didn't recall the way there, or how people stared, or slipping inside after him. She only remembered curling inside the warm blankets and feeling the comfort of having someone nearby.

Not just someone, some silly little voice in her head murmured as she drifted into a deep slumber. *A friend.*

CHAPTER SIX

Alone and Without Allies

Daana wasn't sure how many hours had slipped past. The only thing she knew for certain was that when she awoke, poking her groggy head from the nest of soft furs, there was a pair of wide brown eyes staring back at her.

"Oh good, you're awake!" Rali beamed. The dwarf was stretched on her belly opposite Daana, with her head propped up in her hands. Bare, stubby feet kicked leisurely in the air behind her. Rali's freshly scrubbed skin had a tinge of pink and she smelled vaguely of pine and cedarwood. Her raven hair was free of its usual braid and piled on top of her head in a messy bun.

". . . Curly?" Daana stammered. She was torn between turning her head to look for him and keeping her wide-eyed gaze fixed on the eerily chipper Lieutenant Ralizak.

"Rali!" Curly's voice came from beyond Daana's line of sight. "I told you not to disturb her."

Rali's feet continued to kick the air behind her innocently. "Sorry, bucko. It can't be helped. Most people just find me naturally disturbing."

"Oh my gods," Curly groaned.

Guided by his deep voice, Daana was able to glimpse him from the corner of her eye without having to twist her head. Curly was seated cross-legged near the door with an unusual shade of pink blossoming across his face. "I didn't mean for you to wake up to that, honest." He reached up and scratched the back of his neck, explaining, "She barged in here after you fell asleep. I can't get her to leave."

"Leave? I have nowhere to go! Not after being cruelly evicted from my own bed." Rali flipped over, throwing a small hand over her brow dramatically. "Picture it for me in your minds, me hearties. There I was, clean and freshly scrubbed, eager for some quality time with my bedroll when that blasted Lieutenant Holt marched in. And oh boy, was she all business, set on giving Ellisar a rigorous dressing-down right then and there. Just like that, with barely a word, I was thrown out into the cold like old bathwater! Heartbroken and yearning for camaraderie, I sought my dearest friends."

"Uh . . ." was all Daana managed.

Curly hid his reddening face behind his hands, sighing, "Whenever I don't understand what she's yammering on about, I just assume it's sexual."

"It's not that I mind Ellisar having an active romantic life," Rali carried on, either oblivious or uncaring to their growing discomfort. "But she could go do it somewhere else! Or at least offer to share. Not that I find anything particularly bewitching about Lieutenant Holt, but it's the sentiment that counts."

Daana was learning far more about the private lives of the traveling party than she'd ever imagined. Or desired to know, for that matter.

Lieutenant Ralizak seemed to have misinterpreted Daana's silence as an invitation to expand on the unwanted details. "I swear, that Holt has a working vocabulary of ten words tops. Yes, sir. No, sir. Three bags full, sir. Get her in a room alone with Ellisar and suddenly the woman can speak in full sentences! Between the wanton squeals of ecstasy, of course."

"I hate you so much right now," Curly groaned, burying his face further into his large hands.

Rali's bushy eyebrows pressed together. "What?"

"Can you go be you somewhere else?"

"What are you talking about? We have company. I'm being sociable!"

"She's not your company, she's mi—"

Light flooded around them as the canvas doorway ripped back without warning, cutting Rali and Curly's bickering short. Daana whipped her head around, already gathering her feet beneath her as the drum of her heartbeat blared within her ears. Relief washed over her the moment she realized the stocky figure standing inside the doorway was not Captain Monk nor his men come to collect her. Briony, all five terrifying feet of her, stood with her arms crossed and looking like she wanted to trample something. From the fading pink light backlighting Briony's squat figure, it looked to be nearly dusk outside.

"Miss Blackwater," Rali called cheerfully. "Snuck out from the infirmary again, did you? You must have exceptionally deep pockets. Snag doesn't take on other people's work lightly. I should know. I can't get him to do shit."

With an irritated flick of her ears, Briony's stare shifted from Curly to Rali. "You two, out."

Curly responded with a threatening snap of his tusks. "It's my tent."

Briony met his challenge and raised it. Her hoof stomped with such force the tent poles rattled in protest. "Out!"

"You know what, maybe we should go check on Faris. Make sure he and Rasp are getting settled." Rali promptly stood, still barefoot, and tugged Curly behind her, murmuring under her breath, "It's never wise to argue with a lass when she's got that wild look in her eyes, bucko."

Briony waited until the pair was out of sight before snapping the door shut and stomping over to Daana. The faun dropped to the ground, her arms still wrapped protectively over her chest. She glared up at the rustling roof overhead as she spoke. "For the record, this does not make us friends. I stepped in earlier because it was the right thing to do, not because I like you."

A ripple of anger banished the heartfelt thank-you Daana had started to string together. Her cheeks burned hot to the touch as all sense of gratitude vanished from her mind. "I'm sorry, did I do something to earn this hostility? I don't even know you, and you act like I went and pissed in your morning oats."

"You rip children from their families in the name of the Division of Divination. That warrants plenty of hostility, if you ask me."

Ah, yes. *That.* The heat dissipated from her face as the familiar twinge of guilt clawed to the back of Daana's throat and settled there. Testing the young for magical abilities wasn't the difficult part. It was what came afterward that took its toll. So many children taken from their families. By her own hand, no less. It had been easier in the beginning, when Daana still believed she was helping them. Now . . . now she didn't know what to believe. Each passing day her actions grew heavier, weighing her down like iron chains.

"Why do you think I'm here?" Daana dropped her face into her hands with a groan. "I'm trying to get away from a career as a seeker. This was supposed to be my opportunity to prove to the magic council that I could handle a change of assignment."

"I've given that some thought, actually—why you're here. But before I jump into my theories, I'm obligated to ask what ugliness happened between you and the captain." When Daana made no reply, Briony continued, grudgingly, "I only know what I saw, and what I saw wasn't much. If he overstepped in any way, simply name the body part and I will bring it to you."

"You shouldn't jest like that." Daana peered at Briony through the gaps in her fingers. "Say what you will, but that man is dangerous."

Briony's deep amber eyes narrowed. "Who's jesting?"

Dear gods, she meant it. Daana had grown accustomed to the travel party's crass nature, but Briony was dead serious. Daana's hands fell limply into her lap as she lowered her voice to a harsh whisper. "Are you mad? Do you know what would happen to you if anyone overheard you saying such things?"

"Spare me the concern, seeker, and answer the question. Do I need to cut that man a few fingers short or not? I can aim lower if you'd like." Briony arched one brown-and-tan eyebrow higher than the other, as though Daana's uncharacteristic silence was a challenge. She raised her hand until it hovered above her head. "I'll tell you what. I'll start my hand yea high and move it downward. When I've reached the appendage that is to your satisfaction, simply say so."

"No! That's not necessary, really."

"Are you sure? Final offer."

"Yes," Daana said quickly, before Briony could go into greater detail about the proposed mutilation. "And I appreciate what you did, truly. Thank you. But Willem taught me how to crush a windpipe if I ever needed to. I wasn't expecting to have to use it on the captain. I just froze is all. It won't happen again."

Willem. With the mention of his name, the sinking feeling started all over again. *How am I supposed to do this without you?*

"Mhm, yeah about that. Are you ready for me to burst your bubble yet?" The faun didn't wait for Daana's answer, which was probably for the best given that she didn't have one. Briony laced her fingers together and flexed, causing her joints to crack. "Good. Now, keep in mind most of this is just a working theory, but here's what I have so far. This entire time you have been under the misconception that you were sent to capture the Palace Ghost when, in reality, it lured you here. Disguised as a member of the Division of Divination, of all things."

She had to be jesting this time, surely. Except, even after a span of uneasy silence, Briony didn't backtrack. She only stared back with a particularly patronizing expression. Daana shook her head in disbelief. "That's the most ludicrous thing I've ever heard."

"Alright, let's take this one baby step at a time. Willem had magic. You saw it, I saw it, not so sure if any of the other stragglers at the falls did, but they weren't exactly looking for it, so I can't fault them for that." Briony paused for breath, seemingly realizing just how far off course she'd veered. "Can we agree that Willem was, at the very least, a witch?"

For the sake of hearing where this theory was going, Daana reluctantly agreed. "Yes, fine."

"Why didn't you pick up on his magic sooner then? You're supposedly the division's best seeker, right? The ability to cloak one's power is not a simple task, mind you. Takes a lot of magic to pull off a spell like that. Either Willem was the world's luckiest witch, or he was something much more powerful."

Amid the churning doubt, a new thought flickered across Daana's overworked mind. She latched onto it, even if it only served to distract her from the realization that her partner may or may not have been the very being she had been hunting all along. She narrowed her eyes at Briony. "I don't know who you are. I don't know why you have such a vested interest in my affairs, but I suspect we are on opposite sides of the equation here, at least as far as the Division of Divination is concerned. Shouldn't I be the last person you want to have this conversation with? What do you even get out of this? You're obviously not talking to me because you like me. You've made that abundantly clear already."

"I find it helps to bounce my theories off of someone else. With my usual go-to preoccupied, you're the only other option I've got." The smile the faun awarded her was downright murderous. "Besides, now that you're alone and without allies, you don't really have a choice, do you?"

"I could scream."

"Did that work out so well with Captain Monk?"

Silence, Daana decided, was her best option. That, and a sweltering glare which, alas, seemed to have zero effect on the grinning faun.

"Any idea why the ghost might have lured you here?"

"It didn't lure me!"

"Right. You're still in denial. Moving on then." Briony reached inside her buckled vest and withdrew a tattered green book. She twiddled it between her fingers thoughtfully. "Was Willem the one who wrote this? There's some nasty shit in here. I couldn't decipher the origins, but if I had to guess, it predates the realm."

"Where did you get that?" A sudden burst of pain jabbed her in the heart like a hot poker. Daana lunged for the spellbook, but Briony merely lifted one hoof and planted it in the center of her chest. The faun wasn't even applying force. It was as if sheer will alone was enough to keep Daana's pitiful efforts at bay.

Briony flipped through the yellowed pages, shrugging. "Nicked it off of you after they brought you up from the falls. You know it's charmed, right?"

"What? No!" Daana sat back with a scowl. Her anger was not targeted at Briony, but her own increasingly obvious shortcomings. She was the magic-sensitive one, for crying out loud! She, of all people, was more than qualified to determine if something was spellbound. And yet, something about Briony's amused expression made her stomach twist into knots.

"Do you know what your problem is, seeker? You're so busy proving that you're better than everyone, you forget to use your natural-born talents." Briony leaned forward and whapped Daana on the forehead with the battered notebook. "Think! Use that big head of yours. The book went into the water with you, didn't it? Why hasn't the ink bled? Look at it. The pages aren't even wet."

The journal couldn't be charmed. It was just an ordinary notebook . . . filled with spells that no one at the division had ever seen. Except Willem. The same Willem who may not have been a seeker, or a librarian, or even an actual member of the order. Oh dear gods, how could she have missed something so obvious? Had it all been a ruse? A single act of friendship—that's all it had taken to blindside her.

"I don't know, okay?" Daana wiped under her eyes with the back of her sleeve, attempting to stop the trickle of tears that fell unsummoned. "Can I have it back, please? That's all I have left of him."

"You're forgetting the magic in your stones. That's his, too, I bet."

Daana's teary gaze drifted back to her armlets. The fur blanket had shifted, revealing the bands on her upper arms. She tugged the covers back over her. "I didn't drain him! At least I don't think I did. I—I didn't even touch him. I . . ."

Had she? Oh gods, no. Was his death her fault? Imposter or not, Willem had saved her. And she, in turn, had weakened him when he needed his magic most. Guilt slammed into her like a fist. Daana hunched over, curling her arms around her stomach as she struggled to breathe around the invisible noose that tightened over her throat.

"You're telling me you drained Willem without knowing it? No spell? Didn't even have to touch him?" Briony pursed her lips as she drummed the notebook against the flat of her palm. "Gods, your mother must be an incredible witch."

"No, no more," Daana cried, wincing as she covered her ears. "I don't care who you are. You've done enough. I don't want to hear anymore!"

"Really? That one's not even a secret. All magic-sensitive elves are born of a witch. They absorb their mother's power while in the womb. The stronger the witch, the stronger the child. That's basic magic fundamentals." Briony watched her with an entirely unreadable expression. "She never told you? I mean, given your family's close ties to the Division of Divination, I can understand why. I'm just surprised is all."

"She died when I was young." Daana's thoughts raced to place this piece into the rapidly shifting puzzle. Mother, a witch? Surely not. Uncle Geralt did not share much about her parents, but he definitely would have mentioned that! A bolt of pain surged behind her eyes. Daana dug her fingertips through her hair and pulled, attempting to alleviate the growing pressure. Too much. This was all too much to process. First Willem and now Mother, too? She was going to have an aneurysm if Briony said anything more.

With what might have been a look of genuine pity, Briony tossed the journal into Daana's lap and stood. "I've got to get back to the infirmary. If you're ever really serious about getting out of the seeker business, you know where to find me."

CHAPTER SEVEN

Get Out

The events following Rasp's rescue passed in a nauseous haze. His body felt like a bowl of noodles left to sit in broth too long. Everything was swollen, his legs had gone rubbery, and his poor mind was the functioning equivalent of congealed mush. There hadn't been time to stop and rest after the rescue, however. He remembered that much. The party was off again once the last evacuee was pulled from the crumbling shaft.

Rasp spent the ensuing march sprawled across a makeshift stretcher, drifting in and out of consciousness. He didn't know how long they traveled. It could have been hours, days, years even. Years didn't make sense, given the context, but who was he to judge? Sense had ceased to exist the moment he'd been pulled from the collapsed stairwell still breathing. By all rights, he should have been dead. Then again, maybe he was, and his poor body simply hadn't caught up to speed yet. Waking up dead. What a surprise that would be. Rasp chuckled to himself as the creeping darkness flooded the corners of his dazed mind once more, lulling him into yet another restless sleep.

When Rasp awoke again, still miserably alive, he found the stretcher beneath him had been replaced with a bedroll. Blankets, too. Lovely, thick, only slightly damp blankets. He nestled the coarse fabric against his face and burrowed deeper, intent on never getting up again. He was already drifting off, mouth agape and drooling, when that stupid, nagging voice in the back of his head had to go and spoil everything.

You can't be here.

Couldn't be here? Why the fuck not? He was tired and every muscle in his body thrummed with a deep ache. He'd earned a rest, hadn't he? Gods, he was so tired. If only the little voice in his head would shut up and leave him be.

The little voice, unfortunately, was his own. And it would not be silenced until it had spoken its piece. *Do you even remember what you're running from? You've kept it locked away, but there is a reason the darkness seeks you. It won't be long now. Soon you'll have no other choice but to confront what you did.*

A flash of blinding light flooded Rasp's vision. The roar of thunder followed. It built, growing louder, louder, louder, until every bone in his body vibrated with the same agonizing intensity as the deafening sound rattling between his ears.

Rasp jerked from his sleep with a scream. Waves of pain surged up his spine and shot straight to his head. He screwed his eyes shut, but it did nothing to stop the starbursts of color pulsing in time to the rapid drum of his heartbeat. A pitiful whine escaped his gritted teeth. It sounded like the fading whimper of an animal as the snare caught around its neck pulled too tight.

"Easy, Dinglehead." A warm hand curled around his wrist as another pressed flat against his chest. The pressure wasn't hard, only enough to encourage Rasp to ease back down into the nest of tangled blankets. "You're not going anywhere in this shape. Lie back down. Get some rest."

Rasp seized the hand pressed to his chest and held it. Slowly, his gelatinous mind came around, shifting from his frenzied dream state back into the real world. He could hear the wind batting the canvas shelter overhead and, beyond that, the creak and groan of evergreens as they swayed back and forth in a hypnotic rhythm. The inside of the dark tent smelled damp and slightly stale. There was another scent, too. It hung heavy in the air, irritating the back of his throat as it seeped the moisture from his eyes.

The top of Rasp's palate felt unusually dry. It was as if all the saliva from the inside of his mouth had been wicked away and replaced with cotton. It took several tries before he could get his swollen tongue working again. "I smell fire."

"Wildfire," Faris explained. "It's still burning on the other side of the range. Too far to reach us, luckily. But the wind is kicking the ash our way."

That was certainly going to make slipping away more complicated. Oh well. Rasp would deal with it in due course. For now, he had to focus on the more attainable objectives at hand. Like finding his way out of the damned tent, for starters. Every aching muscle in his back protested as he forced his body upright, attempting to gather his useless noodle legs beneath him.

Faris pushed him back down again, this time with more force. "You don't have to worry about the fire."

Rasp could just barely make out Faris's hazy shape against the gloom. The faun bent over him, working quickly to rearrange the blankets into a loose swaddle arrangement. It was only loose on account of Rasp's squirming, of course. Had he been still, Rasp was certain Faris would have had him trussed up tight like a fly in a web.

"The fire is nowhere near here," Faris assured Rasp, still attempting the most untender tuck-in imaginable. "You're safe. Settle down and go back to sleep."

Safe? *Safe?* What did the fucker know about safe? Nobody was safe. Not so long as he was on this cursed mountain.

"Afraid that won't be happening, Dingle." Rasp slapped Faris's persistent hands away. The blankets, a former sense of comfort, were now utterly unbearable. Heat flushed across his face, stinging his cheeks as a line of sweat gathered along his brow. Everything was suddenly too hot, too tight—the blankets, his clothes, the very skin stretched taut across his aching bones. Rasp threw the covers aside and was already working the constricting fabric of his shirt off over his head when Faris stopped him.

"What are you doing? Stop that!"

"I need to get out."

"Of your clothes? Dear gods, no. Keep those on."

The words left his mouth before Rasp could consider an approach that sounded more akin to reason and less like a rambling madman caught in the throes of cavern fever. "I can't be here, Faris. I wasn't supposed to get this far. I was going to slip away, or run, or . . ."

"Bring the pass down on yourself?" Faris volunteered, still sounding somewhat miffed by Rasp's last-ditch strategy.

Faris would be a little more forgiving if he actually understood what the alternative was. How could Rasp possibly get him to see reason? A mere "ending his life to spare the lives of others" was a gross oversimplification. It went deeper than that. Rasp wasn't just preventing a few deaths, he was trying to single-handedly stave off the very curse he'd been born to fulfill. But Faris saw the good in people. Even in the worst of people. People like him. People destined to bring death and destruction wherever they went.

Rasp ceased his struggle, allowing his shirt to be yanked back down over his torso as his shoulders slumped. "You wouldn't understand."

"You're right. I don't think I'll ever understand why you felt the need to try to bring a mountain down on top of yourself."

"Because I had to!"

An uncomfortable silence slowly inched past between them before Faris said, "I'm sorry you feel like you had to do that, Rasp."

The next pause was even more nauseating than the first. Faris broke the silence eventually, offering something that was probably meant to be comforting. "Look, if it's your brothers you're worried about, just know, there hasn't been a sign of a single Stoneclaw yet. The wildfire may be to thank for that. It's kept the mountain patrol so preoccupied, our arrival may have gone unnoticed. Like I said, you're safe. You don't need to do whatever this is."

"You think it's my brothers I'm worried about?" The uneasiness in his chest refused to settle. It twisted and roiled like a serpent, churning his insides so violently, Rasp didn't know whether to scream or vomit. "It found me, Faris. I was on this cursed mountain for two fucking minutes, and it was already trying to latch its claws into me."

"What did?"

"The darkness!" Rasp's heartbeat pounded harder at the mere mention of its name.

"Just now?"

"No, in the cave. Right after I brought the pass down."

"And did it succeed?" Faris asked. "Did it hook its claws into you and offer you a deal you couldn't refuse? Did you say yes to it, Rasp?

"Of course I didn't say yes! I told it to fuck off and leave me alone."

"Exactly! You did that. You turned it down all on your own. And you didn't stop there, did you? For the gods' sakes, you had one magic lesson and held up the entire pass until everyone—people you wouldn't normally give a shit about—got through. Not because you like them, but because it was the right thing to do."

How was he supposed to respond to that? Nothing Faris had said was mean. It was the exact opposite of mean, in fact. Possibly the nicest thing anyone had ever said to him. And yet, it made Rasp want to crawl out of his skin all the same.

Ugh. Being crushed beneath a collapsed mountain passage would have been so much easier than this. He didn't even know what *this* was. The radiating heat on his forehead slowly cooled as Rasp sat in a stupor, willing his sluggish mind to come up with something, anything, to combat whatever effect Faris's words were having on him.

Faris must have realized it was working, because the little cheat took advantage of Rasp's resulting silence to pile on even more. "You're not what you used to be. You spent your entire life afraid of what you are. And now, now you don't have to fear it. The darkness can't get to you. Your hatred gave it power over you, but you're different now. You've changed."

He wished Faris's soapbox spiel had the intended effect. That it would have helped settle the queasiness trying to borrow its way out of his stomach, but all it did was add a layer of shame to the panic roiling inside of him. Deep down, Rasp knew it wouldn't matter. The dark entity didn't care about change. So long as he was on the mountain, it would keep coming back, wearing him down, little by little, until it saw an opening to finish what he'd started.

Being reformed wasn't enough. Rasp could see that now. Despite all of his efforts to be a better person, to go against everything he'd been brought up to believe, in the end, the only thing he would be remembered for was the curse he was born to fulfill.

There was a strange somberness to Faris's voice, as if he too knew it was all for nothing. He kept trying, though. Which made his next words even more sad. "You're stronger than you give yourself credit for. I wish you could see that."

Rasp meant to only think it, but the thought slipped free of his dry tongue nonetheless. "It's not enough."

"Maybe you're right, Rasp. Maybe being strong isn't enough. But that's why you have people to help you, remember? You've got me, you've got Mother, you've got that magical little bastard we don't talk about." Faris raised his voice, sounding as though he was speaking over his shoulder. "Who, if they just happen to be listening, would have my undying appreciation if they suddenly appeared and, I don't know, helped settle their panicking pupil maybe?"

A moment of silence followed before Faris shook his head with a snort. "Damn, I was hoping that would work."

The last of the heat slowly dissipated from Rasp's face. Faris was right. There were people to help him, at least until his strength returned and he could manage on his own again. As the frantic drum of his heartbeat eased, so too did the crushing pressure building within his chest. The uneasy roiling was still there, but perhaps a little less violent than before.

While he could not allow himself to lose sight of the end goal, he could at least acknowledge that regaining his strength was equally important. For one more night, anyway. Rasp eased back down, wincing as fresh pain flared along his spine. "I'll stay the night," he said weakly. "Because you're scared of the dark and I know having me here helps. But in the morning, I'm leaving."

"If you say so," Faris agreed, pulling the blankets back over the top of him.

Rasp lay in the dark, listening to the wind whipping through the trees. It wasn't long before Faris's throaty snores filled the inside of the tent. Sleep pulled at Rasp, lulling his panicked mind into a false sense of security. But he didn't want to sleep. His dreams were becoming more vivid, playing out images he normally kept locked in the dark, unvisited corners of his mind.

One, in particular, was drawing closer with each sleep. He could feel it crawling about. Its metaphorical claws scraped along the walls of his memory, wearing down the mental block that had been put in place to keep it at bay. The barrier was thinning, however, and it would not be long before Rasp remembered exactly what it was he'd tried so hard to forget.

As his eyes closed for the final time that night, right before the visions of lancing light and roaring thunder overtook him, a new noise reached his ears. It started low at first, a light, soothing pitter-patter. As the hours trickled past, the sprinkle grew louder, drowning out the wailing wind and rhythmic sway of the treetops.

Rasp drifted steadily deeper, pleasantly unaware that outside the rain fell harder.

CHAPTER EIGHT

The Unrelenting Nightmare

The storm raged throughout the night. Rasp heard the pelting rain each time he screamed himself awake. He gave up on sleep after the third such incident. There didn't seem to be any point. He'd rather battle exhaustion than slip into the same relentless nightmare awaiting him each time he closed his eyes.

It was morning now. At least, he assumed it was. While the rain hadn't shown any signs of lessening, the outside world appeared marginally less dark. Rasp was curled on his side, wrapped in a thick layer of musty blankets, staring out at the shifting gray shadows beyond the open canvas doorway. Briony had tied the tent flap shut on her way in, but the wind had ripped it loose shortly after the faun's unannounced arrival. Rasp could hear the canvas flap whipping about in the rain like a battle-torn flag.

"Is nobody going to get that?" Faris said.

The faun's hooves produced a wet squelch against the waterlogged ground as he hurried past to secure the door. The worn floor tarp had held up the best it could against the onslaught, but the sheer amount of water pouring in had overwhelmed it sometime during the night. There was a steady *drip-drip-drip* as puddles now collected on the ground near the corners and by the door.

"Rasp?" Briony's melodic voice came from somewhere above him. The scent of her lilac and rosewater perfume wafted closer, offering a welcome reprieve from the salty musk clogging the air.

Rasp remained as he was, lying on his side, still staring aimlessly at the doorway, slightly miffed that his only source of entertainment had been successfully secured against the elements. He liked the erratic flappy sound. The occasional spray of brisk water against his face was quite refreshing as well.

After all, what better way to distract himself from the dark shadows haunting the inside of his head?

"Rasp?" Briony tried again.

He supposed other people were just as good of a distraction. Except for the part where they asked him questions and expected answers in return. He offered his reply in the form of a grunt. "Hm?"

"Faris says you were up all night, tossing and turning."

"And screaming" was the part Briony left out. Which was kind of sweet, really, considering the faun rarely minced her words. As this was still not a question, Rasp felt no obligation to answer. His remaining strength was better spent staving off the growing need for sleep.

"See?" Faris hissed beneath his breath. "He screamed all night long and now I can barely get a word out of him. He's not well, Briony. He needs sleep but he's fighting it. Can you give him something?"

Barely a word, his ass! Rasp had a particular word for Faris, a full set of them in fact. In the end, with his energy reserves dwindling dangerously on empty, he settled on a response that was substantially less taxing. "No."

"Yes," Faris replied. "You're supposed to be regaining your strength, remember? You can't do that if you drive yourself mad with sleep deprivation."

"Don't care. Not gonna do it."

Briony must have done something to get Faris to button his lip, because it was she who spoke up next, in a tone of voice that was both concerned and infuriating at the same damn time. "Rasp, what's going on? Why won't you rest?"

"I don't need to."

"Ha!" Faris said as he stomped past.

"Are you having nightmares?"

Briony was persistent, Rasp had to give her that. The fact that she sounded legitimately concerned made it hard to stay angry at her. Mother raised no quitter, though. "Of course not, Briony. Thank you for your concern." Rasp raised his limp hand over his head and waved her away. "That will be all. Goodbye."

"This wouldn't have anything to do with a certain dark entity, would it?"

Rasp's eyes shot wide open as he heaved himself upright, throwing an accusing finger in Faris's direction. "You shameless blabbermouth!"

"Over here, idiot," Faris called from the other side of the dark enclosure.

Rasp's embarrassment was easy to ignore, fortunately, on account of the anger currently burning his cheeks warm to the touch. He swiveled around in the appropriate direction, finger still held aloft despite the trembling protest of his noodle-like arm. "Do you have no respect for the sacred pact of brotherhood, Faris? Just because Briony's your fiancée doesn't give you the right to share my dark secrets."

"This is what you're upset about? Not any of the actual problems taking place right now?"

Of course not. That would have taken genuine self-reflection, something Rasp was currently avoiding at all costs. He folded his arms over his chest and scowled. "Why does she know about the dark entity?"

"Everyone in the traveling party knows about the dark entity. Daana read a whole journal out loud about it, remember?"

"Yeah, but none of them took it seriously. Why is Briony acting like she knows it's a real threat?" When Faris offered no reply, Rasp made one for him. "You told her everything I said last night, didn't you?"

"To help you, yes."

He threw his hands into the air above his head. "Unbelievable!"

"You're unbelievable!" Faris's hoof stomped against the ground in response. The impact was less threatening considering all it did was make a squelchy sound, similar to the sort of thing you'd hear around the shit pit after a hearty meal of stewed cabbage. "Quit fixating on the wrong thing. Be mad at me, fine. But if you could please funnel even half of this energy into the actual crisis at hand, we'd both be better for it."

That was a good point. Not in the way Faris intended, but he was right about how Rasp was expending far too much energy on trivial dramatics. He needed to put every ounce of strength toward staying awake. With a final glare, Rasp pulled the blanket over his head and flopped back down onto his soggy bedroll. The fact that the reaction itself was in direct conflict with his vow to stop being so needlessly dramatic was not worth the effort to mull over. He was just a lifeless lump now. Any further argument would be met with the cold, lumpy shoulder.

"Rasp, please," his friend pleaded.

Rasp allowed his silence to do all the talking necessary.

"Do you see what I'm dealing with here?" Faris said to Briony. "He won't sleep, he won't talk to me, and the longer this goes on, the worse it's going to get."

"I can give him something to sleep," Briony said.

"Good."

"Bad!" Rasp disagreed.

Briony's loud ear flap warned them to let her finish. "But all it's going to do is treat the symptom, not the problem. I can't actually help unless I know what is going on."

The pregnant pause that followed was probably meant to break him. As if silence was some sort of big, scary threat. Rasp wrapped the blanket tighter, content to wait them out until they were forced to admit defeat.

The corner of the bedroll dipped as Briony sat next to him. She rested a hand on his shoulder. "Yes, Faris shared with me what happened last night. He brought me to help because he's your friend, Rasp, and he is worried about you."

Faris should have been more concerned with his own welfare. Specifically about what would happen if Rasp let down his guard for even a second. He was doing them a service by not falling asleep. Why couldn't they see that?

"Daana's lecture was not the first time I had heard mention of the dark entity," Briony said. "Our people have always known of the dangers that lurk within the Iron Ridge. You're right to be afraid of it."

If this was supposed to be Briony's version of a pep talk, Rasp didn't think it was working. He kept his jaw locked tight, silently willing the conversation to end.

"They say it preys on your worst fears and uses them against you. What's your worst fear, Rasp?" She patiently filled in the gaps he refused to utter out loud. "I think you're afraid you might be all of the horrible things everyone said about you."

Damn, she was good. Better than she had any right to be. Rasp bit back the impulse to yell at Faris again for sharing all of his secrets. That information was supposed to have been kept confidential between them. Last fucking time he'd open up to anyone ever again. For here on out, he'd be impenetrable—like a rock. A rock without any fears or any need to rely on other people. Or sleep. That was the most important activity to avoid at the moment.

Try as he might, Rock Rasp still had functioning ears. He had no other choice but to listen as Briony voiced his worst fears out loud.

"You're afraid making yourself a better person didn't fix anything. Because even though you changed who you are, it didn't change what you're meant to be."

Or the unspeakable things you've done, his thoughts unconsciously filled in the missing blank. The clawing sensation was alive and well in the back of his mind once more. Rasp could feel it fighting its way out of its box.

Scratch, scratch, scratch, the memory steadily wore away at the last of his resolve. Stifling a whimper, he buried his face into the coarse blanket.

Briony's voice shifted directions, muffled slightly by the blankets encompassing Rasp's head. "He's not well."

"No shit. I told you that," Faris said. "Can you help him?"

Briony's hand still rested on Rasp's shoulder. He felt her fingers drum against his upper arm as she sat quiet, considering her answer. When she spoke again, having settled on an answer, her voice had a noticeable edge to it. Calm, but commanding. "Check outside first. Make sure we're the only ones listening."

Sucking a loud breath through his nostrils, Faris trudged past once more. His hoof steps made soft squelches in the mud as he slipped out into the downpour.

That was odd. Faris rarely followed anyone's commands, certainly not without bellyaching about it first. Something was up. Rasp raised his head from the blankets, calling after him, "What are you—"

"Not yet," Briony ordered.

Rasp fell silent, straining to catch any sounds over the torrential rainfall. Faris returned several minutes later, shaking the droplets from his fur-covered legs with a few vigorous kicks as he shuffled back inside. "We're clear. There are two soldiers posted on watch, but they're tucked under the trees. So long as a certain someone doesn't start screaming, nobody's going to overhear."

What an odd thing to say. What was even odder was what Briony followed it up with.

"Good," she said. "I think it's time."

CHAPTER NINE

What Have You Done?

The rain continued its persistent assault, beating down against the top of the musty canvas tent stretched overhead. While the weather didn't do much to lift the overall mood, at the very least, it served to muffle the heated conversation taking place within Rasp's tent.

"Now you want to do it?" Faris paced back and forth restlessly. "What happened to waiting until the end? That's what you told me when I suggested we pull him early, remember?"

"That was before I saw what he could do!" Briony snapped. Unlike Faris, she seemed to realize her volume was supposed to be kept at an inconspicuous level and adjusted it accordingly. "You were right, alright? Staying the course was the wrong idea. I should have listened. I'm sorry."

Faris grunted his acknowledgment as he continued his relentless pacing. Rasp could sense the faun's mounting frustration, but it was hard to take him seriously when his hoofs kept making wet squelching sounds with each exasperated step.

Squish, squish, squelch.

"I know it's dangerous," Briony said, "but I don't think we have a choice."

Squelch, squelch, squish.

"Look at him, Faris!"

"I am looking at him! I'm the one who brought you in on this, remember?" Faris's wet hoof steps stopped just shy of Rasp's bedroll. "There are too many eyes on us. Acting now is a risk we cannot take. Give him something to sleep and we'll wait for a better opportunity. One that doesn't involve being surrounded by armed soldiers, preferably."

"He's not going to last that long. We have to move now, while he's still in control."

"Then find something that'll help control him."

"Unbelievable," Briony muttered. "You know that's not how this works. And even if it did, anything I can whip up will pale in comparison to what's lurking outside. I don't know about you, but I'm not all that keen to see what happens when your best friend, a highly powerful, highly unstable witch, gets taken over by a dark entity."

Alright, that was it. The final straw. Rasp was a useless lump of a man no longer. If Faris and Briony were going to insist on having a secret conversation in front of him, then they were going to have to deal with the consequences. Consequences such as *tell me what the fuck you two are whispering about so I know how angry I should be at you right now.*

Rasp loosened the tight cocoon of blankets from around his weary body and sat, ignoring the protesting ache that flared in his lower back. The cool air prickled his skin and lifted the hairs on his arm on end. Finding a sitting position that wasn't absolute murder on his sore muscles was a bit of a challenge, but he persisted in spite of the pain. Faris and Briony kept suspiciously quiet as he worked. Fearful, perhaps, in the knowledge that they'd finally awakened the beast and were now waiting with bated breath to see whether it would attack outright or put up a stink first.

"Go ahead with that explanation any time now," Rasp said, adjusting the layers of blankets back over his shivering frame. "I don't care who it comes from, but one of you is going to start talking."

"We're getting you off the mountain," Briony said.

Rasp's heart leapt into his throat. He swallowed it back down, trying to stifle the sudden drumming within his ears that was making it difficult to hear. "To be clear, you mean alive, right?"

"Preferably."

He didn't like how Briony made it seem like an option. "Good start. Keep going."

"We were supposed to wait until we had a path mapped through the ridge, but that doesn't matter anymore. Keeping the entity from reaching you is priority number one."

"I still think we should wait," Faris interjected.

Briony lit back into him with fresh vigor, laying out once more why waiting was out of the question. Her words steadily blurred together, intermixing with the roar of the rain, as Rasp's thoughts turned inward. Thinking clearly had never been so difficult. One by one, he sifted through the world's slowest stampede of runaway thoughts. Countless ideas moved as a single liquid body through his mind, but sluggishly, as if the internal gears were trapped in thick molasses. Something about what Briony said had set off a small flicker in his head and he was determined to root it out.

Like his words, the realization came to him slowly. "You two aren't with the realm."

"We're not," Briony agreed, silencing Faris's protest with a snap of her fingers. "I shouldn't have to tell you why you need to keep that bit to yourself, right, Rasp?"

He countered her question with one of his own. "Who do you work for?"

"Let's just say they're the kind of people that want to keep powerful witches out of the hands of the realm."

While that was an idea Rasp could certainly get behind, it still sounded like the sort of thing capable of coming back and biting him in the ass later on. "And I expect you'll be delivering me to them afterward?"

"The deal was both for you and for a mapped route through the ridge," Briony said. Her confident tone turned to one just shy of disgust. "They can keep their blasted money, as far as I'm concerned. I plan to wash my hands of you the moment we're past the foothills. You're far too much trouble than you're worth. You can be Faris's problem."

That sounded lovely, actually. Too lovely. Which is why Rasp put absolutely no trust in it whatsoever. He swiveled his head, searching futilely for Faris's hazy shape within the surrounding gloom. "You've been awfully quiet, Dingle. Got anything to add? For instance, whether or not Briony's talking out of her ass here? Color me skeptical, but this all seems a little too good to be true."

Faris let out a bleak sigh. While his frenzied pacing had stopped, he was still exuding a rather hostile energy. He obviously didn't agree with Briony's reckless decision to take their chances and split, but the idea of a dark-spirit-possessed-best-friend didn't sound like it was sitting with him any better. "She means every word."

"You're really going to get me out?"

"That's the plan."

It was a poor choice of words on Faris's part. A simple "yes, Rasp. Whatever you say, Rasp" would have been much more concise because Rasp's head was now swimming with new revelations. The thoughts still moved like molasses, but they were there nonetheless. Bubbling to the surface one tiny, slow bubble at a time. "Yeah, about that. Plan implies you put forethought into this. And you never considered, I don't know, mentioning it before?"

"Lower your voice," Faris hissed. "And this is exactly why I didn't tell you. You don't have any self-control."

He wouldn't have needed any had they cut and run from the start. "I asked you to get me out of here back at your village. Why didn't you do it then?"

"Because not everything I do is about you."

Ouch. Rasp's anger subsided to a simmer as a fresh helping of hurt took its place. It was true, he supposed. But being kept in the dark still stung in ways he hadn't anticipated. He allowed his tone to reflect the same self-pity currently filling the hole in his chest. "Better late than never, I guess."

"Please don't start," Faris said. "I'm working to get you out. Be grateful for that."

He supposed he could show a little gratitude. "Thank you, Faris."

"Silent gratitude," the faun clarified. "You saying things like that feels unnatural."

Poor, naive Faris. He had no idea what unnatural was. Rasp graciously demonstrated it for him. He straightened his slumped posture and held his hand over his heart, proclaiming to the heavens, "I will henceforth arise each and every day, singing your praises upon my lips. All hail the great and generous Faris Belfast. May his unending kindness shine down upon us one and all."

"We're running away to start a cult together. Great."

The bedroll shifted as Briony placed a heavy item between her and Rasp. He suspected it was a bag, given the way she was now rustling through it. Rasp ran his hand along the side, confirming that the object in question was indeed a smooth, leather pack of some sort. Briony smacked his fingers away before he could reach inside and discover what sort of fun curiosities she kept on her person.

"No touching," she said.

"You're starting to sound like Faris." Rasp wrung the invisible sting from his fingers as he listened to her work. He swore he heard the pop of a cork followed by the faint pouring of sand. He doubted Briony was constructing a miniature sandcastle in his bed and was therefore forced to ask the painfully obvious. "Now what are you doing?"

"Making you something." There was a sudden trickle of liquid being poured into an empty tin container. After a few moments of vigorous stirring, Briony pushed a cup into his hands. "If we're going to make this work, then you need to be at a functioning level."

Rasp lifted the concoction to his nose and sniffed. It didn't strike him as poison. In fact, it smelled rather nice. He detected notes of honey and chamomile. "Is this going to give me energy?"

"No. It's going to make you sleep."

"Were you even listening?" Rasp lowered the tin cup, mindful not to let its contents spill all over his bed. Had he been capable of finding Faris's bedroll in the dark, he might have thrown it that way. Alas, his poor vision left him with no other choice but to clasp it between his tightly clenched hands, ignoring every impulse urging him to dump it over the top of Briony's head. "That's what I don't want to do!"

Briony grabbed the front of his shirt and pulled him closer, speaking in a harsh whisper. "If we're going to pull this off, then we need you well rested. Listen to the rain outside. No one is going anywhere in this storm, including us."

"But—"

"You trust Faris, don't you?"

Briony released him, allowing Rasp to sit back down as he considered his answer. Trust Faris? The same Faris who had been secretly planning their escape all along without ever once mentioning it to him? What a stupid question. Of course he trusted the devious little cuss. Probably too much, given the new information he'd just received. On the other hand, it did sort of make his best friend more appealing. Rasp liked having an ace up his sleeve, even if it was one he hadn't previously known about.

Naturally, he couldn't admit any of that out loud without it going straight to Faris's already fat head. He pretended to hem and haw before admitting, "If I have to, I suppose so."

"Oh, please," Faris said with an irritated snort. "I'm the only one you trust and we both know it."

"Not true. I also trust Mother."

"Oh, good. I'm on the same ranking threshold as a bird. I feel so honored."

"You should be. Mother's amazing. And, for the record, you actually rank below her."

"Are you two finished?" Briony asked politely.

"No, but carry on anyway. It takes Faris forever to finish." Rasp grinned at her, only slightly disappointed he couldn't see her expression for himself. "But you already know that, don't you?"

Briony spoke over Faris, cutting his complaints short once more. "When it is time to move, trust that Faris will tell you. In the meantime, do not do anything to garner extra attention. Keep your head down. Reacting prematurely will put us all in danger. Do you understand?"

"Yes, ma'am."

She placed her warm hands over his and lifted the tin cup higher. "Faris and I will handle the planning. But that does not mean you get to sit back and do nothing. Your part is just as important. You need to be well rested and have your wits about you."

So, basically, his part still amounted to sitting back and doing nothing. Got it.

"Faris," Rasp said, raising the lip of the cup to his mouth. The drink was cold, but the inviting aroma of honey and chamomile was steadily working its way up his nostrils and warming his inside in areas the liquid would never reach. It didn't taste half bad either. Certainly better than the concoctions Snag had been giving him. "You have my blessing."

"For what?"

"Marriage, of course. I didn't get it before, what you saw in Briony. But I see it now."

The pedantic faun replied accordingly. "You can't see anything."

Oh, but he did. Rasp saw a glimpse of hope. Like a ray of sunshine, it broke through the cloud of misery and breathed fresh life back into his weary soul. Even if it was suicidal, destined to fail, at least it was something.

With a few final parting instructions to keep their heads down and firmly out of their asses, Briony left to attend to her infirmary duties. Rasp refused to sleep right away. The mood in the tent was finally something close to pleasant, and he wanted to enjoy it for as long as he could. He sat nestled in his blankets, slowly sipping the elixir and gnawing his way through a ration of dried fruits and meat, trading increasingly nonsensical quips about Faris's future cult as the roar of the rain battered against the canvas roof.

Sleep found him, eventually. Rasp didn't fight it this time. As he laid down, resting his head between his arms, he knew what nightmares awaited him. But hope was mysterious that way. Even the smallest flicker of light could ward off the creeping darkness until dawn. Rasp closed his eyes and slept, prepared to arise fresh and well rested in the morning so he could thwart the curse of the sixth son one final time.

As his consciousness drifted deeper, shifting from one reality into the next, the insidious clawing in the dark corner of his mind started up again. *Scratch, scratch, scratch*—it steadily wore the walls of its cage thinner. The charms strung through his ears warmed against his flesh, but Rasp was too tired to notice.

"He went this way!" The voice bounced along the surrounding cliffs until it sounded as though his brother was all around him.

They were gaining on him. The ax wound he'd taken to the ribcage had turned his effortless gait into a pitiful hobble. Rasp held his hand to his side as he ran, desperately trying to ignore that the left side of his tunic was drenched with blood. He continued his mad scramble, his boots catching on every protruding rock and root on the way down. The trees were beginning to thin around him. Soon, he would be out from under their protective cover entirely, openly exposed to the dangers behind him.

He didn't have a choice. He couldn't stay back and hide, that would be suicide. His brothers were hunters. They'd follow his trail of blood and see to it that they finished the job good and proper this time.

His heart pounded so hard it felt like it was going to burst. Sharp chest pains added themselves to the steady mix of panic and pain already coursing through his body. Loose scree slipped underfoot as Rasp reached the edge of the trees and plunged brazenly down the barren cliffside. An arrow zipped past, glancing off a shard of stone mere paces ahead of him.

He banked right, zigzagging his way down the mountain in a manner so lacking in pattern that even he didn't know which step would be his next. The clamor grew louder behind him. His brothers shouted after him, assuring him he would not reach the safety of the foothills. He could run, but he could not get away.

An arrow grazed his forearm, ripping away a chunk of cloth and flesh as it skimmed past. Rasp screamed, miscalculated his next step, and fell. He hit the rocky ground and tumbled, head over heels, falling, falling, falling, until a crop of mountain juniper impeded his rolling plummet. Rasp picked himself up, swallowing the taste of blood that flooded his mouth, and staggered on. Tears streamed down his face and clouded his vision as he forced his leaden legs into a hobbled run.

Amid the pain and terror flashing like beacons within his pounding skull, his mind clung to a single thought, repeating it over and over. *What have you done?*

CHAPTER TEN

Distraction

Rain fell fast and hard around her in great sheets of water as Oralia made her way through the densely packed trees. Like the plateau at the base of the falls, this section of the mountain had been carefully sculpted to fit the needs of the mountain folk. Protected by the protruding cliffside from the worst of the winds, the surrounding landscape had been dug up, leveled, and replanted, transforming a formerly steep, precarious mountainside into an ideal hunting ground.

It also made for an ideal hiding place. Sheltered against the elements and surrounded by an abundance of overgrown cover, Oralia estimated the traveling party could remain at rest for another two, possibly three days before they would be forced to move on again. Whether that direction entailed continuing up the mountain as planned or searching for an alternative way down was yet undecided.

The torrential rainfall was throwing an extra element of difficulty into the equation as well. Water streamed off the surrounding cliffs and pooled at the base of the trees, transforming the low-lying areas of the patchy forest floor into a swamp. While Oralia had ensured her camp was set as far from the low areas as possible for just this reason, the encroaching water line crept ever closer. Another day or so of such weather and she would be forced to relocate to higher ground ahead of schedule.

That was tomorrow's problem, however. Camp would hold for the remainder of the day and throughout the night. She had more pressing worries on her mind. Desperate for answers, she'd donned her cloak and staggered out into the rain in search of them.

Oralia slogged across the soggy terrain, ducking between trees to escape the worst of the downpour. The patchy spruces creaked and groaned overhead, their rain-battered boughs swaying hypnotically in the wind. The sweet, refreshing scent of spruce needles was overpowered by the swampy, wet ground. The stench clung to her like a stubborn tick. It would not be long before her own clothes began to smell of mold and mildew.

You only have yourself to blame, her thoughts kindly reminded her. *You could be in your tent right now. Warm and dry, held in the arms of your fuckmate.*

She dismissed the pesky thoughts with a grunt and continued forward, splashing through yet another ankle-deep puddle.

In theory, braving the elements long enough to conduct a patrol of the perimeter should have helped clear her mind. It was supposed to have given her a task, a way to focus her attention on something other than her own rampaging thoughts. And yet, through wind, rain, and relentless mud, Ellisar's warning kept coming back, steadily gnawing away at Oralia's resolve.

"You're in over your head."

Oralia came to a stop beneath the bent bows of a quaking aspen. Her breath puffed into the wet air as she glanced around her, certain no one had followed. No sane person would have tried. The fact that she'd bothered to slip this far out into the trees was probably some testament to her own waning sanity. Nevertheless, it had to be done. If not for the fate of the mission, then for her own peace of mind.

Oralia reached into the front of her tunic, pulled the pendant free, and held it in her hand. The once brilliant powerstone had faded from deep blue to gray. She tapped its smooth exterior with her forefinger, breath bated as she waited for the customary tingle of magic to weave up her arm.

Nothing happened. No yelling. No cursing. No soft words to assure her that her dear friend was alive and well.

"Whisper, I do not know if you can hear me." She felt suddenly ridiculous talking to a hunk of polished stone. Not ridiculous enough to stop, however. She had to know, even if meant confronting the very real possibility that she, her people, the mission, and all that it entailed, had failed. "But my reservations are growing and I desperately need to hear from you."

The sad, dull stone remained sad, dull, and unresponsive in every way.

Iron was lethal to fae. The fact that she was currently standing on a mountain ridge famous for its overabundance of the mineral in question was probably ironic in ways that were lost on her. Oralia hoped it was simply the iron-rich environment weakening the magical connection between her and Whisper. But no matter how she tried to convince herself of this, she couldn't shake the sinking feeling stirring to life inside of her.

Was her dear friend in hiding? Lost? Injured? Dead? Of all those under her command whom she worried about, Whisper was rarely one of them. The fae had lived during the age of magic, survived the extinction of the old ones, and was there to witness the dawn of mortal-kind. A small excursion up a mountainside seemed inconsequential in comparison. And yet, some nagging feeling told her that somewhere, something had gone terribly wrong.

"It is my hope that you are alive and, for whatever reason, simply unable to reach me. I cannot linger in this area for long. I will wait until the worst of the storm has passed. If I have not heard from you by then, I will assume the worst and make a decision accordingly." Oralia paused before adding, "You and I have had our differences, but I have always considered you a friend. I hope it is not goodbye, but if so, I hope you have found your people beyond the planes of this life and are finally at peace."

Oralia meant what she said. She also held out hope that the stone would flash to life and Whisper's irate voice would ripple across her thoughts once more, berating her for daring to wish something so stupid.

She stared at the dull powerstone held within the palm of her hand, knowing it would not shimmer or shine. Oralia waited anyway, holding out, against all odds, that her answer would come.

The minutes slowly ticked by as her boots sank deeper and deeper in the mud. Her cloak was nearly soaked through by the time she tucked her pendant back into its customary place and started back toward camp. Oralia's thoughts started up again as she shuffled with her head bent against the wind and rain.

You're in over your head. You should have turned back while you had the chance. Your greatest advantage is gone and now you, and everyone you care about, are cursed to die upon this mountain.

The euphoria of surviving the crumbling pass had lasted about a day before the harsh realities of her situation came crashing down on her with the weight of a sledgehammer. Her thoughts were a mess, an endless stream of one panicked thought screaming over the others in a desperate bid for her attention. None of her usual tactics for quieting her mind were working either. Mending was out of the question due to the fact that her repair satchel had been misplaced during the shuffle and had yet to turn up. She had her emergency patch kit that was kept on her at all times, of course. But shy of idly stitching leaves together, there wasn't anything to mend.

Distraction via companionship was also out. Her faithful four were busy processing the many traumas from the day before in their own ways. A casual stroll past Ellisar's tent had been enough to convince Oralia perhaps she wasn't *that* desperate for camaraderie. Besides, she had companionship. She'd laid with Sascha thrice already. To the point where he threatened to leave her hands tied if she propositioned him for a fourth. The big lug was sleeping now, safely tucked away in her bed, sheltered from the howling elements. Probably where she should have been as well, but such was the nature of distraction. If you remained idle for too long, it stopped working.

Her stint outside was as much to reach Whisper as it was an attempt to clear her head. Unfortunately, all the fresh air did was make her even more miserable than before. Thanks to the downpour, she could now add shivering to her racing thoughts and the growing tightness in her chest.

Oralia ducked beneath the sagging boughs from one black spruce to the next, feeling fat droplets splatter against her waterlogged hood. The soft mud sucked at her heavy boots with each burdensome step. She pulled her left foot free only to have the right sink a little more. Any more of this and she stood to lose her footwear completely. Fortunately, relief was not far. She could see the beginnings of camp through the gaps in the swaying trees.

With a weary sigh, Oralia wrangled her boot free and pressed onward. She passed one of the posted sentries as she crossed from the trees into the rows of sad, sagging tents, offering him only a nod of acknowledgment. The soldier looked too miserable to care, much less question why his stalwart commander had just returned from an impromptu stroll in the woods. From the looks of it, the only thing preoccupying the poor man's mind was the upcoming shift change.

Oralia's tent was as she had left it, a battered stretch of canvas strung between four poles, sagging in the rain. A sudden gust of wet wind convinced her that home had never looked so inviting. She ducked inside, secured the tent flap, and kicked off her wet boots and outer layer of clothing. Sascha either didn't hear her enter or was too exhausted to sit upright, because he remained as a giant, unmoving lump beneath her furs.

She preferred that, actually. Perhaps if she slipped in unnoticed beside him, she wouldn't have to answer such probing questions as, "Why are you drenching wet? Were you outside? Good gods, woman, have you lost your mind?"

Wearing only a damp undershirt and her wool leggings, Oralia tiptoed over, lifted the corner of the blankets, and eased inside. Her stealthiness was for naught, as Sascha lurched upright with a startled yelp, dragging the majority of the bed coverings with him. "What in the name of chaos?" He searched the inside of the dingy tent for several seconds before his accusatory stare settled on her. "Moonflower?"

Oralia gripped the edge of the fur-lined blanket and attempted to pull it back over her shivering body with limited success. "Go back to sleep."

"Were you just outside?"

"I was, for a time. And now I am not. Lie back down please. You are letting all of the heat out."

"I'm sorry, *I'm* making you cold? Me?" he said. "Woman, your body feels like a corpse against mine. Let's not start pointing the cold finger here."

Oralia had meant to sneak back into bed and wrestle with her thoughts until a restless sleep found her, but the opportunity to lose herself in a petty argument was just as good of a distraction. "A corpse?" she feigned innocence. "How would you know? Have you shared a bed with one before?"

His dark eyes narrowed. "Does present company count? Because trying to turn yourself into a corpse is the only explanation I can think of for being outside in this weather."

Sascha had managed to flip the argument around on her far too quickly. A feat that was as impressive as it was irksome. He didn't need to know that, so in lieu of a reply, Oralia merely snuggled deeper underneath the blankets, silently willing him to do the same.

More wishful thinking, apparently.

"What were you doing outside?" Sascha persisted.

"If you must know, I was conducting a patrol of the perimeter." She added, before he was given the chance to interject with more relentless questions, "To ensure your continued safety. You are welcome."

"Sounds unnecessary."

Try as she might, Oralia could not help the small smile that pulled at the corner of her mouth. "On the contrary. Your continued safety is never unnecessary."

"Mm."

CHAPTER ELEVEN

Doubts

Based on the severity of Sascha's noncommittal noises, Oralia sensed neither of them would be getting any more sleep. With a heavy sigh, he leaned over and rustled through the pack situated near the head of their bedroll. "Sit up."

Oralia slit one eye open warily. "Why?"

"'Why' she says, soaking the bed and everyone else in it." Sascha hooked his hands under her arms and hoisted her into a sitting position. He peeled away the wet undershirt clinging to her cold skin with an ungentle tug and tossed it onto the floor before Oralia even had time to realize what he was doing. "Because if I wanted to lie in a puddle, I would be sleeping outside."

Oralia's teeth snapped together as she pulled the blankets over her chest. Although the strip of linen serving as her bandeau was still fitted in place, she would not put it past him to try to remove it as well. "I can undress myself, thank you."

"Is that so? Could have fooled me." Sascha flung a thick cloth over her head and began towel-drying her hair with the sort of annoyed attentiveness normally associated with chiding mothers. "Considering you're the one who came to bed dripping wet."

There was an inappropriate joke there. One she dared not utter. Undoubtedly Sascha would have found a way to turn it around on her as he managed to do with everything she said. Oralia sat stock-still instead, so utterly confused as to what was taking place that her best option was to wait him out. He would tire of his relentless smothering eventually.

She hoped.

Despite the racing panic taking place inside her head, whatever strange behavior Sascha was displaying might have been working. One by one, the overworked muscles in her back relaxed. Oralia closed her eyes, enjoying the way he worked the cloth through her hair. This was beyond question the best distraction she'd encountered so far.

He made short work of drying her hair. Too short, in Oralia's opinion. Fortunately the patronizing treatment didn't stop once he'd run out of damp hair to dry. Sascha moved down past her neck and between her shoulder blades. The fast, furious speed of his handiwork steadily slowed. He gathered the towel in one hand and wicked away the moisture with slow, circular movements. Oralia neither knew nor cared for the sudden change in tempo. She was fully in the moment, enraptured by the friction of the thick cloth as it brushed against her clammy skin.

Sascha's voice disturbed her still thoughts like a pebble against the water's surface. "You must be ill."

She was enjoying herself far too much to take the bait.

"On the verge of death, I daresay."

Such melodramatics meant Sascha would continue to escalate until she acknowledged him. She kept her eyes closed, mumbling. "How so?"

"You would ordinarily never let me do this."

"That explains it then," she agreed, refusing to let the moment slip away. "My dying wish is for you to keep going."

He did, for a while anyway. Working the cloth up and down her neck, across the bare skin of her exposed shoulders, and over each arm. Somewhere along the way the towel itself was ditched and replaced by the kneading movement of his own hands. The massage started light, but it wasn't long before Sascha's expert fingers discovered all of her hidden areas of tension. He clucked his disapproval as he worked, combining the relaxing magic of his kneading hands while playfully chastising her for not taking better care of herself.

"Out in weather like this when you have a perfectly good watch shift already on rotation. Positively ridiculous."

The lecture itself was easy to ignore. After all, it was nothing she hadn't already heard. Before long, the warm hum of Sascha's voice intermixed with the falling rain outside, creating the most soothing of lullabies. Oralia was on the brink of drifting off when his left thumb dug a little too deeply into a knot buried within the muscle of her shoulder.

Her eyes shot open, sucking a lungful of damp air through her tightly clenched teeth.

Sascha immediately relaxed his grip. "Sorry. Too much?"

"No," she said, her voice barely a hoarse whisper. "Caught me off guard is all."

Sascha resumed his kneading with more gentleness than before, she noted. A shame, really. She preferred when he didn't handle her like a porcelain doll. "It's funny you say that," he said, sounding almost pleased with himself. "I always thought catching you off guard wasn't possible."

Good gods, he was not going to let this go. Whatever *this* was. She didn't even know the cause for his sudden behavior and, already, it was driving her mad. "Alright, spit it out."

"Moonflower, whatever do you mean?" he asked innocently, as if he had no idea that he was being a pain in the ass. A doting one, inarguably. But all of his incessant comments were stemming from somewhere.

"You are upset about something," Oralia said. Not that she necessarily wanted to know, but it would be nice if the comments stopped. Unfortunately, something told her this was more wishful thinking and not the way relationships were intended to work.

"Well, since you asked, I am finding your behavior as of late a little bit"—he paused, as if purposely searching for the word most likely to provoke her—"angsty."

"*I* am the angsty one?" She would have laughed had it not been for the way his strong fingers were working the knot from her shoulder, inadvertently sapping the breath from her lungs.

"Yes."

"Me? What about you? You are the one currently muttering little things under your breath."

"That's pettiness, not angst, dear. They're different."

"Oh good gods, Sascha." Oralia hung her head with a groan. "What can I do to make it better for you?"

"It's not that I don't mind helping you grind through your troubles, Moonflower." The added squeeze to her shoulders assured her that his unique choice of wording had been absolutely intentional. "But I'd like to be able to help in other ways, too. And you don't seem to want to let me."

She feared she knew where this was going and kept her lips sealed.

"You can talk to me, you know." His horrible words were intermixed with one of the best massages she'd ever received, leaving her with severely muddled feelings on the matter. "Talking to me is not unbridled passion, granted, but it does have some unique upsides of its own. Opening up, letting your partner get close to you, who knows, maybe even earning valuable insight along the way."

The tightness in her chest nearly doubled in intensity. The chemical intoxication of adrenaline and relief had faded since he'd pulled her from the collapsed stairwell. And although the underlying sentiments persisted, a small part of her could not help but wonder if she'd made a grave miscalculation in revealing her feelings for Sascha. All the things he spoke of required vulnerability, and Oralia mastered emotional vulnerability as well as one might fare a full-bodied embrace with a cactus.

Despite how her lips parted and her tongue curled against the roof of her mouth, no words flowed forth. That in itself wasn't necessarily a surprise. Still, it would have been nice to offer some reassurance that she'd meant what she said and wasn't currently considering running back out into the rain.

Although, her boots weren't that far . . .

"Oralia."

Too late. Apparently they were doing this. "Yes?"

"I know you keep your cards close," he started, which was silly, because he of all people should have been able to see that she wasn't holding any blasted cards. Sascha must have sensed her underlying confusion because he laughed before attempting again. "I can see there is a lot on your mind and the effect it is having on you. I'm not asking you to tell me everything, but it would be nice, as your future partner in retirement, to be let in from time to time."

If only Sascha knew what he was asking. On the surface, his plea was sweet. Downright endearing, actually. He genuinely cared for her, and she for him. Which was why she couldn't possibly tell him that she had begun to question everything. The mission, the realm, the resistance and their damned road through the ridge. Deep down, she feared Ellisar had been right all along. Oralia should have given up when she had the chance. Her forces were depleted, the person she was supposed to be reinstating to the throne could not be allowed to do so, and now, it was too late to turn around.

If there was one skill she felt she had mastered in her time as the Protector of the Realm, it was the art of partial truths. It was all about maintaining the delicate balance of which truths to share and which to keep to herself. The less specific, the better. She had to say something, after all. She feared that if she made the mistake of looking at Sascha's stupidly handsome face, with his big, imploring eyes, for even just a second, she was going to break.

"I had doubts about this mission from the beginning, as did many others, who told me as much. I did not listen and I am beginning to regret that." She rearranged the fur-lined blanket spread over her lap, not out of necessity, but because it was easier to admit these things without having to worry whether the amount of eye contact she was giving was too much or too little. "My forces are dwindling. We lost eight soldiers to the swamplander horde yesterday and there are many more wounded."

She could have stopped there. Surely that alone had satiated Sascha's need for wanting to be let in, but the tightness in her chest was starting to ease. Setting free some of the rapid thoughts buzzing about within her skull had never been so easy. Proof that she had either lost her touch or something else was afoot. "We were fortunate that the wildfire was keeping the mountain patrol occupied. The rain has changed that. Once the fire is put out, there will be nothing stopping them from resuming their regular patrols. I fear we are days away from being discovered."

Sascha mulled this over for a few thoughtful seconds before asking, "You wish to turn back, then?"

It wasn't a wish so much as it was a fantasy. The pass lay in ruins behind them. Even if they did find a way to tunnel back through, there was still the matter of the swamplander horde waiting for them on the other side. "Turning back is not an option."

And that was just the tip of the metaphorical iceberg. The Stoneclaws were a formidable foe, but they were not Oralia's main concern. They had cast out their rightful leader and she was beginning to think she understood why. Whisper had claimed the boy was powerful. She hadn't realized her dear friend had meant 'bringer of darkness and destruction' powerful. For the gods' sakes, Rasp had held up an entire stone passageway by himself! And lived to complain about it afterward.

If it was true that there was a predatory spirit lurking on the mountain, awaiting Rasp's return, then she was doubly fucked. Had she put too much faith in Whisper's vow to protect the boy?

Her hand went to the pendant hanging from her neck. Perhaps it was Whisper who had put too much faith in her. Somewhere her friend was either dead or dying. Her single greatest advantage was no longer available to her and without it, she felt paralyzed with uncertainty.

Sascha settled down next to her, his large hand closed over her own. He squeezed. Not enough to hurt, but it did succeed in snapping her from the spiral of her own rampaging thoughts. The heat radiating from his skin wormed deep into her flesh, banishing some of the chill from her bones. "If there is anyone who can pull off the impossible," he said, "it is you."

His continued faith in her would have been endearing if she had not found it heart-wrenching. Whisper had made the same mistake and might have paid dearly for it. "How?"

"Ah, you see, that's why I specified you, not me. I'm merely the emotional support partner in this scenario." He gave her hand another firm squeeze and flashed a teasing smile. "I'm good for engaged listening, backrubs, and pushing food in your face when you forget to eat. The strategic planning business is more of your strong suit."

"It does not bother you that I think we are hopelessly doomed?"

"A little. But I also know you well enough to know that you don't give up in the face of insurmountable odds."

There was that phrase again: give up. It was sounding more and more appealing. Perhaps it was time to give that a try. Easier said than done, alas. While her faithful four would gladly jump at the idea of ditching the mission, Captain Monk would undoubtedly feel differently. Even if Oralia could get him to see reason, to give up the mission and return home, he had witnessed what Rasp could do. As a loyal servant to the realm, Monk would insist on delivering Rasp to the capital and into the hands of the Division of Divination. Handing Geralt Lazuli a magically unstable tinderbox was only slightly better than allowing Rasp to fall into the hands of a dark entity.

Then don't tell the captain. Put it in the hands of those you trust. Captain Monk will have no choice but to accept defeat if you no longer have an heir to put on the Stoneclaw throne.

Now that was an idea. Not a good one, granted, but it had potential.

Ever since learning what Rasp was, Oralia knew she would have to remove him from the equation. She'd planned to do so at the end, once tensions had settled and the route through the ridge was established. As those things were no longer set to happen, she supposed there was no harm in skipping some of the steps in between. It certainly beat waiting around pointlessly to die. Who knew, maybe it would even spare countless lives. Not hers, unfortunately. But perhaps that was the price for thwarting the impending apocalypse.

"I know that look on your face." Sascha's teasing was back with a playful nudge. "See? I am helpful to have around. You're already back to scheming."

"I do not have a scheming face."

"Oh, yes you do. The light changes in your eyes, like you've gone somewhere else." He leaned closer, nearly touching his nose to hers. The insatiable scent of mint and cloves filled her nostrils, banishing the last of the tightness from her chest. Sascha showed his upper teeth in an unspoken challenge to be put in his place. "Where did you go this time? Anywhere noteworthy?"

She threaded her fingers through his beard and tugged his mouth close to hers. "Perhaps I was fantasizing about pinning your arms over her head and making you beg."

"And fantasy-me let you do that?"

"Fantasy-you loved it."

Just as his lips brushed hers, Sascha pulled away. "Are you sure you wouldn't rather cuddle? I could hold you in my arms as we talk about our feelings well into the night."

His charming smile combatted her scowl in ways that could only be explained by dark magic. Sascha held her unflinching gaze for nearly ten unbearable seconds before he acquiesced. "No?" He leaned in, nuzzling his face against her neck as he planted soft kisses of affection. "Fine. But one of these days, we're going to do what I want to do."

She did not know how much time she had left, but it seemed foolish not to enjoy it. Oralia gave in to him, holding on to every savory moment for as long as she could. In two days' time, when the weather cleared and she had a better idea of whether or not Whisper would return, she would decide whether to continue or give up. Until then, she would let her charming fuck-mate distract her for as long as possible.

CHAPTER TWELVE

Orcs and Underwear

Daana spent the night tossing, turning, and sobbing into her blankets until they were as wet and miserable as the storm raging outside. It was nearly dawn when she settled into a restless slumber. Her body, having succumbed to exhaustion, lay still, but her mind could not shake her sorrow. She dreamt of Willem, of dancing blue lights, and of a monster with giant, glowing orange eyes. She fought her way through, time and time again, reliving the same nightmare, only to descend into absolute darkness at the end. There, Daana drifted, helpless and without a voice, slowly sinking into the void as fragments of herself cracked and broke away.

Mid-morning came and the light outside shifted from inky black to bleak gray. The rain stayed. Daana hardly noticed it anymore. It was just another useless sound for her overworked mind to tune out altogether. Unable to achieve a fitful sleep, she eventually gave up trying. Daana sat huddled in a mound of damp blankets at the top of the bed instead, feeling both numb and completely raw at the same time.

Poor Curly looked nearly as lost as she felt. He'd kept his word and stayed by her side throughout the night, ensuring the only people who came near were those he deemed trustworthy. The faithful four, trustworthy—huh. Once upon a time, Daana would have found the use of those words in the same sentence disturbingly comical. For the life of her, however, she couldn't remember what comical felt like.

Empty and overwhelmed. Those were the only states of being that still made sense in her steadily shrinking world.

The few times Curly attempted polite conversation were either met with one-word answers or nothing at all. Daana caught only about half of what he said. The drone of his voice melded so seamlessly into the background, she hardly noticed she was ignoring him. Ordinarily she would have felt bad about doing so, but the void had swallowed that feeling as well.

Curly continued to check in on her, undeterred. Oftentimes it was to offer her a sip of water or push a bite of food into her face. Despite his insistence, she didn't feel the normal pangs of hunger. Eating had become a chore, and not just because the majority of their rations constituted salted jerky and slabs of unchewable hardtack. Daana gnawed on the lackluster food throughout the day. With the storm raging outside and little else to do, she didn't bother to move from the bed.

Curly, on the other hand, seemed incapable of sitting still for long. The orc shuffled about their cramped quarters, desperate for any sort of activity to occupy his time. He was knelt in the far corner at the moment, rearranging the assortment of wet garments hanging from the laundry line for what had to be the third time that hour. Without fire to aid the drying process, the task was going slow. Irritatingly slow, apparently, judging from the way he huffed and grunted as he pulled a damp garment from the line, wrung it out between his strong hands, and then rehung it, only to repeat the process from start to finish with the next offending item.

There was a time, not too long ago, when Daana would have been morti-fied to watch a big, burly orc soldier wring out her undergarments. Presently, she simply could not muster the mental wherewithal to care. Besides, there was absolutely nothing sensual about the way Curly was cursing every deity in known existence as he hunched over, ruthlessly wringing the last of the moisture from her wool underpants.

He swiveled his head in her direction, his broad brow winkling in accu-sation. "Are you laughing?"

The strangest of sensations was taking place on her face. For what felt like the first time in ages, a smile had started to form on her lips. Daana waved it away dismissively. "Of course not."

"It's not funny, you know. This is serious."

"It is serious," she agreed. Her voice was foreign to her, as if a stranger had seized control. Daana was simply a passenger now, fated to watch the scene unfold from the back seat of the runaway carriage, too lost in her own misery to fight for the reins. "I can tell by the look on your face."

At least this version of her had a sense of humor.

"Do you know what makes a trip like this go from bad to worse?" Curly demanded, shaking the garment in his hand at her chidingly. "Doing it in wet clothes. The moisture saps all of your heat so your body has to burn extra energy just to keep warm. Out here, in a place like this, a chill is a death sentence."

It was good to see that one of them was still capable of being overly dramatic.

Curly carried on, as his obvious passion for properly dried undergarments lit a fire within his dark eyes. "This shit has got to air dry. Impossible to accomplish when it's pouring buckets of water outside. And don't even get me started on the fire ban. It's like they want us to catch our death!"

"I see." Daana nodded with a sageness befitting someone who actually understood what he was ranting on about. "So you're not just fondling my underwear because you like it, you're actually saving my life. I suppose I should thank you."

"Your what?" His glare shifted from her to the thick, colorful cloth he was currently wringing between his hands. He should have been mortified, and yet, his brow furrowed further over his dark eyes as if this new knowledge was somehow offensive to him. "These are skivvies? I thought this was a hanky!"

Something pinged to life inside of her, like a splash of color in a monochromatic landscape of beige. The sensation was fleeting, lasting only long enough for Daana to reply, "Why would a handkerchief have leg holes?"

"I don't know. I assumed it was poorly designed." Curly stretched the item between his hands, adding, "Just like your underwear, apparently."

"Those happen to be very fashionable."

"Fashionable? Who the fuck cares about fashion on a mission?" The virtues of women's underwear did not seem to be the sort of topic Curly would have ordinarily participated in voluntarily. And yet, he continued, perhaps pleased that he was finally getting something more out of her beyond a blank, vacant stare. "Functionality, support, and comfort. Those are what you should care about in underclothes. Not whatever mockery this is."

The temporary blip within her chest returned, prompting Daana to lift her shoulder in a hapless shrug. "They *are* comfortable. Try them. See for yourself."

He blushed so fiercely, his cheeks were nearly the same color as the petal-pink underwear currently being strangled in his fist. "Are you trying to make my life more difficult? I'm already fighting off allegations that we're a thing. I don't need to add wearing women's underwear to the mix, alright?"

"Does that bother you?" Daana wondered if she could change the blush on his face from pink to crimson. "That the rest of camp thinks we're a thing?"

"Normally I'd tell 'em all to go fuck themselves. But between the murderous looks I'm getting from Monk's people and the questionable advice from my own teammates, I'd just rather everyone stop thinking about me altogether."

Her thoughts refused to linger on the subject of Captain Monk. She would have to deal with the slimeball eventually, but eventually could be saved for later. Preferably when they were within pushing distance of a very steep ravine. Daana addressed the latter half of Curly's rant instead. "Questionable advice from your teammates, you say? Do go on."

"Trust me, I'm doing you a favor by not telling you," Curly assured her as he returned the wool undergarments to the clothesline. He took down her cloak next. It was substantially larger than the underwear had been, forcing Curly to wring it dry piece by piece, starting with the far corner. Water streamed from between his hands and pooled onto the tarped floor as he worked.

Well, that didn't help. She was even more curious now. "They were giving you romantic advice, weren't they?"

"If you call trying to stuff my pockets with sheepskins and a vial of oil *advice*, then sure. They gave plenty. Too much, you could say." Curly unfurled the damp cloak and lifted it above him, scrutinizing his handiwork. The harsh lines of his mouth turned downward into a scowl. "Your cloak is torn."

Daana assumed the torn cloak was Curly's way of avoiding disclosing the true gamut of what sort of questionable advice his friends had given him. Her weary gaze shifted to the dark green garment stretched between his hands. True to his word, the cloak now sported a sizable rip down the back. She imagined it must have happened at some point during all of the chaos the day before. Between running from a swamplander army, being dragged underwater by a monster, and barely escaping a collapsing mountain stairway, she was fortunate that a torn cloak and a few cuts and bruises was the worst she had to show for it.

The same could not be said for Willem.

Oh dear. The emptiness dissipated as her guilt returned with a vengeance, latching its claws back into her heavy heart and chastising her for allowing herself even a moment of reprieve. How could she be so selfish? Here she was, alive and well, enjoying the bizarre company of a new friend, when her partner was dead? She hadn't even gotten to say goodbye. Or thank him for—

"Unacceptable!"

The loud snap of Curly's tusks broke Daana from the start of another emotional spiral. She lifted her head from her hands with a start. "What?"

"You think moisture is a problem now? Wait 'til you try to wear this out in the elements. Defeats the whole purpose of being covered if it's got a giant hole in it!" Curly lowered the garment as he glanced around the cramped tent, looking for something. "Right. Where do you keep your mending kit? We've got to repair this immediately."

"I don't have one."

His dark eyes grew wide in disbelief. "You don't have a repair kit?"

"No."

"Are you trying to be the most useless version of yourself?"

"I don't have any belongings anymore. This shirt"—Daana pulled at the collar of the woven tunic around her neck—"isn't even mine! I'm currently wearing a stranger's clothes because the only ones I do have are sopping wet! Because, in case you didn't hear, I was dragged into a lake yesterday and nearly devoured! So forgive me for having useless underwear, holes in my clothes, and nothing to repair them with."

This was taking somewhat of a dramatic turn, one Daana could not stop no matter how vehemently she tried. The emotional floodgates were open now. More guilt and creeping sadness rushed in to fill her former emptiness. It filled too quickly and started to leak out around her eyes.

Curly's expression softened. "You're wearing someone else's clothes?"

Daana nodded, unwilling to part her trembling lips in the event her treacherous tongue betrayed her again, allowing more thoughts to spill forth that were better left unsaid.

"Do you think they have any extra undergarments you could borrow?"

The way he said it so sincerely forced a squeaky laugh from her throat. Unfortunately, it didn't stop there. The giggle shook loose the tears as well, and it was not long before her restrained laugh transformed into weak sobs. She couldn't hold it at bay any longer. The harder she tried, the faster her unbridled emotions spilled forth. Throughout all of it, all Daana could think about was how stupid this must have looked.

To her horror, Curly settled down beside her, mindful to leave enough distance between them for his repair satchel. He offered her a patronizing pat on the head. "There, there. Don't cry. We'll find you some suitable smallclothes yet."

"I'm not crying about the underwear!"

"Oh, good." He smirked. "Because of all the things to blubber about, panties seemed like a silly choice."

Daana sat straighter, wiping the tears from her eyes with the corner of her sleeve. Several deep breaths got her breathing under control again, mostly anyway. As she had no desire to continue the conversation regarding her unmentionables ever again, she nodded her chin at the garment in his hands. "What are you doing?"

Curly snorted, as if it should have been obvious. He reached into the repair satchel and withdrew a leather tool kit. Flipping it open with a practiced hand, he revealed a small arsenal of pins, needles, and other sewing implants. "Mending your cloak. What does it look like?"

The mental image of a big, strapping orc taking the time to properly mend her clothes was not one Daana had ever envisioned taking up space within her mind. The fact that this was not only reality, but also taking up space within her bed, was something she decided to expel from her thoughts before it could take hold.

What was even stranger was the way she rested her head on his shoulder soon after, whispering a meek, "Thank you."

He whispered back, "Never mention it to anyone."

CHAPTER THIRTEEN

Changing of the Guard

Daana dozed the rest of the morning beneath the mound of blankets in a rare state of sleep pleasantly void of dreams. She would have kept sleeping, too, if it were not for the pair of fervently whispering voices that roused her from her slumber. Managing to keep her eyes open after the third try, she peeled back the warm furs and peered out into her surroundings. It was early afternoon, judging from the grayish light filtering in from outside. The interior of the tent looked nearly identical to when she'd last seen it, with a single, glaring exception.

She and Curly had company, and to describe their visitor's sour facial expression as glaring was an egregious understatement.

Snag was wrapped in a cloak near the tent entrance with his long ears pinned back behind his head. There were dark rings under his eyes and an edge to his tone that suggested he would not be taking shit from anybody, including his closest friend. "So we're a charity now, is that it?" he hissed. "We're gonna take in every sob story we come across?"

"It's not my fault," Curly grumbled. "You started it."

"What are you talking about? I didn't invite no elf woman to come sleep in my bed!"

Daana's heart sank. She had conveniently forgotten this wasn't just Curly's domicile, but Snag's as well. Manning the infirmary had kept Snag away, but he was back now and obviously irritated about having to share his already cramped quarters with an additional body. It seemed her short streak of luck had run its course already. Daana remained motionless, silently debating whether to speak up or simply walk out. The fact that she was wearing nothing more than a thin tunic and form-fitted thermals was making the latter option slightly less appealing.

"You started it when you saved her at the falls," Curly said to Snag. "And don't try denying it, either. Ellisar already told me all about it. Said you braved monster-infested waters to pull 'er out." The orc was back in full uniform, currently struggling to fasten the lower buttons on his shirt jacket. His freshly oiled coat of chainmail was strewn across the floor by his feet.

"Oh my gods, I saved her life. I didn't fucking adopt her. Just 'cause I do the occasional nice thing doesn't mean I want to be saddled with the good deed forever."

The final button was being stubborn. Curly furrowed his brow as his large fingers struggled to thread it through the buttonhole. He kept his concentration on his work as he spoke, gritting out, "She has nowhere else to go, Snag."

"So that makes her my problem?"

Curly snapped his head up at this, dark eyes narrowing. "She's not a problem. She's my friend."

The goblin had only to lift his eyebrows in counterpoint.

"Is it really that much to ask? You're not going anywhere. Just for one evening. Come on, please?"

The revulsion melted from Snag's gnarled face and was replaced with something just shy of pity. "Gods, boy. You've got it bad, don't you?"

"Don't start."

"Oh, no, no, no. If you're gonna insist on making me play nanny to your secret girlfriend, then I get to spout whatever shit I want."

At last, Curly got the stubborn button successfully threaded. The relief in his voice practically bordered on ecstatic. "You'll do it?"

"Just this once. And don't think I'm doing it out of the kindness of my arteries, either. You want me to watch her? Keep her safe for you? Then you're stuck serving as my designated assistant until our official disbandment." Snag lifted his nose into the air with a sniff. "And you can forget all about those lovely rocks I scribble faces on, 'cause your days of bountiful payment are over."

Despite Daana's best attempts to remain inconspicuous, a snickering breath betrayed her. Snag's torn ear swiveled in her direction. His unnerving stare followed a second later, settling on her with a weight that seemed at odds for someone so small. "Look at that, napping beauty has awakened. Sleep well, princess?"

Daana poked her head the rest of the way through the blankets and eased upright. Her eyes roved between the pair as she considered all the ways Snag's question might have been a trap. Still sluggish from sleep, her mind was of no immediate help. Daana faked a yawn, mumbling, "Well enough, thanks."

"Good, good. And the bed, comfy enough for you?"

Her comfort did not seem like something Snag would ordinarily care about. Daana's befuddled stare switched to Curly. "Why is he being weird?"

Snag slammed his curled fist against the ground with such force it made the rings strung through his ears rattle. "Because it's my bed you're sleeping in!"

"Oh." Well that certainly explained his hostility. Also why a number of the blankets didn't quite reach past her toes. Daana sat cross-legged, tucking her feet beneath her body for added warmth. "Sorry about that."

"It's fine," Curly assured her. Although his words were directed at her, his stare bore down on Snag, attempting to pulverize the goblin through unrelenting eye contact from the looks of it. "He wasn't using it anyway."

Snag appeared utterly underwhelmed by Curly's ferocity. So much so, his response came not in the form of words, but by thumbing his nose up at the orc and jutting out his dark purple tongue. The addition of a high-pitched whine, similar to that of a mosquito, was an interesting touch.

Alright then. Apparently she wasn't the only one losing her blasted mind. The mounting pressure had clearly gotten to Snag as well. Blinking back her surprise, Daana opted for a change in subject. The reason for Curly's sudden change back into uniform seemed important enough to bring up. "What's going on? Are you going somewhere?"

"I'm next on watch," he said. "I didn't want you to be alone so Snag here agreed to keep you company while I'm away."

Snag lifted the corner of his lip, flashing a top row of thin, needled teeth. "Reluctantly agreed."

Daana's throat tightened, making it difficult to get the right words out. "You're leaving?"

"It's just the midday shift. I'll be back tonight."

Daana's heartbeat quickened, filling the inside of her skull with its runaway beat. Her sole source of protection would be abandoning her side. She would be alone and exposed. Surely Captain Monk would notice. Would he try to take advantage of Curly's absence and come for her again? The invisible noose around her throat pulled tighter, like a hot vise, as she shrank back into the blankets, fighting for each panicked breath.

"Whoa, easy." In the blink of an eye, Curly was kneeling at her side, his large hand engulfing her own. He squeezed and offered a reassuring smile.

"You'll be safe. I told you once before, if you want scary, Snag's your guy. No one's going to get past him."

Daana's gaze darted in Snag's direction. Scary was putting it lightly. The goblin's gnarled expression looked like he was trying to commit arson through sheer willpower alone. His round, yellow eyes were rimmed red around the edges, a half step shy of bloodshot. Even from across the tent, Daana could see the faint purple vein throbbing on the underside of his neck.

"There's still time to take you to Oralia," Curly reminded her. "You could tell her what happened. She'd sort you-know-who out right away."

And risk Captain Monk retaliating? Daana shuddered. Oralia might have been in charge, but the soldiers were Captain Monk's men. Even Daana did not miss the suspicious glances they gave one another in the protector's presence. "I'd rather just keep my head down for now," she said, refusing to meet Curly's concerned stare as she slid her hand from his grasp and hid it beneath the blankets. "Don't worry about it."

"Daana—"

"Drop it, please." The very mention of it was making her insides want to liquify and trickle out her eyes and nose.

Curly snapped his tusks against his upper teeth, but otherwise honored her wish to let it be. He snatched his chainmail from the floor and stood, pulling the iron-linked coat over the top of his head before threading each burly arm through. "I'll be back later tonight," he said, tugging his cloak from the laundry line and fastening the brass clasp around his neck. "Stay here. Try not to draw any attention."

Knowing Curly, he hadn't meant it as an insult. Still, the comment stung a little. Enough to help push back down her growing sense of unease. "You say that as if I make a habit of drawing attention to myself."

"Talk around camp says otherwise. Something about how you were slinging goblins skyward left and right back at the falls?"

"It was like two! At most."

"Still kinda sounds attention-grabber-y to me."

Okay, that definitely was meant as insulting. Possibly even flirtatious, from the way Curly was now beaming back at her with his widest smile yet. Daana crossed her arms, muttering, "Shut up, Baby Face."

"After you, Princess." Flashing a final, parting smile, he moved to the exit and took his sweet time unfastening the door ties. "You know, Snag, if you're looking for an assistant, Daana would be a good choice. Can spell.

Has handwriting nicer than mine. Probably won't try to snort whatever herbs you're grinding into powder."

A gust of cool air billowed in from the outside, prompting Snag to pull his cloak tighter around his shivering body. Naturally, the goblin wasn't about to let a little drab weather get between him and the opportunity to voice his displeasure. He shook his head at Curly with a disapproving tsk. "Trying to shirk your new responsibilities already, is that it?"

"I think she'd be good at it, is all I'm sayin'."

"I don't tell *you* how to do your job."

"Yes, you do. Constantly."

Snag shooed him off with a flippant wave of his clawed hand. "Will you stop fiddling with the door and go already? You're gonna be late, and I'll be damned if you earn yourself a double shift for being tardy."

"See?" Curly called over his shoulder as he stomped out into the rain. "You're still doing it!"

CHAPTER FOURTEEN

No Touchy

Daana's gaze lingered on the open doorway for longer than it should have, watching as Curly's burly shape disappeared out into the thundering downpour. It was only when she looked elsewhere that she realized Snag was also staring. At her, unfortunately, not at Curly's shapely rear end. The heat from her face shot to her ears as Daana nearly drowned in embarrassment.

The goblin was doing that thing again, where he didn't blink for prolonged periods of time. She hated how effective it was.

"What?" Daana demanded.

"Hurt him and we're going have a problem."

She didn't know which was worse, the fact that Snag had caught her staring or that she was being actively threatened for it. It wasn't like she'd meant to. It had just been there, perfectly level with her line of sight and rather easy on the eyes and . . . never mind. Thinking about it was only making her thoughts stray further into unwanted territory.

Daana shifted within the blankets as she considered the most inconspicuous way to stand and fetch her trousers from the laundry line. On the bright side, Curly had graciously left the tent door unfastened behind him. She could collect her bottoms and simply waltz out if she needed to. "Trust me," she said. "I have no intentions to hurt him. Curly's the only one who's nice to me around here."

With an overdramatic shiver, Snag stood and shuffled over to the billowing doorway. He had the canvas flap secured in only a fraction of the time it had taken Curly to open it. "That's not true. I saved you from a watery grave. That's plenty nice."

"It was nice. Right up until the point you demanded payment for doing so."

He shrugged, allowing a needled smile to cut across his weathered face. "Got to retain my crotchety reputation somehow. If I pulled every nincompoop from danger without demanding recompense, people might start to expect things from me. Can't have that now."

Daana didn't reply, which, for some terrible reason, only encouraged the little scoundrel to keep going. "Look at the shiny side, I didn't throw you back in, did I?"

"No, you didn't," Daana agreed. Come to think of it, she couldn't recall if she had properly thanked him for saving her life at all. Perhaps that was where some of the underlying hostility was stemming from. "And, actually, I really should be thanking you. I'm sorry I didn't do so earlier. The fact is, I wouldn't even be here if you hadn't—"

Snag made a noise in the back of his throat, similar to a cat hacking up a furball. "You can stop right there."

"Why?"

"I don't do sentimental."

Except of course if said sentiment applied to Curly. Daana suspected Snag wouldn't like it if she pointed out the inconsistencies in his behavior, however. She gave his statement the metaphorical equivalent of a poke with a stick instead. "You'll accept money but not a genuine thank you?"

"Money doesn't make my skin feel itchy." Snag returned to his spot on the floor and began rummaging through a pack that looked to be nearly the same size as him. "Now, go back to sleep or cry into your pillow, or whatever things occupy your day. I've got work to do and I don't want to be bothered."

Daana decided to watch him instead.

Snag pawed through his cluttered belongings, rearranging various bundled items onto the floor beside him in his search for whatever it was he was looking for. There was a disturbing amount of razor wire involved in the process. Daana ordinarily would have asked what the wire was for, but this was Snag, and getting the truth out of him was like getting blood from a stone.

She opted for a question slightly less forward. "Haven't you been up all night in the infirmary?"

"Yeah, what of it?"

"You have to be utterly exhausted. Surely whatever this is can wait until you're more"—Daana decided against using the words "of sound mind" and settled on—"rested?"

"Oh, now you suddenly care over how rested I am?" Snag remarked over his shoulder. "But not while you were busy stealing my bed?"

She really wished he would stop bringing that up.

Her reason for wanting him well rested was rather simple, actually. While Snag was currently filling the role of acting medic, his field of expertise was more in line with that of an assassin—one with a penchant for poison, in fact. At the moment, the assassin part didn't bother Daana so much as it normally would have. Having someone on her side who was versed in the art of keeping others away was a commodity she could not afford to lose. It was the prospect of poison that worried her. Particularly the part where she was anywhere near it.

It was not so much of a stretch to conclude that whatever project he was working on would likely involve deadly substances. Rather than dignify the bed question with an answer, Daana redirected with one of her own. "Is what you're working on dangerous?"

"Not sure yet." He glanced back at her, yellow eyes wide and glimmering. "Want to find out?"

"You seem a little jumpy is all. It was my understanding that one needs a steady hand when dealing with poisons."

"Poisons? Nobody said anything about poison, girl. Now stop fretting over me and mind your own damn business." With his arms laden with a curious assortment of equipment, Snag waddled closer to the entrance and arranged his treasure trove onto the flattest part of the tarped floor. Among the array, Daana spied several empty glass vials, a mortar and pestle, a funnel, and what appeared to be a wad of old wool socks.

His dismissive response only served to make her more wary. Daana sat straighter, watching his every move for clues as to what was taking place. Snag was too enthralled with his work to tell her off again. So much so, he didn't even deliver his customary "don't mention I wear these" look when removing his spectacles from his breast pocket and affixing them to his face. A black-and-red bandana followed next, tied securely over his mouth and nose.

The sight of the face covering was worrisome. Daana craned her head back as she checked the tent for areas of ventilation and found none. "Would you like me to open the door for this?"

Snag's thin shoulders went rigid. He whipped his head around, glaring at her from over the top of his reading glasses. "And attract attention? No!"

"I'm concerned about fumes."

"There aren't going to be any fumes. I'm grinding powder. Now stop watching me. It's creepy!"

Daana pretended to look away only long enough for him to stop glaring at her. Snag had to know she was still watching, but perhaps if she refrained from speaking, he'd allow it. He selected the wad of socks from the assortment and unfurled it with care. Her plan to remain inconspicuously quiet worked as well as could be expected, which was to say a generous span of thirty to forty seconds at most.

Daana recognized the dark substance in his hands and uttered the words without thinking. "That's charcoal."

She earned his wrathful gaze once more. Only this time, there was an extra element to his sour scowl. His furrowed eyebrows knitted together into one deep, suspicious line across his wrinkled forehead. "How'd you know that? I thought your specialty was history books and talking all the time."

After having showcased her powers back at the falls, Daana supposed there wasn't any point in sticking to the emissary cover story. Anyone with half a brain would know she was not a political liaison by now. "They kept samples of charcoal back at the academy for spellwork. Never got to use any of it, personally. But I did try to watch whenever the alchemy students would let me."

"Spellwork?" Snag pulled the briquette to his chest protectively. He looked her up and down with the sort of scrutiny typically reserved for drunken mercenaries and wayward swordsmen. His gaze stopped on her armlets. Whatever realization was forming within his mazework of a mind caused his eyes to widen. "So it's true then? All that talk about what happened during the swamplander attack?"

Daana sincerely doubted it. She lifted one shoulder in an overly casual shrug. "Depends on what was said, I guess."

"You a witch?" Before she could answer, Snag followed up with a far more pressing question. "You don't spontaneously set things on fire, do you?"

"Not usually."

In a bizarre turn of events, the assassin-poisoner was suddenly the one side-eyeing the exit, as if debating whether or not to cut his losses and run.

A bad joke, apparently. Daana tried to put him back at ease. "I'm not a witch and I don't set things on fire."

Some of the leeriness softened from his curled expression. Snag ruminated on Daana's answer for several painstaking seconds more before putting his thoughts to words. "Academy trained, huh? Does that mean you're as good at taking notes as you are at interrupting?"

Rude. To be fair, she could see how her perfectly justifiable questions could be misconstrued as a hindrance. "As it happens, I am an excellent notetaker."

Wait, had he changed his mind about making her his honorary assistant? Had she changed *her* mind? Two minutes ago she didn't want to be anywhere near his experiments. The charcoal was piquing her interest, however. From her academy days, Daana knew it had a variety of uses, including smelting and as an ingredient in stomach-soothing tonics. While the former was improbable in this case, the latter also seemed unlikely. Snag may have been a medic in title, but he was far too excited about the project for it to be work-related.

That probably should have worried her. All the entirely valid reasons to quietly excuse herself from the tent, however, were being overshadowed by her growing curiosity. In her defense, Snag had said so himself that he wasn't dealing with poison. Surely there wouldn't be any harm in making herself useful. Perhaps if he viewed her as his assistant and not just "Curly's secret girlfriend," he'd be more inclined to protect her as well.

Yes, there was the main motivator—not curiosity, protection! That was a one hundred percent, absolutely legitimate reason for going along with whatever this was.

Daana gnawed the corner of her lip, trying her best not to appear overly excited. "Are you officially requesting my help?"

With a reluctant sigh, Snag selected a battered notebook and a second bandana from his pile and extended both in her direction. "I've got the strangest feeling I'm going to regret this, but fine, whatever. You can be my temporary assistant. At least until Curly gets back."

Daana's line of sight moved from the items held in his hand to the crowded laundry line hanging a regrettable distance away. "I need to grab something first."

"Such as?"

"Bottoms."

"Ah," he said with a rattling shake of his head. "There's that regret. Right on schedule."

Snag averted his gaze, pretending to rearrange his items around his work station as Daana leapt from the bed and wrangled her thick trousers up over her hips. The fabric was cold and still a little damp in some areas, but she was too thrilled to care. For what felt like the first time in her life, someone had willingly chosen her as their assistant. And not just anybody, either, but an actual expert in a field! The fact that the field in question was poison did little to damper the warm, fuzzy sensation blossoming within her rapidly beating chest.

Fully clothed once more, Daana settled onto the cold ground beside him. She secured the bandana over her face in the same way he had and flipped the tattered notebook to a blank page. Her voice was only slightly muffled by the musty-smelling face covering. "Ready."

Snag placed the precious lump into the bowl of his mortar. With a few practiced turns of the pestle, he had the charcoal broken into more manageable pieces. Daana watched, wide-eyed and with her chalk stick held between her fingers, ready to start recording the moment something exciting happened. Regrettably, it all went rather routine. The briquette pieces broke smaller and smaller, gradually turning to refined powder beneath the crushing weight of the pestle. Snag kept at it, face scrunched in concentration, as he ensured every last lump was ground into the uniform consistency of his liking.

Temporary assistant to the chief medical officer-poisoner was not as thrilling of a position as Daana had hoped. Other than noting that charcoal ground rather well into dust, there wasn't much for her to do. She found herself attempting polite conversation in order to avoid falling asleep. "So what happens next?"

For once, Snag was forthcoming with an answer. "I portion it out into separate vials and from there add additional ingredients, testing for possible reactions."

It all sounded so . . . ordinary. Perhaps Daana had misjudged the assignment and Snag really was making a stomach-soothing tonic. "Is this for medicinal purposes?"

"And waste my ingredients?" Snag set the mortar and pestle aside and began fitting the funnel to the first empty vial. "Gods, no. I'm testing a theory."

"About what?"

"About whether or not charcoal has underutilized uses." He talked while slowly filling each vial, breaking from his explanation every now and then to deliver a set of measurements to be recorded. "I found a small stash of unusual ingredients while we were clearing the cave of booby traps. I suspect they were what might've been used to bring the pass down—a combination, anyway. Didn't get to have a look at the inner mechanisms though, on account of the falling rocks and marauding swamplanders and what have you."

Daana lowered her chalk stick and swallowed the sudden lump in her throat. "Charcoal was responsible for bringing the pass down?"

"That's the theory."

And here she thought poison was the deadly option. Leave it to Snag to prove her wrong as usual. "We're not trying to replicate that, are we?"

"No."

"Oh, good."

"*I* am trying to replicate it. You're taking notes."

She set the notebook down and locked eyes with him. "You can't be serious."

"Hush. Assistants don't speak during experiments."

"Well that would make for a very poor assistant, wouldn't it? How are they supposed to interject when they think something is a terrible idea? Terrible ideas such as trying to replicate whatever it was that caused the mountain to implode on itself, for instance?"

Daana could tell Snag was smiling despite the stained bandana that obscured the lower half of his face. His voice was slightly higher in pitch, bordering dangerously on amused. "Where's your spirit of adventure?"

"It died the moment you mentioned imploding mountains."

"Good. Maybe you'll stop interrupting then."

The promise of protection no longer seemed worth the effort if it involved getting taken out by an unstable experiment in the process. Unfortunately, Daana had nowhere else to go. This tent was her only safe haven, even if it was growing markedly less safe with each passing minute. "First of all, that's not going to work on me. I will interject with safety concerns as much as I like," she said. "Secondly, I have a safety concern. My own, primarily, because it feels like you're tampering with powers beyond your means."

He glanced at her from out of the corner of his eye. "I'm the one tampering with powers beyond my means?"

It seemed rather obvious considering he was the one currently pouring a second, yellowy powdered substance into the first vial. Daana answered anyway, in the unlikely event Snag was not simply being rhetorical. "Looks that way to me."

"Hypocrite."

She sat straighter at the accusation. "Excuse me?"

"You're the one wearing magical armbands. Seems like you're more familiar with the unnatural tampering of power than I am." Snag sealed the first vial with a cork stopper and gave it a vigorous shake. "But what do I know? I'm just a simple gobby scratching out a humble existence fixing other people's problems."

Daana narrowed her eyes at him. Not so much for being called out, but because he was right and she had no way to refute it. "Touché"

"It's pronounced *touchy*. And no, you may not."

"No, I meant . . . never mind."

Snag held the vial overhead, peering at it with an expression that was hard to place. "One capful of ground brimstone added to vial one—write that down."

Daana did so, reluctantly. "What happens if it combusts?"

"I won't be testing that part in here," he scoffed. "Especially not while holding it. What kind of idiot do you take me for?"

"Well you could have mentioned that before, you know."

"I assumed it was obvious."

Daana suspected it had less to do with it being obvious and more with the fact that he enjoyed watching her squirm. She should have bit back her words, but the situation already had her on edge and his continual pokes were not helping. The accusation rolled right off her tongue without a second thought. "I'm beginning to see why you were banished from the flatlands."

Snag's voice dripped with insincerity. "Do you now? Oh, do tell."

"You keep it hidden alright. In fact, compared to the other faithful, you come across as the most normal one. But you're a walking tinderbox, aren't you?"

His eyebrows furrowed not so much in anger as general confusion. "What's that mean?"

"You're unpredictable and liable to get out of hand."

"Well then you'd be wrong."

"You're trying to recreate the same process that imploded a mountain!"

Snag added two capfuls of brimstone to the second vial and gave it a vigorous shake before holding it to the gray light filtering in over his head from the top of the canvas ceiling. His tone implied his ruthless smile had returned, hidden beneath his bandana. "Nah, I meant about the banishment. The official reason they kicked me out was smuggling."

Daana resisted the sudden urge to slam the notebook against her head. "Oh my gods."

"Yes, yes, pray to whoever you like, if it makes you feel better." He uncorked the vial and gave it an experimental sniff. The results must have been underwhelming because the leathery skin on his forehead wrinkled in dismay. "Still doesn't smell right. We're missing something."

"Virgin blood?" she volunteered sarcastically.

"Are you offering?"

Daana snapped her arms to her chest protectively, narrowing her eyes at him. "No touchy."

CHAPTER FIFTEEN

Enchantment

The storm raged all night without any signs of lessening. The inside of Daana's tent was cozy, however, and the warmth of her shared blankets made it doubly so. Sometime during the night she and Curly had gravitated toward one another. She hadn't even realized it, at least not until a loud snore near her head startled her awake. Not startled enough to move, of course. The heat radiating from Curly's body was like sleeping next to a personal fireplace. While the proper thing would have been to increase the distance between them, the proper thing also sounded terribly cold.

Thus, she remained nestled in the curl of his arm, feeling the rise and fall of his broad chest with each slow breath. It was a soothing sensation. Piled beneath a mountain of furs, warm and comfortable, Daana allowed the rhythmic pitter-patter of the falling rain to lull her back to sleep.

Croak!

For a brief moment, her heavy eyelids fluttered open. The blurry shape perched beside Daana was no immediate concern to her overworked mind and she soon slipped back into the dreamless void.

This time the harsh scream of the raven was accompanied by a flurry of wet, beating wings. *Croak! Croak! Croak!*

"What in chaos?" Daana struggled to free herself from the restricting curl of Curly's arm. She sat up, blinking the sleep from her eyes. A quick glance from one sagging wall of the tent to the next confirmed that Snag had already left for his shift in the infirmary. He didn't seem like the type to carelessly leave the door unfastened, which failed to explain why it was currently hanging ajar. Daana eyed the surprise intruder warily. "What are you doing in here?"

Although most of the flock looked indistinguishable from one another, she knew this one to be Mother on account of the missing eye. The large raven ruffled the feathers on her head as she hopped away. Mother stopped just shy of the open door and glanced back at Daana, as though expecting her to follow.

On second thought, it didn't matter what the raven wanted. Daana was tired and the sun was nowhere near being up yet. She could deal with the obnoxious bird in the morning. Or, better yet, someone else could. "Close the door on your way out." Daana collapsed back into bed and pulled the blankets over her head. "I'm going back to sleep."

Her efforts were for naught as Mother swiftly returned, this time with a vengeance. The raven squawked and screamed, pecking at Daana's body through the tangle of thick furs.

"Leave me alone!"

Curly stirred beside her. He stretched his burly arms over his head with a yawn. "Something's attacking its nest."

"It's what?" Daana cautiously lifted her head from the protection of her arms, prepared to duck back under the covers the moment the angry raven relaunched its assault on her. "Do you suddenly speak bird, too? How do you know that?"

In lieu of an intelligible response, the orc rolled over onto his back and started to snore.

Seriously? How was that any help at all? Daana's wary gaze shifted from Curly's still form back to Mother. "You don't have a nest."

Croak!

Daana knew next to nothing about ravens, but this cry seemed different than the times she'd heard it before. Mother sounded neither hungry nor angry, but scared. Scared? Great, now she felt bad for it! This was not how Daana had envisioned spending her morning. "Fine, I'm coming! But this better be worth it."

Grumbling, Daana threw her furs aside. There was no need to dress, as she was currently wearing her only dry set of clothing—someone else's actually, but she wasn't going to dwell on that. Not when she had pestering ravens to focus on. Fastening her belt around her waist and checking to be sure the dagger was still attached, Daana snatched her cloak from the clothesline and shoved her feet into still-damp boots. Tugging the thick hood over her head, she stomped out after the bird into the downpour.

Mother, still softly croaking, hopped along the muddy ground in front of her, leading her through the maze of drooping tents. Daana pulled the fabric tighter over her arms, shivering. "Alright, you have my attention. I'm out of bed and soaking wet, now what? Where are we going?"

Oh good gods, she was talking to a damn bird. Grief was making her fuzzy-brained. *Turn back*, the rational portion of her mind insisted. *Return to the tent and pretend this never happened. Cling to whatever sanity you have left.*

Mother clasped the edge of Daana's cloak in her beak and yanked.

"You know what, never mind. I'm not doing this. Go bother Rasp. At least he'll know what you're saying."

The one-eyed raven dropped the cloth from her beak and jetted upward, beating her wet wings against Daana's face.

Stifling a scream, Daana covered her head and spun around. That was it—she'd reached her breaking point. She was officially done with anything and everything that had to do with ravens! Muddy water squelched beneath her leather boots as she stomped back in the direction they'd come. She was only a few stomps into the return journey when an icy prickle crept up her spine and spread to the back of her neck.

Daana froze mid-step. With ear tips tingling, she glanced warily over her shoulder at Mother. "That's not you, is it?"

Croak!

No, not the raven. This was coming from further away. *Magic*, her sixth sense told her. Dark magic. *Lots* of dark magic. With rainwater collecting on the tip of her nose, Daana reluctantly lifted her finger into the misty air. Her voice was barely a squeak. "You want me to go in that direction? Toward the magic?"

Croak!

Was that a yes? Why did that sound like a yes?

Sucking in a lungful of cold mountain air, Daana tentatively followed. Mother hopped quickly across the patchy, puddle-soaked ground between the rows of weathered tents, leading her all the way to the edge of camp. Mother would have kept going had Daana not hesitated. She braced herself against the wet bark of a paper birch as her eyes roved back and forth across the shadowy landscape. She couldn't see anything of significance beyond the dark, swaying tree forms, but something was out there. She could feel it. The hairs on Daana's arm lifted into the air as the call of magic rippled across her skin.

Mother was growing impatient. The raven fluttered ahead without her, croaking at Daana to follow.

"You're going to get me killed, aren't you?" Following a raven out into the deep, dark woods unescorted seemed like a very poor idea. A wiser person would have turned back around, but the magic danced like a siren song in her ears, impossible to ignore. With a prayer on her lips, Daana sucked in a lungful of soggy, damp air and plunged into the dark woods after her impatient guide.

The forest was suffocatingly dark. Daana slipped and slid as she tried to keep pace with the raven, wincing each time a wet, needled branch whipped across her face. She did not have to rely on Mother's persistent calls to guide her for long. The approaching magic burned bright in her mind's eye, acting as an internal compass for her sixth sense to follow. Reaching an area of the woods where the trees thinned, Daana stopped, panting to catch her breath. A small glimmer of gray light filtered down from between the treetops, scarcely illuminating the patchy woodland floor below.

Squinting through the downpour, Daana saw two shapes standing within the small clearing. The closer of the pair she recognized as Rasp. Barefoot and wearing nothing more than a thin undershirt and trousers, he appeared unaffected by the rain. The other form, Daana realized as she drew nearer, ducking between the dark tree forms, wasn't a person at all. She saw instead a gray, listless shadow. It billowed and swirled around Rasp like a living cloud, whispering strange words in a soft, melodic hum. Daana did not recognize the language, but her sixth sense knew right away what it was.

Enchantment.

Fear lanced up her spine. Seekers were trained to handle witches, not otherworldly entities, especially not ones of this caliber. Power rippled in the air around the shadow. Even from a distance, Daana could detect the stench of sulfur and rotten sewage wafting from its incorporeal body. Panic gnawed at Daana's courage as she glanced back over her shoulder in the direction she had come. Camp was too far. There wasn't time to run back for help, and shouting at this distance would only alert the entity of her presence.

Mother landed on the tree beside her. The raven kept quiet, but the look in her one beady, black eye was a pitiful one. She tilted her head, silently pleading for Daana to interfere.

An incantation from Willem's spellbook formed in Daana's mind unprovoked. For a split second, the grief of losing him dropped in her chest, but there wasn't time to consider what he was or why he'd risked his life for her. Surely such a sacrifice had to have purpose. Perhaps it was time to find out exactly what that purpose was.

Working her dagger from its makeshift holster, Daana raced across the slippery ground with mud and water splattering underfoot. The unfamiliar power in her armlets crackled down her wrists and pulsed across her fingers with an eerie blue glow. Daana dove low, dragging the blade of the dagger into the soft dirt, and etched a crude ring around her and Rasp.

"*Ne intraveritis!*"

The magic responded. Her protection spell sprang up around them in a blazing shield of shimmering blue. The shadow swept forward with dark tendrils of billowing smoke and encircled them. Magic crackled against magic, with sparks of blue piercing through the shifting dark. Daana rose onto stiff legs and braced herself against the onslaught. Sliding the blade back through her belt, she hooked her forefingers together and drew her concentration inward. A second wave of magic burst from her trembling hands and the ring glowed with twice the intensity as before.

Rasp broke from his trance with a startled yelp and seized Daana's arm. She grimaced, feeling his fingertips cut into her skin through the thick wool of her cloak. There was something else too, besides the sudden pain. A crackling heat that burned from Daana's elbow to her fingertips. Easing one eye open, she watched, mystified, as a swirling yellow intermixed with the blue pouring from her body.

There was also screaming. Daana realized it was not coming from her own tightly clenched mouth, but from Rasp's.

"Go the fuck away!"

Rasp didn't speak a spell, and yet, the magic responded. In a flare of brilliant, blinding yellow, it surged from the center of the protection ring and flared across the drenched ground, sending a shockwave of knee-high water in its wake. The darkness shrank back. In a plume of black and gray smoke, the shadow spiraled skyward and fizzled out with a hiss. Twisting and writhing, the remnants of the cloud dissipated into the surrounding shadows until there was nothing left but the roaring pitter-patter of rain.

Daana unhooked her fingers, chest heaving. The dancing waves of blue and yellow light faded to a flicker around them. She turned and, without thinking, struck Rasp in the shoulder with her clenched fist. "You?" she screamed, shaking the sting from her fingers. "You've been a witch this whole time?"

Not just any witch, *the* witch. The one responsible for holding up the mountain passage back at the falls. Magic was like a fingerprint. On the surface, all signatures appeared relatively similar, but someone trained in the art of detection could learn to decipher which signature belonged to which wielder. In Rasp's case, it was less of a magical fingerprint and more akin to a raging warning beacon. His power was raw, untapped, and barely under control.

"Rude," Rasp muttered, rubbing the life back into his shoulder.

Probably wasn't the best idea to hit him, all things considered, but the moment had passed. Daana threw her hands into the air. "How did I miss this?"

First Willem and now Rasp, too? This was clearly the universe's way of telling her she wasn't cut out to be a witch hunter. Perhaps it was time to give the dragon hunting profession a try. She certainly made for good bait.

Mother descended from above and landed near their feet, chattering excitedly.

"Mother? How did you . . . where the fuck am I?" Standing unsheltered from the rain, the answer dawned upon Rasp relatively quickly. He wrapped his arms around his midriff, shifting from foot to foot as he shivered. "Shit! What happened to the tent? How did I get all the way outside?"

Daana considered offering him her cloak, but decided she would rather keep it instead. She'd just saved his ass after all. It was the least he could do. "You were under an enchantment."

Rasp's eyes grew wide. "It can do that?"

In light of the circumstances, he was taking the news surprisingly well. Unlike Daana, who suddenly wanted nothing more than to bury her head in bottomless sand and pretend none of this was happening. "How should I know that? I don't even know what that thing was!"

"The dark entity, idiot. The thing you've been warning me about this entire time? Gods, I thought it was your job to coach me through these things, not vice versa." Rasp folded over, still shivering. "And where in the realm have you been anyway? Don't get me wrong, I appreciate whatever the fuck you just did, but I could have used you during the cave misadventure too, you know. Teaching me one lesson and then throwing me to the wolves does not qualify as an apprenticeship."

"What are you talking about?"

Rasp tilted his head at her, rainfall streaming down his face as his lips pulled into a quizzical frown. "Whisper, so help me, if you're messing with me right now, I'm going to drop-kick you off this blasted mountain."

Whisper? Who in the seven realms was Whisper? Daana blinked the droplets from her lashes as she lifted her chin to the dark sky, groaning, "Oh my gods. You're deranged."

Rasp reached out and brushed the side of Daana's cheek with his fingers. "Why are you disguised as the emissary?"

"Because I am the emissary!"

Rasp's expression changed. The softness disappeared from his brow as his jaws locked together. He seized Daana by the wrists and yanked her closer. "You're not Whisper," he said in a snarl that was more beast than man. "Why do you have their magic? What did you do to them?"

"I didn't do anything to anyone!" She didn't dare pull away for fear his iron grip would tighten. "I have *Willem's* magic. Because *Willem* gave it to me. Right before he fucking died. Magic I just saved your ass with, in fact. I would appreciate it if you would show even a modicum of re—"

"Shit!"

This outburst didn't seem necessarily directed at her. Still, she found it rather rude, considering she'd just saved his life and all. Daana drew herself to her full height and adopted her most authoritative voice. "Unhand me."

"They're gone. They're fucking gone." Despite the fact he didn't appear to be listening, Rasp released her all the same. He slowly sank to the soft ground, muttering a string of unintelligible curses into his hands. "No, no, no . . ."

"Oh no you don't." Daana heaved him upright with minor success. If Rasp went down, she feared she wouldn't be able to get him up again. "We can't stay here. We have to get you back to camp." What to do after that, Daana wasn't sure. She didn't know where Faris had set up his tent. She certainly couldn't bring Rasp back to hers, not with Curly there. Doing so would result in far too many questions. The infirmary? Did she dare drag Briony into this? Snag would be present, too. Involving a member of the faithful four meant involving Protector Dawnsight. An outcome Daana fervently wanted to avoid.

Rasp decided for her. Using Daana as a counterweight, he pulled himself the rest of the way and threaded his arm through hers. "The infirmary," he said. "We have to find Briony."

Well, that certainly made her decision easier. The making it part, at least. The part where Daana accomplished it without garnering unwanted attention was yet to be seen. Perhaps fate would smile kindly down upon her and grant her an uncomplicated task for once. Unlike the last several days, which had all ended a few missteps shy of disaster.

Stop overthinking and go!

Right. Time to start moving, before her refusal to make a decision resulted in disaster. Daana tightened her grip on Rasp's arm and started back toward camp, suddenly painfully aware that she'd never led a member of the blind before.

She hated to ask, but there didn't seem any other way around it. "Do I tell you where to step or . . ."

Rasp clung to her, shivering, as his bare feet sank into the wet mud with every shaky step. "You lead, I follow. Warn me of any tripping hazards. Other than that, just don't walk me off a damn cliff, alright?"

She could handle that. "Right."

"And thanks," Rasp added, under his breath.

It was unwise to thank her for saving his life so prematurely. As much as she appreciated the vote of confidence, Daana was only now beginning to realize just how far out from camp they truly were. She pulled Rasp beneath the overhanging bows of a towering poplar beside her. It wasn't much in the way of shelter, but it at least kept the rain out of her vision long enough to get a better idea of their surroundings. Daana's gaze swept across the dark forest floor as the icy grip of panic flooded her airways. The dark, looming trees were identical in every way, and whatever trail she'd left on her way in had already been washed away by the unrelenting downpour.

Croak.

Rasp's head perked at the sound. "Mom?"

The large, one-eyed raven fluttered down onto a lower branch beside them, shaking the beads of water from her feathers with a disapproving snap of her beak.

He reached out and stroked the top of her head with trembling fingers. "I'm sorry." Tears leaked from the corners of his eyes. "I don't know what happened."

Rasp's trembling was growing worse. Daana feared the chills were already setting in. If she didn't find their way back to camp soon, she would either be returning alone or not at all. Stifling a sigh, she unfastened the cloak from around her neck and placed it over his shoulders. "So you *really* can understand them? The ravens?"

Rasp nearly buckled under the unexpected weight of the cloak. Not that it was heavy, he just seemed to be in the precarious state where a light breeze could have taken him out. He gathered the edges of the warm fabric in one hand and pulled it tight over his body, keeping the other arm free so as not to lose his grip on Daana. "When they want me to."

Croak.

"Mother says 'thank you.'"

Talking birds and evil spirits. It was as if she'd stepped from reality right into a storybook faerie tale. The ending was destined to be one of the dark, grim ones if they didn't find their way back to camp in a timely manner. Thus, rather than reject her newfound sense of insanity, Daana embraced it.

"Can you ask Mother to help me find the way back?" she asked. "I'm a little turned around."

Gurgling a reply, the large raven swooped ahead of them, moving from tree to tree as she croaked for them to follow. Daana tried the best she could, but their progress was slow. Even with the added warmth of her cloak, Rasp shuffled alongside her at a snail's pace. His movements were sluggish and stiff. The added difficulty of navigating the soft, slippery terrain without losing his footing was siphoning his remaining strength.

Daana's eyes strained against the dark as she glimpsed the first signs of camp peeking through the scraggly trees. She increased her pace, all but dragging Rasp in her wake as she tried to pinpoint which of the sagging tents in the distance was the infirmary. Mother's harsh croak rang out ahead of them, its echo muffled by the thunder of the rain.

Rasp jerked Daana to a halt. "Wait!"

Before Daana could demand an explanation, a dark form materialized from out of the brush in front of them, purposefully blocking their path.

"Sergeant Farrow," Daana stammered as blood rushed to the tips of her ears. Something about the situation was off. Her sixth sense was screaming so loud, it nearly drowned out the roar of the surrounding rainfall. "What are you—"

"Save your breath, elfling." Ellisar approached with her longsword drawn.

"Sheath your sword, Sergeant," Daana told her. Her boldness was an act, of course. Not that it would fool Ellisar, but maybe it would buy her some time to figure out what in the chaos was taking place. "We are on the same side. Threatening us is unnecessary."

"Sword?" Rasp repeated, clamping tighter onto Daana's arm.

Ellisar's golden eyes roved between them suspiciously. "Are we on the same side? Finding you two out here in the woods, alone, certainly raises some curious questions."

Rasp was a beat faster than Daana, providing an easy explanation for their sudden disappearance. "Maybe we were fucking. It's not your business, is it?"

"Except you weren't."

Shit. How much had Ellisar seen? Daana didn't know how she was supposed to explain any of what had happened, let alone to someone who had a nasty reputation for stabbing first and asking questions later. "Let us pass. Rasp's not in a good way, just look at him. He needs to be taken to the infirmary immediately."

"Change of plans, I'm afraid."

"What are you talking about? He's not well! Move aside and let me take him—"

Ellisar's blade cut through the air as fast as a viper strike and stopped a hair's breadth from Daana's neck. Ellisar held the sword in her right hand and, with her left, reached out and plucked the dagger from Daana's belt. "To Oralia," she finished Daana's sentence for her. "You can tell her all about your little misadventure in the woods. Let's see how far you can spin your lies before she finally agrees to gut you."

CHAPTER SIXTEEN

The Truth

*S*hit, shit, shit.

This was bad. So, so bad.

One moment, Rasp was burrowed deep within Faris's warm blankets, ignoring the faun's meek protests for personal space, drifting peacefully to sleep, and the next he was freezing his ass off outside being saved by the least competent member of the travel party! He didn't remember waking up, or leaving the tent, or how he got all the way into the woods without slamming face-first into a tree. That probably had something to do with the enchantment, he supposed. This revelation, however, only made the knots in his gut twist tighter. How was he expected to keep the darkness at bay if it could simply seize control without him even knowing?

Oh, and to top it all off, Ellisar had intercepted him and Daana on their way back. The lunatic elf was now driving them straight into the awaiting jaws of the enemy. Had Rasp been caught alone, it might have been possible to explain his disappearance. But now there were two stories to corroborate, and his and Daana's wouldn't align. Oralia would know something was amiss. What's worse, Ellisar wasn't telling whether or not she'd seen what had happened. Even if he and Daana could somehow get their lies straight ahead of time, it would be their word against one of Oralia's top officers.

"Ellisar," Rasp said, his mind desperately grasping for whatever half-baked solution it could find. She'd helped him unexpectedly once before, back in the cave. Maybe, just maybe, if he appealed to her sense of self-preservation, she would let him go a second time. "This is life or death. You have to let us—"

"Shut it."

"You helped me once before. If you could just—"

"That was a one-time courtesy and you fucked it up. I won't be making that mistake again."

The cold air stung Rasp's cheeks as his anger flushed across his clammy face. He raised his voice. "Do you want to die?"

"Do you?" Ellisar replied coldly. "Keep running your mouth, and I'll show you what actual follow-through looks like."

Rasp's response died on his tongue in the form of a whimper.

They were fucked. Absolutely, positively, six ways, sideways, beyond a shadow of a doubt, fucked. Whatever hope Rasp had felt the day before slowly shriveled within his dying soul. Briony and Faris's escape plan was destined to fail. He could see that now. Oralia had eyes on him at all times. Even if he managed to talk his way out of an early grave and the trio slipped away into the night, the protector's people would be on them like fleas on a stray. Ellisar was a damned hunter, for the gods' sakes! She would delight in the opportunity to track him down like a wild beast.

Hot tears streaked down Rasp's numb face as he came to the realization that his options had finally run out.

Mother swooped low overhead, calling out to him.

"How can you say that? You know Oralia's not going to listen." Rasp tightened his grip on Daana's arm as he stumbled along beside her. Cold, ankle-deep mud squished and squelched around his bare feet, attempting to suck him under. Despite the chill that bore deep into his creaky bones, the charms strung through his ear burned hot against his skin.

"They never listen," Rasp said.

Croak!

"Truth? I've been telling her the truth this whole time!" Most of it, any-way. The fuzzy, black cloud of internal guilt started to drift into focus, but Rasp pushed it away from the forefront of his mind with practiced ease. Now was not the time to pry the lid off of that snake pit.

"I assume you're speaking to the bird," Daana hissed beneath her panting breath at him. "But I think it might be best to let me do the talking once we're inside the tent."

"No colluding," Ellisar's harsh voice barked at them from behind.

Rasp clung to Daana for all he was worth as she half-trotted, half-dragged him through the muddled maze of dark shadows back toward what he assumed was camp. The storm had him all discombobulated. No matter how hard he strained, his ears couldn't pick up anything over the thunder of the rain. His nose didn't fare any better. Everything smelled of wet wood and mud. Without his senses to guide him, Rasp couldn't make heads or tails of their surroundings. Ellisar could have been driving them off a cliff for all he knew. Maybe that would have been better.

Alas, their journey did not end with a sudden drop and long fall, but at the front of Oralia's tent. Ellisar shouldered her way past them and threw a wet tarp aside, shoving the pair in ahead of her. Rasp stumbled inside, whipping his head back and forth to make sense of his new surroundings. The interior of the tent was just as dark as the outside. The smell was different though, as the pungent odor of orc musk all but jammed its salty fingers up Rasp's nose upon entering.

"What in chaos?" a male voice rumbled at them.

"Ellisar," Oralia's voice came next, near the same location as the first, laden with equal parts drowsiness and irritation. "What is the meaning of this?"

"Up and at 'em, boss," Ellisar called as she secured the flap shut behind them. "You'll never guess what I found out gallivanting in the woods."

"Could this not have waited until dawn?" The male voice spoke again. It took Rasp's sluggish thoughts a moment to identify the speaker as the camp's cook, Sascha. In the same instant, a much smaller, horrified portion of Rasp's brain now understood *why* the tent smelled of orc musk. They weren't just in audience with the protector, but her private company and, from the smell of it, they'd been awful busy.

"What were they doing outside?" Oralia demanded.

Rasp flinched when he heard the soft clatter of Ellisar's sword being sheathed. Normally this would have comforted him. Regrettably, sword or no sword, it didn't detract from the fact that he was probably about to die. "You'll have to ask them," Ellisar said. "I'm curious to hear what they come up with."

"Thank you for bringing this to my attention, Sergeant Farrow," Oralia said. "Return to your station outside and keep watch. Ensure we are not disturbed. I will signal for you if necessary."

"I brought them in, single-handedly, and now you're asking me to miss the best part?"

"Now, Ellisar."

Grumbling under her breath, the elf stomped back out into the rain.

Oralia paused, ensuring her orders had been carried out, before addressing her present company. "Emissary Lazuli," she said in a voice so fierce, Rasp was certain she could have pinned her victim to the floor with it had she tried. "Care to explain why you and Rasp were outside the perimeter in such inclement weather?"

Poor Daana couldn't seem to come up with an answer that was both believable and skirted the fact that she'd just thwarted an evil spirit from a storybook. She tried anyway, blurting out, "We didn't go together. I found him outside like this. I think he might have been sleepwalking. He seemed very disoriented and I was on my way to take him to the infirmary when—"

"I wasn't sleepwalking."

To Rasp's horror, the soft words had come from his own traitorous mouth. Oh dear gods, it had finally happened. His last shred of self-persever-ance had withered and died. The cold was partly to blame, surely. While the tent was significantly warmer than it had been outside, Rasp's unruly limbs failed to take notice. They continued to shake and tremble with a will of their own. He pulled Daana's cloak tighter over his quaking shoulders to no avail.

He barely had time to register the set of approaching footsteps before the waterlogged cloak was ripped from his back. It was replaced with something significantly heavier. Rasp bit back a protest as his numb fingers roved up and down the fur-lined fabric, quickly concluding that it was not only a bedcover, but still warm from previous use. He was so exceedingly grateful he hardly cared that the blanket smelled of orc sex. In fact, he wasn't even going to think about that pesky detail. Ever.

"When you have finished removing the rest of your wet clothes," Oralia said, snapping Rasp from definitely not envisioning the many private, pos-sibly traumatic, couplings the blanket had borne witness to, "you may go sit with Sascha."

"Excuse me?" the other orc said. "I would at least like to be consulted before you make these decisions on my behalf, thank you."

"Of course. Sascha, will you please keep our guide alive long enough to accomplish this mission so that we may retire together and not die horrid, gruesome deaths at the hands of our enemies?"

"While I fail to see how sharing my bedding prevents any of that, yes dear," Sascha said, his teasing tone clashing against Oralia's authoritative one.

Rasp peeled the wet shirt from his shivering torso and tossed it to the floor. He did the tent the courtesy of covering his lower half with the blanket before wriggling out of his trousers and kicking them away to join the rest of his ensemble. Breathless from the effort and still shivering, he wrapped the blanket tighter over his shoulders and shuffled past Oralia, probing the area around him for the bedroll with his bare toes as he went.

"You claim you were not sleepwalking, Rasp." Oralia kindly reminded him that, despite some mild concern regarding his welfare, this was still an active interrogation and she was going to get her answers one way or another. "I assume you were escaping then?"

"I was not!" He swiveled his head at her and scowled. He hoped the dark, blurry area he squinted at was her face and not her chest, but that was not the sort of thing one uttered out loud. Besides, her accusation kindled a fire in his belly, and he'd rather argue than worry about whether or not he was yelling at a pair of tits. "You know that thing Whisper kept warning us about? Well it's here and it found me. And it's not going to let up. We have to turn around now, before it's too late!"

"You were out in the cold too long. Whatever you thought you saw was a hallucination."

"No, you don't get to act like I'm the crazy one! Go ahead and ask Lady LaPrissy if you don't be—" Rasp's rant was cut short when Oralia hooked her foot behind his heel and swept him to the ground. He fell backward into Sascha with a surprised yelp.

"I changed my mind. You may stop talking now," Oralia said calmly, as if spilling Rasp onto his ass was an appropriate response to the situation at hand. "You are not doing anyone any favors, yourself included, trying to spin such nonsense."

Rasp followed one of her directions, wriggling his body into place beside Sascha with far more elbow than was necessary. Alas, the same did not apply to the "stop talking" rule. "Ask her!" Rasp shouted, pointing in what he hoped was Daana's direction. He wasn't even sure if she was still in the tent, to be honest. Maybe she'd done the smart thing and ducked out when no one was looking. He continued, regardless, because letting go of his mounting rage meant acknowledging the weight that pooled in the back of his throat, nearly cutting off his air. "She saved me, Oralia. Her! Of all people, when it should have been Whisper."

"Be silent."

"Will you listen to me? Whisper's gone!" Rasp gripped the blanket so tight he could feel the color draining from his knuckles. There was a tremble in his voice that hadn't been present before. Try as he might, he couldn't get it to go away. "You can feel it, can't you? They're gone and they're not coming back. I thought maybe this was one of their lessons. That they were punishing me for bringing the falls down, but then that thing came for me. And it almost had me, Oralia. It was that close. Whisper wouldn't have let that happen. And now, the only trace of your witch I can feel is on her!"

From near the entrance, he heard a faint whisper from Daana. "Oralia's witch?"

"We can't keep going. It will be the death of us all. Don't you get it?" The tightness in Rasp's throat was spreading. It moved into his chest and behind his eyes, doubling its pressure until something gave. It wasn't his body that quit on him this time, but his mind. That stupid, incessant cloud that had been hanging around the back of his skull for months now slunk from its dark corner and reared its ugly head.

The truth slipped free from his useless tongue and for once, he didn't try to stop it. What did it matter if they knew? It was all over now anyway. "I've been trying to stop you since Lonebrook, but you wouldn't listen. If the darkness doesn't kill us, my brothers will. Whether the realm reinstates me or not doesn't matter. My people will never accept me. Not after what I did."

Oralia's reply cut through him like a knife. "What did you do?"

"I killed him."

"*Who?*"

The memory was like a half-forgotten dream. Fuzzy bits and pieces that came and went without rhyme or reason. No matter how he tried to arrange them, Rasp had never been able to get the fragments to fit together well enough to glimpse the full picture. Not that he had really tried all that hard before. But now, the memory was clearer than it had ever been, and the real reason he was avoiding the mountains was one he couldn't keep from himself anymore.

Rasp spoke so softly his own ears strained to catch it. "My father. It was an accident. I didn't mean to tap into the dark magic and—"

"Enough! You are feverish and confused." Oralia stormed to the entrance, drawing back the doorway with an exasperated click of her teeth.

It must have counted as the signal because it wasn't long before he heard Ellisar respond. "You called?"

"Go fetch Snaglebrag. Tell him to bring the yellow arrowroot from his kit and any strong sedatives he can spare."

"*Finally.*"

"Wait, I can do it!" Daana's squeak was akin to a mouse who'd realized too late its tail was caught in a trap. "I'd like to be helpful and obviously I'm not any further use to you here, so—"

"You will do no such thing." Oralia assured her with steely confidence. Her voice shifted directions. "Sascha, it grieves me to evict you from my tent, but I suspect I will not be getting any more sleep tonight. If you could locate

Mister Belfast for me and tell him that his charge has been found wandering outside unattended, I would be most appreciative. Have Faris bring Rasp's pack, as well. He is in need of a change of dry clothes. Shoes too, from the looks of it."

The warm body pressed against him moved away and Rasp was cold once more. The orc's rumbly voice now sounded much farther above him. "Is it safe to assume I should find other accommodation afterward?"

"I suggest commandeering Faris's tent. He will not be needing it. Not after the earful I am about to bestow upon him." There was a deliberate pause as Rasp assumed Oralia was waiting for her lover's lumbering shape to disappear out into the downpour before continuing where she had left off. Judging from the severity of her words, they were now being issued through tightly clenched teeth. "What were you thinking, saying all of that in front of him?"

She must have been talking to him, as Daana had uttered a grand total of four words so far. Rasp attempted to match Oralia's tone but failed. If anything, he succeeded only in coming across more miserable than before. "I'm telling the truth."

"*I know that.* What I cannot fathom is why, of all possible moments, it was this one you chose to be completely forthright! I understand subtlety is not your expertise, but the next time I knock your ass to the ground that hard, it means shut up."

Rasp's expression twisted as his sorrow turned to venom. "I'm sorry. I just got snapped out of a fucking enchantment. My brain's a little soupy right now!"

"Then do yourself a favor and stop talking," Oralia said. "Emissary Lazuli, you are uncharacteristically quiet. I would like to hear your version of tonight's events. And do not waste my time with another lie. Your ears change color when you are untruthful, in case no one has ever told you."

When Daana gave no immediate reply, Oralia tried again, this time with a tone that was a few knife strokes short of murder. "My apologies, do you respond better to 'witch hunter'? That is what you are, is it not?"

Witch *what?* Rasp's spine automatically straightened as he waited for Daana's eventual reply. Unfortunately, like Oralia, he kept waiting. Whatever words Daana was attempting to form had seemingly compressed into a solid lump and settled in her throat. He could hear her trying to say something, but nothing intelligible was coming out.

He didn't know why he suddenly felt inclined to help Daana. Maybe it was because she'd gone out of her way to save him first. While that was an endearing thought, the answer was probably much simpler. As it turned out, picking on someone was only enjoyable if he was the one doing the picking. Standing by while it happened to someone else made him feel all squirmy inside.

"Just a thought," Rasp ventured. "Have you considered talking to her like she's a person and not your next victim?"

Grinding her tusks against her upper teeth, Oralia relented with a heavy sigh, "I know you are a seeker, Daana. And I know Rasp is a witch. None of this is a revelation to me."

Well that made one person. Rasp sat dutifully silent, waiting for what would happen next. Hopeful, that if he listened hard enough, he wouldn't have to ask such pesky questions as: *What the fuck is going on? What's a seeker? And where is Faris with my damn clothes?*

Oralia continued speaking to Daana. "I do not like the idea of trusting you, but I am regrettably short of options. As it stands, you may be the only person on this mountain capable of protecting him. I will ask you once more. What happened prior to you barging into my tent?"

Daana's explanation tumbled free in a single, conscious thought strung together without room for extravagances such as breath or discernible spaces between the words. "The raven woke me up, the one called Mother, I think? She led me to the magic and I saw Rasp standing with, well I don't know what it was, to be honest, but it oozed dark magic. Once I realized it had him under an enchantment, I did the only sensible thing and activated a protection spell around him."

When no one else said anything, Rasp held his index finger aloft and contributed his thoughts on the matter. "The sensible thing would've been to run away."

CHAPTER SEVENTEEN

Science

Outside, fast rainfall pitter-pattered against the canvas roof without signs of lessening. The raging storm failed to mask the sudden despair that stretched Oralia's stern voice abnormally thin. "I can no longer reach Whisper, either. I had hoped it was the iron tampering with the powerstone." The protector's tone was bordering on concerned now. "Are you certain Whisper is gone, Rasp?"

"Am I really one step ahead of you on this? Gods, where's Rali when you need her? I feel the sudden urge to gloat." Rasp wrapped himself tighter in the thick blanket with a shiver. After a moment, he remembered that Oralia was awaiting a response and offered it in the form of a grumble. "Whisper was Willem. So yeah, according to all the talk around camp, pretty sure they're dead."

"Um," Daana interrupted, having finally found the courage to speak. "Who is Whisper? It's the fourth time you've used that name and I'm still not any closer to an answer."

"The Palace Ghost," Oralia said. "Whisper was the only person standing between Rasp and whatever it was you encountered in the woods just moments ago. Regretfully, they are gone now. As you are the only other person here versed in magic, my hand has been forced. I must ask for your assistance, Daana."

"Protect him? You mean from that thing outside?" Evidently Daana's mouth was a step ahead of her brain and opened itself prematurely, allowing whatever thought currently was occupying the forefront of her mind to come tumbling out. "Seven realms, is that the spirit from the history book? Oh gods, no. I am not prepared for this."

Oralia's response was cut short by the sudden, splattering footsteps that sounded only moments ahead of the person who barged into the tent unannounced. Two persons, actually, Rasp realized, as he counted footsteps. One was fast and frenzied and the other less panicked, as if being awoken in the dead of night had lost its charm decades ago.

"I don't know how he slipped past me, honest." Rasp should have known the flighty one was Faris. The faun was at his side in the blink of an eye, trying to peel back the layer of old fur blankets as he babbled nonsense. "Briony gave him something to sleep. It wasn't supposed to do this!"

Rasp curled his upper lip, swatting Faris's grabby hands away. "Will you get your paws off me? I am capable of dressing myself, thank you very much!"

"Then why have you been making me do it this entire time?"

"You kept insisting. I thought you liked it!"

"Lower your voices please. Focus on getting dressed, Rasp, including shoes," Oralia ordered. Her voice changed both direction and volume, now barely over a whisper. "The others?"

Rasp heard the flap of leathery ears a split second before he was pelted in the face by a spray of water droplets. From the telltale jingle of earrings, he knew who the second arrival was well before Snag got his smartass reply out. "I missed the part about this being a pajama celebration. I feel so overdressed."

"I can't believe I'm saying this, but some of us would appreciate pants right now," Rasp said, jutting his hand up in the direction he assumed Faris to be standing. Rasp was still on the ground, still wrapped under a blanket and, possibly for the first time in his life, wishing there weren't this many people eagerly lined up around his bedroll while he was sitting naked as a jaybird.

"You're not the only one," Snag murmured. "Kinda hard to take you serious while you're standing in skivvies, boss."

From the light stomping, Rasp assumed Oralia had gone to retrieve her clothes from wherever they were piled on the floor. Instead of undressing, it sounded as though she merely tugged them over what she was already wearing. What was even more strange was the fact that, from the soft, metallic *clink-clink-clink*ing, she was also donning chainmail. "The message, Snaglebrag. Did you pass it along?"

"Yes, yes, super sneaky-like. Nobody saw me."

There was movement at the backside of the tent as the side lifted. Rasp nearly jumped out of his skin when a squat form rolled past, nearly flattening him in the process. The fuzzy, boulder-ish shape rose up alongside him, offering a patronizing pat on the head as it swaggered into the center of the tent. "Ellisar and Curly are waiting at the tree line," Rali said, keeping her thunderous voice notably less boomy. "Is this a real yellow arrowroot situation or are you just clocking our speed again? I get the whole testing us thing, but now, really? I haven't had time to shake off our last death-defying experience."

"It is not a drill. And I apologize for springing this on you so unexpectedly, but our circumstances have changed," Oralia rumbled. "I need you to vacate the Iron Ridge immediately. Take these three with you."

Faris choked on his surprise. "What?"

Daana, shockingly, managed to be more articulate. "We're going back?"

"Hush, children," Rali said sweetly. "The adults are talking."

"What about the pass?" Snag's ears must have been up and fanned wide, because his metal hoops tinkled together with every tremble of his jaw. "We can't exactly go back down it, you know."

Having donned his trousers, Rasp was fighting his way into a dry shirt when he heard this. His voice came out only slightly muffled by the coarse fabric currently refusing to let his head through. His heart, having settled since being death-marched into Oralia's tent, picked up where it had left off with a rapid *thump-thump-thump.*

His encounter with the dark entity had assured him of one thing—the spirit would stop at nothing to get him. If he was going to have any hope of staving off the stupid prophecy, then he had to accept whatever help came his way, including from the very people he'd formerly considered enemies. "You don't need to go back down the pass. There's another trail on the north side of the mountain, into the flatlands."

Faris kicked him with a hiss, but Rasp kept going. "I can get you there."

Oralia and her officers must have been doing that super annoying thing where they conversed without using words because, for a short stint, no one said anything. Rasp finished tugging his head through the opening of his shirt while his brain dutifully filled in the blanks his vision was unable to provide. He envisioned Oralia's expression saying something along the lines of, "There. Rasp knows the way. Satisfied, Snaglebrag?" Whereas the goblin was probably looking at her like she'd sprouted a second head because there was no way he'd ever be satisfied with such a flimsy plan.

Finally, the protector broke the silence, utilizing a tone that was entirely too confident to be genuine. "It is not ideal, I understand. But it may be the only way any of us get off this confounded mountain alive. Between the two of you, I have faith you will find your way. You know the flatlands better than anyone, Snaglebrag. Locate a hideout and lie low. I will rejoin you when possible."

"You're staying behind then?" Snag sounded almost as confused as Rasp felt.

"To lead the main party, yes. We will only slow you down. Speed is of the essence."

"Oralia, no!" This came from Rali. And, judging by the sudden pause, she must have received the mother of all glares for voicing her disagreement. Didn't stop the arguing, however, as Rali immediately switched to one of the orc languages. As Rali neglected to use the words "corpse sodomizer," Rasp understood none of it. It wouldn't have mattered anyway. The dwarf spoke so softly and quickly, he would have caught only a fraction of what was said. From the severity of her gruff tone, it was safe to assume the lieutenant disagreed with the protector's decision.

Oralia replied calmly in the same orc language as Rali. This succeeded only in angering her lieutenant more. They went back and forth for several turns until the issue reached an impasse that, judging from Oralia's unyielding tone, ended on the note of "I am in charge and we are doing it my way."

A pointed cough from Snag interrupted their bickering. "I don't mean to break up your love fest, but . . ."

The fact that he didn't finish his sentence led Rasp to conclude that he was back to substituting words with hand gestures. Rude.

"I don't hear anything," Rali muttered.

"Well then, sounds like the bait just volunteered itself," Snag said. "Go on. Go have a look-see. Prove me right."

"No way, bucko! You don't put your best worm on the hook. Everybody knows that."

"No one is leaving the tent until I say so." The protector addressed the group as a whole this time, finally explaining to the more confused members what the fuck was going on. "I am not above admitting defeat. Continuing this mission would yield nothing but certain death. Faris, Daana, I am tasking the two of you with shielding Rasp from whatever dark magic lurks in these mountains. Under the protection of my faithful four, you will travel ahead of the main party and into the foothills as quickly as possible. If you wish to survive, do as you are told. Understood?"

"We're leaving now?" Daana said. "I mean, I'm not opposed. Don't get me wrong. There are some people here I would rather not see again, but can I at least grab my things first? My spellbook, specifically. For . . . protection reasons?"

That might have been convincing had they all been born yesterday. Evidently Oralia thought the same because her rumbling voice shifted directions. "Ralizak, will you retrieve Lady Lazuli's spellbook for her?"

"As second-in-command, I'll be delegating that task to you, Snaggy."

"No thanks. I barely survived the last errand you all sent me on."

"But—"

Snag carried on, recounting all of his recent encounters with death. "Let's see now, there was the dragon, the rockslide, and the wyrm. Not to mention digging you four out of the mountain."

It wasn't out of character for Rali to disobey a direct order from her commander, but the fact that Snag wasn't giving in after a few halfhearted grumbles meant this wasn't so much an errand as it was a survival mission. Which should not have been the case given they'd been asked to fetch someone's luggage. Rasp stood and instinctively reached for Faris's shoulder. He found it on the second try and, instead of batting him away, Faris placed his hand over Rasp's and squeezed.

They were in agreement then. There was obviously something else afoot but, judging from their covertness, Oralia and her people were keeping it to themselves. Whatever was going on, Rasp hoped the secrecy was to avoid mass panic and not indicative of something far more sinister.

"I can get it myself," Daana was still attempting to talk her way into a swift getaway. "I won't be more than a minute."

"No!" Rali and Snag chorused together.

Oralia was more diplomatic in her response. "You have already had a difficult evening. Ralizak will be happy to do it for you."

There was a sudden intake of air as Rali drew breath for the upcoming onslaught. And then, for whatever reason, thought better of it. "Of course I'll grab the elfling's stupid book. In fact, I'll go ahead and collect all of her possessions while I'm at it." The dwarf stomped toward the doorway with a lot more gusto than was necessary. "What was I thinking? Offering brilliant tactical advice when I could have been carrying baggage all this time? My life's calling, fulfilled at last!"

"Without waking the rest of the camp, perhaps?" From the proximity of her voice, Oralia was now standing alongside the doorway—either holding the tent flap aside as a means to be helpful or attempting to throttle her sassy lieutenant into submission. While Rasp's brain considered both options equally valid, the fact that Rali was still producing noise indicated it probably wasn't the latter.

The dwarf made a sort of mocking sound under her breath as her stomping grew fainter, muffled by the downpour. From the wet splatter of her footsteps, she was only a few yards outside of the tent when Rasp heard a sudden thud, followed by a wet thump. He tilted his head in the direction of the doorway, straining for further clues. Rali's telltale footsteps had fallen deathly silent.

"Faris?" he ventured, hoping someone with fully functioning vision would clarify.

It was Daana who volunteered the missing information. "Oh fuck. Someone jumped her. She's down."

"Seven realms," Snag hissed. "Oralia, that fall looked a little too convincing."

"Oralia Dawnsight!" Captain Monk's voice called from outside. "You are surrounded. Drop your weapons and come out with hands above your heads."

"Under whose authority?" Oralia replied in a tone that did not match her sudden change in demeanor. The large orc shouldered past Rasp with startling speed. The metal ends of her belt clinked together softly as she fitted her sword into place at her hip. He was even more taken aback when he felt her press a blade into his hands. "If any of his people gets close to you, stab them."

"Uh . . ." What was possibly even more confusing than her command was the resulting tingle from blood rushing to a specific area of his body that, by all rights, had no business being awake right now.

"Oh my gods," Faris groaned.

Fortunately, Captain Monk was yelling again, drawing everyone's attention to the more pressing issue. "The authority is mine! I am officially charging you and your ilk with intent to commit treason against the United Territories of the Realm. We already have your dwarf. Surrender Lady Lazuli and the Stoneclaw into my custody if you wish for your lieutenant to live!"

"Seems you were right, Snaglebrag," Oralia said. "Change of plans. I will cut a path through. You get them out. Do not look back, just keep running."

"Mhm," Snag said, as though he were half listening.

"Hey!" Faris cried as his body lurched against Rasp. "I am not a ladder. If you wanted the lantern, you could have just asked."

Snag's feet landed back against the ground with a gentle thud. Had he possessed the ability to see, Rasp suspected he still would not have understood what the goblin was doing. Amid the rustle of activity, he could pinpoint the clink of glass and the soft rustle of sand, possibly powder, pouring from one container into another.

Rasp leaned closer to Faris, whispering, "If he comes at me with poison, I have permission to stab him."

"He's combined three vials of powder into the cavity of the lantern and is now . . . shaking it." Given Faris's sparse description, he too had no idea what was going on but, at the very least, possessed the sense not to admit it out loud.

"Match," Snag said in the tone of voice that would indicate he was jutting his hand in Faris's direction expectantly.

Faris must have forked it over relatively quickly because a spark of flame lit the inside of the tent a split second later. Snag dropped the match into the lantern and then whipped his creation out the door. Everything went dark again the moment he pulled the canvas flap shut behind him. It didn't last, though. Outside, the front of the tent flared bright as day as his creation sprang to life.

Rasp threw his hand over his eyes as the blinding light grew inexplicably brighter. "What the fuck is that?"

"He summoned the sun." Faris sounded mesmerized by the glow. "It's the middle of the night and it's burning as bright as daylight outside."

"Witch!"

Faris smacked Rasp's accusing hand back down. "Science."

"I call it the thunderflash. Induces temporary blindness. Impressive, innit?" The goblin was undeniably pleased with himself. He might have even been smiling. "You all might want to cover your eyes for this next part."

Outside, there was a crackling *pop, pop, pop* as the blinding light undulated from bright to dark with a disorientating strobe effect. Judging from the proximity of Oralia's voice, she had rejoined Snag alongside the doorway. "Snaglebrag," she said, her steadfast tone wavering ever so slightly, "I do not tell you often enough how brilliant you are."

"I get the feeling you're preparing to follow that up with a 'but.' The compliment loses all meaning when you do that, you know."

"I was going to ask if you have any more of those, actually."

"Ah, well, no. Sorry. In my excitement, I sort of threw all of my ingredients together, all mishy-mashy like. I can see now how that might've been a tad excessive of me."

"Effective though," Oralia remarked as the thunder flash continued to spark and boom just outside of the tent. "I do have one small request, however."

"There it is. I knew you'd get around to that 'but' eventually."

"For the love of gods, whatever you do, promise me you will not teach science to Ellisar."

CHAPTER EIGHTEEN

You Are a Dwarf, Not a Chicken

The thunderflash lit the edge of the encampment and the dozen realm soldiers positioned outside the front of Oralia's tent in an eerie, pale glow. The blast lasted for nearly a minute and then, with her enemies temporarily blinded, she slid soundlessly from the doorway. The plan, which was a generous term for the loose series of steps decided seconds prior, went something like: archers first, take out any of the big bruisers along the way, and, if there was time, wring Captain Monk's scrawny neck until he was blue in the face. The remaining soldiers would be drawn into the fight, thus allowing the escape party to make a break for it out the back.

Bounding across the slippery ground with her broadsword hanging from her hip, Oralia reached the nearest cluster of archers and disabled the first with a closefisted slam across the temple. The second tried to run but, disoriented, chose the wrong direction and dropped with a knife-hand strike to the throat. Oralia snapped both bows in her hands as she moved for the third, shattering the ribs, legs, and arm bones of anyone caught between her and her prey. By the time the third archer's arm was dislocated from their shoulder with a sickeningly easy *pop*, the soldiers from the backside of the tent had rounded the corner.

Oralia hurled the screaming archer in their direction and charged, not at the advancing line of soldiers, but toward Captain Monk. Despite suffering the aftereffects of the thunderflash, his sword was drawn and he stood grinning, eager and waiting like a fucking madman. His wide-eyed lieutenant reached him first. Yelling something Oralia did not hear over the commotion, Holt dragged the protesting captain into an awkward retreat. On Lieutenant Holt's order, an orc soldier dutifully stepped between them and cut off Oralia's swift advance.

The clang of steel against steel rang in Oralia's ears. In three fluid movements, Oralia knocked the sword from the orc's grasp and slammed her knee to his groin. Gasping, the soldier folded over, leaving him susceptible to a blow to the head from Oralia's heavy pommel that dropped him the rest of the way to the ground. Captain Monk, alas, was already gone, slipping away cowardly between the rain-battered tents.

Planting her right foot firmly in the wet ground, Oralia pivoted with a wide swing that sent the advancing soldiers scuttling several steps backward. From the collective terror shared among their expressions, facing the Protector of the Realm was a simple matter of following orders and not necessarily a choice. Oralia's sharp eyes caught movement from behind, watching as a fourth shape picked itself up from the mud and slunk closer.

"Drop your weapons." Oralia spoke it as a command, not a suggestion, in exactly the tone of voice a nervous soldier would respond to without question. "And I will let you live."

Alas, their hesitation cost them. With an infuriated roar, the small shape leapt at them from behind. Rali's short sword slashed across the lower legs of the first soldier. Screaming, the elf fell into a puddle of bloodied rainwater. Rali was already on to the next. The human that turned to attack her was run through at the navel. Oralia neatly dispatched the remaining soldier with a merciful clip to the jaw, sparing them from her lieutenant's wrath.

"I was trying to avoid a senseless slaughter," Oralia snapped.

Rali wrenched her blade from the slack body of the second soldier. The stench of blood now permeated the air, intermixing with the rain and earthy stink of wet soil. "They attacked me unprovoked and now they die. It's not senseless. It's perfectly logical!"

Rali broke from her rant to address the oncoming dwarf soldier who barreled at her for the simple fact that she was, in theory, a better target than Oralia. It was a mistake the dwarf soldier would not live to regret. Roaring, Rali dropped low at the first mistimed swing of their ax and took them out at the knees. The pair tumbled across the wet ground with Rali screaming dwarfish obscenities with every punch.

"Incapacitate. Do not kill." Oralia spun and deflected a blow from the human soldier who had circled around behind her in an attempt to catch her unaware. She blocked their second stroke and then slammed her blade against the wooden shield, driving the soldier back in a shower of painted splinters. "It is not fair to take it out on them when it is me you are angry with."

"I can be mad at two things!" Rali had the dwarf's head sandwiched between her bloodied hands and twisted until they stopped writhing. "While we're on the subject, I couldn't help but notice you didn't stop to check on me first."

"You faked that fall!"

"So? Your lack of concern still stings, Oralia. Almost as badly as you trying to make me fly the coop!"

"You are a dwarf, not a chicken!" Oralia hooked her foot behind the soldier's heel and swept them to the wet ground. The soldier threw up their shield, blocking a blow that would have otherwise proved fatal. Frustrated by her own carelessness, Oralia hammered at the shield as a means to vent her mounting fury. "You cannot fly."

"It's a metaphor!"

"Metaphors cannot fly either!"

"Oh my gods! What I'm trying to say is, if you're going down, then we're going down together, understood? No more of this lone martyr shit." Rali rifled through her dead opponent's pockets for keepsakes. Something outside of Oralia's field of vision caused the lieutenant to lift her head. Rali's eyes widened and she jumped to her feet, abandoning the body where it lay. "Archer incoming!"

Oralia dove to Rali's side. She meant to grab only the shield, but ended up hefting both the shield and its wielder in front of them. The heavy wood shuddered under the solid *thud, thud* of the arrows burying into it from the other side. One of which, from the screaming, she assumed had also caught her luckless opponent in the back. Oralia crouched low, ensuring the small shield protected most of Rali. From her scowl, the dwarf did not appear to appreciate her generosity.

Oralia peeked around the edge, prepared to duck back behind the splintered barrier the moment another arrow whipped at them. Whitefern stood tucked against a tree with a third bolt already nocked. From the calculated glint in her eyes, the elf scout anticipated Oralia's next move. "Try to charge me," Whitefern called from behind the tree, "and I'll drop you both before you get halfway."

Rali kept her voice low enough for only Oralia to hear. "She's bluffing. It takes four arrows, minimum, to stop an orc in a full rampage. Keep your head and neck shielded and the odds are in your favor."

"If I have the shield, then you are exposed." By contrast, it only took one arrow to kill a dwarf. Rali was quick, but even she couldn't outrun death.

Oralia glanced over her shoulder and her frown deepened. A pair of stooped figures darted along the edges of the rain-battered campground, using the surrounding trees and tents to mask their movements. "We have another two flanking us."

"Surrender, now!" Whitefern emphasized her point with her third arrow.

The iron arrowhead ripped through skin and flesh as it grazed above the leather greave on Oralia's shin. She lurched a half step forward, but caught herself, hissing through her clenched teeth as searing pain flared up her right leg. Oralia shifted her weight to her left foot, blinking away the hot tears that leaked from the corner of her eyes, threatening to obscure her vision.

Dark blood gushed from the fresh wound. Already, Oralia could feel the sticky warmth saturating the thick fabric of her pant leg as it trickled down her shin. Rali's concerned stare moved from the gash back to Oralia's face, meeting her eyes. "I think we might be backed into a corner here, boss."

"My gods, Ralizak. Have you finally run out of bright ideas?"

"Run out? No! I already gave you my brightest idea and you . . ." Rali's voice trailed. She tilted her head as a calculating expression formed across her brow. "Is it just me or is the ground shaking?"

The ground trembled beneath her feet. At first, Oralia thought perhaps it was the earth itself shifting deep below her. This line of thinking was promptly extinguished from her mind the moment she heard the accompanying roar. It was a chilling, blood-curdling sound that made the hairs on the back of her neck stand on end. Oralia made the mistake of making eye contact with her lieutenant, whose bloodied face was now pressed into an amused smile.

Rali pursed her lips thoughtfully. "Is that what I think it is?"

"Do not waggle your eyebrows at me."

"It is, isn't it?" The two black, fuzzy caterpillars on Rali's forehead continued their suggestive dance. "And you said having a fuckmate was a bad idea."

Oralia whipped her head over her shoulder to check the position of the soldiers behind them. Wide-eyed and with faces drained of color, the pair threw down their shields and ran, vanishing into the surrounding line of dark trees. The shaking below their feet grew stronger, creating ripples in the deep puddles strewn across the ground. Whitefern sprinted past in a blur of brown and tan clothing, followed closely by possibly the most beautiful sight Oralia had ever set eyes upon.

Sascha tore after the soldiers with his tusks bared and snarling like a wild animal. He upended tents, bushes, and entire trees as he grabbed at his fleeing prey. Sascha wasn't armed. There wasn't any need to be. Trees, boulders, his victim's own detached appendages—all were readily available weapons to a rampaging orc. Oralia knew, deep down, the proper thing to do would be to call him off. But she couldn't help but watch, utterly entranced, for a few seconds longer. It was a tender moment made less enjoyable by Rali, who clung to Oralia's upper arm with a death grip, stifling snorts of laughter.

Oralia covered Rali's eyes with her hand. "Not a word."

"This is really putting the hanky in your panky, isn't it?" Rali attempted to pry Oralia's fingers apart in order to peek through. "Look, I'm no expert, but I know a catch when I see one. He can cook, he ties people that annoy you to stumps, not to mention that thing with his tongue that makes you squeal—"

"Ralizak!"

"Yeah, like that. But usually it's his name, not mine." Rali settled back on her haunches, grinning. "Come on now, Moonflower. Your fuckmate just went on a rampage to save our skins. Surely that's reason enough to admit you might be in love, hmm?"

"I am not going to dignify that with an answer." Clicking her tusks, Oralia stood and slung the shield over her shoulder. She didn't normally carry one due to their cumbersome nature, but with the amount of arrows being shot at her as of late, she was beginning to reconsider her previous stance. It was a pity this one was so small. The fact that the wood appeared to be several years past its prime bothered her more than the fresh coat of blood that obscured the front emblem.

The sigil of the realm soaked in blood and wielded by its former protector. Something about that seemed horribly ironic.

"Check on the others, Ralizak." Oralia called over her shoulder as she limped in the direction her lover had gone. "See if the escape party got away safely. I will find Sascha."

CHAPTER NINETEEN

Mutiny

Dawn was still hours away. Between the dense trees and the roiling storm clouds overhead, the forest was suffocatingly dark even for someone who possessed excellent night vision. Pain rocketed down her right leg as Oralia limped in the direction Sascha had gone. Light or no light, his trail was not difficult to follow. The search reminded her of the faerie tale stories of children lost in the woods, leaving a trail of cookie crumbs to mark their passage. Only in this case, instead of crumbs, Sascha's trail consisted of broken branches, shattered logs, and more than one obliterated tree.

The fluttering in her stomach had died down to a churning unease by the time she found him. Sascha was slumped beneath the quaking bows of a black-and-white birch, breathing heavily through his tusks. To Oralia's relief, he appeared unharmed. Currently, the only blood she could smell was her own, still slowly trickling down her leg. Sascha heard her approach and lifted his head. Their eyes met and Oralia realized he shared the same look of dread that hung heavy in her soul.

Naively, she had hoped to avoid this. That, through some ancient alignment of the stars, he would remain at her side always. But that was the yearning of a hopeless romantic. Unlike her faithful four, Sascha had only ever been allowed to see one side of her. She may have played the part of the unyielding Protector Dawnsight well, but that's all it had ever been. An act. A complicated performance meant to deceive the masses, Sascha included. Regretfully, somewhere along the way her feelings for him had turned real.

Deep in the unvisited corners of her mind, she had known it would never work. He loved Oralia Dawnsight, the loyal, faithful servant of the realm, not the traitor. But that was the nature of hope. You clung onto it as long as you could, dreading the day the harsh sting of reality slapped you back to your senses.

Oralia's gaze flickered to Sascha's clenched hands, noting the lack of blood once more. "The scout?"

"I don't kill our own. Not even for you. You know that."

"What did you do?"

"I chased her—"

She locked her jaw, speaking through clenched teeth at him. "What did you do after I excused you from my tent?"

"I did as you asked!" Sascha met her stare with defiance. He managed only a few withering seconds before his shoulders slumped in defeat. "And then the captain and his lieutenant found me. I thought it odd they were up at such an hour, but I didn't have any reason to suspect it would lead to this."

"What did you tell him?"

"The truth! What else would you have me tell him, Oralia? How am I supposed to keep on top of your games if you don't trust me enough to involve me in the first place?" There was hurt in his eyes, and in his voice, and in the way his lower jaw trembled. With a pained grimace, Sascha averted his gaze to the ground. "I mentioned that the guide was acting erratic. Something about magic and wanting to turn back. I told them that you'd sent for the medic and had it handled. I don't understand why the captain intervened like he did, but . . ."

Sascha's hands trembled. Whether it was a symptom of the rampage slowly fading from his system or due to what he was about to ask, Oralia didn't know. Some cowardly voice within her head told her to turn and run before the truth revealed itself.

"Are you going to tell me what this is about? *Really* tell me?" he demanded. "I have served under Captain Monk for several tours now. While I have called a number of his decisions into question, the man respects the hierarchy. He would not have challenged your authority without cause. I was forced to pick a side without knowing the stakes. I would like some sort of assurance that my loyalty to you was not misplaced."

Oralia took a breath. Not due to a lack of air, but because she needed time to decide on an answer. The seconds slipped past slowly. First one, then two, all the way to ten before she delivered it, with a sigh that was rattled deep in her bones. "In light of our recent losses, I made the unilateral decision to withdraw from the ridge. Continuing on would be suicide. I gave orders for my four to whisk Rasp off of the mountain so that we would have no other choice but to turn back. Captain Monk has never been keen on losing. I suspect he caught on to what I was doing and rallied a mutiny to stop me before my people could slip away."

"And the part about the dark magic? What was that about?"

"I fear the pressure has gotten to Rasp. His mental state is swiftly unraveling. It was the final nail in the coffin, so to speak."

The moment of silence that stretched between them was difficult even for Oralia to withstand without flinching. She found herself holding her breath once more. While she did not know what Sascha's exact reaction would be, she held no disillusions as to where it would end. Come fury, confusion, or disappointment, ultimately the weight of his response would crush her.

"You . . . you used me to retrieve Faris for you." Sascha's dark sable eyes darted back and forth across the moss-covered ground as he fitted the missing pieces of information into place. He reached an eventual conclusion and lifted his chin until his horrified gaze met her own. "You made me complicit in your schemes."

"Unknowingly complicit."

He bared his tusks. "That doesn't make it any better, Oralia!"

She winced at his volume. The fact that it was deserved did not make it any easier to bear. "I know. I am sorry, truly. But I did so to protect you. I did not realize the situation would escalate this qui—"

A horrific shriek lit the air. It sounded like the unfortunate offspring of a dragon and a tone-deaf bird. The call died away moments later, the horrific sound still ringing in Oralia's ears, leaving only the uncomfortable pitter-patter of the rain between her and Sascha. Oralia studied his crushed expression for a second longer, wishing she could be the version of her he wanted. The version he deserved.

"That is Ralizak's signal," she said. "She must have found the others. I cannot stay."

Oralia turned and limped back the way she had come as the sinking feeling in her chest threatened to swallow her whole. With each painful step, their future together, the future she wanted, slipped like loose sand between her fingers. Grief transformed to anger as patches of heat broke out across her clammy face. She walked on, with the cold air stinging her cheeks, silently cursing herself for being so stupid.

Why in the seven realms of chaos had she bothered to come after him anyway? She could explain until she was blue in the face but, in the end, it wouldn't matter. Sascha had fallen for a version of her that didn't even exist. No amount of justification could ever repair that. Their relationship had been over the moment she made the call to evacuate the ridge. She should have just let him go. It would have been kinder to them both.

"Oralia, wait!"

Oralia halted, unable to turn around, suddenly grateful for the rain that helped disguise the tears trickling from her eyes. She prided herself on her words and yet, for the life of her, they simply would not come. Oralia stood silent like a damned fool instead, feeling as though she was caught between two worlds and on the verge of losing both.

"That's all you're going to say?" Sascha's voice was husky from the aftereffects of the rampage, but at least he wasn't yelling. Not yet, anyway. His wet footsteps were heavy and sluggish, but gaining on her nonetheless. "Not even a 'thank you for saving my skin, Sunflower'? I promise to make it up to you with lots and lots of intimate cuddling'?"

An involuntary whimper caught in her throat. Oralia forced it back down with a dry swallow. "Thank you, Sascha," was all she could manage at first. It took several painfully silent seconds for Oralia to compose the rest of her racing thoughts into a logical order. "I am afraid I can only offer my gratitude. If you turn back now, you might just make it off of this accursed mountain alive."

"Yeah, that's not happening." He bumped her shoulder with his as he strolled past. It wasn't hard, but it still made her lose her balance.

In more ways than one, because now it was she who was utterly confused. "Sascha—"

"This signal of yours, Moonflower," he called over his shoulder, refusing to slow down. "Is it supposed to sound like a dying bird?"

Oralia scrambled to catch up to him, unable to control the unmistakable flutter in her voice. "Screech owl."

"Mhm, subtle."

"Rali did a very convincing peacock for a while. Ellisar convinced her to retire it. With the aid of a knife, of course."

"Of course."

Oralia winced. Normally she would not have included that last detail, keeping it securely to her thoughts, but the inside of her head was drumming almost as loudly as her heart and, currently, nothing was behaving as it should. Sascha included. The big lug had glimpsed who she truly was for the first time, and still, he stayed. Logic decreed Sascha should have turned and fled the moment she'd admitted to making him complicit in her schemes.

"Sascha, you don't—"

He swiveled his head at her and held his finger to his lips, motioning to keep quiet as his long strides slowed to a crawl. "We're nearing camp,

Moonflower," he reminded her softly. "Best not to draw any attention to ourselves in case there's a welcoming party waiting for us. You can thank me profusely once we're past."

Good gods, she was behaving like a wet behind the ears cadet, not the battle-scarred leader she was supposed to be. Oralia assumed the lead position, weaving in and out of the trees at an ungainly jog, and grimacing with each burdensome step. She took them around camp in the event the scattered soldiers had regrouped on familiar ground. She neither saw nor smelled any trace of the enemy soldiers. Not live ones, anyway.

On the other side of the abandoned campground, tucked just beyond the first row of shaggy trees, Oralia stumbled across the first of many bodies strewn haphazardly across the wet ground. Her gaze lingered a little too long on the bloodied face of an elf soldier, his dark eyes wide and staring lifelessly back at her. The deep puddle forming around his head had taken on a murky red color. She looked away with a sigh. Another senseless death that could have easily been avoided had his commanding officer not been a nitwit.

Judging by their proximity to the rows of upturned tents, this was where Ellisar and Curly had been waiting for the rest of the evacuation party. Whatever force Captain Monk had thrown at them clearly had not been enough. The carnage was entirely one-sided.

Sascha stooped to collect a long-handled battle ax from its fallen owner. Despite its intimidating size, the weapon still looked comically small in his hand. Satisfied with his selection, he fell back into step and the pair plunged deeper into the brush, following an obvious trail of death and destruction.

Oralia waited until they were a sensible distance from camp before airing her misgivings. "May I talk sense into you *now*?"

"You can certainly try."

She whipped her head over her shoulder at him, dread still alive and fluttering in the pit of her stomach. "Sascha, you do not have to do this. This is not your fight."

"You forfeited your chance to surrender. If you challenge him again, Captain Monk will kill you."

"Just as he will kill anyone caught fighting alongside me. The precise reason, my love, that you should not be here."

"Your what?" An impish smile banished some of the despair from Sascha's handsome features. "I have to say, I do like that better than what you normally call me."

Oralia stopped running and whirled around at him, snapping her tusks in frustration. "Stop being ornery for one damned second and think this through!"

Sascha slowed to a stop, chest heaving in and out from exertion. Even with a leg injury, Oralia easily outpaced him. "I have thought this through, Oralia. I'm not leaving. If I do, you die. And if I get down onto my knees and beg and plead for you not to go back into the fight, you still die. Because no matter what you feel for me, it will never rival the love you have for that strange little family of yours."

"That is not—"

Sascha silenced her with a single, cutting look. "I have accepted my place. As I have accepted that the only scenario in which any of us avoid a gruesome death is to face Captain Monk together."

"I . . ." Oralia found herself unable to finish whatever foolish sentiment her mouth had started.

"Oh my gods, just shut up and kiss him already!"

Oralia scoured the low-lying shrubbery for signs of her eavesdropping lieutenant. While her vision found nothing, her nose told her the dwarf was hunkered down in the thick mountain ash only paces ahead. Despite the mud that cloaked most of Ralizak's scent, the faint odor of stale barley beer was a lingering one. Oralia clicked her tusks in exasperation. "Tell me you have not been listening to our conversation this entire time."

"Nah, just the good bits." Rali popped up with a brimming smile. "Where did you find him again? More importantly, do they have more?" She leapt from the wet shrubbery and started off without them, managing to do so while jogging backward. A feat that was as irritating as it was impressive. "And how much of my soul do I have to trade to get one?"

Oralia pretended to not have heard a single one of Rali's prying questions as she trotted behind her. "You signaled, Lieutenant?"

"It's always work, work, work with you, isn't it? You've got to learn to stop and enjoy the banter, boss. Especially when it's coming from me." The look Oralia delivered must have been one for the record books, because the dwarf suddenly remembered her report. "Captain Monk's got the escape party pinned down about a quarter mile from here. They're holding for the moment, but the captain's got numbers on his side."

"How many? And for the gods' sakes, turn around! I am not losing you to a sprained ankle."

"Rough estimate, I'd say about a score or so. It was hard to get an accurate count with all the milling about. The key players were Captain Monk,

Holt, and two archers. The rest appeared to be a mishmash of foot soldiers."
Rali managed all of this between short, panting breaths.

The sounds of the approaching scuffle grew louder. Through the spindly green and black trees, the pre-dawn gloom gradually gave way to light. Following Rali's example, Oralia slowed her pace and crept the rest of the way to the edge of the makeshift battlefield, utilizing the surrounding trees and overgrown thickets as cover. What little sound the trio made was drowned out by the fighting.

Rali pushed the tangle of thorny branches aside with her hands to get an unobstructed view of the fight. "Shit." The color drained from the dwarf's bloodstained face. "Holt's got Curly down!"

"Ralizak, wait!"

Oralia grabbed for Rali, but it was too late. The dwarf slipped her grasp and sprinted headlong into the melee. There wasn't time to stop and strategize. Their cover was about to be blown, and she had to make the most of it before the rest of Captain Monk's soldiers caught on. Cursing, Oralia unsheathed her sword and barreled through the wet underbrush after her. The branches that ripped at her flesh and clothes went unnoticed. The call of war was already coursing through her veins, drowning out the pain.

Something caught her sword hand with such force her fingers spasmed. The weapon dropped from her grasp a split second before she was jerked backward. Oralia whirled around, still trapped firmly by the wrist. Her gaze traveled from her arm to Sascha. "What the fuck are you doing? Release me!"

"Oralia," he pleaded. "Surrender, now. While your family is still breathing."

The words slid from between her tusks with a hiss. "Whatever foolish act you are about to attempt, reconsider."

"Please don't make me do this."

CHAPTER TWENTY

Red Mist

His deep, sable eyes gazed back at her, begging her to see reason. For several heartbeats, Oralia's surroundings stilled to an eerie calm. Sascha's mouth opened slowly, and words spilled forth, but she did not register them. And then, as if to counteract the momentary lapse, time sped forward and Oralia's shield was slamming into his nose. She struck the ground on top of him in a tumbling, cursing spray of blood and wet pine needles.

"Oralia," her brain told her. That's what Sascha had said a split second before the takedown.

After her second unsuccessful attempt to bludgeon him to death with the shield, Sascha ripped it free and flung it aside. She retaliated with a closed-fisted slam to his temple. The impact lessened his grip on her wrist and Oralia pulled free, desperate to put distance between them. She may have been the more accomplished fighter, but he had a significant size advantage. Getting away was priority number one, and then she could think up some clever way to dispatch him.

Sascha caught her by the ankle and dragged her back down. She clawed at the ground for traction and struck with her other foot, kicking with all of her might. All the while her mind kept interjecting unhelpful pieces of information through her rapidly running thoughts.

"Oralia, forgive me," he'd said.

Forgive him? He would be lucky if she buried him when she was done picking his shattered skull from her knuckles! This was why she didn't do commitment. This was why she didn't have friends! This was why all the good things in life had passed her by!

But you love him.

Had. She had loved him. She *thought* she had loved him. For all of two seconds before the bastard turned on her! Oralia became vaguely aware that she was on top of him again, tearing at Sascha's face with her bare fingers. There was a metallic taste in her mouth, to which of them it belonged she wasn't sure. Nor did she care. The awareness of her surroundings faded into the background as the red mist of war assumed control. The change strengthened certain abilities—speed, reaction, coordination—while cutting off the parts that would only serve as a hindrance on the battlefield.

A blistering heat surged through Oralia's veins as the rampage took hold. To the seventh realm with love, she was going to rip his tusks from his jawbone and use them to mince his body into unrecognizable pieces!

"Oralia!" Sascha's voice sounded strangely far away.

Why the fuck was he still trying to reason with her? Why couldn't he just shut up and accept that she was going to rip him limb from limb?

"Oralia, stop! They'll kill him if you don't!"

Fuck. Something was wrong. Not just with the situation spiraling out of hand around her, but deep within her mind itself. The fury bubbling up inside was overpowering her better judgment. Already, logic and reasoning had gone completely out the window. She was teetering dangerously on the verge of losing total control. An orc caught in a blind rage was more lethal than any weapon. Soon, Oralia would not be able to distinguish friend from foe, slaughtering both alike indiscriminately. She had seen entire military units wiped out by a single orc caught in the throes of a rampage gone wrong.

Breaking from a rampage too early came at its own cost. The adrenaline pumping through her veins would be rerouted to her head, resulting in a brain fog that rivaled even the worst of hangovers. But she didn't have a choice. She had to know what the fuck the idiot was shouting at her about. Channeling the last of her focus, Oralia's consciousness surfaced back to the outside. The transition struck like a punch to the gut. She doubled over, choking back a throatful of stomach acid as her blurred surroundings started to spin. Flashes of light danced along the edges of her vision.

Sascha grabbed her from behind, trapping her arms at her sides, and forced her to kneel. Even while she was trying to kill him, the big oaf was gentle. As if he actually cared. If he had cared so much, he would have stayed out of her blasted way!

"Gods dammit," he snarled, struggling to keep her on her knees. "Stop fighting me and answer her!"

It was only then that she became aware of the other voice drifting in and out of hearing, like a fly buzzing from the other side of a glass windowpane. Oralia's dazed stare followed the noise to its source: the wide-eyed Lieutenant Holt. Holt had her left arm hooked around Curly's neck. Her right hand held a blade pressed to the underside of his throat. There was a soldier positioned on either side of Curly, holding him back from tearing into her.

Lieutenant Holt was screaming, "Call them off! Call them off or he dies!"

Oralia's concentration shifted across the battlefield, attempting to piece together whatever the fuck the lieutenant was up in arms about. Oralia knew the goings on around her were happening in real time, but her mind slowed them, playing out the events at a snail's pace. She found Ellisar first—a blur of bloodied steel and golden hair as her longsword weaved in and out of the air around her. She whipped and whirled in tight circles, meeting the blades that came at her from both sides. And then there was Ralizak, who was steadily working her way toward Curly. No wonder Lieutenant Holt was scared shitless. From the trail of mangled bodies behind her, Rali was out for blood.

Oralia's gaze drifted in search of the others and found them near the center of the chaos. Snag had rigged a triangle defense formation with Daana and Faris. The trio, outmatched in both numbers and physical stature, seemed to be relying on a combination of speed, timing, and downright luck. Faris wielded a stolen spear and, together, he and Snag were keeping the enemy at bay. Even hapless Daana, sporting a gash across the left side of her ribs, was still attempting to weave magic despite the visible stutter in her hands.

A tall figure cut in front of Oralia, obstructing her view of the battle. "Protector Dawnsight!" This shrill voice, Oralia realized, belonged to a red-faced Captain Monk. He paced back and forth in front of her, waving his sword in the manner of someone quickly losing control. "Call him off!"

Him? Him, who?

Movement from the corner of Oralia's eye caught her attention. Was that a black cloud?

No, Oralia realized, as her vision came into focus. Birds. An angry, screaming flock of ravens swarmed like a miniature thunderhead on the far side of the battlefield. Rasp broke from the swirling mass of swooping feathers and talons. Yellow magic arched between the stolen blades in his hands as he threw himself at the terror-stricken soldiers with unbridled rage written across his blood-spattered face. He moved without rhyme or rhythm, fighting with such unpredictable insanity the enemy seemed incapable of touching him.

Ah, that would be the "him" Captain Monk was screeching on about. The Iron Devil had finally come out to play. And what he lacked in tactical precision was made up for by the highly volatile magic seeping from his skin. *Fuck.*

"Oralia!" Sascha's burly arms shook her, as if attempting to bring her back to sanity. "Call them off. For fuck's sake, surrender! They will kill Curly and then they will kill you."

Clarity struck like a bolt of lightning, jolting her back to her senses. Some of the fog lifted and Oralia threw her head back, thundering, "Lieutenant Quartz Ralizak, Sergeant Ellisar Farrow, Corporal Snaglebrag Flint—"

"Chief Medical Officer Snaglebrag Flint!" Snag's voice hailed from his corner of the triangle formation.

"—stand down!" Her three obeyed, albeit grudgingly. They were versed enough in unspoken commands not to drop their weapons. For the moment, they simply stopped fighting. Faris and Daana followed suit. To Oralia's surprise, even the ravens stilled to a hostile silence. The birds settled in the boughs nearest to Rasp, all watching her with their feathery heads tilted, ready to take flight once more at a moment's notice.

With adrenaline still raging through her system, Oralia lifted her chin to Monk and flashed a smile. "In case it is the last time you have the privilege of hearing it, *that* is how one commands the battlefield, Captain."

"I hope you enjoyed it," Captain Monk snarled. "As that command will certainly be your last."

Oralia spoke with a calm collectedness that was sure to drive him mad. "Let me and my people go, Captain, and you might make it to the foothills before the Stoneclaw patrol comes to collect you. I assure you, if they were not on their way before, they most certainly are now. That, or waste your time killing me. I am sure you and all," Oralia paused, counting aloud to herself, "one, two, three . . . ah, eleven of your remaining soldiers can hold your own against an army of mountain folk warriors. My meager force gave you enough trouble on their own, but I am not one to rub salt into fresh wounds."

"Sir," Lieutenant Holt said.

"Not now!"

Oralia continued, "Leave me and my ilk here and we can buy you a small window of escape."

"And leave you to turn and follow us?" Captain Monk scoffed. "I think not!"

"Sir!"

Oralia looked up at him thoughtfully. "Do you think I lasted as Protector of the Realm for two hundred years by chasing after every foe who bested me in battle? That is how one earns an early grave, Alin. If you hope to inherit my title, you must first learn the art of survival. Retreat while it is still an option. My faithful and I will lead the mountain folk in the other direction, toward the flatlands. Let us go, and you and I will never cross paths again."

"I want the Stoneclaw." Captain Monk glanced over his shoulder at Faris and Daana. "And the girl, of course."

Daana's voice rang out from somewhere behind Faris. "Over your dead body!"

"Sir, the Stoneclaw!" Lieutenant Holt screamed. "He's glowing!"

Both Oralia and Captain Monk whipped their heads in Rasp's direction. The ravens were working up into a second flurry. They screeched and croaked, swooping in low, slow circles. Rasp stood at the center of the chaos with a sword in one hand and Oralia's knife in the other, his red-stained chest heaving. From the bodies half-submerged in the puddles around him, Oralia suspected the blood was not his own. Raw magic poured from his fingertips and wove into the cold air, intermixing with the current of dark wings and feathers.

"If you want me so bad, Captain, come get me yourself!" The pulsing yellow light grew stronger with each word from Rasp's curled mouth. The one-eyed raven, Mother, landed on his shoulder in a flutter of dark wings. She jabbered excitedly in his ear, bobbing and dipping her head to make her point.

Oralia did not have to understand raven to know the source of Mother's panic. She too could sense that Rasp was on the verge of losing control and raining all of chaos down on top of them.

"You have made your point, Rasp. Stand down. I will handle this." Oralia ignored the sudden ache in her shoulders. With her adrenaline fading, her whole body would soon be feeling the effects of her escapades. Her weary stare transitioned from Rasp back to the red-faced captain. "The mission is over, Alin. You have no use for him. Take Lady Lazuli and we will part ways without any more senseless bloodshed."

"And let you walk away with the greatest asset the realm has ever seen? I think not, Oralia. The boy is mine."

"He is not an asset, Alin. Look at him! He is a disaster waiting to—"

"Stop talking like I'm not here!" Rasp screamed.

A pulse of lightning crackled overhead, silencing the remaining words from Oralia's useless tongue. The gathering grew eerily silent, every fear-stricken face highlighted by the glow of Rasp's increasing magic. Clouds of wispy yellow light lifted from his shoulders, shimmering like heat from a hot body on a frozen day. "Call me boy again," Rasp snarled, lifting his left blade in Captain Monk's approximate direction, "and I'll strike you down where you stand."

"Rasp," Oralia started, squirming against Sascha as she tried to stand. She managed to only get one leg bent beneath her before he forced her back down.

"No, I'm done listening to you, too. I'll handle it from here, thanks."

The grip on Captain Monk's sword was so tight that all color had drained from his knuckles. There was a noticeable tremble in his hand as well. Not due to fear, Oralia sensed, but fury. "With what? You may have magic, but you have no idea how to use it," Captain Monk bellowed back. "Make no mistake, you are not the one in power here, boy. Cut the theatrics and I'll ensure that you and Mister Belfast survive what is about to happen."

An unsettling smile pulled across Rasp's bloodstained face. "Will you now?"

Mother reacted before Rasp could finish raising his hand. She took to the air, beating her wings against his head in what could only have been a mother's reprimand. Rasp's magic withered beneath the onslaught as he threw up his arm, shielding his face. "Stop interfering! I've got it handled!"

Croak!

Mother got through to him somehow. Rasp lowered his arms, wearing a dark scowl, as the surrounding magic faded, withering away until all that was left was the faint afterglow of light around his fingers. Satisfied, Mother dropped to the ground. She hopped along the muddy forest floor near Rasp's feet, still chattering. Her harsh calls were echoed by the flock.

Rasp raised his voice to be heard over the din. "She says I can't kill you with magic. So if you're interested in living, Captain, take the protector's deal."

Captain Monk looked almost thoughtful as he considered his response. "I feel like you're not taking this as seriously as you should," he said at last, with an idle wave of his hand. "Kill the bird. Show the boy I mean business."

Rasp lurched half a step forward, screaming for Mother to take flight. The raven bent her legs beneath her and launched her feathered body into the air. An arrow caught her midjump. A pitiful squawk escaped her beak as Mother fell earthward, still flapping her useless wings in a futile attempt to escape the inevitable. She struck the ground with a wet thump and then went still.

For a breath, the entire forest stilled until the only sound was the pitter-patter of the rain. Rasp edged a step forward, his eyes desperately moving back and forth across the puddled ground for signs of her. "Mother?" His voice cracked the moment his foot touched her lifeless body.

Oralia tore her eyes from Rasp to Captain Monk. "You fool!"

"Now that I have your attention," the captain said, "you may want to reconsider your options."

"Mom?" Rasp wasn't listening. "Mom, wake up." He dropped to his knees, collected the fallen raven, and held her to his chest as tears trickled down his blood-splattered face. Streams of yellow magic leaked from his trembling body as his grief grew, pooling over the wet ground like oil on water. It rippled from him, spreading in gentle, lapping waves.

Oralia watched in horror as the magic swept across the swampy woodland floor. "You just killed us all, Captain."

The crimson tint bled from Captain Monk's face, replaced by ghostly white. His eyes widened as realization sank in at last. "Make him stop! Protector Dawnsight, I am ordering you to make him stop or I'll . . . I'll . . ." Desperate, Monk raced to Lieutenant Holt's side and seized the dagger from her hand. "Command him to stop or your orc dies!"

Faris broke from the triangle formation and struck out across the slick battlefield. Magic pooled around his hooves, slowing his progress as he fought to reach Rasp's side. "Rasp, stop!"

A final surge of yellow magic pulsed across the ground. It washed over the gathering like a silent tide and disappeared into the trees. At first, there was nothing. Only silence. And then, high above, in the distance, a thunderous *crack* rang out. The deafening, splintering snap of falling trees grew unmistakably louder. The mountainside shook as the wind whipped with sudden force, ripping branches from the surrounding forest.

Faris dropped to his knees, shaking Rasp's slumped form. "Don't do it!"

"Call it off!" Captain Monk raised his hand to strike.

Oralia saw the flash of steel as Monk's blade plunged downward. She lurched forward, ripping free of Sascha's grasp as she raced for Curly. The surrounding uproar grew strangely dim. Arrows zipped at her from two different directions. A bolt bit into her thigh with blistering pain, but did not slow her. Curly searched the crowd for her, his face pale and panic-stricken. For half a heartbeat, their eyes met. Oralia was nearly to him when sound returned to the forest. Above them, a wall of water rolled down the mountain and slammed into her.

CHAPTER TWENTY-ONE

Loose Ends

Pain was the first sensation to return to her. It started as a dull ache in her bones and crescendoed into a symphony of agony that pulsed through every fiber of her body. Groaning, she eased her heavy eyelids open. The surrounding gray light bore deep into her skull like a hot ice pick. Daana shielded her hand over her eyes to lessen the pain. Her arm, crusted from elbow to fingertip in mud and pine needles, was unrecognizable to her.

She studied her fingers, dazed. How in the gods did this happen? Also, where in the seven realms of chaos was she? Why couldn't she remember getting here? And why the fuck was she soaking wet? In addition to the agony running rampant through her body, Daana was also unbearably cold. Her wet clothes clung to her clammy flesh like a second skin. Each weighted limb trembled as if it had a will of its own.

The blasted rain had stopped. Daana only realized because she would not have otherwise been able to hear something moving through the brush toward her. Squinting her eyes against the harsh morning light, Daana twisted her head in the direction of the sound and nearly screamed when a lancing pain shot down her neck. Some buried instinct told her not to draw attention to herself. She bit her bottom lip, riding out the waves of agony in silence as her eyes darted back and forth, searching the washed out forest for signs of movement.

It was not long before a pair of soldiers crept out from between the low-hanging trees only yards from where she lay. Aside from the usual filth associated with travel, their uniforms appeared relatively clean. Unlike her, they were not coated from head to toe in mud. That meant something important, surely, but for the life of her Daana couldn't remember why. It had to do with fighting, and water, and . . .

Oh, right. The magically-induced flash flood that had washed away the makeshift battlefield. That certainly explained the chill in her bones and why she hadn't called out to the pair upon detecting them. Pushing the hazy memory from her mind, Daana focused the few functioning brain cells she had left and willed them into action. Slowly but surely the identities of the soldiers unfolded before her. She recognized the first elf as Whitefern, Captain Monk's lead scout. Her companion, Crim, limped at her heels. Straining her ears, Daana was barely able to make out their hushed conversation.

"Can we go, please?" Crim hissed, wringing his hands. "You and I both saw the same thing. A wall of water, Fern. A wall of it! This whole trip's been one bad omen after the other. Let's cut our losses before the next disaster gets us."

"Stop your sniveling and look for survivors."

While these two hadn't been present during the final standoff, there was no question as to where their allegiances fell. Swallowing the whimper that threatened to burst from her mouth, Daana pressed further into the rough bark of the black spruce behind her. There wasn't much cover, but if she remained still, there was a chance she would go unnoticed.

"Slight problem with that plan," Crim carried on. "Captain told us to kill the protector, remember? Suppose we find him first. What are you going to say? 'Oh, so sorry, sir. We were going to do it, you see, but then we got chased off by the cook. Did we mention he wasn't armed? Oh, and by the way, he may not actually be on our side like he clai—'"

A twig snapped behind her. Daana turned to find a small, bearded man working his way around the back of her tree. He froze, as equally surprised as her, and for a split moment their eyes met.

Run.

Daana lunged upright, every muscle in her legs screaming as she forced them into a run. The man seized her by the elbow and yanked her backward. She pivoted, using the momentum to come back around swinging. Her fist smashed into the man's bulbous nose. Pain rocketed down her arm from the impact.

"Fuck!" she shouted, certain she'd just broken a number of the finer bones in her hand. While Willem had done her the service of teaching her where to punch, he'd neglected to mention how to do so without injuring herself in the process.

On the bright side, she wasn't alone in her suffering. Cursing, the human stumbled several steps backward, consequently loosening his grip on her elbow. A crackling, hot energy swelled within Daana's furiously beating chest. The little voice in her head commanded her to flee once more. *Run, run, go!*

Daana yanked free of the man's grip and staggered sideways, willing her aching legs to take flight. She made it a single step before a new agony erupted across her lower ribs. Daana dropped uselessly into the mud, gasping as her body spasmed uncontrollably. She glared up through the swell of hot tears that clouded her vision. Whitefern stood over her, backlit by the soft morning light, swinging a long-handled dagger nonchalantly in her hand.

"You're lucky that was just the hilt. Try your luck again and I'll stick you with the pointy end." Whitefern's unconcerned gaze moved past Daana to the human who was bent over against a tree. "She get you good, Obi?"

The man was busy feeling his nose. "Like getting punched by a baby."

Crim peeked his head out from behind the lead scout. His wide-eyed stare shifted from Daana to Whitefern, murmuring, "I'm a bit jumbled from this morning still. Why are we threatening the emissary?"

Whitefern's reply was cold. "She chose a side. The wrong one, unfortunately."

"Oh." Realization broke across Crim's dull features and his eyebrows lifted nearly halfway up his forehead. "And now you're thinking she might be our ticket back into the captain's good graces, yeah? Gotta be honest, I'm not so sure a pretty piece of tail is gonna be enough to save our necks, Ferny."

Oh, fuck no, Daana thought, narrowing her eyes. Over her dead body. Or theirs, preferably.

"Stay back!" she snarled, checking her stones. There was still magic. Not a lot, but enough to take down two targets at least. She would have to outrun the third. Daana flexed the stiffness from her numb fingers as she waited for the trio to make their move, attempting to decipher which of the three scouts would be the slowest.

"*Our* necks?" Whitefern said, wrinkling her nose at Crim, ignoring Daana's pathetic attempt at intimidation. "Find your own trophy. This one's mine."

"Yours?" Obi shot her a wrathful look from beneath a shaggy set of eyebrows. He placed his hands at his sides and widened his stance. "I was the one who found her. She's mine."

"You lost your claim the moment she popped you in the nose."

"Dammit, Ferny, this ain't right." Crim slunk out from behind Whitefern with his head tucked into his shoulders, still wringing his grime-covered hands. "I don't like the palace brat any more than either of you, but she didn't do nothin' to us. You know what the captain's going to do to her. The man's gone mad."

Whitefern's grim expression remained unchanged. "Better her than me."

"Look, just hear me out, alright? We don't even know if the captain is alive. After that flash flood, it's a miracle we found anybody still kicking. I say we take the girl and get the fuck off this mountain. The three of us deliver her back to Sunstorn safe and sound and let her uncle pay us a boatload of coin for our trouble." He tapped his fingertips together as he peered up into Whitefern's face pleadingly. "Filthy rich sounds better than dead to me."

"He's right," Daana interjected. "Uncle would pay whatever you asked."

Obi curled his lip at her with a scoff. "Is that before or after he cuts off our heads?"

Daana gathered her knees beneath her, wincing at the sharp stabbing sensation that rolled across her rib cage. "I will vouch for you. You have my word. A glowing review for the three of you. You'd be hailed as heroes of the realm."

Whitefern considered this proposition for several painstaking moments. Whatever her thought process was, her bleak features revealed nothing. Reaching her decision, the elf slid her dagger into its sheath and retrieved a length of cord from her pocket. "No."

Crim's lanky arms dropped to his sides. "What do you mean, no?"

"And risk the captain coming after us? What do you suppose he'd do if we're caught trying to sneak his prize back to Sunstorn without him? I, for one, want to keep my skin." Whitefern reached for Daana, snarling, "Raise your hands, elfling. And I don't want to hear another word out of your mouth or I'll bind that shut, too."

It was now or never. Magic surged down Daana's forearms and crackled between her fingertips. She flung her hands in front of her to direct the blast, shouting, "*Avalore!*"

Whitefern was a hair faster. The elf scout threw herself sideways and rolled. Dodging the worst of the magic, she came up on one knee, bow in hand. An arrow thudded into the trunk behind Daana, nicking her ear as it zipped past. "I'll put the next one through your leg, I swear it!" Whitefern's harsh stare flickered from Daana to Obi. "Don't just stand there, idiot! Grab her—"

A blurred object whipped through the trees and smacked into the back of Whitefern's head with a wet *thunk*. She lurched from the impact and then righted herself. Blood bubbled from her open mouth and the elf swayed, as if unsure if she was actually dead. With a gargled noise rattling deep in her chest, Whitefern collapsed. A hatchet, splattered in blood and sunk to the iron head, protruded from the back of the elf's skull.

Movement caught her eye. Daana turned, breath drawn, realizing the silent shadow that broke from the surrounding overgrowth was already at the halfway mark and gaining. The lithe figure sprinted with a longsword raised at the shoulder, feet barely skimming the surface of the wet ground. Crim saw the charging warrior and dropped flat on his stomach, covering his head with a whimper. Obi was still fumbling with his sword by the time the shadow reached him. A flash of steel cut through the air in three effortless slashes. With a pained wheeze, the human slumped face-first into the puddle beside Whitefern.

Ellisar spun, arching the blade around at Daana. The point of her bloodied steel stopped just short, hovering a fraction from her nose. The elf's golden eyes narrowed, daring her to make the next move.

"Thank you?" Daana stammered, hopeful a show of gratitude would convince her rescuer to stop acting like a dick.

Ellisar said nothing in return. She only stared, as if contemplating whether she wanted to kill her victim outright or toy with her first.

"Are you fucking kidding me?" Daana wasn't so much shouting at Ellisar as she was at the situation in general. "I was escaping *with* you! Do you not remember?" Okay, now she was shouting at Ellisar. Unfortunately, it still wasn't doing anything to lower the elf's blade. "At any point during this entire trip you could have killed me. Why did you wait until now?"

Somehow Ellisar managed to shrug without lifting her shoulders. "Just taking care of a few loose ends."

A third voice shattered the deadly standoff. "Ellisar, don't."

Tearing her eyes from the huntress, Daana's gaze dropped lower and found the source of the interruption. With her attention focused on Ellisar, she'd failed to notice the second shadow that had slunk from the tangled undergrowth. Snaglebrag stood tucked beneath Ellisar's raised right arm. His knife was pressed to her upper thigh.

"You might have enough time to kill me before you bleed out," he said with remarkable calmness. "But you still die. Put the sword down."

CHAPTER TWENTY-TWO

Complicated

Seven realms, Daana cursed. Out of the frying pan and into the fire, it seemed. Just her luck.

Daana remained frozen with her hands lifted pleadingly in the air above her head. She didn't know why Ellisar wanted her dead or why, conversely, Snag was keeping that exact scenario from happening. What Daana did know, however, was that now was not the time to bring either one into question. She waited instead, with her heartbeat pounding in her ears, watching as the elf and goblin remained locked in a deadly standoff.

Ellisar stared straight ahead, her icy glare boring invisible holes into Daana's forehead. Her long blade hovered at the tip of Daana's nose. A simple thrust was all it would take for the invisible holes to step neatly over the threshold from figurative to deadly. "What's she to you, Snag?"

"You heard the others. She's valuable."

Oh, great. Apparently she was still a hostage. Better alive than dead, at least.

"Bullshit! I saw you dive in after her at the falls. Once is a fluke. But this is twice now you've risked your hide to save her." While Ellisar kept her blade perfectly straight, there was an undeniable waver in her voice. "If you've gone and double crossed us, I swear, I'll string you up right next to her."

"It's not like that," Snag said. "I know her from before."

"Before what? Before you sold your soul to the realm? Before Geralt got to you? Before I cut your fuckin' head off? Which before, Snag?"

Daana was as confused as Ellisar. There wasn't any prior history between her and Snag. For the gods' sakes, they'd only officially met, what, a week ago? Two, at the most? Good grief, that seemed so long ago now. Caught in her own spiraling thoughts, Daana failed to notice that her hands had steadily dropped lower.

Unfortunately for her, Ellisar noticed rather quickly. She bared her teeth, snarling, "I see those hands! You even think about hitting me with magic and you're dead, elfling!"

The threat appeared to snap Snag out of his stupor. "Look, she's the reason I got stuck in the realm, alright?"

"And that makes you want to save her?"

"It's complicated!"

"What in the seven realms of chaos has gotten into you two?" A third form materialized from the brush. Like the others, Rali's chainmail was caked in mud and grime, making her nearly indistinguishable from her surroundings. Despite the fresh head wound split across her brow, Rali's stride had not lost its usual swagger. Her clomping footsteps halted paces from the cowering scout and her gaze dropped, as did her expression. "Hello, idiots!" She gestured to Crim's huddled form with both hands. "You missed one! Why are you trying to kill each other when there's a fresh body right here?"

"Don't kill me, don't kill me, don't kill me!" Crim's dark eyes searched the dwarf's face for a shred of mercy. Whatever answer he found in Rali's toothy smile, it must not have been of the merciful variety because the elf rolled swiftly to his feet and took off at a speed born of sheer desperation.

"Have you gone daft? Could either of my two top sprinters stop whatever it is they're doing and go after him, please? Or you know, pick up the dead one's bow and shoot him before he gets away, maybe?" When neither Snag nor Ellisar responded, the dwarf threw her hands over her head and started after Crim herself. "Unbelievable! Demotions all around, you hear? Don't bother killing each other because when I get back, I'll do it for you!"

Ellisar's gaze dropped to Snag, whose blade was still held firmly against her thigh. "You said you got kicked out of the flatlands for smuggling."

"Technically, true. It's not my fault none of you thought to ask what I was smuggling." Snag's uneasy gaze followed the length of Ellisar's sword until he reached Daana. "You're going to lock up your shoulder holding that position any longer. Lower your blade and I'll lower mine. If I wanted you dead, I would have severed your spinal cord and been done with it."

Ellisar went silent as she considered his offer. Her stony expression revealed none of what was going on behind her eyes. At last, the taut muscles in her forearm relaxed and her arm fell to her side. Daana's gaze followed, realizing the elf's knuckles were drained of color from holding the heavy blade aloft. There was a subtle twitch in Ellisar's fingers that she hadn't noticed before.

Relief flooded Snag's gnarled face as he stepped swiftly out of Ellisar's reach and planted himself between them. As promised, his dagger returned to its sheath.

Whatever game Snag was playing, his bluff was good. None of what he was saying was true, but Daana had the sense not to state this fact out loud. Alive was alive, after all. It didn't matter that her salvation came at the hand of a lie. For now, she would simply play along and wait for answers later. Or run when no one was looking. Also a good option.

If looks could kill, Daana was certain she and Snag would have dropped dead right then. Ellisar's eyes had changed from pale gold to a deep, blazing color. "What are you telling me, Snag? Am I supposed to believe you got banished for moving rich brats across the border?"

"Not brats. Just *a* brat. This one, specifically." Snag gestured over his shoulder at Daana with what had to be feigned confidence. After a few seconds of heated silence, his resolve withered and he volunteered more information unprompted. "I didn't know who she was at the time, alright? If I had, I would've asked for double. She was a damn tot for crying out loud. Could barely babble coherently. And anyway, I didn't think it was going to get me banished. I was just supposed to move the child from the flatlands to the capital and get paid. That's it."

"Who hired you? Geralt?"

"Not per se. It was less of a contractual obligation and more of a spur of the moment, make it up as I go along, and don't get caught sort of thing."

Ellisar gazed over the top of him at Daana in the same manner a hungry hawk watched a field mouse. "I'll just take a little off the top. Her ears, I think. Maybe that'll jog your memory."

"There was this ship, you see. Got caught in a nasty storm and sank just off the coast. We had bodies washing up for weeks." Once started, Snag seemed incapable of stopping the flood of information that poured from his mouth in a single, conscious stream. "A bunch of us were combing the beach for whatever was salvageable and came across a child. I was put in charge of keeping her alive while the others figured out who to contact for ransom money. We knew she was from the realm, which meant somebody had to be missing her. The sheriff caught wind of what we were doing and demanded we surrender the elfling over to the proper authorities. He obviously just wanted the reward money for himself. A fight broke out and they were all so busy knocking each other's teeth in, no one saw me slip out the back with the child.

"Eventually, someone noticed I was missing, because it wasn't long before I had half the flatlands on my tail. I knew they'd kill me if they caught up to us. Her, too, through pure incompetence, probably. I kept low and snuck my way into the realm. It took three blasted months to reach Sunstorn. I managed to haggle my way into a personal appointment with some uppity head of something at the palace and—"

Ellisar raised her eyebrows. "The Speaker of the People?"

"Again, I didn't know that at the time," he grumbled with a flick of his wrist. "There were a lot of people running back and forth. It was complete madness. By that point, I was more focused on making sure no one pulled a knife on me than keeping track of who was who. Finally, the elf in charge came strolling in and thanked me for my service. He gave some long explanation about how the child had been abducted and to protect everyone involved, I was not to breathe a word of what happened to anyone. He made that part very clear. Under pain of death and whatnot. They gave me a sack of money, I handed over the toddler, and we all went off on our merry way."

"That's not true!" Daana was horrified to realize it was her own voice speaking the words. Evidently Snag's weave of lies had gotten too absurd for even her to maintain her silence.

Snag whirled around, pointing his clawed fingertip at her accusingly. "I'll have you know, after everything I went through, your uncle shorted me! He paid only half of what we agreed on. I'm not making that mistake a second time."

Ellisar, with her thin mouth pressed into a tight line, appeared to be deep in thought. "And this all happened because of a shipwreck? What kind of vessel did you say it was?"

The goblin was too busy itemizing his bill on his fingertips to listen. "The money doesn't even begin to touch the pain and suffering. Since I brought you back, I've been run out of multiple towns, had three businesses burned down, and on top of it all, a bunch of assholes demolished my house by baiting a dragon through my blasted living room! And then they took advantage of my destitution and convinced me to join them!"

"Snag!"

"What? I'm in the middle of airing my grievances. To which you have contributed enormously, I might add."

"The ship! What kind?"

Snag glared at Ellisar for interrupting his tirade, lifting one scrawny shoulder higher than the other. "It was a big wooden thing that floated. Or did, anyway, until it didn't."

"It wasn't flying any particular colors?"

"I saw it in pieces, El. It could have been in the shape of a giant duck for all I know."

Ellisar's unnerving stare settled over Daana. "How old are you?"

Daana didn't see how that was pertinent. But, not wanting to find herself on the wrong end of Ellisar's sword again, volunteered the information willingly. ". . . Seventy-six?"

And then the impossible happened. Ellisar's face betrayed her. Her eyes grew wide and her jaw dropped ever so slightly, leaving an open mouth from which no words passed. This was rectified several moments later when she threw her head back and cursed to the Goddess of Chaos above. The elf turned, long hair swaying behind her, and kicked at the mud as she ran through every expletive in her expansive repertoire. When finished, Ellisar simply started from the beginning again.

CHAPTER TWENTY-THREE

Tadpole

Soft soil squelched beneath her boots as Ellisar stormed up and down her chosen strip of stomping ground. Snag watched her unusually loud antics with his hand hovering over the hilt of his bone-handled dagger. For the briefest of moments, his eyes darted in Daana's direction. "Is there something significant about your age?"

Daana was so desperately lost in the tangle of new information, she feared she would never be found again. A shipwreck? She'd never been on a ship in her life. And she certainly hadn't washed ashore and traveled through lawless territory as a toddler. Snag was confused. It was someone else. It had to be. She'd been born and raised in the Sunstorn Palace. This wasn't something Uncle would have kept from her.

. . . Just like all the other important stuff he had kept from her.

In the midst of the storm raging within her thoughts, the old fragment of the song came back to her:

Ta home ya return,
Happy and spoiled rotten.
Little tadpole, little tadpole,
Will I be forgotten?

Daana clamped her eyes shut and summoned the face that accompanied the lullaby. From the dark recesses of her memory, it came to her, slowly. She saw the blurred outline and twinkling glimmers of light. Starlight—she once thought. Daana eased her eyelids back open, stifling a nervous laugh as the image shifted from the plains of memory into reality. Not starlight, she realized, but jewelry. Jewelry that had once shimmered and caught the sunlight, now as battered and tarnished as its owner.

An owner that looked on her with a familiar softness she had failed to recognize before. Daana sank to the ground and landed hard on her ass. The undignified landing brought back the pain in her side. She clutched her ribs, wincing. "You called me tadpole."

"My utotrian wasn't very good back then. I asked your name, but between you an' me, I couldn't tell what you were saying on a good day. Had to call you something." His demeanor was different than before. The old Snag would have marched up to her and demanded to see what was ailing her without concern for bedside manners or propriety. Now, fiddling with one of the bangles in his ear, Snag acted strangely reserved. "You want me to take a look at that for you?"

Holding her breath, Daana peeled back her wet tunic and exposed her battered ribcage. She didn't want to look for fear of what she might see. When he gave no indication of how severe the damage was, she opened one eye and chanced a quick glance. Other than a small, superficial cut, her insides had not turned to outsides. A wave of relief washed over her.

Snag crouched as he studied the bruising that bloomed in great black and blue patches across her left side. His jagged mouth twisted downward, asking, "Does it hurt when you breathe?"

"Yes."

"And what about when I do this?" He jabbed a finger into her ribs.

A gurgled scream escaped her mouth as Daana lashed out with her foot, attempting to push the unhelpful goblin out of arm's reach. She missed and rolled onto her side instead. "Oh my gods, what is wrong with you?"

"Your first broken rib, how adorable. Should we write that down in the baby book, maybe?"

Still on her side, Daana pulled her knees to her chest, whimpering. "Why does it feel like I'm dying?"

"That's called pain. You'll get used to it." Snag unslung the waterskin from his hip and offered it to her. "Here, this'll take the edge off."

Daana took a slug, expecting the fiery bite of alcohol to slide down her throat. Whatever it was she swallowed, it was certainly not booze. Her hand flew to her mouth, fighting the sudden urge to gag. The taste was bitter, like rancid almonds, and made her stomach lurch in protest. "That is horrid."

"Willow bark tea. Extra strong. The taste encourages better choices. You know, if you're lucky enough to make them again." He waved his clawed hand at her dismissively. "It's a broken rib, not the spotted plague. You're fine."

Daana stared at the ground as she forced another sip of the foul brew. "Why didn't you say something before? About finding me, I mean."

"What part of 'under pain of death' do you not comprehend?" Snag curled his nose at the question. "And what was I supposed to say? 'Hello, strange elf woman. You may not remember me, but I stole you when you were real little like and we went on a three-month journey together. You cried most of the time and at one point I lost you in a swamp, but we had some good times. Say, do you still enjoy eating bugs? Have you learned to use the toilet yet?'"

"I did not eat bugs."

"Oh yes you did. Snails were your favorite. I'd be lucky if I got half my catch in the cook pot before your grubby little hands snatched 'em up. You'd suck 'em right out of the shell." He accentuated his last point with a horrifically wet, slurping sound.

Daana's stomach was starting to feel ill again. "Alright, I get it. Stop."

Ellisar, having finished her fit of rage, froze mid-stride on her way to rejoin them. She stared at Snag with an expression of absolute confusion. "What the fuck are you doing?"

"Demonstrating how one eats raw snails."

Ellisar brushed several strands of mud-crusted hair from her face, huffing, "We don't have time for food. Rali hasn't come back yet. We need to regroup and see about finding the others."

Snag stood and adjusted his stance, jutting one foot out in front of the other as he crossed his bony arms over his leather cuirass. He indicated Daana with a tilt of his head. "Only if 'we' includes her."

"On one condition," Ellisar said. "You don't tell anybody else about your history with the girl. Not Curly, not Rali, and especially not Oralia. If they ask, you're keeping her for the ransom, clear? They can't know about your deal with Geralt."

"Do you know something I don't?"

"Goddess, I hope not." Ellisar paused, as if realizing she'd uttered this out loud instead of keeping it to her thoughts. She fought off the imploring looks from both Snag and Daana alike before conceding the matter with an uncharacteristic stomp of her foot. A splatter of mud accompanied her mounting frustration. "It's only a hunch. Ashwyn would know more, but without her, I can't be sure. So no, I don't actually know anything. Not yet."

Ellisar was hiding something. It was as plain as the scowl on her face. Daana persisted. "Then tell us what your hunch is."

"Put a muzzle on it, princess. I've already agreed to let Snag bring you along. Don't make me reconsider my generosity."

Normally Daana would have left it alone, especially since it was Ellisar making the threats, but she could see that the elf was on the edge. Ellisar's hands were held stiffly at her sides and trembling. It was risky, sure, but it was also very likely the only opportunity Daana would get to question Ellisar while she was under obvious duress. The hairline cracks were beginning to show and if Daana kept up the pressure, there was a chance Ellisar's determination would crumble.

"Who am I, Ellisar? And what the fuck does it have to do with a boat? You obviously know something. And I'm not going to let up until you give me an answer."

"She sounds awful serious, El," Snag said. "You sure you don't want to make your life easier and just come out with it?"

"Lower your voices, the both of you. You're going to attract the enemy."

Daana drew her upper lip back, flashing her upper teeth in a manner that she hoped looked intimidating and not constipated. "Tell me what you know!"

"No!"

"Then I guess I'm just going to keep asking you, over and over and over and over again until you—"

The hairline cracks were more severe than Daana realized because Ellisar's entire facade came crashing down in the blink of an eye. She threw her hands high over her head, shouting, "Fine! You're someone important, alright? Or were—I think. If you are who I think you are, then the absolute last person you want to know is Oralia."

Daana opened her mouth to volley a series of follow-up questions, but there was no need. Ellisar provided the answer willingly. "She killed your mother."

"Mother?" The words unraveled from Daana's tongue like a loose thread from a poorly knit sweater. "But uncle said Mother died on the road journeying from—"

"Yeah, well your blasted uncle didn't tell you about the boat wreck either, did he? Or the goblin that smuggled you across the border, or the fact that you're not even Lazuli blood!" Ellisar had that look on her face again. She had said too much.

Sensing she'd wrung as much information out of Ellisar as was physically possible, Daana realized the rest was up to her. "Briony said all magic-sensitive elves are born of a witch," she said more to herself than the others. Her thoughts took the beginnings of an idea and ran wild with it. "Which means my mother was a witch, a powerful one at that. And Oralia kills witches."

Except for Rasp and the Palace Ghost and—that wasn't important right now! She was onto something. *Focus!*

Daana closed her eyes with a shaky breath and focused. Silently, she willed all of the whirling thoughts in her brain to align into some sort of a discernible order. Her mother, witches and Oralia; something about a boat and the flatlands; and her age—why was her age important? And the blood part, something about not being a real Lazuli? If she and Uncle Geralt weren't related, why had he claimed her as his own?

The answer hit her like an open handed slap—one that kept slapping, over and over and over. Daana's eyes snapped open with a start. Her words vacated her mouth not so much as a question, but a scream. "My mother was Larkspur Denari?"

Ellisar's teeth gritted against one another in a pained expression of regret. Not so much for Daana's outrage, perhaps, but because she had been the one to give the secret away. Ellisar glanced over her shoulder, as if debating whether or not this was an appropriate time to cut and run.

"Ellisar!"

"Alright, yes. I think so. But for now, that's all I can tell you," she said, still looking as though she wanted to be anywhere but here. "If you want to live long enough to get answers to all your stupid questions, then save them for someone who gives a shit. For now, you do as I say, when I say it. Keep your fucking head down and your mouth shut. Ashwyn will be able to tell you everything once we get back to Sunstorn."

"Ashwyn?" A second revelation started to brew within the violent churning behind Daana's eyes.

"That counts as a fucking question!"

"Oi, shut it, both of you." Snag's ear shot straight into the air in a flurry of dancing bangles and hoops. He held his hand aloft and listened. Other than the whistling wind whipping through the treetops, Daana heard nothing. Finally, after several excruciating seconds, Snag turned back to Ellisar, unperturbed by her withering stare. "Tell me you hear that?"

"I don't hear shit, Snaggy. But if it'll get Miss Suddenly-Has-A-Brain off my back, then I'll tell you whatever you want me to."

"It's Rali." Snag fastened his waterskin back over his hip and took off on all fours at an awkward bound. For such a mismatched stride, it was remarkably effective. He skirted to a rough halt just shy of the tree line, as if remembering the others did not possess his keen sense of hearing. "She's calling for me," he said. "I have to go."

"Are you forgetting something?" Ellisar gestured to Daana.

"It sounds bad, El. Take Daana and follow my trail. Carefully, in case it's a trap. And if you show up without her, so help me, I'll—"

Ellisar waved him off. "You'll make jelly from my eyeballs, I get it. Go!"

He imparted one last concerned look over his shoulder before he charged headlong into the thorny undergrowth and disappeared from sight.

CHAPTER TWENTY-FOUR

Like a Warm Hug

Un-fucking-believable." Ellisar clenched and unclenched her trembling hands. "He leaves me to play nanny? Me? The one who was threatening to kill you only moments ago?" Her glare settled on Daana, as if the situation was her fault somehow. "You really should pick better protectors. This borders on negligence."

If it were anyone else, Daana might have extended her hand in a silent plea for assistance. The only kind of assistance Daana could expect from Sergeant Farrow, however, was a helpful shove over the nearest cliffside. Gritting her teeth, Daana gathered her knees beneath her and began the agonizing process of pushing to her feet unassisted. The pain radiating from her ribcage nearly dropped her. She persisted, knowing that if she collapsed now, her guide would not hesitate to leave her there.

Daana moved through the washed-out forest, navigating the fallen trees and muddy debris with painstaking care. Ellisar trotted ahead unconcerned. Just when Daana feared she'd lost her guide completely, she spied the impatient elf leaning against the papery white-and-black bark of a birch tree, waiting for her.

"Why are you walking like a geriatric turtle?" Ellisar asked with her arms folded over her narrow chest. "You're an elfling. You're supposed to be spry."

The realm's best information had placed Ellisar's age somewhere in the six hundred range. Daana hated that someone who was five, possibly six, times her age, could sprint uphill through the mud without breaking a sweat. "Snag thinks I broke a rib."

"I could remedy that for you."

More death threats, lovely. Daana never thought she would live to see the day that Ellisar Farrow grew predictable. "You know, I think I preferred you as the hostile quiet type."

Ellisar's hand disappeared within the confines of her jacket, searching for what Daana hoped wasn't a knife. Ellisar produced a leather pouch instead, and set about peeling a dried leaf from the inside with painstaking care. Wordlessly, she offered it to Daana without the anticipated taunting or exaggerated eye roll.

Daana raised her eyebrows at the strange offering, squeaking, "More illegal substances?"

"Your mother would be rolling over in her grave right now."

She scowled at the remark. "Excuse me for exercising a little caution. You just tried to kill me, remember?"

Ellisar pressed the shriveled leaf into the palm of Daana's hand as she shouldered past, grunting, "Threatened to kill you. Not tried. Had I wanted you dead, you would be."

Daana limped after her. Her wide-eyed gaze lifted from the leaf to the back of Ellisar's head. The older elf was already gaining ground ahead of her. "Will you at least tell me what it is? Or what it does? Or how I'm supposed to take it?"

"Stop using your mouth for talking and chew it."

Daana bit back the thousand remaining questions that leapt to the tip of her tongue. Interrogating Ellisar was, admittedly, a poor idea. It would only cement the sergeant's dislike of her, possibly enough to abandon her. Daana wouldn't be able to find her way without Ellisar's help. And she certainly couldn't make it on her own, either. Not without the possibility of running into Captain Monk along the way. That prospect terrified her more than ingesting a substance of questionable origins.

Swallowing her trepidation, Daana tucked the leaf between her molars and gave it an experimental chew. The taste was pleasantly sweet. A welcome relief compared to the willow bark tea, anyway. Daana chewed as she walked, watching her body for signs that the remedy was working. The strange buzzing sensation that danced across her tongue was the first thing she noticed. But her ribs ached less and her feet suddenly weren't so heavy. It wasn't long before Daana found herself closing the gap between them.

"Ellisar!" Rali's voice rang out across the still forest. From the proximity, the dwarf wasn't far.

Ellisar broke into a run. Without thinking, Daana pushed through the last of the pain and raced after her. The pair sprinted across the mud-covered ground. Ellisar hurtled over fallen trees and branches as though they were minor inconveniences. Daana, sensibly, went around. She didn't know where she was going, but her guide seemed to have an innate sense of direction.

They found Rali crouched on the ground beneath the broken branches of a sagging balsam poplar. Snag was beside her, digging furiously through his kit while cursing every chaotic deity of the seven realms. Curly was slumped against the trunk between them. The bloodied chainmail on his chest heaved in and out with each fast, labored breath. He watched Daana and Ellisar approach. His eyelids were drooped and his stare unfocused.

Ellisar shoved between Rali and Snag and took Curly's head in her hands. Her eyes searched his ashen face. "What the fuck is this now? You big, dumb baby. You aren't supposed to fuck shit up without me!"

Curly's trembling lips parted, but only an agonized whimper came forth.

"Gods dammit, don't get him all riled up again, El! We're working to get you through this, alright, Curly? Just focus on breathing. You can do that for me, right? Breathe." Rali glanced out of the corner of her eye at Snag. The worry that shone in her face had been carefully removed from her voice. "You got a status for me?"

"There's a fucking hole in his neck with blood coming out. What more do you want me to tell you?" Snag was furiously mixing a compress in a small wooden bowl. Finished, he applied the sticky green-and-gray paste to the wound with his hands. "I could use some help, actually. Someone want to be useful and hand me the damn bandages?"

Feeling as though she'd stepped from the real world into a dream, Daana's limbs responded before the rest of her realized what she was doing. She dropped down into the mud and pulled a roll of cloth from Snag's open bag. "Here. What else do you need?"

"Got any fucking miracles on you?"

With a distressed grimace, Curly reached up, slowly, and placed both hands over Snag's wrists. He pulled the goblin's hands from the wound with more exertion than it should have taken.

Snag's lower jaw trembled with fury. "I'm trying to save you, idiot. Let go!"

Breathing short, raspy breaths through his tusks, Curly stared back at him, arguing in his own stubborn way. His black eyes softened and he looked tired, as if any moment now his eyelids would shut and he would drift quietly to sleep.

"Whatever the fuck you think you're doing," Snag's voice was low, like a growl, "stop it right now."

A pitiful whine escaped Curly's slack mouth. It made the flicker of hope in Daana's chest turn to stone. Hot tears slipped unbidden from her aching eyes as she realized what he was asking.

Snag must have realized it too, because he whipped his head back and forth with force. His tarnished hoops rattled in an eerie symphony of jingles and chimes. "No, I can't! I won't! Don't look at me like that."

Curly said nothing. There was no need. His somber expression communicated more effectively than words could have.

Ellisar dropped back on her haunches grimly. Her eyes flickered to the dark red stain that coated the skin around Curly's neck. Blood had spilled down the front of his chainmail, transforming the aged steel from gray to a dark brown, almost black. "He's right, Snag. You'd only be stretching his time out a few hours at most. There's no coming back from this."

"No! You don't get to take his side on this! Nobody here's qualified to have an opinion except me. And he's not dying unless I say so!" With his hands balled into fists, Snag tore free of Curly's weak grasp and spun around at Daana. "Don't sit there slack-jawed, girl. You have magic, don't you? For the gods' sakes, use it! Fix him!"

The rage that glowed within his yellow eyes sent Daana scuttling backward. Fear bubbled up from her gaping mouth. "I—I can't. It doesn't work like that."

"What good are you then? Why in the seven realms of chaos did I stick my neck out for you if you can't manage even the simplest—"

A gravelly click disrupted Snag's tirade. Daana looked to Curly, realizing the warning sound had come from him. With a pained huff, he jutted his bloodstained hand in her direction. Daana took it, taken aback by the strength that, even now, clung to his flesh with the same stubbornness as its owner. Curly pulled her to his side and then slumped back against the tree, exhausted by the effort.

"I'm so sorry." Daana rested her head on his shoulder as the sudden, swelling pains in her chest made filling her lungs next to impossible. The streams of tears slipped freely from the corners of her eyes and clouded her vision. She didn't know what else to say. There weren't words to make any of this better. There was nothing she could do to fix it, either. She was utterly helpless. Her only recourse was to hold his hand and offer whatever comfort she could for what little time he had left.

Across from them, Ellisar and Rali were holding a hushed conversation. Fast tears rolled from Rali's red-rimmed eyes. Ellisar may not have been crying, but her expression was equally as bleak. After some heated back and forth, Ellisar ended the argument with an angry whisper and reached for Snag's leather pouch. Snag saw what she was doing and dove to recover it, but the elf was quicker. Ellisar withdrew a vial from his meticulously labeled selection and returned to Curly's side.

"Don't worry. Auntie's got you. One last one for the road, yeah?" Ellisar slid in on the other side of Curly as she worked the cork stopper free with her teeth. "You remember the mushrooms? Those were shit compared to this. Forget about seeing all the colors, mate. You're going to feel them. When the euphoria hits, it's like a warm hug."

Curly whimpered something Daana was unable to decipher. Rali moved beside Ellisar and took his free hand. She squeezed it, trying to smile as the color drained from her cheeks. "It's okay, love. She'll understand. Leave the explaining to us, okay? Do what you need to do."

Curly's teary eyes shifted to Snag. He let go of Rali and reached for him, wheezing softly. Snag looked the other way, pretending not to see.

"For fuck's sake, Snag!" Ellisar bared her teeth at him. "He's not going to go unless you let him. Get your sorry ass over here and give him a proper send-off!"

"No."

"What do you mean no?"

Snag stared hopelessly at his feet as his long ears drooped behind him. His voice was small, like a skiff caught in a hurricane, fighting the mighty ocean swells that threatened to drag it under. ". . . I'm not ready."

"Snaglebrag, please." The free-falling tears had left trails in the mud and dirt that caked Rali's face. Her chest heaved in and out as her breathing grew fast and labored. "This isn't about you. This is about him. And if his dying wish is to have you by his side, then you're going to come over here and hold his fucking hand and tell him he made you a proud papa!"

Her words broke him. Snag's rigid posture changed and, for a brief moment, it looked as if he would crumple into the ground. Biting his trembling lower lip, Snag's dragging steps drew closer. He took Curly's outstretched hand and collapsed against him. Whatever final words passed between them were muffled by Curly's bloodstained armor.

When they had said their goodbyes, Ellisar tipped the vial to Curly's lips. She waited until the glass was empty and then rested her forehead against his, closing her eyes. "You know where to find us. Follow the lights. We'll be home soon."

Before Daana knelt a very strange family. Not one built on blood or covenant, but forged from circumstance. To know family was to know love. And in knowing love, inevitably, one met loss. On that quiet summer morning, with the wind rustling the treetops overhead and birdsong in the distance, she watched this bizarre family grow one member smaller, and the tear in their souls infinitely larger.

Curly lifted his head from the heavy blankets, groaning. He could hear the floorboards creak as the others moved unquietly through the house like a stampede of wild boars. They were up to something, surely. Protector Dawnsight usually had his ass out of bed by first light. She only ever let him sleep in when the others were too hungover to crawl out from whatever hidey hole they'd bunkered down in for the night.

Maybe she thought he was sick. He was, in a way. His throat was raw, and it felt like someone had filled his chest with stones. Homesick, he'd heard it called before. Home? If it were not for the creeping sadness that pulled tight at the base of his neck, he might have laughed. He didn't have a home, not anymore. No home. No family. All he had now was an overbearing commander and her small legion of loyal imbeciles.

Curly debated whether to go back to bed, but decided that today, of all days, was not the one to endure another tiresome lecture. Besides, he could smell pork and onions simmering from the kitchen. A full stomach was better than wallowing in self-pity, anyway. Curly rose from the bed and dragged his reluctant feet toward the door. He froze, certain he heard soft laughter coming from the other side. Probably another one of their stupid pranks. For being several times his age, Oralia's warriors were no better than children. Lethal, ugly children.

The edge of his mouth curled into a devious smile. Perhaps it was time to play a prank of his own. Returning to his bunk, Curly removed the flask from his pack and slipped it into his pocket. Just because he was spending the winter solstice trapped with the company from the seventh realm of chaos didn't mean it had to be all bad. He crossed the creaky floorboards once more and reached for the tarnished door handle.

He paused, blinking his eyes in disbelief. What in blazes was with all of these colored lights? Had they already slipped him something? Is that what the laughter was about?

Curly opened the door and the warm glow from the hearth illuminated the room. The smell of apples and fresh-cut spruce filled the air. Four familiar voices hailed him, beckoning him further inside. Maybe they weren't so bad, after all. A little weird. But he could get used to that. Curly crossed

the threshold, mesmerized by the dancing light of the paper lanterns, only
vaguely aware of the soft voice ushering him from the beyond:

> *O dear friend,*
> *We wish you might stay.*
> *Twilight draws near,*
> *Your curtain on its way.*
>
> *Hold my hand, don't fret, don't cry.*
> *Though this may feel forever,*
> *'Tis only a short goodbye.*
>
> *Wait along the crystalline shore,*
> *Where the waters meet the moon.*
> *Watch the colors dance against the sky*
> *and know,*
> *We'll be home soon.*

CHAPTER TWENTY-FIVE

Iron Devil

Rasp's consciousness unfurled from the safety of the internal fetal position and slid warily to the forefront of his mind. His body was cold and his clothes were drenched and clung to his clammy flesh like a second skin. The memory of what happened, how he'd gotten here, was like a familiar scent on the breeze. It was faint, but recognizable. And each time he nearly remembered what it was he'd forgotten, the thought slipped back into the unreachable recesses of his memory once more.

Something had happened. And for whatever reason, his mind was protecting him. Again. Just like it had with Father.

What have you done?

Guilt gripped him. The invisible fish in his lower gut that gummed his intestines in times like this was gone. A badger had taken its place, ripping him to shreds from the inside until his stomach was full of a thousand tiny, leaking holes. What had he done? What was his mind protecting him from this time? Rasp pushed himself upright, groaning as the needling pain of life returned to his numb extremities.

He was wet and smelled like mud and soil. Wet. Wet meant water. Something about water. A whole lot of it. He remembered the snapping crack of trees and the roar of fast-moving rapids right before the icy swell took him under. There was something else, before that. A sound. No, a voice. Someone had been yelling at him. Not Oralia, she was always yelling at him. That wasn't out of the ordinary. Someone who didn't normally yell. They were panicked, Rasp remembered that.

"Faris!" Rasp screamed as he lurched forward onto his hands and knees, searching the area around him for any telltale sign of his friend. "Faris, are you here?"

It was coming back to him in fragmented pieces now. Faris had reached him only seconds before the flood hit. Rasp's magic shielded them for a ways, but the strain had been too much and his mind had slipped quietly into its safe place soon after. He may have lost track of time and place, but he knew Faris was nearby. Rasp wouldn't have let go. Not of Faris.

Rasp scrambled forward on all fours. Water sloshed around his knees as he attempted to make sense of his surroundings. Beneath him, his fingertips sank through a thin layer of mud and wet sediment until he hit solid rock. The only light source he could make out was coming from the side, not above. The air was wet and musty and the steady *drip-drip-drip* of water echoed all around him. A cavern, he realized. He'd been washed into one of the many natural rock recesses carved into the face of the mountain by the annual snowmelt.

"Faris, if you can hear me, say something!"

"Don't," a voice spoke, heavy and labored, as if talking had become an unbearable task, "talk to me."

Rasp whipped his head toward the mouth of the cave. Other than the contrast of light to dark, he saw nothing. He crept forward on all fours, willing his numb limbs to move faster. "Now's not the time to be dramatic, Dingle. Are you hurt? Keep talking and I'll come find you."

"Stay. Away."

Rasp faltered. His palms sank further into the cold muck as the hope in his chest shriveled like overcooked onions in a pan. "Faris, whatever I did, I—I'm sorry."

"I said stay away!"

A heaviness flooded his insides, pouring through every guilt-riddled hole until he was drowning from the inside. The weight dragged him down, down, down, until Rasp's lungs were so compressed, he could barely fill them. The water—that had been him. He'd lost control. Again. There was something else, too. Something his mind refused to unlock. Why had he summoned the water? Dammit, he'd been so careful!

"It was an accident. I didn't mean to—"

"To what? Kill everyone?" Faris screamed. His voice reverberated against the walls with such magnitude, sheets of loose sediment rained down from the ceiling and pitter-pattered against Rasp's shoulders and head. "Is that what you didn't mean to do, Rasp? Fucking kill everyone?"

A chill snaked down his spine and spread to his chest. The cold combatted the strange burning sensation emitting from his ears. Rasp's tongue faltered as he processed Faris's words. He didn't kill everyone. He was reformed now. He was good.

Except for some of Monk's soldiers. He might have killed them. His memory was still a little hazy on the details. But they'd attacked first! That was justified, wasn't it? Right? He was still good, wasn't he? He'd tried. Didn't that count? He hadn't meant to unleash his magic. He couldn't even remember why he'd done so. But it had been an accident, he was certain of that. And accidents didn't count. He was still good. He was good. He was good . . .

Rasp sank lower into the mud as his limbs gave out beneath him. The stale air was thick and difficult to breathe. He pulled his knees to his chest, gasping to quell the sudden fire in his lungs.

"My father wanted to kill you. Did you know that? He insisted we cut your throat the moment he discovered what you were. It was me who said no. I was the one who said you could change. That maybe if you were shown some damned compassion you could learn to be better." Faris wasn't yelling anymore. His voice was cold, calm, and like a knife, it cut deeper with each bitter word. "I should have listened to him. What I would give to go back and set things right."

The tightness in his chest spread to his throat. Rasp clawed at his neck, opening and closing his mouth uselessly. Hot tears streaked down his panicked face. The little charms threaded through his ears burned like blazing coals against his skin. Still good. He was still good. Faris was just panicking. He didn't mean what he was saying. He'd snap out of it soon and everything could go back to the way it was.

"I used to feel sorry for you. All those stories of how your father treated you, I couldn't help myself. But he wasn't the bad guy, was he, Rasp? He knew what you were, just like my father did. And that's why you killed him. He saw your rottenness for what it was and you got rid of him before he got rid of you."

Rasp gasped for breath. The cold muck pooled around him, pulling him deeper, deeper, deeper. "That's not true."

"Of course it's true! That's what you do. You kill people. You killed your father. You killed your mother. You killed all of our friends. And if I hang around here any longer, you'll kill me too."

Mother? He hadn't killed Mother. She'd died of summer fever before his sixteenth year. Rasp had been responsible for many horrible things in his life, but not Mother. He would have never hurt her. She was his only protector. Even in death, her raven was never far.

In fact, why wasn't she here now? She never missed the opportunity to give him a righteous earful for losing control.

The final piece of the memory fell into place. *Oh no. Oh no, no, no.*

"I'll admit," Faris said, "all this talk about being good, about being better. You had me convinced. I thought you had changed. The sad thing is, I think you actually tried. It's probably the first time you've put effort into anything in your life."

Oralia had worked a deal. Monk was letting them go. All he had to do was shut up and let her do her thing, but he couldn't do that. Rasp had to go and fuck it up! And now they were all dead. And Mother . . . Mother was gone. There was no second afterlife. A soul couldn't come back a third time. Killing made you a murderer. Wiping a soul from existence made you unforgivable.

"You failed because your good isn't good enough."

Unforgivable. He was unforgivable. Rasp drew into himself, attempting to shut Faris out. But the voice was all around, impossible to ignore.

"You will never be good enough!" Faris thundered until the surrounding rock trembled. "You cannot change what you are. You were born a curse, you will live as a curse, and you will fucking die as a curse."

The heaviness pulled him further into the abyss. A familiar tingle washed over his skin as magic leached into the cavern from below. Its dark tendrils wormed through his aching bones until his entire body pulsed with hot rage. The magic whispered into his ear. It pulled at his fingertips, urging him to reach out and accept it.

It can all go away, the magic promised.

"No!" Rasp screamed, tucking his head into his arms and willing the darkness to subside.

"No? No what, Rasp? No, you don't want to kill people? You don't want to bring death and destruction everywhere you go? It's too fucking late for that!"

No one will ever hurt you again. You only have to say yes.

Pain. Pain was the only way to save himself. Rasp raised his hand to his lips and bit down, shuddering silently as a wave of agony rippled down his arm. The warm taste of metal pooled across his tongue.

"I'm done, Rasp." Faris said tiredly. "I should have never come here. I'm going home before you curse me, too."

They hurt you and then they leave. But you do not have to be alone, Stoneclaw. I will not demand you to be something different. Something that you are not. I accept you as you are.

The pain wasn't working. Rasp dug his fingers into his forehead, screaming, "Shut up! Shut up! Shut up!"

He was still good. He was good.

Accept what you are.

He was a good person who sometimes did bad things. That didn't make him bad. It made him complicated. His father's death had been an accident. The villagers claimed it was his curse that had killed his mother. His son, too. But those weren't his fault. They were . . . they were just bad things that happened to good people. Bad things that always seemed to happen when he was around . . .

"Faris, please," he sobbed, drawing his legs to his chest. "Please don't leave. I can't do it alone."

There was no answer.

He sank deeper into the churning pit of despair. Magic rippled across his blistered skin, soothing the burn. It felt good. He was tired of being strong. He didn't have the fight to resist any longer. Maybe he'd gotten it wrong. Maybe good wasn't what fate wanted from him. Not everyone was born to be better. There had to be villains, too, didn't there? There couldn't be heroes without villains. His entire life he'd been called a devil. Maybe it was time to stop running and accept the role fate had assigned him.

Stillness filled the cavern, until even the steady *drip-drip-drip* of the water faded. Rasp shut himself off to the outside, shrouding himself in numbness. In the distance, through the quiet nothingness humming in his ears, the soft croak of a raven rang out.

CHAPTER TWENTY-SIX

The Incessantly Talking Beanpole

Oralia awoke with her head pounding and every bone feeling as though it weighed twice what it should have. Her hair and clothes were damp and plastered to her skin. The potent stench of old blood and body odor struck with such force, her mouth immediately filled with acid as her stomach attempted to upend itself in a single heave. Clamping her eyes shut, Oralia fought the rolling sensation in her gut until it subsided. It wasn't until after the nausea faded that she was able to ease her heavy eyelids open again.

Spots of light danced overhead against a dark background. When her vision stopped swimming long enough to adjust to the gloom, she found herself in a narrow room bathed in pale, flickering torchlight. Above her, the walls stretched nearly twelve feet in height and were carved from great slabs of red-gray stone. The ceiling and the cold, pitted floor that stretched below her appeared to be fashioned from the same material.

A low hum droning on in the background alerted her that wherever she was, she was not alone. Through half-closed eyes, Oralia tilted her head to try to pinpoint the source of the annoying disturbance. Pain erupted across her stiff neck and she grimaced, holding back a snarl. It was only after the agony died down to a dull throb that she was able to take in the finer details of her surroundings.

The noise was coming from a pair of shadowy figures standing on the other side of the bars. *Unimportant,* her overworked brain decided. *Forget the noise and focus on the bars. More specifically, how to get out of them.*

Several uniform rows of iron bars made up the front and sides of what was now very obviously a prison cell. Whose prison this was, she didn't know yet, only that she was on the inside of it and, regretfully, the bars appeared well set and rather sturdy. From her current position, sprawled across the stone floor, she saw the room appeared to have only one entry point. There wasn't anything remarkable about the heavy wooden door across from her, other than the fact that if push came to shove, she was fairly certain she could kick it down on her own.

That plan relied on her ability to get past the bars first, however. A prospect that wasn't looking particularly fruitful at the moment.

Sudden movement on the edge of her peripheral vision caused her to freeze. Through slit eyes, she watched as one of the shadowy figures stalked past the front of her cell. He was human and either didn't notice that she was awake or didn't care. Regardless, Oralia remained perfectly still, content to play dead for as long as possible.

She waited until the guard resumed his position before continuing her visual sweep. She counted four other cells spanning the length of the room. A generous walkway ran parallel to the bars, ensuring the guards could move freely along the front of the cellblock without being accosted. There were four prisoners in total, including herself. Two of which were Captain Monk's soldiers and the other—the current occupant of the cell closest to Oralia—was of no importance as he was already dead to her.

None of her faithful four were present. Gods willing, they had survived the flood, regrouped, and were already halfway down the mountain. Oralia had already issued them orders to go on without her. With the exception of Rali, the command to save their own skins didn't normally need repeating with her crew.

For a long time Oralia remained still and merely watched, making mental notes of anything significant. The posted guards came in pairs and spent most of their shift playing cards and sneaking swigs from a flask. They were absent at the moment, having been dismissed by the well-dressed man pacing outside of the cells. He was a slim, gangly little thing. All bones, no meat, like a walking, incessantly talking beanpole.

The man appeared to be a taller version of Rasp—save for the mop of long brown hair on his head and the fact that his facial features hadn't been rearranged by someone else's fist enough times to be noticeable. This newcomer's shared resemblance told her that he was a Stoneclaw and that this place, by extension, was the Stoneclaw dungeon. If this were the case, how the fuck had they gotten her here? Better yet, how did they get *him* here?

Against her better judgment, her gaze swept over Sascha's still form. He was hunched over near the back of his cell with his head buried in his hands. On instinct, she almost called out to him, but then she remembered she wanted him dead and snapped the words back into her infernal mouth. There was a possibility she could strike an alliance with Sascha and the two of them could manage an escape together, but she wasn't sure she would be able to abstain from strangling him through the bars long enough for that to happen.

"And another thing—"

Gods, was the beanpole still talking? Oralia might have learned the man's actual name had she bothered to listen. That, however, was entirely too much effort and she concentrated her stare on the splintered cracks running the length of the ceiling instead. This particular human wasn't in charge. She'd encountered enough leaders to recognize the difference. He may have been higher up, given the way the guards obeyed his command, but it was the sort of authority that came with being a member of the royal family and not overall competence.

The ancient door creaked open and a second figure sauntered into the sparsely lit cellblock. She assumed that this was another member of the Stoneclaw family based on his confident demeanor. Unlike the beanpole, this human appeared as though he would be significantly harder to snap in half. He was a few inches taller than the other, with a round stomach, stout arms, and legs so bulged in muscle they strained against his comically small clothing. In addition to a head of long brown hair, he sported a neatly braided beard that reached somewhere past his collarbones. A convenient handhold, Oralia noted, in the event he gave her a reason to swing him by it.

"Bil said he'd caught the protector. Had to come see for myself," the new arrival murmured, swaggering up to the bars with his hands placed at his belt. "Gods, look at the size of her. I knew she was supposed to be a big un', but I didn't realize they'd meant behemoth."

Ah, also not in charge, Oralia concluded, from her position stretched across the stone floor. Like his chatty companion, the newcomer was currently standing slack-jawed in front of Sascha's cell. Not only did the pair wrongfully assume that size equated rank, they obviously could not tell a female orc from a male, either. Somewhat insulting, considering Sascha had a beard, but who was she to complain?

It was odd that Sascha hadn't bothered to correct this misconception yet. The Protector of the Realm was enemy number one as far as the Stoneclaw clan was concerned. They were keeping her alive for a host of reasons, many of which undoubtedly involved various forms of torture. Oralia would not have blamed Sascha for giving her up. Their last encounter had made it very clear that whatever had previously existed between them was over. And yet, the fool continued to sit silent, as though he had already accepted his fate.

Was he protecting her?

Don't get all sentimental for him now, idiot. You made that mistake once already and look where it got you.

Closing her eyes, Oralia extinguished all thoughts of Sascha from her mind. All of her remaining mental energy was redirected to the dilemma at hand. *Someone* among the Stoneclaws had known who she was. Said person was clearly not either of the two currently strutting in front of the cell beside her. Perhaps it was finally time to set the record straight and request an audience with the real ringleader.

Oralia sat upright, fighting the urge to scream at the pain that flared across her aching shoulders. She opened her eyes with a pained grimace as her hostile gaze settled over the Stoneclaw pair. "Gentlemen, I am afraid you are mistaken. While the orc in front of you is as you say, a 'behemoth,' *he* is not the Protector of the Realm."

Both brothers whipped around in her direction, mouths hanging agape.

"As a token of my appreciation for your hospitality, I will gift you his head." Oralia ignored the look of hurt that crossed Sascha's sullen features, adding with a tight smile, "I imagine his skull would make a very nice cauldron."

The bulky man closed his gaping mouth as several thoughts darted behind his eyes. One of them must have landed, because he seized his brother by the arm and gave him a ruthless shake. "Have you been talking to the wrong fucking orc this whole time?"

"No!" The beanpole wriggled free of his brother's grasp, mindful to place an adequate amount of distance between them as he massaged the soreness from his arm. His accusing glare shifted back to Oralia. "Why in the realm didn't you say something earlier? Are you trying to make me look like an idiot? This is your plan, isn't it? Undermine the head of power right from the start."

"The head? Lingon, please, everyone knows you're the ass of power."

"An' you know what you are, Mul? You're the tit of power. That's what you are!"

Dear gods. These were the proud offspring of the great Paler Stoneclaw? These had to be the rejects, surely. Every family had them. If there was one thing imbeciles responded to, it was a show of true power. Oralia leapt to her feet, tusks splayed, and thundered, "Where is the other one?"

Both men jumped as if they were children caught stealing from the cookie jar.

"Who?" Lingon ventured, peeking out from behind Mul's hulking shoulders. Cowardice aside, how he had managed to dart behind his older brother in the span of a single heartbeat was rather impressive as far as speed went.

"You are Lingon. He is Mul. There's supposed to be one more of you. A third living Stoneclaw brother. Where is Bil?" Oralia accentuated her question with a loud snap of her tusks. The way the ominous sound bounced along the stone chamber was not a touch she'd intended, but was rather effective nonetheless. "I will not waste my time squabbling with underlings. Fetch me your leader."

Lingon puffed out his scrawny chest and strutted in front of the bars with a confidence that stemmed from the fact that Oralia was in a cage and he was not. "Bil's not the leader. We all are."

"It's a joint coalition," Mul grunted.

"Yeah," Lingon agreed with a bob of his head, long hair swaying around him. "So if you have something to say, you can say it to us."

Rasp had more brains than these two combined. Oralia was not sure she wished to live in a world where the prime example of Stoneclaw leadership came from the same man who possessed a moral objection to pants. "How unusual. The mountain folk have always served a single leader," Oralia said calmly. "Am I to understand that it now takes three men to fill the role of one? I suppose that is what happens when you try to usurp the silver-haired. After all, running your own brother down a mountain because fate chose him over you could not have been without consequence."

Their faces went noticeably pale. Admittedly, it was difficult to determine how much of that was due to the poor lighting. Mul's question died on his lips. "How did you . . ."

"A word of advice, gentlemen." Oralia leaned casually into the bars. "When staging a coup, it is important to ensure the heir to the throne is actually dead before trying on his crown."

The puff in Lingon's chest deflated in a single exhale. "Actually?"

Mul stormed toward her, his eyes wide, like a lone stag about to face down a pack of hungry wolves. "What are you talking about?"

"After you killed your brother, Rasp, the silver-hair did not choose another. Did you not consider that odd?"

Lingon seemed to catch what she was implying faster than his brother. The slender man had a handful of long hair gripped in each tightly clenched fist, practically melting to the floor. "Oh fuck, oh fuck, oh fuck. He's alive, Mul. He's alive! I told you we should have decapitated the body!"

The larger brother wrinkled his nose into a snarl, displaying several spade-shaped upper teeth. "What business is it of the realm?"

Oralia matched the coldness in his voice. "Bring me Bil and I will tell you."

Mul withstood her unflinching stare for several seconds before storming back toward the entrance. He snatched Lingon from the floor and dragged him by the arm in his wake, ignoring his brother's feeble protests. The ancient door opened and closed behind them with a deafening slam. Out in the hallway, from the other side of the wall, their loud footsteps grew quieter as the pair took off at a panicked run.

CHAPTER TWENTY-SEVEN

Traitor

Oralia's shoulders slumped with exhaustion. Standing was proving too much for her weary body. The gash in her thigh where the arrowhead had nicked between her leather braces flared with agony. With her armor stripped away, Oralia could see someone had cleaned and wrapped the wound. An indication that, at the very least, the Stoneclaw brothers didn't want her dead. Perhaps she was reading too much into it, and the medical attention was simply to ensure she did not die of infection prior to the execution.

She pressed her weight against the bars, fighting the urge to bash her head into them. Movement from the corner of her eye caught her attention. "Stare at something else," Oralia muttered. "Or I will pluck your eyes from their worthless sockets."

Alas, Sascha knew a bluff when he heard one. His brow wrinkled into a disapproving scowl. A bruised line cut across the bridge of his nose, courtesy of several repeated encounters with the blunt edge of Oralia's shield. The deep blue and purple color matched the bloodied claw marks around his eyes. "My skull would make a good cauldron," he repeated, his voice low and rumbling. "Really?"

"A chamber pot would have been more fitting. I feared they would not have known what that was."

"Oralia—"

"No," she snarled. "You do not get to do this. You do not get to explain yourself after what you did!" She knew Geralt had planted a spy in the traveling party. Never in a thousand years would she have suspected Sascha. In hindsight, it was obvious. But that didn't lessen the sting any. "This whole time I was naive enough to think you had volunteered for this mission. That you had done it for me. Gods!" She struck her clenched hand against the iron bars and grimaced at the pain. "My own lover, a spy."

"I am not the traitor in this scenario." Sascha gathered his feet beneath him and stood. It was just as well that their captors had vacated the cellblock because, iron bars or not, he still cut an intimidating sight. "I gave you the chance to come clean and tell me everything. You lied to me, remember? This is on you, not me."

"Forgive me for trying to protect you."

"Protect me? Oralia, you are the reason I am in this mess!" Sascha's face was doing that pitiful thing that made the insides of Oralia's stomach sink lower. Even now, the impulse to offer him comfort was sickeningly strong. "They came in the dead of the night. They dragged me from my bed and brought me before the Speaker of the People. He claimed you were a traitor and that I was somehow complicit! I defended you. I told him that his information was wrong. That you were innocent. I struck a deal to save both of us."

She raised her eyebrow at him. So much for not doing this. She was invested now. That, or she was still seething from earlier and simply wanted a deserving person to release her pent-up rage upon. "Both of us? How does spying on me benefit both of us?"

"It was the only way to prove you were innocent. I knew any information I collected would be worthless. It wasn't supposed to go down like this. I was supposed to prove that your loyalty was still to the realm and not to whatever . . . whatever in the seventh realm it is you're actually doing." Oralia's prolonged silence must have struck a chord because Sascha lifted his chin, studying her expression with a sudden, panicked desperation. Whatever it was he saw, it made his jaw quiver. "Captain Monk ordered his people to kill you. Had he had his way, you would have died back at camp. I convinced him to let me bring you in alive instead. I couldn't save you from the consequences of your betrayal, but I could at least ensure you and your people weren't slaughtered without a trial."

Stupid, stupid, stupid. You should have seen this coming.

Despite her insistence that they would never again be whatever they were before, Oralia's heart disagreed. Even now, with hot rage churning in the pit of her gut, her stupid feelings for Sascha persisted. She could feel them crawling up the back of her throat, easing the burn that singed her insides. But she wouldn't allow it. The fact remained: he'd turned on her. And there was no coming back from that, no matter how adamantly her foolish heart protested.

"I just want to know why." Sascha's broad shoulders slumped. "I knew things changed after Ashwyn, but I didn't think . . . this is just . . . how did it get this bad?"

This, Oralia decided, deserved an answer. "I saw firsthand what Geralt Lazuli and the Division of Divination were doing to the very people I was supposed to be protecting. I could not in good faith call myself the Protector of the Realm while turning a blind eye to Geralt's abuse. I tried the diplomatic route and it got me nowhere. This was the only way to protect those who needed it most."

It was his turn to remain quiet, prompting more from Oralia. "He Is assembling an army of witches, Sascha. Where do you think all of the graduates of the magical academy go afterward? The magical order has no outside oversight. Every time I petitioned for transparency, Geralt shut me out. I fear it will not be long before he has the numbers to overthrow the current powers and claim the United Territories for himself."

"And this was your solution? Instead of turning the new witches over to the division, you've been killing them? Is that really what you consider protecting the people, Oralia?"

"He really believes that is what I have been doing this entire time?" This solicited an unexpected laugh from Oralia. Gods, the power of a bad reputation was worth its weight in gold. She expected the witch-killer masquerade to last a few years, a decade, at most, but certainly not this long. "Am I partly responsible for the recent decline in magic? Yes. But I did not kill them. I have spent the last sixty-some-odd years smuggling our witches beyond realm borders. I helped the resistance build a system for getting people out. My collaboration has been kept anonymous, of course. Even to those operating secretly within the realm on the resistance's behalf."

His jaw dropped in disbelief. "You turned in Ashwyn for attempting the exact same thing!"

"That part was her idea, actually." After the massacre in Sunstorn, Ashwyn knew Geralt would never give up the chase. She was the one who insisted Oralia deliver her and Ellisar to the realm for trial. With the main conspirators dead, Geralt would lower his guard, believing the rebellion had been successfully culled. Oralia, meanwhile, could continue to operate in secret—right under his pompous nose. "Turning in my own sister ensured that the realm would have no reason to question my loyalties. I have to admit, as much as I hated the plan, it was effective."

Oralia saw the disgust on his face and dismissed the look with a flippant wave of her hand. "Do not look at me like that. Ashwyn's sacrifice ensured the lives of thousands of others. And if it makes you feel better, Geralt never killed her. He has been using her to try to control me ever since."

"Feel better?" He gripped the bars so tightly the iron groaned in protest. "Ashwyn was as much of a sister to me as she was to you! I have grieved her loss every single day since the massacre. You do not get to dismiss my pain, especially when you could have ended it by telling me she was alive from the start."

Having spent so much time around the emotionally stunted, it was easy to forget that her poor choices affected others outside of her inner circle in ways she had not intended. Oralia thought she had done a decent job of keeping her relationships at arm's length, but evidently she was a failure in that regard as well.

"I'm . . . sorry." Ugh, this felt so wrong! If only the ground would split open and swallow her whole, then she wouldn't have to put words to the guilt trying to claw its way out of her chest. She wasn't ready to let go of her anger. Not yet, maybe not ever, but it felt wrong not to acknowledge that she'd contributed equally to their downfall. "Not just about Ashwyn, but everything."

"You are going to owe so much more than that when this is through," he said, after an unbearable stretch of silence. "But, seeing as you're finally being honest with me, I have more questions. For starters, why are you here on the ridge? The speaker thought it was a power grab. That you were here to recruit the Stoneclaws onto your side. What are you actually here for?"

As it turned out, discussing her betrayal to the realm was far easier than sorting through the clusterfuck of emotions waging war on one another within her head. Oralia was grateful for the chance to shove her feelings aside in exchange for cold, hard facts. "Do you know how long it takes to smuggle even a handful of people to safety? Getting through the United Territories is arduous enough, but it is the mountains that present the biggest issue. Going around the ridge takes three weeks alone. And that is not accounting for any unexpected hiccups along the way."

Sascha, fortunately, could follow a line of reasoning to the end without having to be told each minuscule step in between. "You're cutting through."

"My final gift to the resistance," Oralia said, studying her nail beds, as the alternative was looking at Sascha and she certainly couldn't bear any more of that. "Or it was supposed to be anyway, before I learned perhaps a little too late that there is something far more dangerous than Stoneclaws lurking here."

"The dark magic your guide was rambling about?"

"Precisely. I had hoped if I could get the boy off the mountain in time, I could spare us. But Captain Monk botched that one. And now, I am afraid, it is much too late."

Sascha parted his lips to say something, but Oralia lifted her palm, silencing him. There was a growing commotion coming from the outer passageway. That was the beautiful thing about stone, everything echoed. After some heated shouting, the door flung open and a short, fat man barreled inside, flanked on either side by the Stoneclaw brothers. Mul and Lingon panted while trying to keep up with the newcomer's effortless stride.

"Bil, I assume," Oralia said when the man came to a sudden stop at the front of her cell.

Fate had a cruel sense of humor. Not only had it skipped over the eldest Stoneclaw brother as the bearer of the silver-hair, it had awarded him hardly any hair at all. Aside from a small crown of thinning curls around his ears, the man was bald. He was little, even smaller than Rasp. Standing on the very tip of his toes, Oralia would have placed him just a hair over five feet.

"Did you tell these two idiots that Rasp is still alive?" Bil demanded, demonstrating perhaps one of the qualities Oralia cherished most: the ability to skip the introduction and get to the fucking point.

"I did."

The edge of his lip lifted in a snarl. "And how do you know this to be true?"

"Because the realm tasked me with reinstating Rasp into power. And, if I may cut your questioning short, your brother is also already on the ridge. Additionally, he was not in a good state last I saw him. It will not be long before the magic consumes him. If I were you, I would be considering how to evacuate your people while you still have the chance."

"Lies!" Mul said, his booming voice echoing across the barren stone. "Don't listen to her, Bil. This is just a ploy for us to give up our territory. An obvious one, if you ask me."

Bil peered up at her through dark, shrewd eyes. There was more than a flicker of intelligence here. Nay, Oralia saw a damned wildfire. If there was any hope for the mountain folk, it rested in this man's hands. Bil's gruff voice cut back in. "Do you have any proof of this?"

"Your secret passage through the falls was a well-kept one. Without Rasp's assistance, I can assure you, the realm would have never discovered it." Oralia watched Bil's face for tells. Flattery apparently wasn't enough. She was going to have to rely on fear and superstition to persuade him. "Surely you have noticed the irregularities taking place on your mountain? It was Rasp who caused the flash flood that scattered my forces. And the rockslide at the falls the day before that."

Lingon's eyes grew wide. He leaned closer to Bil, whispering fervently into his ear at a volume he mistakenly assumed Oralia would not hear. "The birds. Remember, I told you I saw the ravens? They're back. It was an omen."

Oralia did not wait for his fervent whispering to stop. She merely spoke over the top of him. "Ask yourself this: If Rasp gives in to the magic, what is the first thing he is going to do? Where is he going to go? Is it in your brother's nature to show mercy? Or do you think he will come after the very people who betrayed him in the first place?"

"He was a witch! We were justified in what we did," Mul said with a stomp of his foot. "Father was already preparing to throw him out. Except Rasp went and killed him before he could give the official order."

"I believe you are only proving my point," Oralia replied. "Your brother will be coming for you. Leave, now. While you still have the chance."

All three Stoneclaws raised their voices to shout at once. A deep rumble started from far below them, drowning out the noise. It grew in intensity until the very walls quaked in protest. The hairline cracks running the length of the ceiling buckled beneath the pressure as broken slabs of stone toppled from the ceiling. Rubble struck the ground and shattered into thousands of tiny pieces. The flickering torches mounted near the entrance flared, their tall flames licking the splintered ceiling. And then, with a hiss, the fire flickered out and the narrow room went black around them.

CHAPTER TWENTY-EIGHT

Run

Faris braced his shoulder against the fallen branch and pushed with all his might. To his dismay, the log remained unbudged. The faun's chest heaved with effort as he gathered his strength and threw his entire upper body into it once more, gnashing his teeth together until they felt like they were going to crack and splinter from his mouth. The log took no notice, remaining as it was, a giant hunk of broken tree, pinning his right leg beneath the soft mud. Faris tried again, and again, and again. His efforts were to no avail. The fallen branch did not budge. And nor did he, still trapped firmly beneath it.

"Muck it!" With an infuriated scream, Faris collapsed against the swampy ground, momentarily defeated. "I'll just lie here and die, then!"

His broad shoulders sank deeper in the slick mud. Its coldness seeped through his wet clothes and into his flesh, worming deep into his aching bones. He was covered from head to hoof in the sticky brown muck. So much so, to a passerby he wouldn't even look like a living being in need of help. Thanks to the added layer of grime covering his body, he was just another piece of the monotonous brown landscape. Unremarkable. Unnoticed. Destined to lie here forever under the crushing weight of a tree until death claimed him.

This was it, Faris decided. His final resting place. He'd tried to call out for help initially, but no one came. It wasn't until his voice had gone raw from screaming that he realized there probably wasn't anyone left to help.

As he lay there, resigned to die, his thoughts could not help but return to the moment everything went wrong. More wrong, he supposed. If he really wanted to start at the first mistake, it would have been the second he agreed to go on this cursed mission. He wasn't going to go that far back, though. That required too much self-reflection. Instead, he replayed the end of the battle over and over, wondering what would have happened if he had just acted a little sooner.

He should have seen Mother's death coming. But, paralyzed by fear, he hadn't even realized what Captain Monk had done until after the raven's crumpled body had struck the ground. Still, he could have moved faster. Gotten to Rasp sooner, maybe even stopped the flash flood that followed. If nothing else, Faris could have at least held onto his friend a little tighter.

He reached Rasp seconds before the water hit, but the current proved too strong and they were ripped apart almost immediately after. The flood carried Faris for what felt like forever. Finally, moments before he was certain his burning lungs were going to collapse in on themselves, the water subsided and he found himself alone in a washed-out patch of secluded forest. His right leg was pinned beneath a monstrous branch. He'd managed to dig the left one out, but the ground beneath his right hoof was not dirt, but stone.

Stuck between a rock and a hard-on.

The memory caused an involuntary laugh to burst from his mouth. "That's how the saying goes," Rasp had insisted to Snag. "I'm not the one who makes these up. Ask Faris, he'll tell you."

Faris rested against the wet, debris-littered ground with a sigh, feeling the back of his skull sink a little further. Gods, even now he missed that idiot. Partly because Rasp could have lifted the tree off of him without even thinking about it. But also because now, after months of being the man's shadow, Faris felt like a part of him was missing. He'd never met someone so completely without moral objection to causing the most trouble possible. Faris hadn't meant to like him. Rasp was just supposed to be a job. A punishment, actually, if he was being honest. But the shit they got into together came so naturally, liking him had been easy.

The crooked smile slipped from his lips as an invisible weight settled in his chest. *We're not going to see each other again, are we? And now I'm going to die out in the wilderness alone, stuck under a tree because of you.*

He should have been mad, but all Faris could feel was the hole in his chest hurt a little more.

An approaching sound pulled him from his internal wallowing. Faris's ears flickered in the direction of the commotion. Twigs and branches snapped beneath heavy feet as something lumbered unhurriedly in his direction. The smell hit him next. An unholy mix of musky fur and a pungent, earthy stink. Faris was too terrified to cover his nose. Prey instinct kicked in and he remained frozen, feverishly praying whatever beast was ambling in his direction would pass him by unaware.

From the other side of the fallen branch, a large, fuzzy head lifted into view. For a few terrifying heartbeats, their eyes locked and neither moved. The bear uttered a low growl which, admittedly, was difficult to hear over Faris's own shrill scream. Startled, the bear ducked out of view. A few moments later, after remembering which of them possessed skull-crushing jaws, it returned. It placed both paws firmly onto the log as it began the laborious process of hauling its gigantean body up and over.

Pain erupted across Faris's trapped leg. "No, no, no!" he shouted, clawing at the soft ground in a futile attempt to gain traction. "I get to die in a big, fabulous house surrounded by money. Not like this! Eat me and I swear, I'll turn into a warbear just to eat you back!"

The bear raised its paw to strike. A white projectile whipped through the air and stuck deep into its foot pad. A second and third caught it in the nose. With a pained huff, the bear pushed off of the log and turned tail, disappearing into the surrounding undergrowth in a blur of brown fur.

Green and yellow leaves, slick with mud, stirred into the air. They floated above Faris's head in a dancing cloud of swirling debris before the wind picked up, blustering them out of sight. The gale grew stronger and, with a sudden *whoosh*, the air current swept low and lifted the creaking log several inches from the ground. Faris scrambled out from under it seconds before the branch came crashing back down and splintered across the muddy forest floor.

With his heart thumping deep in his chest, he whipped his head around, simultaneously grateful and fearful to know to whom he owed his life. A small figure stood stooped with their hands tucked into their sleeves. Their head was concealed by a thick maroon hood, but Faris recognized the silvery eyes glaring back at him.

"You?"

"Unfortunately so," Whisper rasped, glancing around them as if only now remembering what they were looking for. "Where is the little bird?"

"No idea. We got separated during the flash flood."

The fae's slumped posture went rigid. The sudden movement cost them, and they doubled over immediately after, gritting out through clenched teeth, "You weren't supposed to leave his side!"

"Well excuse me for getting washed down the mucking mountain. I tried to hold onto him the best I could, but it turns out you need your arms to swim!" Faris searched his clothes. He found a few silver coins jingling in his pocket, but he supposed offering a fae silver might be misconstrued as insulting. Grudgingly, he pulled the last of his cigarettes from his coat and tossed it at Whisper. The rolled paper was damp and possibly useless, but without his traveling pack, it was all he had. "Here."

Still doubled over in pain, Whisper stared at the strange offering resting at their feet before their befuddled gaze shifted back in Faris's direction.

"I know better than to owe a favor to a fae," he explained, trying to say it in a manner that sounded more grateful and not accusatory. "That is my payment for you helping me."

With great, painstaking care, Whisper straightened their posture, looking exhausted from the effort. "I am not here to trade trinkets with you, faun. I had hoped to reach the little bird in time, but alas, as you are no longer with him, I fear I am too late. I will not demand a life debt even though it is my right to do so. Instead, I humbly ask for your assistance."

"Please tell me you want to go back down the mountain." Faris considered fetching the cigarette. It was his last, after all. And it was only a little damp. It would be a shame to let it go to waste. Whisper was watching him with that predatory look in their eyes, however. He decided it would probably be best to wait to reclaim it until their back was turned.

"First, I will need your help locating the young Lazuli. As she carries my magic, I can track her whereabouts. Getting there in a timely manner is the issue." Whisper drew back their cloak, revealing a black, oozing sore along their ribs. "My ability to travel quickly has been compromised. It took nearly all of my strength to get over the falls. I must preserve the rest for what is to come."

Faris was too preoccupied with the wound to fully process the fae's ominous words. "That's iron poisoning."

"It is."

"You're dying."

"I am."

When there was no further explanation, Faris was forced to ask, "Shouldn't you be a little more concerned about that?"

"The course of death for my kind is a lifetime compared to yours. There is still time to make this right. Stop stalling and help me find the young Lazuli."

For several breaths, Faris stared without speaking as he considered how Lady Lazuli fit into the equation. Whisper was well aware of what Daana was, including the talent that had made her the top seeker within the Division of Divination. The words *pet project* slid forth unsummoned from the vast catacombs of his memory.

She's been a part of Whisper's plan all along. If you were a manipulative, powerful fae bound to a powerstone, what would you be using Daana for?

The answer, he realized, was simple. "You're going to use Daana to set you free."

"Attempt to," Whisper admitted. "It has never been done before. No mortal has ever had reason to try."

"She was sent here to capture you, specifically, in case you've forgotten. She has no reason to trust you, let alone help."

For a moment, the fae only looked at him with what might have been sympathy in their eerie, shimmering eyes. At last, Whisper said, "She will help because the alternative is annihilation." The fae limped toward him, grimacing with each burdensome step. "The young Lazuli is many things, but not vindictive. She can feel the magic on the mountain changing, just as I can. She is not the one I will have trouble convincing."

Run. Prey instinct coursed through Faris's thoughts as his heartbeat suddenly doubled. *Run and don't look back. Go, now!*

CHAPTER TWENTY-NINE

Like a Brother

Faris remained frozen. No matter how fervently the instincts clawing at the inside of his skull commanded him to run, he was powerless to move. The icy grip of fear cinched tighter around his throat as Faris realized he was about to be asked to do something unthinkable.

Whisper limped closer, stopping until there were only a few, insignificant paces between them. From beneath their heavy hood, the fae gazed up at him earnestly. "We were supposed to protect him, you and I. And we failed. There is only one way to rectify our failure."

Faris narrowed his eyes. "Stop talking in riddles and say what you mean."

"Your friend must be stopped by any means necessary."

It was progress, but Whisper still wasn't saying what they meant. Not all of it, at least. As much as Faris tried to keep his tone civil, it came out a few decibels shy of a scream nonetheless. "How can you say that? We haven't failed. We haven't even tried anything yet! Maybe instead of jumping to conclusions we could try, say, I don't know, finding him first?"

"The magic within the mountain is changing, faun. I can feel it. The little bird was the one who awoke it in the first place. It called to him before. I could sense it, even from a distance. But now it has stopped and there is only one explanation. I fear the darkness has found its vessel."

The invisible noose pulled tighter around Faris's neck. "No."

"It is too much to ask of you, I know. But your friend is already gone. Releasing him will be an act of mercy."

"Don't do that. Don't sugarcoat it. At least have the decency to say what you mean. You don't want to release him, you want to *kill* him." An angry snort rattled up from the depths of his chest, alleviating some of the tightness in his throat. "Secondly, you don't know any of this for certain. There's no way of knowing if he's given in or not. I know Rasp, and he is a stubborn piece of shit when he puts his mind to it!"

There was that pitiful look again. It made Faris's blood boil beneath his skin. To add insult to injury, Whisper's voice was infuriatingly soft. "I never fully understood your relationship with the little bird. I knew it didn't stem from a sense of duty or honor. Not even riches, as you claim. But I see the reason now."

"Stick to the subject."

Whisper said nothing, resigned to a stoic silence. Their patronizing expression spoke volumes all the same.

"Fine! You want to go there? Then we'll go there! Rasp is the closest thing I have ever had to a brother and I would do anything to save him!" Faris took a brazen step forward and struck his hoof against the wet ground, ignoring the shock of pain that radiated up his sore leg. "Is that what you wanted to hear? That I actually care what happens to him? Because it sure as chaos doesn't seem like you do!"

Try as he might, Faris couldn't stop the sudden deluge of vitriol and venom that poured from his tongue. "Everyone is just using him for their own gain. You, the dark magic, the realm, my own muckin' parents! I thought I could stomach it. That maybe if I protected him, I could make it better somehow. But I . . . I don't think I can anymore."

His nostrils flared as a cold stone settled in his gut and Faris found himself reevaluating what had just come from his mouth. It was the first time he'd ever put words to any of this, but it existed, nonetheless. He couldn't recall exactly when Rasp had made the transition from that annoying human he had to keep from walking off a cliff to someone he would protect with his life—but it was something he could no longer deny. He and Rasp fought like cats and dogs half the time, sure. But that's what siblings did. And they always made up in the end.

Except some gnawing sensation in the back of his skull was telling him that this time wouldn't be like the others. That maybe there wasn't any going back from this. He shoved the thought back down, allowing his anger to return. "And now that we're done discussing me, we can go back to talking about Rasp. More importantly, we can discuss ways to prevent the annihilation of mortal-kind without having to—"

A low rumble built from below. It reached the surface with a sudden, shaking jolt, threatening to split the ground beneath their feet. *Crack!* The black spruce overhead snapped under its own weight and listed toward them with an eerie, creaking groan. Faris threw Whisper over his shoulder and bolted. The spruce struck the forest floor behind them in a cascade of broken branches and loose needles. Around them, trees teetered and fell at random. Faris darted between the chaos, wide-eyed, dodging falling limbs in a mad scramble for safety. Tiny claws gripped his shoulder as his burden grew inexplicably lighter. He looked at Whisper from the corner of his eye, realizing the fae had assumed the form of a white weasel and was clinging to him for dear life.

After several frantic twists and turns through the trees, the rumbling stopped. Faris did not. He maintained his breakneck pace, clearing entire patches of washed-out forest floor in a series of effortless bounds. Stopping meant acknowledging what just happened. If he kept moving, then he didn't have to think about it. He didn't have to consider why the entire mountain was shifting beneath his hooves. There were two possible reasons. One of which was natural and the other . . .

The other meant something very bad.

That wasn't possible, though. Not Rasp. He'd changed, Faris had seen it with his own eyes. This had to be a trick. "How do I know the ground shaking isn't because of you?" he shouted at the beast clinging to his neck. "Can you prove this is Rasp and not just another one of your attempts to manipulate me into doing what you want?"

To his astonishment, Whisper's voice rippled across his thoughts. **I assure you, if I could use my magic in that capacity, you would not be carrying me up the fucking mountain right now!**

He hated that Whisper actually made a good point. So, naturally, he chose to ignore it and focused on running for his life instead.

Faun!

Faris barely noticed the burning ache in his muscles as his spring-loaded legs launched him up and over a fallen tree. He sailed high over the spindly branches before crashing back down among a tangle of raspberry bushes. He pressed on, ignoring the thorns that ripped at the fur along his ankles. He didn't mind the pain. In fact, he welcomed it. Perhaps if he could make his outsides hurt worse than his insides, this would all go away.

That was wishful thinking, of course. And, as if on cue, his mind decided now was the perfect time to run through the many reasons why he could never do what Whisper was asking of him.

Rasp believed Faris's family saved him. What he didn't realize was that he, in turn, had saved them too. Faris's mother and father were so preoccupied fighting Rasp, they'd finally stopped fighting each other. Caring for the injured mountain man had forced Faris back into the Belfast family home as well. A place he'd formerly avoided as fervently as one might a rabid dog. The endless lectures from his father about going down the wrong path and doing something productive with his life petered out until they stopped completely. His mother could suddenly look him in the eye again. Little by little, the weight of being the Belfast family disappointment had slowly lifted away.

For the first time in years, there was laughter in the house again. Mum remembered how to smile and Father ventured out from the solitude of his study more and more. Rasp helped fill the hole none of them realized had gotten so big. The Belfast family would forever mourn the loss of its daughters, but in an unexpected way, his parents had gained a son. And Faris, a brother.

A brother he was now being asked to kill in order to set things right again.

Faun, stop, Whisper pleaded as their claws dug deeper into Faris's cloak, piercing the skin underneath. **Faris Belfast, come to your senses!**

Against his will, his footsteps slowed until his hooves gave out beneath him entirely. Faris caught himself against a splintered tree stump and lowered his shaking body to the ground. The rapid thump of his heartbeat drummed within his ears. His forehead was slick with perspiration and burned to the touch. Whisper slunk down his arm and dropped onto the ground in front of him with a disapproving hiss.

Faris buried his face into his trembling arms. "Find someone else."

I do not take any pleasure in what I am about to do. Left unchecked, the darkness will spread. Your people, your family, anyone who means anything to you will fall victim to its power. My magic alone is not enough to stop it. I need whatever help I can get. If you care about him, truly care about him, then you will do this not for yourself, but for him.

Faris spoke between shaky gasps of breath, trying to convince Whisper as much as himself. "It's still him though, isn't it? At least on the inside? I could talk him out of it. He listens to me."

I am counting on it.

Faris lifted his head from his arms. "But you said—"

You only need to get him to drop his defense for a few seconds. I will take care of the rest.

"What? No! That's not what I meant! You want me to distract him while you swoop in for the kill? That's not—"

This is not an easy choice, but it is the one we must make. I do not have the strength to defeat the darkness on my own. You are the key to this.

"I don't want to be the key!"

We have no other option.

"Yes, we do! We could just not do anything. I could turn around and go home and forget about all of this." The argument wasn't any stronger on the outside than it had sounded within it his head, but it was all Faris could think to say. He knew he was losing the argument. As did Whisper, judging by the way the weasel tilted its head at him in a manner that looked downright patronizing.

And by doing so, you would be condemning the rest of mortal-kind. Is that what you want, faun? When Faris offered no rebuttal, Whisper's silken voice flowed across his thoughts like water over glass once more. **Make no mistake, we will only get one chance at this. If we fail, the darkness will grow stronger. I fear all will be lost after that. I wish there was another way, I do. But this is it.**

How had it come to this? Faris wasn't a killer. He was a vegetarian, for muck's sake! He refused to squash the spiders that got stuck in the wash bowl every morning. The first time he'd seen Rasp kill a squirrel, he'd boxed his ears and insisted on holding a private burial for it afterward. He didn't kill. He couldn't. Especially not Rasp. He'd threatened to more times than he could remember, sure. But that was just talk. And when it came down to it, that's all Faris was. Stupid, showy talk. This was one situation even he couldn't talk his way out of.

Whisper drew no attention to the fact that they'd won the argument, having successfully broken Faris beyond the point of protest. With a sad little nod of its head, the white weasel scrambled back up Faris's arm and curled around his neck. **I am sorry, faun. But we cannot linger any longer. Come, I sense the young Lazuli is not far.**

CHAPTER THIRTY

Mangy Dogs

alk the plank, ye mangy dogs!" The harsh clang of metal striking metal echoed across the creaking forest. The sound was accompanied by the occasional cry of pain and a slew of nonsensical curses from Rali. "What's that? Had enough? Yer lookin' a little green around the gills, matey!"

Daana peeked through the thicket of tangled, thorny branches, watching Ellisar and Rali's antics with growing trepidation. Grief came in many forms, but killing anyone they happened upon seemed like overkill. Not that she was going to be the one to bring it to their attention, of course. She'd stared down the wrong end of Ellisar's blade already once that day and had no desire to tempt fate twice.

During the search for their missing members, the group had stumbled across Lieutenant Holt's makeshift camp. A temporary truce was the only way forward, Holt insisted—to which Daana wholeheartedly agreed. Ellisar and Rali felt differently. With her sword in hand, Ellisar charged, intent on laying waste to the remaining realm soldiers. Lieutenant Ralizak grudgingly followed. Rali's hesitation was not in objection to the senseless slaughter, but at the lack of a plan. Her teammate, currently a whirling, blur of steel and death, seemed content to formulate her strategy on the go. A strategy that appeared to depend almost exclusively on excessive stabbing.

Beyond the thicket, Daana watched Rali duck the oversized battle ax that swung over the top of her head in a blurred arc. The dwarf popped up along the orc's left flank and slashed at him with her shortsword, hollering, "Do that again, bucko, an' I'll keelhaul yer scurvy ass!"

Ellisar glared over her shoulder at the dwarf, neatly sidestepping Lieutenant Holt, who attempted to run her through from the front. "For the last time, I don't sound like that!"

Dancing out of the orc's reach, Rali turned and brimmed brightly back up at her elf companion. The glimmer of madness in Rali's dark brown eyes was unmistakable even from a distance. "Not yet ye don't," the dwarf said with a cackle. "Give it time. I'll coax the ol' Cap'n Pride out of ye yet."

The juxtaposition of the lighthearted banter paired with their unquenchable thirst for violence was what Daana found most unsettling. Rali and Ellisar volleyed insults back and forth between strikes as if nothing had happened at all. As if, hardly a few hours before, they'd not been huddled together saying their goodbyes to one of their own. The baby of their odd family—the inadvertent glue that had bound these highly caustic individuals into a single, tight unit—was gone. And without Oralia to keep them in hand, the loose threads were beginning to unravel at a speed that was unsustainable.

Daana did not know which would succumb first: the pair's ability to keep fighting or their mental fortitude.

Ellisar's dry voice carried on the cool afternoon breeze, snapping Daana from her thoughts. "Rali, if you spent less effort sounding like an idiot and put it toward fighting, we'd be done by now!"

"Why does our theoretical win depend on me? Yer the dumbass who rushed in without a plan!"

"You never stick to any of your plans anyway! You can't fault me for skipping to the fun part."

From what Daana could see, Lieutenant Holt's strategy appeared to be based not around winning but tiring the murdersome pair past the point of exhaustion. Holt pitted her enemy's lack of organization against them. She kept her bedraggled unit tight and running like clockwork, all while waiting for the precise moment to break away. That moment was now, apparently. Holt seized the lull in action and turned tail. She pulled the orc into a run alongside her, yelling at the others to retreat. The remaining soldiers followed suit without hesitation, as lingering even a fraction longer guaranteed a merciless death for anyone caught lagging behind.

"Gangway!" Rali smacked Ellisar on the rump as she barreled past, dodging left to miss the retaliatory swing from the flat of the elf's blade. "Move yer tailend, swabby! The enemy's fleeing off the port bow!"

"Stern!" Ellisar snarled, rubbing the sting from her ass. "You mean stern. Bow is the front!"

"It's my imaginary ship. I decide which side is the back end! Now stop yammering and get yer back end in motion!"

Ellisar took up the chase after her. "You're beggin' to be hung from the yardarm!"

"Ha, there's the ol' Cap'n Pride! Right on cue."

Daana watched the pair sprint after the fleeing soldiers until they were lost from sight altogether. She glanced concernedly at Snag, who stood beside her with his mouth held in a loose grimace. "They've gone mad," she said, ignoring the twinge in her side that was becoming more prevalent with each word she spoke. By her estimation, it had been several hours since she'd taken Ellisar's mysterious leaf remedy. The numbing effects were already beginning to wear thin.

When Snag said nothing, Daana tried once more to elicit a reaction from him. "You can see that, right? Please tell me I am not the only sane one left."

With Rali and Ellisar listing wildly off course, it left her and Snag to act as the voice of reason. Which would not have been so daunting if it were not for the fact that Snag had stopped speaking altogether. He couldn't even muster the energy to offer a halfhearted shrug. He simply stared. Not even at her, but seemingly *through* her, with a vacant look in his eyes.

"You haven't said a word in over two hours."

Snag's hollow stare shifted directions and, without a word, he was off, slowly trailing the path of destruction left by the others.

"Snag, talk to me, please!"

The goblin picked his way through the surrounding thicket with pains-taking care. Not out of concern for the thorns, Daana suspected, but for the fact that he did not want to be caught following Rali and Ellisar *too* closely. And then, by some miracle, he replied. Daana barely heard his hushed voice. It was smaller and raspier than usual, as if he was trying to talk around a throatful of sandpaper. "What do you want me to say?"

"Something, anything! They won't listen to me. You are the only one capable of putting a stop to this." Gods, had talking always been this much work? Daana was expending twice the energy for half of her normal output. She stumbled along the swampy ground as she spoke, growing more desper-ate with each pained word. "This isn't fair. The soldiers aren't the ones who killed Curly."

Snag flinched at the name, but said nothing, still moving ahead of her at a steady pace.

"We are in enemy territory," Daana said, trying to appeal to his failing sense of self-preservation. "Fighting is only going to draw unwanted atten-tion. If those two keep this up, we'll have the Stoneclaw army on us within the hour. If you won't do it, at least tell me how to rein Ellisar and Rali in myself."

"Can you summon a random wave of water? That seemed to work sufficiently last time." Ahead of her, Snag was already clear of the thicket and slipping soundlessly between a row of shaggy trees with needles so dark, they looked more black than green. His green skin and muddied clothing were making it difficult to keep track of him as he slowly trudged further and further out of sight.

"I don't have that kind of power."

Daana kept one hand firmly pressed to her side as she followed, all the while wishing she'd asked for a second dried leaf from Ellisar. Daana could still breathe without passing out, but the steadily growing stabbing sensation in her side warned that the full brunt of her pain would be back with a vengeance soon. She doubted Snag would leave her behind, but the prospect of getting stranded alone was not one she could afford to be wrong about.

She hurried to catch up to the goblin, panting, "And even if I did, my magic is depleted. I have one good spell left in me and then that's it, gone."

"So use it," Snag countered.

"It won't be enough."

"Well then, it's settled. We do nothing."

"That's your plan?"

He spun around, hoops jangling from his ears as he threw his arms out from his sides. Snag's glimmering eyes were wide and tinged pink from the tears that, even now, slipped free unabated. "You're right, alright? We need to get out of here. I'm not arguing. But those two are working through something right now and getting between them and their methods—as questionable as they might seem—is only going to result in more bloodshed. My own, specifically. And I would like to keep as much of my necessary fluids in my body as possible. Understand? The best we can do is wait for it to run its course."

They did not have that sort of time to waste. Already, Daana's keen ears picked up the sounds of yet another battle growing in the distance. It was a miracle the Stoneclaw patrols hadn't discovered them yet. With the way Lieutenant Ralizak's booming voice carried, Daana was certain the neighboring territories had already begun to receive mixed reports of an impending pirate invasion.

She opened her mouth to state as much, but her protest slipped uselessly from her tongue. What started as a small tremble beneath her muddied boots quickly turned violent.

Oh no, not again. Daana instinctively threw her hands over her head. Already, this tremble felt stronger than the last.

The treetops rattled overhead as needles and loose debris beat down on them like dry, prickly rain. A warm tingle blistered across her skin and spread from her fingertips up the length of her forearms. The pain that followed struck her low. Daana dropped, covering her ears as her sixth sense set off alarm bells within her throbbing skull. The dark magic was much stronger than when she had first felt it.

"Daana!"

Daana couldn't hear the rest of Snag's shouting over the high-pitched ring in her ears. She squinted at him through the pain, attempting to piece together what he was frantically gesturing overhead about. She glanced up in time to see a massive tree hurtling toward her. Her feet responded before the rest of her caught on to what was happening, but it wasn't enough. She was about to be flattened, and her confounded legs couldn't even move fast enough to prevent it.

Something grabbed her from the side, and the mossy landscape shifted out from under her with unimaginable speed. Daana didn't question it. She slammed the soles of her feet against the quaking ground in an attempt to keep pace, vaguely aware that some outside force was doing most of the heavy lifting.

Faris's distorted voice blared into her ear. "Tuck and roll!"

CHAPTER THIRTY-ONE

Whirlwind

Daana didn't know where Faris had come from. Or what his warning meant. Nor did she have time to ask, much less prepare for what horrors awaited her. With his shoulder wedged securely under her arm, they crashed headlong through a cluster of flowering snowberries and burst out the other side down a sudden, steep drop. Daana ground her heels into the crumbling cliff, attempting to prevent them from plummeting over the edge. An unhelpful shove from Faris sent them both sailing over it, screaming.

Every bounce was excruciating. Daana nearly bit her tongue in half as she tumbled downward. Horsetail ferns and roots protruding from the cliffside whipped at her flailing body like claws. She hit the bottom and rolled. And rolled. And kept rolling, until her tortured body lost all momentum. With a feeble groan, she slid to a standstill at last. That was, until Faris slammed into her, sending her sprawling a few extra feet from the momentum.

"Muck, that hurt." From the corner of her eye, Daana saw Faris's blurred shape attempt to sit upright. His sense of balance failed him and the faun flopped back over, retching the sour contents of his stomach onto the grass between them.

Daana hardly noticed the hot smell of rancid bile. She stared up at the gray sky above her instead, mesmerized by the twinkling yellow lights that danced across her disoriented vision like fireflies in the night. The euphoria of confusion lasted only a few seconds more before reality came crashing back down in the form of excruciating pain. Every part of Daana's body was screaming, particularly her ribs, which she was quite certain had shattered into powdered pulp from the impact of the fall.

There was a metallic taste in her mouth, too. Daana wiped the crimson trickle spilling from her bottom lip with the back of her hand and inspected it. "Why did you just send me over a cliff?"

"You're right. I should have let those trees flatten you," Faris managed between continued heaves of wet vomit. "You're going to owe me so much more than just land and a title after this."

Daana's gaze shifted to him. Her reply, laden with equal parts vitriol and fury, disappeared with a sudden gasp. "What in the seven realms is that on your shoulder?"

"Oh, still there, is it? Damn." There was a weight of grimness to his voice, as if the line wasn't intended to be a joke. Faris reached up with a shaky hand and touched the small, white creature wrapped around his neck. The weasel chittered angrily at him in response. "I was sort of hoping it was just my imagination."

"Gods' sakes, Faris. Could you have picked a worse escape route? It's a wonder neither of you snapped a neck on your way down." Snag bounded from the thick bushes above and skidded down the slope on all fours, demonstrating a controlled plummet that made Daana's bones envious. The goblin's gaze flickered past them, and the mild annoyance wrinkled across his brow turned to horror.

Daana looked behind her and gasped.

She and Faris had unknowingly bounced into the very midst of the battle waging between the remaining realm forces. What's worse, they'd managed to crash land on the *wrong* side. For the moment, the warring soldiers appeared to be frozen in time as everyone, including a very confused Rali and Ellisar, simply gawked at the pair's unexpected entrance.

Faris lifted his horned head, peering through a clump of white hair that was plastered across his dirtied brow. His hands gripped the wet soil beneath him. "Muck. As if this day could not get any worse."

Rali cupped her hands to her mouth, calling to them, "We're going to have to work on your surprise attack, swabbies. A for effort, though!"

Lieutenant Holt saw her opportunity and lunged, grabbing for the pair before they could regroup. Faris dodged her grasp and went careening into the surrounding undergrowth with an orc soldier in hot pursuit. Daana darted in the opposite direction, but Holt's iron grip clamped onto her shoulder and spun her back into range. The last of Daana's magic pooled in her fingertips as the deflection spell formed on her lips. Holt's knee slammed into Daana's chest, rendering the spell to ash on her tongue. Her breath left her body in a single, pained exhale.

"Wait," Daana pleaded. No matter how she tried, her lungs refused to fill. She forced the words around shallow, wheezing breaths as waves of agony spread from where the lieutenant struck her. "The mountain. Something's wrong. The magic is changing. Can't you feel it?"

Lieutenant Holt wasn't listening. With her captive subdued, she turned her attention to the real threat. "Her life for ours," Holt panted, wiping the beads of sweat rolling from her brow. "Call off your attack and everyone walks away from this alive."

Rali's baritone voice rang across the small clearing as clear as a bell. "You can have her!"

"Ellisar, please!" There was an element below the panic in Holt's voice. It was difficult to pick out, especially now that Daana's legs were attempting to give out from beneath her, but the note persisted. A sort of hurt flutter, like a butterfly with a crumpled wing. "I don't want to fight you. No one benefits from this. I am begging you, let us walk away."

Through her pained vision, Daana saw Rali turn and smack Ellisar across the shoulder. "El, you scurvy sea dog! You went and let another one catch feelings, didn't you?"

The ensuing argument faded to a hum as the landscape shifted out of focus around Daana. She blinked, unsure if what she was seeing was real or proof that her mind was now as broken as her body. Black, vaporous clouds swept across the muddy ground, blanketing the forest in a shroud of shifting darkness. There was that noise again, too. The same gods-awful buzzing whine from before. It grew louder, filling her ears with static until the very ground reverberated beneath her feet.

She watched wide-eyed, mouth slung open but unable to speak. The high-pitched hum grew deafeningly loud as the mist encircled her feet, wrapping tighter, tighter, tighter. A blistering heat erupted across her bare skin as the darkness channeled upward. It engulfed her, digging its invisible claws into her flesh, searching for a hold.

Daana clamped her eyes shut. *It's not real, it's not real, it's not real!*

The command slid unbidden from her open mouth. "Stop!"

All at once, the humming dropped. The blistering heat that burned her skin faded until the only pain left was the steady throb coming from her ribs. When Daana opened her eyes again, the writhing darkness was gone and the forest appeared as it had before. Except for the gaggle of fighters, perhaps, who gawked at her as though she'd sprouted a second head. At least they were listening now.

"For fuck's sake," Daana said. "Stop fighting! Can none of you feel it?"

She received nothing but blank stares in return.

"There is something worse coming. I can feel the dark magic growing. It's changing. It wants you to waste your energy fighting each oth—"

"Enough!"

Daana doubled over as Holt's fist drove into her stomach. Despite every effort to scream, the only sound that managed to escape her tightly clenched teeth was an agonized moan. The muscles in her abdomen spasmed beyond her control as hot bile flooded her mouth and coated her tongue in a mix of blood and stomach acid.

Tears stung her eyes as her head sagged toward the ground. Lieutenant Holt wrangled Daana's body into position until she hung limp in front of her like a shield. The crushing pressure of the lieutenant's arm pressed to her chest was all that kept Daana from sliding face-first into the mud. It felt like a thousand hot needles piercing her stomach all at once. The throbbing ache in her skull melded Daana's vision into a buzzing blur of dancing shapes. She could no longer make out what was going on. She heard shouting in the background, but it sounded strangely far away.

Disconnected from the surrounding chaos, her consciousness drifted like a dandelion seed on the breeze. Looking down, Daana noticed the lovely contrast between the bright green foliage and the deep red splotches that painted the ground between her feet. She choked back a sob as she stared transfixed at the growing pool of crimson. Why had she never taken the time to appreciate the colors before? Time—she used to have plenty of that. For some reason she wasn't so sure that was still true anymore.

Lifting her chin, Daana's gaze moved aimlessly across the battle-torn landscape. A flash of white caught her wandering eye. Odd. It appeared to be moving. Not just moving, but drawing closer, in fact. White, white, white. What was white and moved like lightning? She was certain she'd seen this flash of lightning before. It used to make her angry, but now, for some perplexing reason, she felt something else. The fast-moving blur inspired a small lift in her spirits.

Daana snapped from her daze with a choking start. "Faris?"

Having lost his pursuer, Faris had circled back around and was running toward them shouting something about this being a horrible plan. Faris cleared the line of confused soldiers in a single bound and skidded to a halt at the very center of the fray. With his barrel chest heaving, he threw a small ball of fur high over his head. Daana's gaze followed the animal as it slowly ascended beyond logical means. It stopped. For a split second, the creature glowed a brilliant sapphire blue before dissipating in a churning swirl of smoke. The shifting tendrils snaked tighter, swirling, swirling, swirling, as the rapidly expanding cloud gained speed.

The wind whipped a tuft of matted curls across Daana's tear-streaked face. Fallen leaves lifted from the forest floor as the gentle gust grew to a howling torrent. Leaves gave way to dirt, and dirt to stones, until entire branches were snapped from their trunks and swept into the raging air current. Daana ducked instinctively as the bits of debris whizzed past with alarming speed, but there was no need. She could see the others being struck and blown back, but the current moved around her, sparing her from the onslaught.

A crackle of blue magic preceded the final gust and, with a deafening *boom*, a shockwave of wind erupted from the very center of the dark swirl, throwing everything not rooted to the ground several yards back. Lieutenant Holt's grip on Daana slipped, and she was ripped away by the current.

Magic rippled across Daana's skin until every hair on her arms stood on end. She glanced at her forearms, watching mystified as her jeweled armlets glowed with the same dazzling blue. Her gaze continued down, realizing her feet were currently fixed in place by Faris. She wasn't sure how he'd gotten there, but the faun clung to her knees for all he was worth, as if she was anchoring them to the ground and not the other way around. Snag was alongside them as well—eyes wide as his ears caught the wind like miniature sails.

Shielding her eyes from the torrent, Daana peered across the wind-ravaged battlefield. The only fighters still holding their ground were Rali and Ellisar. The elf huntress was knelt in a half crouch with her head bent against the gale and her blade stuck deep into the soil for leverage. Her golden hair whipped in the air behind her. Rali was stretched on her belly only paces from her elf companion, clawing desperately at the dirt for traction.

"Alright!" the dwarf threw her head back, screaming. "Alright, you've made your point. We get it! Rein in it already!"

CHAPTER THIRTY-TWO

Beginning of the End

The wind dropped and a figure materialized from the center of the smoky haze. Their cloak billowed as they touched down into the trampled mud, as though gravity was an option and not a requirement. "I go missing for three days," the singsong voice thundered. "Three days! And this is what I come back to? Your leader is missing, the little bird has given in to the darkness, there is cursed magic bringing the mountain down beneath your very feet, and what is it I find you two doing?"

"What we're good at!" Ellisar snarled.

Neither Ellisar nor Rali attempted to move. Daana was unsure if this was a precautionary measure, in the event the wind started up again, or was simply out of fear of the small, spiny being that limped toward them with dead set purpose. The creature looked like the unfortunate offspring of a blue elf and a porcupine, leading Daana to conclude that whoever had come up with the name Palace Ghost had clearly never seen the ghost itself in person.

Unlike her, who suddenly couldn't tear her gaze from the frightening creature.

"Acting erratically is your forte, yes," the ghost said to Ellisar. "What is your excuse, dwarf? You are better than this."

Rali planted her face into the upturned dirt, offering a muffled, "I don't want to talk about it."

The ghost hobbled along the strip of dirt in front of Rali, ranting, "Your responsibility is to lead in Oralia's absence. Is this what you consider leading? You are supposed to talk the elf from the edge of insanity, not hold her hand as you jump over it together! The only one here spewing a lick of sense is the elfling! Why is it that I am forced to side with the Lazuli child, the blood of my sworn enemy, when my allegiance is supposed to be to you? This is embarrassing for both of us."

"Piss off, Whisper." This came from Ellisar. Who, from the looks of it, was back to trying to stab holes in things with her eyes. "We just lost Curly. Do you want to be the one to tell Oralia her baby boy isn't coming home? Neither do we!"

The white quills running down the back of the ghost's head rattled in a disquieting manner. "I am sorry for your loss," they said softly. "But senseless carnage will not undo what has happened. I assure you, you will get your opportunity to fight soon enough. There are more pressing issues at hand."

"I knew it!" With the possibility of getting swept off the mountain no longer a threat, Snag dislodged himself from Daana's side. He approached the others, clenching and unclenching his clawed hands with each angry stomp. "Whatever's happening isn't over. You're here because all of chaos is about to be turned loose, isn't it?"

Ellisar whipped her head in Snag's direction, confusion wrinkled across her sweat-soaked brow. "Since when do you know about Whisper?"

"Here's the thing." The previously sad, hollow version of Snag was no more. In his stead was a rabid goblin who looked like he wanted to sink his needled teeth into someone's leg and give it a good shake. "None of you are good at hiding secrets! See these ears? They catch every hushed little whisper the two of you think you're passing in private. So all those little dirty secrets like—oh, I don't know—the fact that Oralia's got a magic necklace, or that it's attached to a psychotic shapeshifter, or that you two have been helping her aid the resistance all this time. Guess what? They're not secrets! Not to me, anyway. Was cute watching you three try an' be sneaky about it, though."

Daana clenched her jaw in order to contain her surprise. Her efforts probably weren't doing much in the way of her face, but at least it kept her from letting loose the stampede of thoughts running wild across her mind. A quick glance downward confirmed that not only was Faris still clinging to her legs, but he appeared to be almost as confused as she felt. She took some solace in that. Not much, but some. After all, it was nice not to be the only one left out for a change.

Rali was still strewn across the swampy ground. Her jaw swung open but, for possibly the first time ever, nothing of substance came out. "But . . ."

Ellisar seemed to be faring only slightly better than her companion with Snag's unexpected reveal. "You knew this whole time?"

"How stupid do you think I am?" Snag threw his clawed hands in Rali's direction. "She talks to Oralia's necklace like it's a person! It wouldn't be so strange if she regularly held drunken conversations with any other inanimate object, but no, just that one. Honestly, it wasn't that hard to put together. I just stayed out of it 'cause the pay was regular and none of you asked me to get involved."

Having said his piece, the fire within Snag's belly quelled as his uneasy gaze shifted to Whisper. He admitted, somewhat reluctantly, "I also might have pulled a knife on this one a few years back. Shit got weird real fast."

A weak smile flickered across the ghost's weary expression. "Among all the mighty hunters ever sent after the ghost, it was the one not looking that found me. Using not magic, but his nose."

"Fae have an irregular smell," Snag explained, scratching the back of his neck as Rali and Ellisar simply gawked at him in disbelief. "Sort of like fruit and moss mashed together. Anyway, I helped this one find a way to cover it up so no one else would notice."

"You knew this whole time?" Ellisar repeated, as though her mind had not yet moved on from the concept.

Deciding he'd answered enough, Snag dismissed her stunned question with a wave of his hand and set his sights on Whisper instead. "You've come out of hiding. Which means whatever we're up against is bad. I'm afraid to ask what it is, though."

The ghost's melodic voice rang out loud enough for all those gathered to hear. "The prophecy has been fulfilled. It is the beginning of the end, unless the little bird can be stopped."

Ellisar stood, tugging her blade from the wet soil and attempting to clean it against her pantleg. She succeeded only in spreading the caked filth from her trousers onto the bloodied steel. "The little what?"

"Rasp," Faris clarified, glumly. He clung to Daana's knees with his eyes screwed shut—as if refusing to acknowledge what was going on around him would somehow make it cease to exist. "The magic that curses this mountain has got a hold of him."

"Bucko?" Rali raised her head, her jaw trembling as she blinked heavily at the ghost. "This is a rescue mission, right? We save the Dinglehead and everything goes back to the way it was?"

The ghost only looked at her with a solemn expression.

Rali rushed to her feet, thundering, "Right, Whisper?"

"I'm afraid the magic on the mountain has already changed. It has its vessel now. The only way the dark entity can be stopped is by eliminating the little bird."

"No! We just had to put one down. Don't make me do it again. Not bucko. I can't stomach losing another." Rali's teary-eyed stare shifted to Faris and her expression curled into a snarl. "Why aren't you saying anything? This is your boy they're talking about!"

Faris only sagged closer to the ground.

"Traitor!"

"Quartz Ralizak," the ghost's eyes flared silver as it spoke her name as a command, "silence."

Rali's mouth snapped shut. Her eyes bulged as a red tint flushed across her dirt-speckled face. Although no intelligible words came forth, it was not from a lack of trying. She worked through several muffled grunts and groans, growing visibly redder by the second. With a final, dramatic stomp, the dwarf spun around, gesticulating her point to Ellisar through a series of rapid hand movements.

Whisper's gaze shifted to Ellisar but the elf was a hair quicker. "Keep my name out of your fucking mouth!" she said, crossing her forefingers at the knuckle and holding them aloft like a shield.

"Stop acting like a fool and I won't have to."

Rali stomped closer, performing another series of frenzied gestures. Whether Ellisar was translating this out loud or merely speaking her own thoughts didn't seem to matter because she and Rali appeared to be on the same page. "Just because you have magic doesn't put you in charge. You can't just leave and then show up again with absolutely no explanation and expect us to fall in line. Shit has changed. We're done."

This statement earned a definitive nod of approval from Rali.

"I just had this blasted argument with the faun and have neither the time nor willpower to rehash it again, so allow me to make it very simple for you." The spiny creature took a brazen step forward, their white quills lifting in an unspoken challenge. "The darkness has taken its vessel and unless we stop it, the rest of the world will pay the price. None of you may care about anything outside of yourselves, but your young orc friend did. You want to honor his death? Make it mean something? Then do what he would have done and protect the good people still left in this world while we have the chance!"

Ellisar and Rali exchanged quick looks. The furrow in Ellisar's brow lessened as guilt filled in around the corners. "That's not fair. You can't play dirty like that, Whisper."

"What I am asking is unthinkable, I understand. But this is bigger than any of us. The fate of mortal-kind is at stake. If we fail, there may not be another chance to right the wrong."

As quickly as it had started, the argument was over. Ellisar and Rali had lost. The former fire burning within their eyes turned to ash at the realization that this was one circumstance even they could not fight their way out of. Rali bit her lower lip, seemingly unable to communicate what she was feeling with limited hand gestures. Tears rolled down her dirtied face as she staggered for Ellisar, her short arms thrown wide.

"No, no, no—" Ellisar tried to run, but got caught around the waist in Rali's crushing embrace all the same. The elf's ears burned red as she squirmed uncomfortably in Rali's unrelenting grasp.

"I require your assistance most of all, young Lazuli."

To her horror, Daana realized the ghost was now speaking to her. Shit. She had been so caught up in the theatrics, she had forgotten to run. Not that it would have been very easy with Faris clinging to her like a lost child. Still, she could have at least kicked him off and tried. Too late for that now.

She stammered a hasty reply, "I—I've used up all of my reserves and—"

The ghost held aloft their gnarled hand, silencing her. "As I have told you many times before, your worth cannot be found in power you do not possess."

There was a familiarity in the way they spoke. The ghost didn't look like Willem, but the words were undeniably his. Or, conversely, perhaps she had it the wrong way around. Willem's words had been the ghost's all along. And to think, this entire time she had been chasing the only person from the division who seemed to give a damn about her. Daana might have found this ironic had she not been consumed by terror instead.

"I do not need a witch." The ghost stared at her unblinkingly with weary, solemn eyes. "I need you. You taught yourself how to separate magic from its wielder. It is my hope that, in a very short amount of time, you can learn the reverse."

Daana's voice was as small and weak as she felt. "And if I can't?"

"Then there will be no stopping the entity."

Ah, of course. The fate of mortal-kind was hinging on an ability she'd never even tried before. In other words, they were doomed. Daana's stare shifted between the petrified faces gathered around her, realizing they sensed it as well. At least, for what seemed the first time since the start of the trip, possibly her whole life, she was finally on the same page as everyone else.

CHAPTER THIRTY-THREE

Wake Up

What have you done?

Rasp's thoughts were no longer a whisper, but a relentless scream, drowning out the erratic gallop of his heartbeat and short, panting breaths. His inner voice had escaped its cage and there was no putting it back now. It bore its claws deep into his panicked mind, slowing it, clouding it, clogging the internal gears until the most he could do was place one leaden foot in front of the other as the voice raged mercilessly behind his eyes. *Run all you like. Run until you have no strength in your legs to carry you. It won't matter. They know what you did.*

They know what you are.

"Shut up, shut up, shut up!" Rasp hissed. He staggered another step, right hand clutching the wound on his side as his vision started to swim. Another step, that's all he could do. One, and then one more, again and again and again until he couldn't manage a single step further.

They're not far behind. They won't let you get away. Not after what you did.

"I didn't mean to do it. It was an accident. He made me—"

The loose scree shifted beneath his boots, stealing the remaining words from his mouth. Rasp lost his balance and slammed hard on his ass, sliding haphazardly down the steep, angled cliff face. He threw his hands out on either side of him. His fingertips clawed into the rocky mountainside, shredding the skin from his unprotected palms as he desperately grabbed for any handholds to impede his plummet. Finally, with his heels dug into the earth, upsetting loose rocks and rubble all the way down, his tortured body slowed to a full stop.

Rasp remained there for longer than he should have, lying stretched across the stony ground, feeling every excruciating rise and fall of his narrow chest. The sheer terror of nearly slipping off of the face of the mountain exerted its toll on his fraying nerves. Rasp's arms and legs trembled beyond his control.

You're only delaying the inevitable, his inner voice said. *They will do far worse than throw you off a mountain when they catch you. They know what you are now. They will not let you live.*

"I'm not anything," Rasp protested, weakly. "I didn't mean to do it. He made me! It was either me or him and I . . ."

There was no point in finishing his sentence. He could argue with himself until he was blue in the face, but it wouldn't change the fact that his inner voice was right. His brothers would cut him apart piece by piece for killing their father. Accidental or not, they didn't care. The witch accusation had been the final nail in Rasp's coffin. His brothers would show no mercy the moment they caught him again.

A few more furious swallows of cool mountain air helped quell some of the fire burning within his lungs before Rasp eased upright. He glanced over his shoulder, confirming the lethal trio were not yet bounding down the steep mountainside after him. He'd outfoxed his brothers for a moment, having thrown them off his scent by circling back and utilizing one of the hidden game trails snaking along the eastern cliffside. It wouldn't be long before they caught on, though. All the more reason not to linger for even a second more—no matter how badly his broken body pleaded with him to give up.

Rasp stood, clenching his teeth to hold back the scream as his intestines threatened to spill forth from the gaping hole in his side. He pressed his trembling hand firmly to the wound, smashing everything back into place. He'd torn one of the sleeves from his shirt and fashioned it into a makeshift bandage to keep from bleeding out. That hadn't been too long ago. Half an hour, at most. Already, the bandage squished beneath his touch, wet and dripping with blood. An ill sign, unfortunately, but he didn't have the time to stop and mend the wound properly.

He had to put as much space between him and the Iron Ridge first, and then maybe he could start a fire and cauterize the damn thing shut. Once ensuring his guts were still safely housed inside of his abdomen and not spilling free, Rasp braved his first step and staggered onward. By some miracle, he'd nearly reached the foothills in one piece. He could see the start of the great forest dotting the green and gray landscape below. All Rasp had to do was make it into the trees. It wouldn't take much to give his brothers the final slip after that.

Moisture trickled along the inside of his thigh. Fearing he'd soiled himself, Rasp glanced down and realized the truth was far, far worse. The blood oozing from below his ribs had fully saturated his shirt and makeshift bandage. Dark red-brown trails leaked from the bandage, steadily creeping down his right leg. The sight made his knees buckle in protest. Rasp caught himself against a boulder, narrowly avoiding a second head-over-heels tumble down the steep cliffside.

Shit. Forget giving his brothers the slip, Rasp would be lucky if he reached the forest ahead of them at this rate. Outrunning his pursuers was out of the question now. Rasp's panicked mind scrambled for alternatives, settling on one that, if not good, at least passed for semi-feasible. He would hobble his way into the woods, find a stream to disguise his trail, climb up a tree somewhere, and then bunker down for the night. He could wait them out after that. Tend to his wounds, catch his breath, who knows, maybe even avoid bleeding to death in the process. In the morning, he would climb down again and find some other way to escape mountain folk territory with his head still attached to his shoulders.

Gathering his dwindling strength, Rasp pushed off from the boulder and staggered on his way once more. He kept his eyes fixed on the trees as he half-hobbled, half-slipped further down into the basin of the mountain. Hope drew closer with each agonizing step, and yet he could not shake the gnawing dread that ballooned inside his chest. Something was terribly wrong. The day was warm with the sun high above him, beating down upon his shaven head with the full weight of its late autumn glory. By all accounts, he should have been drenched in sweat, on the verge of overheating, but it was as if all of the warmth had been sapped from his body.

A miserable chill bore deep in his aching bones. Rasp's clothes felt wet. And not just the portion of his shirt saturated with blood, but everywhere. His coat clung uncomfortably tight to his arms and shoulders, weighing him down like that time his brothers had filled his pockets with stones. Rasp swore even his socks squished with each agonizing step. It would not be long before the shakes really set in. If he didn't find somewhere warm to bunker down before nightfall, he wouldn't make it to morning.

The steep terrain beneath his leaden feet gradually gave way to flatter ground. A towering line of dark spruce and yellow and orange tamaracks rose up before him, marking the beginnings of the great forest. Again, for the second time, it occurred to Rasp that something was amiss. He blinked the dust from his weary eyes, convinced his vision was suddenly plagued by hallucinations. The long expanse of trees stretched on either side of him appeared as they normally should—tall, towering conifers, spruces, and birch, all with their autumn foliage on full display. The section of the forest directly in front of him, however, was eerily different. The trees were dark and sagged under an invisible weight, drained of their usual vibrant colors. Despite the overhead sun, Rasp could see tendrils of mist roiling at the base of their sickly trunks, churning the mossy ground to shadows.

Fuck that. Being actively hunted was nightmarish enough, he didn't need to make it worse by hobbling headlong into what was clearly a haunted forest. Rasp started to limp toward the stretch of woods untouched by the blight, but the darkness was growing. It outpaced him, claiming each healthy stretch of wilderness before he reached it.

He stopped, utterly stumped, surveying the spreading decay as the flicker of hope fizzled out within his aching chest. Strange words slipped free from Rasp's mouth unchecked. "It didn't happen like this."

Happen like this? His own words caught him by surprise. What in the realm was he on about now? Nothing had ever happened to him like this before. It was new. It was terrifying. It was—

Your only hope, his inner voice whispered. *You have no other option. You're only wasting time. Go, now, before they find you.*

Rasp stared at the decayed forest as he considered whether or not he was truly this desperate. Regrettably, his inner voice was right. He couldn't turn back and he couldn't risk standing out in the open questioning his waning sanity any longer, either. His brothers would be upon him soon. The only way to save his skin was by going forward.

Clutching his injured side, Rasp slipped between the unwelcoming trees and into a world of perpetual darkness. The usual pungent scents of forest rot and decay were strangely absent. In their stead, all he could smell was the musty stench of old water runoff. That, too, didn't make sense. Just like how Rasp was now convinced the inside of his boots had somehow turned to puddles. His numb feet squished each time he applied weight to them.

Gods, maybe he had wet himself. Surely that was something he would have noticed? But why wasn't it warm? This was all making as much sense as a juggling bear in a tutu—

Croak!

Rasp flinched, snapping from his runaway thoughts with a sudden jolt. He twisted his head this way and that, searching for the source of the sound. Amid the undulating shadows, he spied the faintest outline of a raven perched in the boughs above him. Rasp squinted harder, straining to make out the bird's shape, but his vision was growing fuzzy around the edges. "Who are you?"

Croak, the unfamiliar raven replied.

"Wake up?" Rasp repeated as a fresh wave of unease flooded his insides. "What do you mean wake up? Who even are you? You're not supposed to be here. It didn't happen like this!"

Like this? Again, his own words caught him by surprise. What the fuck was going on? This had never happened before. Rasp was certain he would have remembered being hunted down like a fucking animal. Wait—was this the blight? It had already laid waste to the trees. Was the blight working its corrupt magic on his feverish mind too?

The raven flapped its wings with a feathery snap, screeching at Rasp to heed its warning.

"I'm not dreaming! This is real. I have to . . ."

A growing clamor near the edge of the trees caused Rasp to fall silent. "We know you're here!" a voice called out to him. "You think some haunted trees are gonna keep us from you? We're coming, Raspy. Run while you can."

"I—I have to go." Rasp tried to blink the growing haze from his eyes. The shadows around the edges of his vision were spreading, merging together to block out his surroundings. It was like trying to peer through smudged glass. With his left hand stretched out before him, Rasp stumbled deeper into the cursed forest. The shouts from his brothers echoed around him. The woods warped the sound, making it impossible to pinpoint from which direction they were coming.

Straight ahead was his only option.

The numbing chill spread throughout Rasp's trembling body, sending every hair on end. The base of his ears burned with a warning sensation that felt oddly familiar but, for the life of him, he couldn't remember why. His haphazard trail led him further into the unrelenting dark. He heard the flutter of the raven's wings as it followed, but he could not pick it out from his pitch-black surroundings. His sense of vision was nearly gone. Rasp could barely see anything more than a few steps ahead and even then, it didn't constitute much more than shifting shadows.

Croak.

"What?"

Croak, croak, croak.

"I . . . I can't understand you." Rasp's shaky steps faltered as he came to a stop. He moved his head back and forth, searching for the bird among the unyielding gloom. The effort was to no avail. "What are you saying?"

The raven repeated its dire warning, but all Rasp heard was obnoxious bird sounds. A sudden sense of loss flooded his foggy brain. That wasn't right. But . . . but why? Birds made bird sounds. Why would he expect anything different? What kind of idiot thought they could talk to birds?

The low-lying mist crept up from the damp forest floor and enshrouded him. It stung the exposed skin on his hands and arms as it weaved upward. Rasp tried to shake off his growing chill, but the mist expanded, enveloping him in its icy embrace. Coughing the frosty moisture from his lungs, he staggered forward, wafting it from working its way into his mouth and nose as he blindly navigated the dark forest.

"I have to keep going," Rasp repeated his instructions to himself lest he forget that part, too. "I can't let them catch me."

And so he continued, whispering the words as more and more of his reality slipped from his feeble grasp. "Keep going," he rasped, blindly shuffling through the impenetrable darkness. "Can't catch me."

The dreaded moment came and his legs, at last, gave in to the inevitable. Rasp crumpled to the ground with a whimper. "Can't . . . keep . . . going."

His head felt like an iron weight. Rasp strained to lift it, eyes roving across the tangle of shadows, desperate for something, anything, to remind him of why he was here. He searched, hope shriveling within his soul, and found nothing. His world, and everything he knew of it, was gone. There was only him. And there was only darkness. The faint sensations of anger and fear pinged within his fading mind, urging him to not forget, but for the life of him, he couldn't remember what they were for anymore either. His memory turned to dust as the churning dark closed in.

Rasp heard the raven's final plea before he was swallowed by the void. His internal voice stirred to life in the back of his head one final time before it, too, succumbed to the dark. *What have you done?*

CHAPTER THIRTY-FOUR

In the Dark

The cellblock was dark. No one had bothered to relight the torches after their flames had gone out. To be fair, there was no one left to relight the torches anyway, at least not on this side of the prison wall. The mountain tremor had cut Oralia's conversation with the Stoneclaw brothers regrettably short. The trio had fled before the walls stopped shaking, with the guards practically nipping at their heels, leaving the prison cellblock dark and unattended.

Oralia presumed they were all running frantically up and down the stone hallway, along with what had to be every other member of the mountain folk clan. From the sounds of it, there was a damn stampede taking place on the other side of the wall. She understood the chaotic fever but, still, a little light would have been a nice gesture. It wasn't every day the Protector of the Realm had the honor of being crushed to death inside your dungeon.

Normally she would not have been bothered by the dark, but her thread was being difficult and a decent light source would have helped remedy the situation. Oralia sat cross-legged on the stone floor, attempting to slip the fraying tip of her thread through the eye of an impossibly small needle. So far, all previous attempts had ended in failure. Resolute, she wetted the tip of the floss between her lips and tried once more.

"Even now, after everything we've been through, you never cease to astound me." Sascha paced the dark cell beside hers, testing each metal bar as he strode past. Despite his valiant efforts, the iron refused to bend beneath even his gargantuan hands.

That didn't stop him from continuing to try, Oralia noted. Poor fool. He probably still thought there was a chance they were going to make it out alive. That opportunity had fled along with the Stoneclaws, leaving her, Sascha, and the other two hapless prisoners in the dark to die.

"Damn it, woman!" Sascha whirled around at her, snapping, "The mountain is falling apart on top of us and you're sewing. Could you not think of a better use of your time?"

"Mending," Oralia corrected. "I am not sewing. I am mending."

Or would be, had she been able to get the blasted needle and thread to cooperate. The mountain folk had stripped her of her sword, chainmail, and anything else that could be used as a weapon, including the amulet from her neck. The emergency patch kit she kept tucked on the inside of her jacket had been missed, however. Not like it mattered. There wasn't much damage she could inflict with such a small needle and thread.

"Oralia."

If Sascha lumbered any closer she could try pricking him with her tiny needle, she supposed. Perhaps that would give him the motivation he needed to break down the bars. He'd probably bring the ceiling down as well. If nothing else, it would at least eliminate all of the tedious waiting. That was the worst part. The waiting uselessly to die.

"Oralia!"

Oralia bit her bottom lip and squinted, failing to thread the needle for the umpteenth time. In a strange reversal of roles, it was she who offered her response in the form of a noncommittal sound. "Hm?"

"The roof is caving in on top of us," Sascha reminded her. "Another good shake like that first one and we're dead."

"Then I shall die with perfectly mended clothes." Aunt Maeve would have argued with Oralia's rather loose definition of "perfect," but she was being recalcitrant, so it didn't matter.

"So you've given up then. Is that it?"

"What would you have me do? Yell? Scream? Slam against the bars?" Sascha seemed to be doing enough of that for the both of them. Oralia failed to see how adding to the noise would help prevent the inevitable. "You die your way. Leave me to die mine."

She could feel him watching her. If it was a glaring contest the fool wanted, then she was happy to oblige. Sascha wasn't one of her faithful four. He didn't have the years of tolerance under his belt needed to withstand the full force of her death stare. A firmly pressed brow and curled upper lip would be all that was required to submit him. Grinding her tusks against the flat of her upper teeth, Oralia lifted her jaw and locked eyes with him.

Her heart dropped the moment she did. It wasn't a challenge she saw etched across his stupidly handsome face. Sascha's big doe eyes were rimmed in white. His slate gray skin looked chalky, almost pale. It wasn't big, burly Sascha who gazed back at her, but the shy baker boy from her childhood. The same nervous youngling who used to follow her in and out of trouble like a lovestruck puppy. Chance had made them neighbors, but it was something deeper that kept pulling Sascha back into her life. Something Oralia didn't want to admit she still felt for him. Did he feel it, too?

The walls rattled, releasing a cloud of dust and debris as a minor aftershock pulsed through the surrounding rock. The trembles had been growing more frequent since the first. Oralia tore her gaze from Sascha and searched the buckled ceiling for signs of worsening. The ceiling wasn't yielding yet, but it wouldn't be long before it gave in to the mounting pressure.

Poor baker boy, Oralia thought. *There will be no following me out of this one.*

The ancient door flung open with a shrill creak just shy of a scream, allowing a channel of pale light to flood the room. The thin, weasely shape of the younger Stoneclaw brother pounded across the stone tile, dodging the bits of rock that littered the floor. The echo of his boots marked his swift passage. "Fuck, fuck, fuck, fuck," Lingon chorused under his breath as he approached Oralia's cell, producing an iron key ring from his cloak. After several failed turns, the lock popped open with a metallic *clunk!* Lingon moved to unlock Sascha's door next, still chanting a soft, "Fuck, fuck, fuck . . ."

"You and you," Lingon said, pointing to the orcs. "Come with me. Let's go."

Oralia tilted her head at the remaining prisoners huddled near the back. From the pair's whispered conversations, she'd overheard that the human was called Zev and the dwarf Beryl. Whatever prior allegiances had existed between her and Captain Monk's forces were severed now. Still, it wasn't their fault their captain was a power-hungry maniac. It seemed only fair to give them a fighting chance. "And them."

"I don't need them," Lingon snarled. "I need big, strong orcs. Now come on. Get a move on before this place comes down on top of us."

Sascha kicked the cell door open and stepped free. "Good sir, you are aware that the time to negotiate was before you unlocked our cells?"

"This isn't a negotiation."

"And if I say otherwise, what are you going to do? Lock me back in?" Sascha's harsh expression dared the slender man to try.

"For fuck's sake." Lingon planted his face into his hands with a moan. "I'm a little frazzled at the moment. Give me some leeway here, alright?"

Sascha towered over the small man by an impressive three and a half feet. A single blow alone could have reduced Lingon to a pile of broken bones and oozing innards. In true Sascha fashion, however, the imposing orc settled for a polite throat clearing, as if reminding Lingon that he was willfully choosing the high ground, for the time being anyway. "Temporary leeway granted. Now, about those other cells then?"

Lingon jerked his hands from his face and placed them at his hips, instinctively widening his stance. The effect was similar to a lap dog attempting to stare down a lion. "I'm still in charge here! Just because you're free doesn't mean I take orders from you."

"That was a suggestion, not an order. Believe me, you'll know the difference when you hear it." They stared one another down for several seconds before a single raised eyebrow from Sascha convinced the Stoneclaw to change his tune.

"Alright, alright, alright! As a show of good faith, I'll let the others out, see?" Lingon scurried to unlock the remaining cells, grumbling beneath his breath. "Calling an emergency evacuation. Brilliant idea, Bil! Get the whole stronghold in a fuckin' panic. Oh, what's that? All the donkeys bolted? Oh, no, no, no. Don't worry about it. You two go ahead an' sit around scratching your asses while I figure out a solution to get us down the mountain alive!"

Oralia folded her mending kit neatly into its pouch and stood, donning her torn dress jacket. She opened the door with less dramatic fanfare than Sascha had, preferring a more casual approach. "Family can be so inconsiderate at times," she said, issuing a pensive sigh. "I have but a single sister and she is a constant headache on the best of days. I cannot imagine how you fare with so many siblings."

"Lady, you don't know the short of it." Lingon jerked open the door of the final cell, glaring at its occupant as if his current dilemma was their fault somehow.

With Lingon momentarily distracted, Sascha swiveled his head in Oralia's direction and locked eyes with her. Wordlessly, his expression pleaded with her to save whatever insanity she was attempting for a more appropriate time and place—one that involved fresh air and not being crushed to death inside of a dungeon, preferably. *The mountain is coming down,* he managed to convey with a lifted brow alone. *The others are free. For the love of gods, can you leave well enough alone and not jeopardize this for us?*

Oralia ignored him. While it was true that the ceiling was most certainly coming down, it still had a ways to go. Besides, she rarely got the opportunity to employ her charming card and this seemed like just the mark to practice upon. "Lingon, you are, as they say, a man of action, yes?"

The Stoneclaw stared up at her with his eyebrows scrunched together. "Of course I'm a man. Are you implying I look like a woman?" His hands once more went to his hips in a manner that seemed to be in direct conflict with his objection to his supposed femininity. "If this is about my long hair, I'll have you know it's all the rage right now and happens to frame my face magnificently. So I don't want to hear it."

Admittedly, her charm may have been a little rusty. In her defense, there was only so much she could do with an audience of this intellectual magnitude. Oralia interrupted Lingon's tirade as politely as possible. "I meant that you are the one that gets things done around here."

"Oh." He blinked. "Well yeah. I'm here, aren't I? I suppose that qualifies."

"Indeed it does." She was remembering why she left the charm to Rali. This was downright infuriating. Still, she needed information before he reunited with his brothers and one of the smarter ones interfered. "I imagine your brothers do not even notice your contributions."

"You mean they use my hard work and take all the credit for themselves? All the damn time." The heart of the mountain rumbled overhead. Lingon craned his head back and stared at the buckled ceiling, as if suddenly remembering there was something dangerous he was supposed to be avoiding.

"Do they know you are here now?" Oralia persisted. If Sascha had been any closer, she was certain he'd be stomping her foot right now. For the moment he was having to settle for a commendably formidable, yet ineffective, glare.

"Psh!" Lingon waved his hand over his head dismissively. "Do I look like the kind of leader who asks permission? I see an opening and I take it."

"Of course." Crumbling mountain aside, this was shaping up rather nicely. Oralia had just been set free of her cage and the rest of the Stoneclaw siblings were none the wiser. Best not to rush it, however. Not until she had a better idea of what was taking place. "And in what way may we be of assistance to you, sir?"

"We'll discuss it on the way," Lingon said, darting back toward the open door with his hood pulled over his head, as if this would somehow protect him from a slab of falling stone.

Shaking his head at her in disbelief, Sascha followed. The realm soldiers, Zev and Beryl, traded uneasy looks before tripping over one another in a mad dash to form rank behind Sascha. Oralia was the last to exit, ducking in order to avoid hitting her head on the petrified doorframe. The adjoining tunnel was carved from the same dull, red-gray stone of the cellblock. Lanterns lined the walls, illuminating a passage wide enough for two humans to pass comfortably. This of course meant Sascha had to walk sideways to avoid scraping his shoulders. The few mountain folk still moving along the lower tunnels pressed flat against the walls as the strange entourage passed.

"I need muscle," Lingon explained, his nasally voice echoing due to the cavernous nature of the surrounding rock. "I've got a cartload of the old and infirm that can't make the trek on their own. Normally we'd have donkeys for this sort of thing, but some idiot went and left the stables open. They bolted the moment that first shake struck and now all that's left is a bunch of chickens. Chickens won't get our people down the path in time, but two strapping orcs might."

"You intend to use us as cattle?" Oralia said.

Lingon glanced over his shoulder at her, grinning like a fox. "Asses, technically."

What was it Rasp always said? Oh yes, she remembered now. "Pass."

CHAPTER THIRTY-FIVE

Ye of Little Faith

The dingy air was still and wet. A thick bough of spiced spruce hung between every third lantern—a measure meant to disguise the musty odors associated with a life spent underground. For Oralia, the overpowering aroma only added an obnoxious layer of nasal burning to the overall experience. She considered covering her nose, but realized this would probably come off as offensive. And, considering she'd just turned down Lingon's request for aid, did not want to risk adding insult on top of injury.

Lingon waved to a group of awestruck mountain folk civilians as they passed, as if to say: *Rest assured, this was completely my idea. I have it under control. Please don't tell my brothers.* Despite his calm demeanor, Oralia could smell a sort of salty, sour odor emitting from his body.

"That's not how this works," he hissed the moment they were out of hearing. "I let you out. You have to do what I say. You're the prisoner, remember?"

"And yet, it is you who is currently outnumbered." Oralia peered down her nose at him and said, "Unarmed and without backup, I might add. This was very poorly thought out."

"I have a blade!" Lingon pulled aside his gold and emerald cloak to reveal the dagger hanging from his side. It was a lovely, curved weapon with a leather-wrapped handle and a jeweled pommel.

With a single, well-timed swipe, Sascha neatly relieved the Stoneclaw of his sole means of defense. Sascha traded quick glances with Oralia, affording her an unspoken look of *I hope you know what you're doing, because you're going to owe me big for this.*

Lingon's eyes bulged as a scarlet hue flushed across his cheeks and nose. He stamped his foot, shouting, "Alright, fine! This was poorly thought out. Let's hear your plan then."

Oralia marveled at the absurdity of the situation. This was by far the most calm and orderly escape she had ever attempted. By all rights, her captor should have sounded the alarm by now. Perhaps the others were too busy to respond. Perhaps Lingon suspected he would get run through with his own dagger if he did so. Neither possibility, however, explained why he didn't simply run. Surely he could navigate the labyrinth of underground tunnels better than any of them.

"To start," Oralia said as she slid past Sascha and assumed the lead position, "I think I will look for the exit."

Lingon steepled his fingers beneath his chin as he shuffled alongside her. "And you intend to find it how, exactly?"

"My nose. This way smells like fresh air," she replied, noticing the way his scowl deepened. One didn't have to possess an intricate understanding of tunnels to know which way led to the surface. "I would like to find my chainmail and a suitable weapon along the way, if you would be so kind. It will be difficult to hold your brother off for any significant amount of time without them. As you well know, the success of your evacuation depends on a good diversion."

From the way his sour expression lifted, Lingon's thought process went something along the lines of: *Oh? Oh. Ohhhhhhhh.*

Oralia offered him a smile, taking care not to show too many teeth. "Find my weaponry, and I will tell your brothers it was your idea."

She expected him to demand an explanation, to question her motives, at the very least exhibit some form of hesitation—hand-wringing, shifting his weight from one foot to the other, an unconscious clenching of the jaw, anything. Lingon, instead, took an abrupt turn and beckoned over his shoulder to them. "Come along, this way. Chop, chop! I want to see some hustle. We don't have all day, you know."

They moved along, switching from long stretches of hallway to a spiraling staircase and back again, plunging ever deeper into the heart of the trembling mountain. Having grown bored of the repetitive landscape, Oralia happened to glance upward and catch the reflective shimmer of blue glass. Squinting, she realized a large glass orb hung above her, strung from the ceiling with an iron chain. It was not the only one of its kind, either. Peering harder, Oralia could make out an entire line of them suspended from the ceiling, following the curve of the hallway.

She had seen similar devices in the main building of the Division of Divination during one of the few times she'd been allowed to tour the academy's grounds. The orbs had been crafted by the division's artificers and, powered by magic, served as an alternative to candle chandeliers. Two points of interest stood out to her regarding the ornate glass bulbs currently stung high over her head. The first was that they were unlit and covered in dust, an indication perhaps that they had seen decades of unuse. Secondly, what in the name of chaos were they doing here? If these were indeed magic lanterns, the Stoneclaw mountain stronghold was the absolute last place Oralia expected to find them.

"Lingon," she said, breaking the uncomfortable stretch of silence that had been hanging over them since the staircase, "what is the purpose of those?"

He glanced over his shoulder at her confused. "Of what?"

She pointed to the ceiling with her finger. "Those."

His eyes narrowed, following the direction of her finger all the way to the dark ceiling. "Oh, the baubles?" Some of the leeriness slipped from his face as he offered her a dismissive shrug. "Beats me."

"How long have they been there?"

"Mom claimed the original Stoneclaws built 'em. Said they were a part of the lost history that went up in smoke when the records room burned down. She was always on us about revering the pieces left behind by our ancestors." A mischievous smile pulled at the corner of Lingon's thin lips. "Pretty sure Mom just said that to keep us from lobbing rocks at 'em, though."

Lingon started off once more, calling over his shoulder at them to stop dillydallying and get a move on. Oralia followed, craning her head from time to time in search of any other oddities. The rest of the journey passed without incident and, after several twists and turns more, the hallway deposited them in front of an impressive set of iron double doors. Lingon briefly fumbled with the keys before throwing open the entry to the fabled Stoneclaw armory.

Lingon unhooked a lantern from the wall and led them inside, booming, "Welcome to the fun room!"

Oralia followed with her lower jaw held slack in disbelief as the warm glow of the lantern reflected from wall to wall, glistening against a sea of polished steel. The room stretched on and on, with the glimmer of steel growing fainter in the distance. For such a small nation of people, the mountain folk armory was larger than it had any right to be. There was enough weaponry on hand to outfit a modest-sized army four times over. Oralia's stunned gaze swept across the cluttered armory. The rumors claiming that warfare was the mountain folks' favorite pastime were far more accurate than she'd previously given them credit for.

What was even more remarkable than the sheer volume of weaponry was the variation. It was as if the Stoneclaws had stolen both armor and weapons alike from any battle they'd ever fought and hauled it back to their mountain lair. There were ancient bill hooks, iron caltrops, and entire collections of shields sporting the emblems of former nations that had long since been swallowed by the expansion of the United Territories of the Realm. In the far corner, Oralia swore she spied the dismantled carcass of a former trebuchet, now reduced to rotting pieces of wood and iron, leaning against the wall.

Rows of towering racks took up the majority of the space, evidence that at one time someone had tried to keep the hoard organized. From the armory's current state, however, Oralia suspected the original system had been ditched in favor of a more haphazard approach along the lines of "pile it wherever it might fit."

Lingon squeezed himself through a small channel that snaked between the random piles of abandoned weaponry. "Your shit got tossed somewhere near the door, I imagine. Feel free to have a look around if you like." His next words were spoken beneath his breath, laced with an unmistakable edge of melancholy. "Such a waste leaving all of this here behind."

Oralia watched from the corner of her eye as Sascha and the others moved to explore. Fearful of having a mountain of rusted armaments collapse on top of her, she kept her exploration strictly to the visual kind. As her gaze slowly traversed the mounds of equipment piled haphazardly throughout the vast room, her stare eventually settled on a set of shelves carved from the surrounding stone itself. Various clay and glass jars littered the shelves, entombed in a century's worth of dust and cobwebs.

Oralia stepped closer, selecting one of the ceiled jars from a shelf and gingerly removing its dust-laden lid. An alarmingly familiar scent assaulted her senses, burning as it clawed its way up her nose. Oralia blinked the tears from her eyes as her mind struggled to place why the overpowering stench of rotten eggs was familiar to her. Her sluggish brain followed several lines of thought before the answer struck her—Snag's concoction. The faint yellow powder within the jar was one of the ingredients he'd used to rig his thunder flash at the start of the mutiny.

She quickly resealed the clay container and returned it to the shelf as her wary gaze moved up and down the rest of the collection. Like the glass baubles lining the passageway, these too appeared to not have seen use in ages. After having witnessed the sheer chaos Snag's single contraption had caused, Oralia decided it was probably for the better.

She felt a small twinge of regret in her gut at the mention of his name. It was a shame Snag and the rest of her faithful weren't here to see the armory. Curly would have clambered over the others to find the biggest, most impractical weapon possible. Rali would have insisted on naming it something that would later have to be explained to Oralia in private. Snag and Ellisar would be standing in the corner taking bets on who would lose the first finger to it. Curly, himself, probably. Faris would have found a way to sell the brothers their own weapons at twice their worth and Rasp . . .

Rasp.

She grimaced at his name. The damn boy was like mold. Off-putting at first, but the more time you spent around him, the more he grew on you. It was bad enough he'd wormed his way into her tight-knit crew, somehow he'd managed to infiltrate her thoughts as well. *I am sorry that it has come to this. You were trying to warn me all along, and I did not listen. And now one of us is not making it off this mountain.*

"I'll be damned." Mul's baritone voice preceded the heavy footsteps that entered the armory behind them. "You actually convinced her? I bet Bil two chickens that she was gonna crush you."

"Ye of little faith." Lingon sauntered back toward the front of the armory, skirting loose pieces of weaponry as he turned his nose into the air with a sneer. "Of course I convinced her. I am the best, after all."

Oralia's gaze settled over the slender man. Lingon instinctively shied several steps away from her, pretending to find a sudden interest in the collection of spears leaning haphazardly against a buckled table buried beneath a mountain of chainmail. "Convinced me of what?" she rumbled.

The start of a smile pulled at his thin lips. "Leading the fight against Rasp, of course. You agreed to stay behind and pose a distraction while the rest of the clan evacuates the mountain. Have you forgotten already? Silly Protector."

Lingon reached toward her with his hand, seemingly intent on adding insult to injury with a patronizing pat to Oralia's arm. A loud snap of her tusks caused him to reconsider. Oralia bore down upon Lingon with the full weight of her glare, realizing that perhaps he was not nearly as incompetent as she first thought. No wonder the little maggot hadn't sounded the alarm. This had been his plan all along.

She narrowed her eyes at him. "There never were any carts, were there?"

"You ever try to pull a cart down a mountain? Yeah, me neither. For good reasons."

Oralia wanted to ask how Lingon knew she would volunteer for the upcoming fight. She abstained from this line of questioning, however, certain the reply would not be an actual answer so much as another reason to punch him in the face.

Lingon provided one anyway, his smile spreading until it was mostly teeth. "I know a sucker when I see one."

Do not strike the man who released you. Do not strike the man who released you. With this helpful advice ringing through her head, Oralia turned to face Mul instead. "Lingon was incredibly convincing. Hardly had to say a word at all."

Mul's thick eyebrows furrowed at his younger brother. "This doesn't make you the leader."

Lingon opened and closed his hand like a mouth, producing a mocking whine that Oralia suspected was supposed to be a poor impression of his sibling. "It's alright, Dingle. I'd be jealous too if I were you. And anyway, how's the evacuation going? Did you manage to get Granny out of the wine cellar yet? She's a feisty old bird."

The burly man's brow furrowed further, until his beady eyes were nearly indistinguishable from his eyebrows. "There was a disturbance up top." He looked to Oralia, crossing his hulking arms over his broad chest. "Friends of yours, I suspect. Your goblin told me he was gonna hang me with my intestines if I didn't release you unharmed."

Her goblin? A mix of dread and hope flickered to life as Oralia's heartbeat doubled. She moved to what looked to be the newest mound of weaponry piled near the double doors and rooted through it for her belongings. She threw her coat of chainmail over her head before securing her sword and leather greaves and braces. "Sascha, Zev, Beryl, gather your things. We are leaving," Oralia said, already directing her steps toward the exit. She acknowledged Mul with a single nod. "Take me to them."

"Oh, I take orders from you too now, huh?" Mul turned and stomped out the double doors. His stride was only half of hers, and Oralia caught him in several easy steps. The throb in her leg was still present, but barely noticeable. Perhaps her body had simply accepted the fact that as far as pain went, this was only the beginning.

Lingon fell in step on Oralia's left. His curved dagger had been replaced by a longsword and there was now a quiver slung over his shoulder and a compact bow held loosely in his dominant hand. She hadn't realized it before, but he was wearing lightweight chainmail beneath his lavish cloak. Her gaze shifted to Mul, who led the small procession. He was dressed similarly, but with twice the weaponry, including a pair of battle axes strapped to his back.

"That is a lot of weight to carry for an evacuation," she said.

This earned a scoff from Mul. "You think we're going to let you have all the fun?"

Clearly they had differing opinions as to what constituted fun. From Lingon's grim expression, Oralia suspected he had weighed the outcomes and had come to the same grisly conclusion as her. This was not a battle. It was a last stand. A last stand fated to go unrecorded by history, as everyone on their side would likely be dead by nightfall.

CHAPTER THIRTY-SIX

A Complicated Joke

Along, winding staircase led them to the surface. Oralia passed between another pair of massive iron double doors and out into the adjoining courtyard. For a brief moment, she saw nothing but blurred outlines as her vision coped with the dramatic change in lighting. Gradually, the scenery around her shifted into clarity. Behind her, the entrance to the Stoneclaw stronghold was carved into the face of the cliffside. Its front steps overlooked a large, open plateau with neat rows of carefully manicured trees and stacked boulders encompassing the lot, shielding it from the high winds.

Bil Stoneclaw, the eldest brother, stood in full battle dress at the edge of the muddy courtyard, barely visible through the gaggle of soldiers flanking him. A motley crew of mud-covered figures was positioned across from him with the tree line at their backs. While most held their weapons at the ready, the situation appeared to have reached an uncomfortable stalemate.

Snaglebrag stood out front as the group's chosen spokesperson. A role for which he had not volunteered, based on the way Ralizak had one hand firmly clamped to his elbow, anchoring him in place. "Oh, thank the gods." Snag's narrow shoulders drooped when he saw Oralia approach. "I made some very bold threats. None of which we'd be able to back up. I wasn't sure how long I had before they figured out it was all a bluff."

The mountain folk entourage stood to attention as Oralia neared, gripping their weapons in anticipation for a fight. A word in the stolac tongue from Bil dismissed the bunch. Oralia could not help but notice the collected expression of disappointment the warriors shared as they trudged past. Even in the midst of a crisis, their instinct to take down the biggest fighter seemed impossible to ignore. It was a shame they looked to be leaving. Stoneclaw warriors were renowned for their unrivaled savagery on the battlefield. Their participation would have, at the very least, ensured the evacuation party reached the foothills before Rasp finished decimating Oralia's pitiful forces.

"This is them?" Bil said without lifting his calculating gaze from Oralia's small company. "The mighty army the realm sent to overthrow us? Frankly, I'm embarrassed for you."

"There are more here than I expected." Among them, Oralia spied Daana and Faris huddled near the back, trying to draw as little attention as possible. It was a matter of who was missing, however, that gave her cause for concern. She tipped her head in respect to the Stoneclaw brethren. "My warriors and I will hold off Rasp for as long as we can. You had best take your people and leave while you can."

"Me an' Lingon are staying." Mul stepped forward with his barrel chest proudly puffed. "Bil, you lead the others to safety."

"I don't know what in the realm has gotten into you, but that's not what we agreed!"

Bil's protest was cut short by Lingon. "You're outnumbered on this one, Dingle. If someone's got to lead the evacuation, it should be the most capable. Mul and I will make sure you get a decent head start."

"Just to be clear." Mul drove his forefinger into Bil's chest. "This doesn't make you the leader. Not unless we die."

"Which we will," Lingon assured him with a nod of unsettling confidence.

Oralia left them to their farewells. She pressed past toward her ragtag crew. Only three of her four were present and accounted for. Her panicked gaze settled on Rali, silently probing for an alternative explanation. The dwarf's bloodshot eyes filled with tears and she looked away, unable to hold her stare. Before she could ask, Oralia felt a small hand touch her own. Snag stood silent alongside her. A solemn shake of his head was all that was necessary to communicate the worst.

Whatever pain Oralia had felt before was nothing like this. A suffocating pressure ballooned inside her. It pulled tight at her airway and climbed higher, building up behind her eyes until it hurt to keep them open. Speaking had never been so difficult. A thousand rampaging questions caught in her throat but stopped at her tongue. When Oralia found her words again, her whispered voice did not sound like her own. "Was there anyone with him? Tell me he did not go alone."

Snag nodded, grimly. "We saw him through to the end. Said our goodbyes. Yours, too."

No, no, no, no. Not like this. It wasn't supposed to happen this way.

All former sense of duty faded away. Oralia didn't know whether she wanted to run or start smashing things. Instead, she stood locked in place, unable to scream around the suffocating pressure. Swallowing the lump that had formed like a stone in her throat, Oralia pulled Snag into an embrace. He slumped into her, his small shoulders shuddering.

Rali stumbled over next. She wiped a grubby hand under her eyes and threw herself wholeheartedly against them. Ellisar appeared perfectly content to linger on the outskirts, glaring purposefully in the opposite direction. This was remedied by Oralia, who merely reached over and directed Ellisar's reluctant steps into the huddle with an ungentle tug.

"I hate this," the elf said after a moment of strained silence. "And I hate all of you."

"Go walk a plank, Cap'n," Rali sniffed.

"Make me."

"Why can't you go five bloomin' seconds without ruining the moment?"

"I didn't even want to be in your stupid moment."

"Well now you're going to be in it even more!" Rali threw her arms around Ellisar's waist and squeezed. "How's that, huh? Embrace your feelings, Ellisar! Embrace them like you're embracing me!"

Half a minute, Oralia noted, as she yanked the struggling pair apart before one of them lost an eye. A record, really. Her tear-filled gaze moved across the strange assortment of warriors as she pieced together some semblance of a plan. Before her stood three traitors to the empire, two realm soldiers, a cook with allegiances that swung somewhere in between, a swindler, two Stoneclaws, and a witch hunter—it was like the start to a very complicated joke. And, like the inevitable punchline, she did not foresee a promising ending.

Does it even matter? They're all going to end up like Curly anyway.

Seven realms, not now. She couldn't give in to the crushing weight that clung to each bone, threatening to drag her under. Someone needed to lead, gods dammit. And for some reason they were all looking expectantly in her direction. As if she had any idea how to make this better. How to make their deaths mean something.

Oralia snapped her eyes shut, slowly counting down the seconds as she hammered the intrusive thoughts back into submission. "This is not a fight I expect to win," she said, failing to control the waver in her voice. "I will not ask any of you to stay. Those who wish to leave, do so now."

When she opened her eyes again, she was surprised to find all of the same faces staring blankly back at her. No one had taken the opportunity to leave. Idiots. "Sascha"—Oralia refrained from the unhelpful addition of "you damn fool"—"that was your cue to leave. Take Daana, Faris, and the captain's troops and evacuate with the mountain folk."

If only you had thought of involving him before. But you were too stubborn to ask for help. And now Curly's dead because of it. Because of you. The realization struck her low and Oralia felt the pull of the spiral begin to drag her under.

It wasn't fair! It wasn't supposed to have happened this way! She had tried, hadn't she? She'd sent Curly off with the evacuation party. He was supposed to have gotten away. And then he could have ditched the realm and his old way of life and made something of his own. She was the one who was supposed to have died on the mountain, not him!

"Moonflower." The rumbly voice snapped her from her spiraling thoughts. Her gaze lifted to meet Sascha's, realizing she'd failed to notice the monstrous hammer that hung loosely in his hand. A souvenir from their trip to the armory, no doubt. How exactly the mountain folk had gotten the weapon inside was a mystery, as it was far too heavy for a human to drag, much less wield. Sascha had a shield too, one with a dense size and shape more akin to a door than the standard round. "That's thoughtful of you, truly. But I'll be seeing this one through to the end."

A trickle of warmth seeped into the ice that rendered her frozen. The heat did little to disperse the suffocating tightness. It only intermixed, slowly turning the ice in her veins a little less cold. Her lungs were still heavy and weighed twice what they should have, but she found herself able to breathe a little easier. She gawked uselessly at Sascha, unable to look away. Every fiber of her being wanted to be held in his arms and just let go, not caring what happened afterward.

But there wasn't time.

Just like there wasn't time to argue over the fact that the stubborn fool was staying. And perhaps, in some small way, she was relieved. That meant something, didn't it? Maybe she hadn't fucked it up as badly as she thought. Unfortunately, there wasn't time to get to the bottom of that, either.

Oralia turned to the others, sighing, "Do the rest of you feel similarly?"

There was a general murmur of agreement. She expected Captain Monk's soldiers, Zev and Beryl to walk, but they didn't. Perhaps they'd already come to the realization that no one, including the Stoneclaw evacuation party, was getting off the mountain alive. "Very well. Then we must make the most of the limited time we have. Ellisar, go scout the best vantage points for the archers. Mul, take Snaglebrag down to the armory. Show him the wall of powders."

Snag's weary stare lifted to meet her own, entirely too beaten down to muster his usual toothy smile. "Powders?"

Oralia placed her hand on his shoulder, practically engulfing it. "Build whatever depraved devices your heart desires."

"Oh," was all the sad little goblin, a shadow of his former self, could manage.

By some miracle, Mul kept whatever combative reply was curling over his tongue to himself. With a resigned shrug, the burly man started off, beckoning for Snag to keep up or get left behind. Oralia watched the pair disappear between the iron double doors as she issued the last of her commands. "Ralizak, organize the rest and start forming a defense strategy."

"Aye-aye, Cap'n!"

Oralia's weary gaze settled over Faris and Daana, and her tongue failed her. What to do with these two? She could tuck them out of sight until the battle was over, she supposed. That way, there would be someone left to warn the neighboring territories of the impending danger.

"I'll take it from here, old friend." This, strangely, seemed to come from a small rodent perched on Faris's shoulders. The creature scurried down his arm and leapt, shifting forms in a haze of blue smoke as it drifted toward the ground. Whisper landed lightly on their feet before her.

A sudden swell of relief washed over Oralia. Some of it must have leaked through her grim expression, transforming it from somber to hopeful, because Whisper took an immediate step backward, rattling their quills with a venomous hiss. "Don't even think about it. Attempt to embrace me and I'll hex you."

Oralia settled for a faint smile instead. "It is good to see you, Dear Whisper."

"Yes, yes, don't waste my time with heartfelt emotions. We do not have long. I can feel the dark magic drawing nearer." The small, hooded figure limped toward Oralia with a scaled hand pressed to their side. Blood seeped through Whisper's tunic along their ribs, staining their fingers black. Whisper met Oralia's concerned stare with a harsh look of their own, warning her not to ask.

She did so anyway. "Whisper, are you—"

"I said not to waste my time!" Whisper barked orders over their shoulder. "Faun and elfling, to me. We have work to do."

Daana emerged from the back of the gathering. She walked with a noticeable limp, but seemed to have fared the dangers of the mountain better than Faris. He trudged after Daana with his arms wrapped protectively over his chest and head down. He did not appear injured and yet, the spark was gone from his dull eyes. Not hurt, Oralia realized. Dead inside.

Me too, Faris. Me too.

Already, she could feel the creeping sadness crawling its way back up her throat. Oralia shoved it down once more, attempting to keep her head in the game. She could grieve when she was dead. For now, there was work to do. "Whisper, what do you need?"

Whisper's steely gaze swept across the muddied lot. "Something less open. What I am about to attempt has not been done before. It requires absolute concentration." They added, with an air of reluctance to their melodic voice, "I also do not wish for your forces to witness it in the event it fails. It would be very bad for morale."

Oralia caught the flash of dread that darted across Daana's face. Perhaps it would be better if she saved her line of questioning until they were out of hearing. "Lingon?" Oralia called, turning in the direction of the younger Stoneclaw sibling.

Lingon, having already decided Ralizak was beyond his skill level, was currently sizing up Faris with a fixed, calculating expression. He appeared annoyed at having his work disrupted. "I believe you meant, Lingon, *sir?*"

Oralia ignored everything he said. "This stable you spoke of, is it still standing?"

"Are you proposing a roll in the hay, Protector?" Lingon abandoned his efforts and strutted toward them, grinning. His stare settled on Daana and his pearly white smile widened. "The cute one can join too, if she wants."

Daana raised her palm only to have it slapped back down by Whisper. "Let the stupid one die in battle."

Lingon jumped at the sight of Whisper. "What in the realm is that thing?"

"The stables, please," Oralia rumbled.

Lingon led them around the side of the cliff face, muttering something in stolac under his breath. Despite his grumblings, Oralia noticed his pace had doubled. Either he was eager to prove himself helpful or, the more likely scenario, he was eager to rid himself of his present company. He stopped at a pair of wooden doors set within the rock face and kicked them open, throwing his arms wide with a sarcastic flourish. "Your stables, madam."

The smell of musty straw and animal dung filled her nostrils as Oralia inched carefully inside. Like the main stronghold, the stables were carved into the rock. The low ceiling and abundance of wooden beams spanning from top to bottom made it seem less likely to collapse, however. Not the best choice but, given the circumstances, their only one on such short notice. She looked to Whisper for approval. "Private enough for you?"

"It will do."

CHAPTER THIRTY-SEVEN

The Last One

Whisper hobbled past Oralia into the dingy stables and came to a stop near the middle of the straw-littered ground. The fae's tight grimace failed to reveal any of the thoughts flickering behind their silvery eyes as they surveyed the cramped enclosure. The space was small and without windows, rendering the interior both dark and thick with the warm, earthy stench of livestock. There was a feed trough to the left, one for water at the back, a sealed door beside it, and a few half walls erected to the right of the stable that, until very recently, might have served as donkey pens. The rest of the stable was left open, allowing for the smaller animals to wander at will.

There were no animals left now, either having bolted at the first sign of trouble or been taken by the evacuation party. The scattered piles of dung, feathers, and chicken shit were all that remained of the stable's former inhabitants.

"It will do," Whisper repeated once more, sounding as though they were attempting to convince themselves more than anyone else. The fae lifted their scaled forefinger and pointed to the empty pail resting alongside the doorway. "Faun, fetch me a bucket of water."

For several painstaking seconds, Faris stared back at Whisper with an empty expression and dull, lifeless eyes. Oralia had seen the look on many a battle-shocked soldier before, and feared Faris was simply too far gone to respond. She stooped to collect the bucket herself, fingers only inches from the iron handle, when the faun lashed out with his hoof and sent the offending pail sailing across the room. It struck the wall beside the water trough with a wooden *thunk* and then fell to the ground among a bed of matted hay and stray clumps of dung.

Having made his disapproval clear, Faris stomped across the dirty stable floor after it. He filled the empty pail from the water trough and then deposited it at Whisper's feet with a scowl that said: *Order me around again, and next time it'll be you, not the bucket.*

Whatever strife had existed between Faris and Whisper appeared to have doubled in Oralia's absence. For what reason, she decided she did not wish to know, nor get involved. There were far more pressing matters at hand. "Whisper, I assume you have a plan. Whatever it is you intend to do, I would like to hear it now."

"I do, of sorts." Whisper produced a drawstring pouch from their cloak and poured the contents into the water pail. The fae formed their fingers over the mixture into a sign and the water turned to a rapid boil. "The dark entity is powerless without a vessel. The boy may be magical, but—"

"Unbelievable!" Lingon snarled at Oralia from the doorway. "You brought a fucking witch onto our sacred soil?"

A single, withering glare from Whisper was all it took to convince the mountain man to go air his muttered grievances outside. The fae slowly twirled their finger in the air above the pail, churning the boiling mixture without touching it as they picked up where they had left off. "Magical or not, the little bird is still human. In theory, if enough damage is inflicted to his body, he will no longer be able to serve as a host. Thus, rendering the entity defenseless."

Oralia had known it would come to this. That, in order to defeat the dark magic, they would have to kill Rasp. But acknowledging an idea and accepting it as an irrevocable fact were two different beasts. It had been easy to compartmentalize at first. To defeat the evil, she had to kill the evil. Simple. Except it really wasn't, because this was no longer a faceless evil. This was someone she'd come to know and—in a small, practically nonexistent way—respect. Rasp had been a thorn in her side from the beginning, sure. But it was the thorns in life that she often found herself at home with.

Poor Faris. No wonder he looked torn between succumbing to shock and wanting to trample something. None of the legends had mentioned that in order to prevent the end of times, one had to kill their best friend. This knowledge, unfortunately, made Oralia's next words all the more difficult to say. "Whisper, I do not need to tell you how powerful Rasp is. Even with my best at my side, we will not be able to hold him for long."

The contents of Whisper's water bucket turned a brilliant shade of red. Gathering a fistful of loose straw, the fae dipped the ends into the mixture and began painting what looked to be some sort of rune on the compacted dirt floor. "Alone, not a chance. Together, my power paired with your forces"—Whisper imparted a halfhearted shrug—"maybe?"

Ah. So they, too, knew to expect a grisly outcome. She wasn't sure why she felt a sliver of comfort from that. Perhaps the lack of hope made it easier to accept the inevitable. After all, what was the point of avoiding death when the only option left to run was toward it?

Oralia's stare shifted from Whisper's work to Daana, who stood just inside the doorway, looking every ounce like a lost lamb. Coated from head to toe in a mix of mud, bruises, and various plant life, Lady Lazuli was hardly recognizable. "Are you going to tell me what your pet project is doing here?"

Whisper stood back and scrutinized the large, spherical symbol painted across the filth-caked ground. "I believe the elfling has the capability of freeing my magic from the powerstone."

That was it. One neat sentence. No lengthy explanation or details as to what exactly freeing them encompassed. Oralia narrowed her eyes at Whisper in a way that was not so much accusatory as it was morbidly curious. "How long have you had this planned?"

"The battling a dark spirit part was fairly recent, but the rest? Decades."

"If I release you of your debt, you will no longer be beholden to me. To whatever happens next." She wouldn't fault Whisper for turning and fleeing the moment they were no longer bound by a life debt, but she got the sense her dear friend intended to stay. "Unless I am mistaken, you do not have a stake in this fight. Why fight at all?"

"My stake is the same as yours. Survival."

Oralia attempted to piece together what this meant without having to ask it out loud and risk the embarrassment of an obvious answer.

"Not just my survival, old friend," Whisper said, sparing Oralia from having to seek clarification. "That of my people as well. If I wish for my kind to make a comeback, I cannot allow an ancient predator to rise from the dead and strip the world of the magic we require to live."

"You do not want competition, is what you are really saying."

"While that is partially true, I am mostly trying to avoid becoming a food source myself. Fleeing would only delay the inevitable. If there is ever a time to defeat it, that time is now, before the entity is allowed to grow stronger."

Oralia had no response to this. The realization that a powerful magical being might walk away from the fight no matter the outcome tugged at the back of her mind. Surely Whisper was the better option. The fae may have despised mortal-kind, but Whisper didn't want them dead. Maybe both magical creatures would die fighting each other. Perhaps everyone involved would perish and it would be a moot point. At least in death she wouldn't have to feel the weight of her decision slowly mashing her insides to pulp.

"Fine," she said at last.

"Fine," Whisper repeated. The fae clasped their hands behind their back as a familiar, mischievous smile pulled at the corners of their blue mouth. "Now, our circumstances may have changed, but the terms of our contract are still the same. In order for my power to be returned to me, I must be released from my bond with you. Have you conceded your title as Protector of the Realm yet?"

No blasted capes, no parades, no ceremonies that dragged on for half a day. Under different circumstances, Oralia might have enjoyed her retirement ceremony. At that moment, however, the only thing she felt was the hurt tearing her apart from the inside. She swallowed the growing lump in her throat, praying she could keep the grief at bay until the action started. The feelings would be easier to ignore once she was fighting for her life. And afterward, well, it probably wouldn't even be an issue.

At the very least, she could strive to make her resignation as official sounding as possible. "I, Oralia Dawnsight, hereby renounce my duties and title as Protector of the Realm. As such, the requirements for our contract are satisfied. You, D'zeahr Vaspor"—Had she awarded them the nickname Dear Whisper because it sounded like a horrific mispronunciation of their real name? Yes. Was it terribly unclever? Yes. Had it ensured that while she did not use the fae's actual name, she still remembered it after sixty-eight years? Also, yes—"are released of any and all obligations to me."

Oralia reached for the stone around her neck only to remember it was still missing. "Shit."

The quills on Whisper's head lifted into the air with an aggravated rattle. "You've been my stone's keeper without fail for over half a century. And *now* is the time you decide to lose it? When all of mortal-kind is at stake?"

"I did not lose it. It is momentarily misplaced."

"Then hurry up and un-misplace it!" With a violent shake of their head, Whisper turned and motioned for Daana to stop doing her best impersonation of a statue and join them within the rune circle. "Young Lazuli, come, step inside the symbol. I will go over the necessary procedures with you while our valiant leader remembers where she left the one absolutely irreplaceable item our entire plan hinges upon."

Oralia snapped her teeth as she considered where in the name of chaos her necklace could have gone. The amulet had not been among her belongings in the armory, leaving her to conclude that it had found a convenient home elsewhere. Someone's pocket, most likely. Her wrathful stare settled on the now empty doorway. She could smell Lingon lingering just on the other side, far enough away not to be associated with the use of magic, but no doubt close enough to overhear every word.

"Lingon Stoneclaw," she thundered, "where is my necklace?"

"How in the realm would I know?" The man in question came swaggering around the corner, hands stuffed in his pockets as he lifted his upper lip with scorn. "Do I look like a common thief to you? I am a proud mountain folk warrior and heir to the Stoneclaw throne. What use would I have for a stupid trinket?"

"That trinket is worth more than—"

"The necklace is a powerstone," Faris cut in, every word laced with exhaustion. He raised his shaggy head, allowing his empty gaze to move from the ground to the open doorway. Lingon's annoyed expression remained unchanged, prompting Faris to clarify in terms the mountain man would be more inclined to understand. "It holds magic."

"For fuck's sake!" Lingon fought with his hood in order to free himself of the offending object. He hurled the opal at Oralia, snarling, "You really should put a warning on that thing! I'm going to have to scrub my skin to the bone to get the wickedness off."

Faris's ears flickered as something stirred to life inside of him. The faun's mouth drew into a curled snarl as he moved, stiff-legged, in Lingon's direction. A glimmer lit within his dull eyes. Oralia recognized the expression. It was the same look Ellisar wore right before entering a room that, inevitably, would have to be mopped of blood afterward. Usually twice over. "This is on you. You know that, right?" Faris said. "If you'd just accepted him for what he was, none of this would have happened. A little mucking compassion, that's all it would have taken! This isn't just Rasp's fault, it's yours, too!"

Lingon tilted his head, his long hair cascading over his gaunt face. He appeared not afraid, only slightly amused. "What's it to you, goat-man?"

"It didn't have to be like this. If you and your muckin' family had pulled your heads out of your asses, I wouldn't have to be here right now! Nobody would be asking me to kill my best friend!" Faris lowered his horns, as if he were preparing to charge. "Make no mistake, I'm not doing any of this for you. If you and your brothers are still standing by the end of this, I'll finish all of you myself."

"You have said your piece, Faris." Oralia stepped between them, cutting off the faun's advance. "That is enough. Stand down."

Faris might have stopped, but Oralia saw the way his calculating stare studied the surrounding stable, already considering every other alternative route around her. She had size and strength on her side, but he was undeniably faster. Oralia glanced over her shoulder at the scowling human. Lingon stood at deceptive ease, pretending to be oblivious to the danger while his right hand hovered near the hilt of his sword.

"Lingon," Oralia rumbled. "You are needed back with the others. Go. I will rejoin you shortly."

"I'm only doing it because it's my idea." He threw his finger into the air as he turned swiftly on his heel and stomped away, his green-and-gold cloak fluttering dramatically in his wake. "Not because you're telling me to!"

Oralia drew the wooden doors shut behind him as her stiff shoulders fell forward with exhaustion. She didn't know what she was supposed to say. Faris deserved something, at the very least. She turned to him and said, "Faris, I—"

"It's not fair," he blurted out as moisture collected along the edges of his red-rimmed eyes. "He's been screwed over by anyone he's ever cared about. The people who were supposed to protect him, didn't. And now . . . now I get to be the last one." Faris's arms slumped to his sides as tears trickled down his cheeks. "My voice is going to be the last thing he hears, telling him that everything's going to be okay. That if he just lets go, we can make it all better again. And even though he's the most scared he's ever been, he'll stop and wait for me to set things right. And he'll keep waiting. Not realizing that his body's gone cold and that the one person he trusted did him in far worse than any of the others."

The invisible walls within her mind gave way as the crush of pain surged up and over the sides, flooding her head with every thought Oralia wanted so desperately to keep under lock and key. The shock nearly took her out at the knees. *Your voice should have been the last thing Curly heard. You should have been there when his body went cold, but you couldn't even manage that. He died without ever knowing what he meant to you!*

She couldn't hold it back anymore. Years of pent emotions rose up and rebelled against her. Grief slammed into her all at once, crippling her from the inside. Oralia managed a single step forward, barely able to speak around the swelling in her throat. "I know, Faris. And I am sorry for it."

"A lot of mucking good that does, doesn't it? I'm sorry, too. But it doesn't change anything. I still have to kill him, Oralia!"

First Curly and now Rasp. No matter what you do, they drop like flies around you. She placed her hand on Faris's shoulder and uttered the only words that were immediately available to her. "I know."

"I don't want to kill him."

When, deep down, you know it should have been you. Oralia blinked, heavily, fighting tears of her own. "I know."

Faris wiped a grubby hand under his eye, sniffing. "You're really terrible at this."

The reflexive "I know" caught in Oralia's throat and went unsaid, silenced by the sudden shriek that filled the stable, amplifying in intensity as it bounced off the bare stone walls.

Daana's hand shot to either side of her forehead as she doubled over, dropping to her knees in the middle of the rune circle. "Ah!" she gasped, digging her fingertips into her temples to alleviate whatever invisible pain was coursing through her skull. "No, no, not again. It's back! Get down!"

Oralia's glare jumped to Whisper, wondering if this was their doing somehow. Her answer came a split second later when, from the depths below, the mountain roared to life. The thunderous creak and groan jolted upward, drowning out Daana's scream with a deafening rattle. Thick sheets of dust and debris shook loose from the rock walls and clouded the interior in a fine layer of red-brown sediment. Oralia watched the ceiling with her breath drawn, waiting for the shake to subside, hoping the ancient wooden beams would hold against the onslaught. Gradually, the tremble died away, leaving a stable full of dust in its wake.

"Muck," Faris said softly, eyes darting back and forth as he unwrapped his arms from his head. "That felt like the worst one yet."

"Young Lazuli?" Whisper placed their hand tentatively on Daana's shoulder.

The elf lifted her head, filthy hair plastered across her sweat-soaked brow as her wide-eyed stare darted in the direction of the doorway. Her voice was small, barely a whimper. ". . . He's here."

A thunderous blast erupted from the outside, filling the room with a deafening roar, as something struck the surrounding cliffside. Shockwaves from the impact rippled through the mountain's core. The ground lurched violently beneath Oralia's feet, throwing her sideways as the walls shuddered in protest. She staggered several steps, managing to keep her balance and not tumble haphazardly across the ground.

One side of the double doors opened and shut with a slam behind her. Turning, Oralia discovered Lingon had darted back inside the stables to escape whatever in chaos was taking place outside. The small man stood with his shoulder pressed against the aged wood, using the door to prop his body upright as his scrawny chest puffed in and out, struggling to catch his breath.

Lingon's eyes were wide and filled with fear. His startled gaze navigated the musty stables without rhyme or reason, never settling on any one thing long enough to hold his attention. His mouth opened and closed like a fish, but no words slid forth, as if he was having trouble coming to terms with what he'd just witnessed.

"Lingon?" Oralia prompted.

He flinched, snapping out of his stupor, suddenly aware the entire room was staring expectantly at him, awaiting an explanation. "... So, uh," Lingon started, tongue unconsciously darting from his mouth to lick his trembling lips, "interesting turn of events."

"He has arrived sooner than expected," Oralia said. "We have gathered as much."

"Well, yes, he has arrived. Stuck at the lower barricade at the moment, but it won't hold long. That's for certain," Lingon managed between ragged gulps of air. "And my gods, he's got it out for your lot. That first blast nearly took the top of the mountain off! Witches, I'll tell you, if I had a chicken for every—"

"Lingon! Your point, please."

Lingon's thin lips parted in an uneasy smile. "Whoever that is out there, he's not my brother."

CHAPTER THIRTY-EIGHT

A Familiar Silence

The scent of spruce and wet soil danced on the breeze. Outside, paper birch and poplars shuddered in the wind, their spindly branches rattling like a symphony of dry bones. Rasp was curled on the damp cavern floor with his knees pulled to his chest. He was still wet. Still miserable. But a little less so than before.

He longed to smile, to laugh, to taunt the darkness that despite everything it threw at him—the fear, the fury, the recurrent nightmares that played out each and every time he closed his eyes—it had failed to break him. He held strong against its influence and awoke in the same musty cavern as before, still clinging to his sanity, uncorrupted by the spirit's promise of power. But no smile pulled across his trembling lips. Rasp's strength was gone, sapped away by the wet clothes clinging to his shivering flesh.

A suffocating weight hung heavy in his chest. The heaviness reminded him that, for all of the recent trials and tribulations he'd overcome, there was one final monster left to confront. He'd kept the truth tucked away in the dark recesses of his mind, content to continue living a lie for as long as he could, but all that had done was allow it to rot and fester. There would be no moving forward, not until he faced what he had done. Unfortunately, knowing what he had to do didn't make it any easier.

"I know you're there," Rasp said, not bothering to lift his head from his arms. "You've been following me since Lonebrook. Do you plan to stay silent forever?"

He heard the faint ruffle of feathers, but nothing more.

"Withholding. Classic you." Gritting his teeth, Rasp heaved himself into a slumped sitting position. He considered returning the silent treatment, but the hurt that ravaged his insides was still raw and aching. As with a festering wound, the only way to rid his body of the pain would be to cut the cyst open and allow the infection to drain. "Why? Why do you suddenly give a shit now? You never cared before."

Still nothing.

Rasp had held off the dark entity. Wasn't that enough? Had he not finally proved he'd changed? That he was capable of being good? What more could anyone possibly want? "If you're expecting an apology, then it's only fair that I get one, too. It wasn't easy for me either, you know. You kept pushing, pushing, pushing. You never listened! I had no one after Mother died. I needed you and you abandoned me!"

The rhythmic *drip-drip-drip* of water beading from the ceiling echoed from the back of the cavern. Outside, the wind whistled against the cliffside. Rasp's soul longed to be out there. To shake off this damned chill and bask naked in the warm sunshine, away from this stupid cave. Away from the stupid raven and its stupid silent disapproval that hung thick in the air like smoke from a green wood fire. The weight in his heart, alas, was as heavy as his numb, unmoving legs. There would be no running. Not this time.

"The only time you ever spoke was to tell me how terrible I was. How I wasn't living up to expectations. Nothing I did ever made you happy. Is it any wonder I stopped trying?" The old poison that pooled in his gut, left to fester and rot, stirred to life. It churned and boiled, clawing upward. Rasp felt the heat spread to his chest. His neck was tight and his throat was inexplicably raw. "For the gods' sakes, quit with the silent judgment already! I'm sorry, alright?" The poison spewed over the top of his tongue. It flooded his mouth with the burning taste of stomach acid. "You had as much part in this as I did!"

For some incomprehensible reason, it was at that moment, on the verge of losing control once more, that Whisper's advice slunk from the folds of Rasp's memory: *Fear and anger make you vulnerable, little bird. That's how the darkness found you. So long as you allow your emotions to control you, so too, can the dark.*

The heat swelling inside of him subsided. Rasp's chest still ached, but it was a different sensation. Cold. Empty. A void that even pain couldn't fill. Rasp's trembling lips parted and the words flowed free on their own accord, unobstructed by the fury that had held them back for so long. "You and I never got along. I—I don't know what I was thinking that day. But with Mom gone, I had no one to confide in. I thought that maybe you of all people, my own damn father, could possibly understand what I was going through."

It had been an exceptionally warm day. Rasp had climbed to the base of the falls to speak to his father alone, away from the watchful eyes of the clan. He remembered the rushing water and the deceitful way the current moved—swiftly, quietly, strong enough to pull even the best swimmer under. He remembered the cool spray of the falls as it rolled over him in great misting clouds. And how the sunlight shimmered across the bubbling surface of the deep, churning pools. His father had been in unusually good spirits that afternoon. Paler's even-temperedness had given Rasp the courage necessary to speak. Hopeful that today of all days, his father would be in the mood to listen.

"I waited until you landed that big fish, knowing it'd tire you out. And then I waited some more, because if there was anything you and I were ever good at, it was fighting about everything but the real issue. Addressing that would have meant acknowledging that I was different from you. That your son, your own blood, born of a mighty Stoneclaw leader, was everything you feared most. I don't blame you for hating me, because I hated me, too. But my magic wasn't the reason I was there that day. I was changing. Things I couldn't explain were starting to happen and you were supposed to be the person I could confide in."

The change had been innocuous to begin with. So what if a few of his hairs had changed color? Perhaps he was going gray. It wasn't unheard of. At least he wasn't balding like his brother Bil. Rasp did everything in his power to hide it. He cut his hair short and rubbed dye into his scalp at night, hopeful that by rejecting the change, it would choose another. It did not. By the summer's end, his hair—not gray, not white—was the same striking silver color as his father's. Fate, Rasp feared, had marked him the next leader of the Stoneclaw clan.

"You lost your shit when I told you," Rasp sighed, closing his eyes and hugging his arms tighter to his chest. "You accused me of using witchcraft. That I'd somehow discovered a way to usurp my brothers and claim the throne for myself, completely negating the fact that I didn't want any of it to begin with! I tried to tell you as much, but you didn't listen. Which shouldn't have been a surprise because you *never* listened."

Rasp had seen his father fly into a rage countless times before, but never like that. As an obedient son, Rasp was expected to bend to his father's will. But Paler's accusations had lit a fire in Rasp's soul that would not be stifled. And so, instead of backing down, he screamed back. His father had not taken the affront to his authority lightly. With water splashing underfoot, Paler had charged, spewing horrible, hateful poison. His father's first swing missed, but the second landed. Rasp retaliated with a fury of flying fists, and the two rose and fell over each other in the shallows of the pool.

Around them, the wind had picked up, chopping the surface of the normally calm waters. It wasn't until the sky had grown noticeably darker that Rasp bothered to look up. Thick, black thunderheads hung low over them. Rasp had been so fixated on the growing storm he'd forgotten to keep his guard up. His father's fist slammed into his jaw and dropped him.

He remembered slipping beneath the surface. There had been a sudden tightness in his chest and his skin felt like it was on fire. It was at that moment he heard the entity's voice for the first time. That damn, soft, soothing whisper in his ear. It promised to make it all go away. Rasp didn't remember agreeing to anything, but all went strangely calm after that. Through the murky water, as Rasp slowly slipped into the darkness, a strobe of blinding light erupted across the top of the churning pool.

"I'm sorry." Rasp's chin sank against his chest. "I didn't mean for it to happen. I didn't. I swear."

A pair of trappers had been the first to stumble onto the scene. They found Rasp sprawled across the bank, barely conscious. Paler was half-submerged in the shallows next to him. When his body was pulled onto the shore beside Rasp, it was black and blue with a strange, branching pattern that weaved across his chest. Rasp didn't miss the suspicious glances the pair cast his way. Had he had a better grasp of his faculties, he would have cut and run right then.

Rasp's brothers were brought to the falls, and it wasn't long before the accusations started. He denied any wrongdoing. It was the lightning that had taken their father's life, not him. Surely they weren't accusing him of being able to control the weather! And then one of them said it. The word he hated so passionately—*witch*. The more they used it the angrier he got, until he screamed so loudly the surrounding trees began to splinter and crack. There wasn't any use fighting the allegations after that. For the second time that day, Rasp found himself fighting for his life.

"You know what hurt the most?" Rasp said as tears slipped down his clammy face. "After everything that happened between us, all the pain and grief and suffering, I thought this was the way it was supposed to be. That family was something meant to be hated. And then I woke up in a house that wasn't my own, with people who had every right to despise me, and they didn't. For six months, I listened to a father treat his son like an equal, and not something to be ground under his heel. The parents actually spoke to each other. Spoke, not screamed. And then they did the unthinkable. They treated me the same.

"I didn't have a name for what I was feeling. It was so completely foreign that I lashed out. For months, my blood seethed under my skin because I couldn't make sense of what was happening to me. But they didn't push me away or shut me down. They were patient and kind and gave me the space to figure it out on my own. Eventually, I realized whatever that feeling was, I liked it. But accepting that hurt, too. Because it meant acknowledging it was something I'd been missing all along. I used to lie awake at night and think: Why couldn't my family have been like this? What was so wrong about me that my father couldn't love me? Had his father not loved him, either?"

There was a flutter of wings as Rasp felt sharp talons grip his pantleg for balance. The lump in Rasp's throat grew painfully tight. "I'm sorry that no one ever accepted you for what you were, Dad. That no one ever told you it was okay to be different. And that you had to live your entire life hiding it, thinking you were cursed. You were surrounded by a wife, children, a whole village of people, and not a single one of them actually knew you. I can't imagine how lonely that must have been."

The raven shifted its feet nervously over Rasp's knee with a soft croak.

Whisper suggested that Rasp had inherited his magic from his mother, Tal. Rasp had never considered where he'd gotten his magic before. He'd assumed it was simply a thing that happened at random. A punishment from fate, as it were. But the more he considered it, the more he realized the truth went deeper. Maybe, just maybe, it was the reason his father tried so hard to push him in the opposite direction. Perhaps the Stoneclaw curse was not the passing down of magic from one generation to another, but the ingrained hatred and self-loathing that accompanied it.

"I don't expect you to forgive me for what I did. But I'm trying to change, I really am. It's just so fucking hard."

Father hopped from his knee to Rasp's shoulder and burrowed his feathered head against Rasp's jaw, uttering soft, melodic sounds. Rasp's throat pulled tight again. Fat, salty tears slipped from under his eyes and collected on the tip of his chin unabated. Rasp had waited all of his life for this moment. He'd expected to feel triumphant, or validated, or, at the very least, a little less like a flaming pile of shit. But the emptiness that had taken up residence in the center of his chest still hung heavy.

Reconciliation did not spell redemption, not from everything Rasp had done that terrible day. He may have had Father's forgiveness, but that wouldn't matter if the darkness wreaked havoc upon the land unchallenged. The darkness he, and he alone, had unwittingly unleashed. "Dad?" Rasp ruffled the top of the raven's feathery head as he steadied his shaky breath. "I think I have to do something stupid."

Croak?

"Flee?" Rasp repeated, confused by Father's suggestion. If anything, fleeing would have been the *smart* option. "No! No more running."

Father begged to differ.

"You're not being helpful right now." As much as Rasp wanted to leave the ridge behind forever, forsaking the will of fate and the miserable part in which he was intended to play, doing so would be fulfilling the very prophecy he'd spent his life fighting. "Look, accident or not, I'm the one who awoke the spirit in the first place. I think that means I have to be the one to make it go away, too."

Father was, understandably, less enthusiastic about this revelation. He did not mince his words, filling the cavern with the echo of his protesting croaks.

"I know I can't see!" Setting aside the sting of Father's harsh words, Rasp conceded that the blasted raven had a point. Even with Father's guidance, he wouldn't be able to reach the village in time. They needed an additional pair of hands to guide him, else by the time the pair fumbled their way to the peak, there wouldn't be anyone left to save. "I think we might need some outside help."

With a shrill screech, Father took swiftly to the air and exited the cavern in a flutter of fast-beating wings.

"That wasn't an invitation for you to leave!" Rasp stood on trembling legs, managed one step, and collapsed back into the ankle-deep water. How exactly was he supposed to defeat a powerful spirit when he didn't even have full control of his own limbs? "Fine, I guess I'll just stay here then!"

CHAPTER THIRTY-NINE

Into the Mountain

Staying put, as it turned out, proved unbearable. Not just because it was boring, but because staying in the water would spell certain death in a matter of hours. Soaked to the bone and shivering, Rasp dragged his soggy ass toward the mouth of the cavern. His numb fingers bore deep into the wet silt, scraping along the bottom for a hold, before using his dwindling strength to haul his body forward through the wet muck. His feet helped the best they could, but they'd be lucky to get a participation trophy at this point.

"Great talk, Dad," Rasp muttered as he struggled along, ignoring the stench of mud and filth-riddled water that inched its way up his nose. The taste was substantially worse—like copper coins fished from the gutter. This probably should have been his cue to stop talking, but he had years of pent-up anger to work through in a very limited timeframe. "You ignore me for years and then, after we finally start to reconcile, you up and abandon me! Again!"

Granted, the raven had promised to come back, but Rasp wasn't assigning any merit to his father's words. They had a mountain of issues to overcome before they could start breaking ground on the "trust" bridge.

If only Mom was here.

The thought struck like a boot to the face. Rasp's crawl slowed to a stop. The cold mud pulled at his numb hands as the sounds of his panting breath echoed around him. Mother. She wouldn't be able to help him. Not this time. Not ever again. While the easiest thing would've been to let the growing weight in his chest take over, that didn't feel right either. She'd helped him get this far. It only seemed fair to make her sacrifice mean something.

I'm sorry, Mother. I'm going to try to make this right.

He'd die trying. Hands down. No questions asked. But perhaps in death they'd find each other again. And, after all the heartfelt declarations were said, Rasp could rub it in Mother's face that he tried and *still* failed. Also, he'd like to see anyone else do any better! After all, he'd single-handedly held off the spirit of the mountain! Who else could claim to have done as much? No one, that's who! And then he'd add that there wasn't any point in her arguing because he was already dead and she'd just have to deal with it.

Oh, how that would set her off. A faint smile pulled at the corner of Rasp's mouth as he envisioned all of the inventive ways Mother would rip him a new one. Knowing her, she'd tell Rasp to undead himself, march right back up to the spirit, and demand a rematch. "And don't bother dragging your sorry corpse back here until you get it right!" she'd say.

Their ensuing, entirely imaginary, argument gave him the motivation he needed to keep going. The sad part was that Rasp was losing. To himself! Or a figment of himself that had been shaped by his mother. He didn't want to delve too deep into the complexities of it. How could he when he had an imaginary argument to lose?

By the time Rasp dragged his uncooperative body to the mouth of the cavern, he could hear Father's harsh calls ring out in the distance. The obnoxious croaking grew louder as the raven drew closer—much like the irritated voice accompanying him. "Alright, alright! I'm coming!" a familiar voice shouted. "This had better be worth it, Chicken Liver. Just because I'm a vegetarian doesn't mean I won't make an exception for you."

Rasp raised his head from the cradle of his arms as the telltale sounds of someone clomping through the wet brush grew louder. Although he recognized the voice, the fact that the nearing footsteps were being produced by hooves was what ultimately confirmed his suspicions. "Hermit?" Rasp called out weakly. "Is that you?"

"Stop calling me that!" Briony's hoof struck the ground. Her warning was accentuated by an irritated snort, although there wasn't as much gusto to it as usual.

"And it's actually you, right?"

"Do you ever ask questions that make sense?" Briony's hooves click-clacked against the stone as she neared. The subtle notes of lilac and rose-water greeted Rasp as she bent over, hooked her hands under his arms and heaved him, wet and dripping, from the flooded cavern floor. "Of course it's me. Who else would it be?"

The terrain shifted below him. Rasp's useless legs went from being dragged over soupy, silt-and-muck-covered stone to being dragged over the firmer, less soggy ground that stretched outside the mouth of the cavern. He tried to assist Briony the best he could, but all that really amounted to was not resisting as she heaved his deadweight along. She dragged him beyond the cave, all the way out into the sun, cursing with each burdensome step, before finding a suitable rock to prop him up against.

Rasp slumped against the slab with a grateful sigh, breathing far too hard to express his gratitude properly. The stone at his back was warm from the sun. Its heat seeped through his sinew and bone, spreading like a slow-moving fire as it sparked some of the life back into his unruly limbs. Whatever this magic was, he needed more. Without thinking, Rasp slithered up and across the stone slab, spreading across its flat surface like a lizard in the sun, willing his numb flesh to leach its warmth.

With the heat of the rock below and the heavenly kiss of sunshine beating down on his unprotected face from above, the jammed cogs within Rasp's mind started to slowly pick up speed again. He didn't have much time, and there was a lot to catch Briony up on, but it seemed prudent to first double-check that the person he was speaking to really was who she claimed to be. "One last time, just for clarity's sake," Rasp said, flipping over so he could warm his front without having to shield his aching eyes from the sun. "You're the real Briony Blackwater and not some spirit masquerading as her in order to trick me, yes?"

"Oh you poor thing." Briony wrangled the wet cloak from his back and set about wringing it dry. Rasp could hear the gush of water as it splattered against the ground with each strained twist. "You hit your head too hard, didn't you?"

"What? No!" Unnecessary insults aside, her response did help assure him that this was indeed the real Briony. Not even the disembodied spirit of an ancient evil could match the faun's sugary-sweet rudeness. "I'll have you know the spirit disguised itself as Faris once already. I'm just making sure it's actually you, is all."

The spirit had been damn near convincing, too. If it weren't for a few discrepancies in vocabulary, Rasp would have been fooled. Briony felt real, however. And while the dark entity seemed capable of altering its voice, he doubted it would be able to mimic a person's smell. Or the way they manhandled him with ungentle care. Or said mean things to him.

Briony's warm breath puffed against his neck as she knelt down beside his basking rock. The irritation from her voice was gone in an instant, replaced with grave concern instead. "The spirit did *what?*"

"Disguised itself as Faris?" Rasp shifted positions, turning his head in order to speak to Briony face-to-face. The effort exhausted him. He rested his cheek against the rough stone and closed his eyes as he recalled the finer details of his encounter with the dark entity. "Said some very hurtful things, too. Almost had me."

Rasp expected her to call him crazy, to insist that he was out of his mind and suffering from the aftereffects of being in the water too long. In a way, he sort of hoped she would. It would be somewhat of a relief to learn all of this was nothing more than a figment of his own demented imagination. Alas, it was not so. Briony's strong hands scooped him up from under his arms with fresh vigor and started to pull, seemingly uncaring of the fact that he hadn't regained the strength necessary to stand, let alone walk.

"Alright, that's it. We're getting you out of here. Come on, up, up, up. Let's go."

Rasp dug his fingertips into the rough stone, clinging to it for all he was worth. His attempt was pathetic at best, and the lovely warmth of his sunning rock slipped from his grasp all the same. "Briony, no! I can't leave."

"Yes, you can. I'll drag you the whole way if I have to."

Rasp didn't have the energy to spare, not with what was to come, but he'd fight her if he had to. Somewhat ironic now, considering only a day or two ago he'd practically jumped at her idea to whisk him off of the mountain.

"Let go!" Rasp wriggled out of her grasp and dropped back down into the dirt with an undignified hiss. He saw her blurry shape lurch in his direction and scuttled backward until his shoulders struck stone. "I'm serious! I can't go. I have to stay and make things right again."

His pathetic attempts must have struck a chord because she gave up trying to nab him. Briony then did the unthinkable—she stepped back and attempted to win him over with reason instead. "If what you're saying is true, then you can't stay here. You are the biggest source of magic on this mountain. Just because you held it off once doesn't mean it won't be back. We have to get you out of here, now."

"It already found someone else."

The resolve in Briony's voice dissipated like a candle in a downpour. "It did?"

"I can feel it. The magic's changed."

"Are you sure?"

"Briony, the last thing you are is an idiot. Do you really think my people would have settled on a mountain that moves this much? Yes, I'm sure." Rasp added, with a shudder, "This whole place feels like it's going to come down any minute now."

"All the more reason to get out of here, right? If the mountain's due to come down, what good is it to stay?" Briony was practically pleading with him now. As if, with just the right combination of words, Rasp would see reason and ditch his suicidal plan. "Wanting to live isn't cowardly, you know."

"No," Rasp said. "No more running. I'm the one who woke the spirit from its slumber in the first place. Even if I don't stand a chance against it, I have to at least try. I need help, though." He reached out with his hand, hopeful she wouldn't take it as an opportunity to drag him by it again. "Can you get me to the village?"

Although Rasp couldn't make out much more than her hazy outline, he was certain he saw her shoulders slump in defeat. "I don't know the way."

Croak!

Rasp flinched, realizing he'd forgotten Father was present. In Rasp's defense, he was used to the raven watching from afar, content to be of no help whatsoever.

Father descended from wherever he'd been perching nearby and landed between them, jabbering at a volume that was difficult to decipher.

"Is that why the magic brought me here?" Rasp said, wiggling the tip of a finger into his left ear to alleviate some of the obnoxious ringing. "You know, that would have been helpful to know earlier. You really need to work on your communication skills."

Croak!

"Fine! *We* need to work on our communication skills. Happy?" Batting the chattering raven back, Rasp gathered his trembling legs beneath him and stood. The heat from the sun had wormed deep into his flesh, reviving his muscles enough to be able to manage slow, agonizing steps. Exhaustion still weighed on him like an invisible anchor, but maybe if he didn't think about it and just kept moving, he could fool his legs into carrying him all the way to the village.

Rasp stumbled forward, one hand stretched out in front of him as Father's feathery shape hopped along in front of him, marking the way with sounds. With both his mind and extremities working somewhat functionally again, Rasp supposed it was time to check if that *other thing* had returned as well. He flexed his fingers and then formed a fist, summoning his magic.

Nothing happened.

Damn, he thought, deciding it was best not to let the others in on the fact that his only means of defense was still taking a nap. Intentional or not, the flood had overextended his magic. He didn't know when it would return.

Nor did he have time to sit around and wait. Wringing the soreness from his wrist, Rasp hugged the wall as he inched his way back into the dark, gaping mouth of the cave. Behind him, he felt the warm kiss of the sunshine fade from his shoulders for what he assumed would be the last time.

"So"—Briony trailed behind him with slow, reluctant steps—"I realize you and Chicken Liver must have had a moment of clarity there regarding the whole 'I don't know the way' thing. But, as someone who cannot understand birds, do you think you could expand on that for me? Primarily why we're venturing back into the creepy cave, for example?"

Oh, right. Rasp supposed the person whom he'd roped into serving as his unofficial escort deserved to know what was taking place. A part of him could not help but wonder if it would be the final nail in his proverbial coffin. Briony hadn't agreed to help, and just because she was still hanging around didn't mean she intended to stay. Rasp sincerely hoped his next words would not give her the push she needed to turn tail and run.

"Father says this isn't a cave, it's an emergency tunnel. If we follow it, we should find a hidden stairway that connects to the main stronghold."

"Can't help but notice your generous use of 'we' here, boy."

"To be honest, I don't know what I could say to convince you, Briony. You don't seem like the type to give a shit about the fate of the world." Rasp reached the entrance to the cave and sought the wall, easing one foot down into the cold water from whence he came. He looked over his shoulder in her direction, having nothing but a halfhearted smile to offer. "No offense."

"Plenty taken," she assured him with a resounding ear flick. "I suppose that makes two of us, doesn't it?"

"That's good, right?" Rasp extended his hand in her direction one last time. "That means they'll never see us coming."

Briony stood at the mouth of the cave, her squat form backlit by the sunlight spilling in from the outside. Her only response was an irritated snort.

"Please help me?"

Briony considered his offer for a few agonizing seconds before she slapped his outstretched hand aside and stomped past, splashing her way deeper into the dark cavern. "I have two questions," she said, her voice echoing along the cavernous rock. "First off, you've been letting us call your father Chicken Liver this whole time and never thought to say anything? Seems a bit childish. And secondly, your plan is to travel inside the mountain? The one that's been shaking on and off for the past hour like it's going to come down on top of us? Do I have that right?"

Father landed on Rasp's shoulder and shifted his weight between his clawed feet until he found a more stable perch. Rasp fought to keep his expression straight. Of course he'd allowed his father to be referred to by such a demeaning name. He hadn't had a reason to care before. In fact, he still found it humorous. With Father resting so dangerously close to his ear, Rasp decided it would be best to keep this bit of information to himself.

He used the wall as a guide as he followed the angry splash of Briony's steps. "Travel through the crumbling mountain, check!"

"As opposed to going—oh, I don't know—a way that's not going to result in our grisly deaths?"

"Oh no, our deaths will be grisly regardless of the path we choose. It just happens that this way might be the quickest." Rasp was grateful when Briony didn't ask him to clarify if he meant the quickest way to the village or the quickest way to die, because the answer was undeniably both.

"Alright," Briony conceded in a voice that implied she was convincing herself more than she was him. "If I'm going to get us through the mountain, then I'm going to do it my way. This is not going to be a scenic stroll. We're hoofing it. Understood?"

He felt like kissing her, a reaction that probably would make her turn tail and run. In lieu of inappropriate gestures of affection, Rasp settled for a wan smile. "I'm going to regret asking for your help, aren't I?"

"Oh, yes. I'll make sure of it, if it's the last thing I do."

CHAPTER FORTY

That Thing

Rasp and Briony stood at the bottom of the hidden stairway with dirty water lapping at their ankles. Deep, endless dark stretched before them. In that moment, Rasp felt like a mouse about to scurry from the safety of its hole, knowing there was a cat lingering somewhere nearby. To be clear, he didn't want to do this. The entire mission thus far had amounted to little more than a series of decisions made for him. The few choices Rasp could claim as his own had been born from sheer desperation. This decision was unlike those because, for possibly the first time, he had other options.

Desirable options, in fact. Ones that wouldn't kill him. He could simply walk away and no one would stop him. No, it was worse than that. He had a guide willing to *help* him walk away. It seemed unnatural to sprint toward the danger, willingly, when the alternative required nothing. No effort. No blood. No sacrifice.

Briony's whispered voice broke the looming silence. "Before we rush headlong into the mountain without a hope or a plan, do you have anything to light the way? As the eyes of this suicide mission, mine don't work so well in the dark."

Croak!

"Oh, well that's helpful," Rasp said. "Father says there's a stash of torches hidden here somewhere."

Under his father's direction, Rasp searched along the wall with his hands. His fingertips found a break in the rock face and ventured inside, feverishly hoping it was a torch he was grasping and not a mountain viper. Fortunately, the object didn't sink its fangs into him when Rasp pulled it free from the crevice with an ungentle tug. "You don't happen to have any matches stashed somewhere around here too, Dad, do you?"

For all of his father's faults, he had been a prepared man. Under Paler Stoneclaw's unwavering leadership, the mountain folk clan had thrived. Paler kept the border patrols on a tight schedule, ensuring their pesky neighbors never ventured any further into the Iron Ridge than the foothills. He stored food and firewood for winter, and was the first to volunteer for a friendly territory raid anytime his people's resources threatened to run out. All of this to say, Rasp was utterly shocked by the raven's reply that, no, he had not housed any matches in the damn cave. Any Stoneclaw worth their salt should have been able to make fire from the resources around them, Father insisted. Adding, with a disgusted shake of his feathery head, how quickly it had taken for "this generation" to go soft.

"You stored torches, but not matches?" Rasp said, realizing yet again how preparedness was not always indicative of intelligence.

Croak!

"It's an emergency tunnel. Sort of defeats the purpose, does it not?"

"Alright lovebirds, give it a rest." Briony promptly relieved Rasp of the torch gripped in his hand. "I'll take that, thank you. Even without matches, it seems unwise to let the unstable fire elemental hold the torch."

A few scrapes of Briony's flint later, and there was a crackling flicker of light. The warm yellow-orange glow pushed the prevailing darkness to the far corners of Rasp's muddled vision. He locked his arm through Briony's and pressed close as they started up the stone stairway together. He blinked, trying to ignore the way the harsh smoke from the torch made his eyes water. "You're doing that thing again, Briony."

"What thing?"

"That thing where you let on that you know way more about me than you should," Rasp explained. "How you just called me a fire elemental, for instance."

"Did I?"

An *unstable* fire elemental, to be precise. But, for the sake of his shriveled ego, Rasp decided he'd let that particular detail slide. "You haven't seen me use fire."

"Chalk it up to a lucky guess then, shall we?"

Rasp's reply turned to ash on his tongue as Briony lurched forward without warning, pulling with the full force of a mule team. He bit back his surprise and forced his legs into an awkward jaunt. The bottom tread of his boots barely scraped against the stone steps before pushing off, often skipping two and three at a time to the next. His strength was returning to him. Rasp's feet no longer felt like useless weights. They had graduated to heavy weights. More helpful than before, but still rather unwieldy.

Father did not appreciate the rough jostling and took wing ahead of them. He greeted them at the top of the first stairwell with a cackling *croak, croak, croak!*

Rasp tugged on Briony's arm. "When we reach the fork in the passage, he says to go right."

The faun merely grunted as she banked right, lugging Rasp with her as if he was nothing more than an inconvenient piece of luggage.

The long stretch of carved passageway reverberated their footsteps until distance swallowed them completely. Rasp had always hated that about the cave system—no matter how much ruckus he made, it'd never kept the silence of the void at bay for long. It consumed all: sound, warmth, light. And, soon, himself as well. Icy tendrils of dread crept across his mind, blanketing his thoughts in the realization that this was no longer his childhood home but a tomb.

"So, Briony." Now seemed like an excellent opportunity to strike up a friendly conversation with his guide. If he was lucky, maybe it would devolve into a spat and divert his attention from the existential dread that hung thick over his head. "I'm a reasonable man. I'm willing to overlook the fact that Faris violated the rules of best-friendship and told you more about me than he should have."

"Here we go," Briony groaned.

"You obviously know more about me than I know about you. Therefore, in the spirit of fairness, I think it's time we corrected the imbalance of information. Starting with, who the fuck are you? And don't bother with the herbalist cover story, that ship has sailed."

"I *am* an herbalist."

"Mhm. An herbalist who has extensive knowledge of all things magical, routinely threatens to remove her patient's body parts when annoyed, and only ever came to town in the dead of night to meet with Faris in the old barn out back. Nothing remotely suspicious about that."

Briony, too, seemed grateful for the distraction. Rasp could tell by the way her melodic voice sounded even more irritated than usual. "Does it really matter right now?"

"It's only fair. Faris told you all of my secrets."

"You can't call your magic a secret when you keep showing everyone!"

A small rumble tore through the rock. Bits of loose stone rattled free from the ceiling and pitter-pattered against Rasp's head and shoulders.

Instinctively, Briony quickened her already breakneck pace. Rasp willed his legs to match her momentum. His limbs grudgingly obeyed. Not because they had a choice in the matter, but because Briony pulled at that speed regardless and he either kept pace or got dragged helplessly in her wake.

The heart of the mountain trembled around them with a low, deafening rumble. It lasted only a few seconds more before it died down and the eerie silence returned. The prospect of being crushed to death seemed to have taken its toll on Briony as it was she, not Rasp, who broke their lapse in conversation. "I suppose it doesn't matter," she sighed. "Seeing as we're not long for this world anyway."

"That's the spirit!"

"If you absolutely must know, I'm a smuggler."

The quake had kicked up a cloud of chalky dust, which made talking slightly more difficult than it already was. Rasp scraped his tongue against the roof of his mouth, attempting to wipe away the gritty film that caused every word to taste like iron and dirt. "Now that you mention it, I do recall something about you mapping a route through the ridge. Whatever you smuggle, it must be worth a lot of money to go through all this trouble."

"People, Rasp. I smuggle people."

On second thought, perhaps enlisting Briony's help had been shortsighted of him. Rasp's mind ran through several possibilities, each darker than the last, before he gave up trying to decipher the meaning behind her words and simply asked. "You don't mean like slaves, do you?"

"No! Gods, I'm not that terrible of a person. I meant witches." There was another hesitant pause before Briony offered her explanation in less cryptic terms. "I help move the magically-inclined through the Mossborn territory and get them to my contact in Adderwood. From there, they're smuggled out of the realm. I use my training as an herbalist as a cover. It's not uncommon to get stopped by soldiers along the way and it's a lot more believable if they think I'm out in the woods gathering herbs or traveling to the next village over for a client."

"Oh thank gods." In the wake of his relief, Rasp's hazy mind gave up questioning Briony's ethics and set about wading through the deluge of provided information instead. Some rarely used portion of his brain arranged each new detail into place until the chaotic swirl resembled several lines of solid reasoning. Sadly, the thought that shot out of his slack mouth was not any of the intelligent ones. "Wait, does Faris know he's engaged to a criminal smuggler?"

Briony's arm went rigid against him. "You really are oblivious, aren't you? Faris and I aren't romantically involved."

Rasp lost his footing and nearly tripped. He caught himself against the wall, inadvertently yanking Briony to a halt beside him. "Then why all the one-on-one meetings? And flowers? And the way he always protected you? How do you explain that?"

"Because I'm his boss!"

Still didn't explain the flowers. "Partner, Briony. Most people in relationships refer to themselves as partners."

"I know this is your way of admitting you're wrong without admitting you're wrong." Briony yanked his unwilling body back into motion. The click-clack of her cloven hooves bounced along the stone passage ahead of them until those, too, were swallowed by the all-consuming void. "But it still makes me want to kick you."

Perhaps it was time to stop talking and listen. Which probably had more to do with the fact that Rasp barely had enough breath to keep moving and couldn't afford to waste it on speaking. Luckily for him, Briony was just angry enough to spill more without being prompted.

She rattled off an explanation as she adjusted their pace from a crawl to a jog, "If you absolutely must know, my relationship with Faris was just a cover. Pretending we were seeing each other made our dealings easier to overlook. Running an underground operation doesn't come cheap, after all. I've got to cover food, lodgings, and the occasional bribe. The Belfasts help out any way they can, but it's never enough. To make up for the losses, I've been bringing back contraband and letting Faris handle the distribution side of things. He's got a talent for it. His mother and father don't approve, but they can't exactly turn me in without incriminating themselves."

"I'm supposed to believe Faris's parents knew about all this?" No way. No fucking way! Faris, a criminal? Absolutely. That checked out. One hundred percent, no questions asked. But Rasp refused to believe that Trant and Novera Belfast had been in on it, too. They were practically saints! Always going on about the merits of pacifism, and overcoming one's past for a better future, and if he could please put his pants back on, as apparently their household was a civilized one. For the gods' sakes, they barely tolerated cursing! Rasp couldn't imagine Trant and Novera Belfast turning a blind eye to an illegal smuggling operation when the mere act of calling their son "a pasty-livered little fuck" required a fainting couch.

"Knew about it? Dear boy, they *started* it. The smuggling witches part, anyway." Briony paused, out of kindness, probably. As if she was giving him a moment to come to terms with the fact that everything Rasp knew had just been flipped on its head. There wasn't enough time left in the world to manage that successfully, however. And, after several excruciating seconds of silence, Briony carried on. "Trant and Novera lost two daughters to the massacre in Sunstorn. They vowed to do what they could to keep it from happening to others. They've been using Lonebrook as a secret outpost for the resistance ever since."

A croak from Father warned that it was time to give up the lovely, flat terrain in exchange for yet another set of spiraling stairs. The cramped stairwell twisted upward, trapping the smoke of Briony's torch until Rasp was certain his airways had caught flame. Up ahead, he could just hear the feathery snap of Father's wings as he led the way.

"You're still with me, right?" Briony gave Rasp's arm an ungentle shake.

"Yeah."

"Just checking. You're being less combative than I expected."

"I'd be more combative if I could breathe," Rasp assured her as he sucked a mouthful of dingy air into his scorched lungs.

At the very least, the inability to speak allowed him time to think. A nagging thought untangled itself from the back of his mind and slid to the forefront of Rasp's consciousness, offering up a long-forgotten memory. He recalled his final weeks in Lonebrook with the Belfasts. More specifically, how a key member of the family had gone missing the exact moment the realm arrived. Novera's strange disappearance had always irked him, but he'd never fully grasped why.

The pieces were beginning to shift into place, but the puzzle still wasn't clear enough to make out. Rasp tried harder, focusing on the clues he did know. Faris had claimed his mother was a teacher of some sort. Rasp had heard her refer to her students a number of times, but he'd never actually encountered any of them. Her classes were always held out in the woods, surrounded by nature, away from—

Oh dear gods. Rasp couldn't help but scream the answer aloud as the light finally dawned within his dim thoughts. "Novera was a witch!"

Briony sounded awfully smug for someone who was about to die. "Finally figured it out, did you?"

How had he missed that? *How?* Had he really been so swept up in his own self-misery that he didn't notice he'd been sharing a household with another witch for half a year? Gods dammit. Certainly explained why devious little Faris knew so much about fucking magic. "Did Novera know what I was?"

"Obviously."

"Well why didn't she say anything?" Having someone he actually liked guide him through the clusterfuck of wielding unimaginable power would have been so much more helpful.

"Because, even now, you still can't say the word without flinching."

"Can too."

"Then say it, Rasp. Admit to what you are."

"I'm . . . awesome."

"Exactly," Briony grumbled. "Novera couldn't say anything because you weren't ready. She tried to get you to come around without having to spell it out. Your head is as thick as a rock, though. You never quite got it and she had the sense not to push."

"So she knew full well what I was and *still* handed me over to the realm?" Rasp tried to ignore the twinge of hurt that ignited within his rapidly beating chest. But the pain was contagious. It spread to the rest of his aching limbs until his entire body yearned to curl into a ball and let the worst happen. He couldn't give up, though. Because he was a good person, and apparently good people weren't ruled purely by their ego. Idiots. And now he, Rasp Stoneclaw, the former Iron Devil and scourge of the mountain folk, listed among their ranks, making him the biggest idiot of all.

Gods, staying a selfish asshole would have been so much easier.

"Actually," Briony said, "Novera wanted me to smuggle you across the border to the resistance. Thought she could strike a trade with their side. In exchange for protection and teaching you how to use your magic, you could help them map a path through the ridge safely."

That sounded horrible. Slightly less terrible than his present situation, but horrible nonetheless. "And what prevented that from happening?"

"Trant. He was more practical. He argued that if they offered you to the realm instead, they would carve out the passage through the Iron Ridge for us."

The hurt felt less twinge-y and more akin to a full kick in the teeth now. Rasp recalled the dark spirit's words, and how it'd claimed that Trant knew what Rasp was and wanted him dead for it. Manipulation or not, he couldn't help but wonder how much of that had been accurate. Trant obviously hadn't felt any remorse about selling him out to the realm. If Rasp had been wrong about Trant, did that mean he'd been wrong about Faris too? Did his supposed best friend use him just like everyone else?

What does it matter? You're dead anyway.

Still, it would have been nice to have been liked by *someone* before he sacrificed himself for the greater good. "So this whole time they were just using me? A convenient means to an end?"

"At the beginning, maybe. But then you got your claws into them and they realized there was an actual person under all your issues. It was too late to call it off by that point. The realm was already on their way. So they did the next best thing they could think of, and made sure Faris went with you."

"Pretty sure I was the one who bargained for Faris to come."

"Of course you did, sweetie." Briony offered him a patronizing pat on the arm as she pulled him along beside her. "I'm sure nobody spent weeks beforehand subtly feeding you that idea until you believed it to be your own."

"You're very mean. Now I'm glad Faris isn't marrying you."

"What can I say? Nice people don't last in my line of work."

For the sake of the argument, Rasp pretended to entertain the idea. Even though it was obviously wrong and nobody could have possibly been that many steps ahead. "Why was sending Faris the next best thing?"

"For protection, mostly. He was supposed to try and keep your magic a secret." Bathed in the warm, red-orange glow provided by the torch, Rasp was almost certain he could see Briony shaking her head. "Poor, Faris. I'm afraid the odds were stacked against him on that one."

If that was supposed to make Rasp feel better, it didn't. "That's it?"

"I wish. Gods, he never shut up about you. Always Rasp this and Rasp that. The two of you were starting to sound like an old married couple." And, as annoying people were wont to do, Briony answered Rasp's question with one of her own. "Faris never told you the plan for after the realm reinstated you into power?"

Rasp realized he'd never bothered to ask. After all, he hadn't intended on ever getting that far. He was supposed to have thwarted the realm, gotten away, and Faris would have returned home no worse for the wear. Rasp had simply assumed that Faris's plan had been the same. It was undeniably brilliant, after all. There simply hadn't been a need for a backup plan.

His lack of a response only fueled Briony's annoyingness. "What's that? You never asked?" She feigned surprise. "I guess Faris isn't the only bad friend."

"Okay, so maybe I could have been a little bit more attentive. I'm sorry. But please, enlighten me. What was Faris planning to do once he reached the mountain?"

"Well, for starters, he knew your grand escape was going to fail. He had some contingency plan for when things settled down. Something about you and him and—oh, I don't know—escaping, using you to create unimaginable wealth, wreaking havoc across the land? It's all a bit fuzzy, to be honest."

Amid the swirl of questions spinning within his head, a single thought rang louder than the others: *Does this mean he didn't actually hate me?*

Rasp dared not state this aloud. Instead, he settled for a belligerent, "Seriously, Briony? That's all you're going to say?"

She was back to smiling now, like the cat that'd finally eaten the canary and blamed it on the dog. Rasp could practically feel the smugness in her tone as her voice echoed along the cavernous mountain passage. "I guess you're just going to have to ask him yourself."

"I'm never going to see him again!"

"Not with that attitude you're not. But, and hear me out here, maybe you could try accepting what you are and using that inner power of yours to get us through? Hmmm?"

Rasp rolled his head back with a low groan. "Ugh."

"Or don't. And just die a needless death, never knowing if your best friend was actually your best friend or not."

"Oh my gods, fine!" On some invisible cue, as if his power had merely gone dormant, waiting for a moment of resigned acceptance, additional strength returned to his legs. Rasp's feet didn't feel as heavy now, and even his breathing had eased to a comfortable level. Gods, maybe there was something to this self-acceptance crap. Not that he would be caught dead admitting it.

A fresh sense of determination flooded his weary bones as Rasp's pace quickened. "I'll accept being a you-know-what if it means I get to rub it in Faris's face at the end of this."

"I do hope you're talking about your magic."

"Briony, there is a time and place for dick jokes!" Which was anytime, anyplace, as far as Rasp was concerned. He was simply mad that he hadn't thought of it first. With the faint buzz of magic returning to his fingertips, and his soul a little less weighted than it had been before, Rasp raced deeper into the rumbling mountain. The yellow-orange glow of Briony's torch bathed the walls in pale, flickering light as he sprinted a little bit more eagerly toward what would surely be his doom.

CHAPTER FORTY-ONE

Focus

ocus. Daana let out a slow breath as she concentrated on the instructions given to her by Whisper. *Move the power within the stone back to its owner. That's all you have to do. Easy-peasy.*

Except it wasn't easy-peasy because it was taking nearly all of her dwindling concentration to stay on task. Leaving an even smaller portion of concentration left over with which to complete said task. Daana screwed her eyes shut, repeating the instructions within her head lest she forget what she was doing. *Move the power within the stone back to its owner. Move the power within the stone back to its owner . . .*

Warm magic prickled across her skin, prompting Daana to ease one eye tentatively open. The opal hanging from the chain around her neck now glowed. Shimmering glimmers of light radiated from the stone and danced across the grime-covered walls in a cascade of shifting blue shapes. The glow grew brighter as magic spread from the powerstone and poured through her until the very molars within her mouth pulsed with its energy. The sensation was unpleasant, though not painful, like biting into a hot turnover and discovering a chunk of uncooked potato.

Daana's stomach didn't merely growl, it roared. Gods what she would give for a chunk of potato right now. She couldn't recall the last time she'd eaten. Escaping death on an empty stomach was making it difficult to do anything right now. And yet, here she was, attempting to prevent the end of civilization without food to fuel her dwindling resources, or a sip of water to wash away the taste of blood and soil from her mouth, or—

Not now! Daana's thoughts snapped her from the visions of hot potato turnovers smothered in gravy. *Stop complaining! We can eat after we're done. Focus!*

How she was expected to do that when there was so much activity going on was beyond her. Her surroundings, the small animal stable, had grown more crowded. Noisier, too. Which certainly said something about Lieutenant Ralizak's character, as she was the only new addition. Having just arrived from the lower barricade, Rali brought news confirming that the person wreaking havoc on the mountain was, in fact, not Rasp. In true Rali fashion, however, she was not giving up any of the details without an award-winning, melodramatic performance.

"And then he did this thing with his hands and black clouds shot up at us and—" the dwarf stood at the entrance between Faris and Oralia, regaling the account with an abundance of animated hand gestures and sound effects. Lingon, refusing to partake in "blasphemous magicry," lounged just outside the open doorway, puffing on a pipe. His smoke drifted in on the breeze and filled the stable with its thick, fetid smell.

"You already said that!" Faris was trying, unsuccessfully, to draw the more important details out of Rali. "Who, Rali? Who did the spirit use as a host?"

"I was building to that! Gods, Faris, where is your sense of dramatic timing?"

"Ralizak!" Oralia snapped, teeth snapping against one another in exasperation. "So help me, I will promote Ellisar over you this instant."

"Nice try. You're not the protector anymore. You don't have that kind of power."

Oralia's dark, slate-colored eyes narrowed. "I will promote her to best friend."

"You wouldn't dare." The dwarf's mouth dropped open in disbelief. Regardless of the validity of the threat, she hastened her story along nonetheless. "It's Monk, alright? I hope you're happy. There's no point in continuing my dramatic retelling now that you've gone and ruined the punchline."

Oralia did not appear to care. She whirled around, knuckles dug so deep into her temples they would surely leave indents. "Whisper, how is this possible? I thought the spirit only worked if it found a magical vessel. It was the entire reason I opted to move Rasp and Daana off of the mountain ahead of the traveling party."

"Well, that and to take the girl hostage," Rali added. She caught Daana's sideways glance and heaved her shoulders into a shrug. "What? This is how you win wars! Be grateful she wanted you alive. I argued for the alternative."

Deal with it later. For now, focus. Daana shut her eyes and took another calming breath. She drew herself inward until the only sound she heard was the slow beat of her own heart. *Focus.*

"You were correct in doing so, old friend." Whisper's singsong voice pulsed in time with the magic pumping through Daana's veins. Like a beacon of light, it broke her concentration and pulled her back onto the outside. "Unfortunately, it appears they were not the only magically-inclined beings in the travel party."

For fuck's sake! Daana's brow pressed firmly together as she plugged her fingertips into her ears in an attempt to tune out the surrounding conversation. *Focus, focus, focus.*

"Are you telling me Captain Monk is a witch?" Oralia's voice was now directed at her. "Daana, did you know this?"

"No, I didn't!" Daana's eyes snapped open at the accusation. Knowing would require having been involved in the Division of Divination's plans. The *real* plans. As she now understood it, Daana's position had been the equivalent of a pawn. No, less than that. She was the equivalent of a pawn captured two moves into the game without strategic reason. "I didn't know about Captain Monk. Just like I didn't know about Whisper or Rasp. At this point, I think it's safe to assume I know nothing. Including how in the seven realms I'm supposed to be channeling the power in this stone back to the witch it belongs to with all of you standing around distracting me!"

All eyes were on her now, including Lingon, who poked his head around the door to see the reason for the sudden commotion. Daana, mildly aware that the stone hanging from around her neck was pulsing blue, clenched her hands and said through gritted teeth, "I would appreciate it if all of you took this conversation elsewhere. I cannot be expected to help prevent the impending annihilation if I cannot concentrate!"

Whisper was seated cross-legged in the circle with her. With a look that might have been concern, the ghost placed its scaled hand over her own. Their words were directed at Oralia. "Monk is not a witch, old friend. And the young Lazuli is not to blame. I, myself, did not realize what the captain was. Not until it was too late. Without magic to betray him, no one here had any way of knowing he was a seeker."

So much for taking the conversation elsewhere. Despite her perfectly reasonable outburst, Oralia and Whisper seemed content to continue talking over her. Great. Just great. Daana absolutely *loved* it when no one took her needs into consideration.

Across from her, Oralia shook her head in disbelief. "Whisper, you were masquerading as a member of the magic council. How could you not have known?"

"Because I wasn't meant to. No one was. Someone worked very diligently to keep the captain's records confidential. I suspect those responsible plucked him from the order and planted him in the military many years ago. He rose steadily through the ranks without garnering attention, waiting for the day his training would prove useful." Whisper pushed to their feet and grimaced. The fresh bandages wrapped around their ribs were already beginning to seep black with blood. Whisper paused, their expression curled in thought, as they turned back to Daana quizzically. "You had a name for this type of seeker, young Lazuli. What was it again?"

"A shadowman." She'd been right about one thing, apparently. Daana may not have gotten the identity of said shadowman correct, but the Division of Divination *had* sent one. It was some small consolation knowing that she wasn't the only one fooled by Captain Monk's feigned incompetence.

"Not that I don't find all of this blasphemy absolutely riveting," Lingon said, blowing a puff of foul-smelling smoke in their direction. "But it appears the lower barricade has been breached."

"He's already made it through the razor wire? Snag was supposed to signal!" Rali stomped past him in order to get a better look.

"I mean, the treetops are on fire. I don't know what constitutes a signal to you realm folk, but I thought it got the point across well enough."

Rali lingered in the doorway with her hand resting on the hilt of her shortsword. "Well, that's us then. You ready, boss?"

"Not boss." Oralia stepped out between the double doors past her. "As you so kindly reminded me, I am no longer your commanding officer. If you insist on calling me something other than my name, however, I do like the sound of 'friend.'"

"D'aw, look at you, gettin' all sentimental on me. Should we hold hands and skip our way onto the battlefield, *friend?*" Rali pulled the doors halfway shut behind her, offering Whisper a pleading look. "Don't take too long with the whole magic stuff, alright? We're already one short out there and I'm not as spry as I used to be. Plus, if Snag kills Monk with his contraption, none of us are ever going to hear the end of it."

Whisper offered a solemn nod in response.

The dwarf's stare transferred to Daana. "Lady Lazuli, you were a horrible hostage. And I take back what I said about offing you. You're alright in my book. Which, by the way, if you end up writing one, do try to play up my bits, will you? Brilliant, charming, better than Ellisar in every way, etcetera?"

A final farewell, Daana realized. A heaviness churned within Daana as she realized this was the second goodbye she had given that day. It didn't hurt as badly as the first, but perhaps that was simply because the painful part hadn't happened yet. "Of course, Lieutenant."

"Faris, it was an honor. And you can keep the damn jacket. Even though sacrificing my ass technically puts you in my debt." Rali drummed her fingertips against the aged wood, choosing her next words with some difficulty. "If you find bucko when all of this is over, smack him upside the head for me, yeah?"

"Yeah."

"Tell him I'm proud of him and that he's not as fucked up as he thinks he is." The doors sealed shut with a soft shudder. "And in case you ever find a nice gent who treats you what you're worth, Quartz works as a boy's or girl's name. Just sayin'!"

A flush of pink crept over Faris's nose as he cleared his throat and stared up at the ceiling, avoiding Daana's impolite stare.

Rali's booming voice grew softer in the distance. "Benton Oralia Quartz Snaglebrag Farrow! Rolls right off the tongue, don't you think?"

CHAPTER FORTY-TWO

Rage

Oralia, Rali, and Lingon were gone, on their way to intercept Captain Monk and do whatever in the gods' name they intended to do—it probably would have helped had Daana been able to fully comprehend Oralia's battle strategy. Impaired by exhaustion and the parasitical drain of brain fog, Daana considered it some small miracle she'd managed to retain the portion of the plan that involved her. This, of course, was probably because it amounted to little more than "move magic from here to here." Unfortunately, she wasn't following through on her part so well. Her concentration was spent, unable to stay on task as her listless gaze wandered the dingy stable at will.

Faris stood slumped against the heavy wooden doors. Exhaustion had taken its toll on his normally fixed expression because, for possibly the first time, Daana realized she could read his face. Among the expected mix of dread and terror, she saw what might have been the tiniest ounce of relief. The fact that he was no longer being asked to kill his best friend seemed to have rekindled some of the light in his pale eyes.

"Young Lazuli?"

Daana flinched at the voice, remembering once more that she was supposed to be doing something.

Whisper limped into the center of the circle and knelt in front of her. For several uncomfortable seconds, the fae stared at her without speaking. Whisper's silvery eyes were old and tired. Amid the weariness, Daana recognized a familiar sharpness. The sting of loss pulled at her heart once more as she realized why. She wanted to look away as the hurt grew heavier, but the familiarity pulled her in, reminding her of the old friend whom she would never see again.

Had Whisper always been Willem? Was this person the same one who welcomed her into their library and provided a small shelter from the cruelty of the outside world? If so, had that merely been a part of the ruse? Kindness as a means to manipulate her? Kindness or not, she was really getting sick of everyone just using her to get what they wanted. At this point, she'd jump to help the next person who flat-out stated what they intended to use her for. At least that way she wouldn't have to constantly question where she stood.

"No wonder you cannot focus. Your thoughts are moving so rapidly, it's giving me a headache."

Whisper's words yanked Daana from the brink of an internal spiral. Even now, the fae's soft voice still caught her by surprise. How such a pleasant, lulling sound could come from such an unnerving-looking being was jarring. Daana's heartbeat thumped loudly in her chest as fresh heat rushed to her ear tips. She bit back her lashing response in favor of something less insolent. "It's rude to read my thoughts without asking. Those are private."

And now, once more, you sound like a child. Bravo, Daana. Bravo. Should have gone with the nasty remark and been done with it.

"I did not find it all that nasty," Whisper assured her.

And they're hearing all of this. Fuck.

And that.

Fuck.

Whisper gathered Daana's hands into their own and squeezed, drawing her attention. "You want to ask about Willem."

Is that what she wanted? To be honest, she couldn't seem to hold onto a single thought thanks to the sudden stream of mental diarrhea clogging the inner workings of her mind.

"Begin and I will tell you."

That seemed like the opposite of focusing, but at this point anything would have been better than what she was currently doing. Daana took another deep breath, held it, and exhaled slowly. Once more, the opal hanging from the chain around her neck flared a brilliant sapphire blue. The magic burned like wildfire as it pooled in her chest. Its heat traveled the inner pathway of her veins and spread to her extremities.

"I did not invent Willem Foss," Whisper began. "He was a real person. An aspiring apprentice with the Division of Divination at the time, in fact. I encountered him in Adderwood after laying waste to the party of seekers sent to capture me. Willem, like you, had started to realize that the division's mission was not what it seemed. He did not wish to pursue a career ripping witches from their families in the name of the realm."

Whisper's words didn't sap her concentration. They slipped over the surface of her mind like a leaf moving along the top of a smooth flowing current. As Whisper talked, the magic from the stone seeped down Daana's forearms and gathered in her fingertips. Her bones ached and her muscles twitched and seized under the strain, but she held fast, listening to the soothing words that whispered inside her throbbing skull.

"I needed a way to infiltrate the division, and Willem wanted a different life. So we made a trade. His identity for a new start. I spent many months in Adderwood with the lad, learning to replicate his likeness. Shapeshifting is like anything else, it takes practice and patience. Smaller bodies are easier to replicate. No one notices if your mouse isn't quite right. But get a detail wrong on a person, and suddenly the entire realm knows."

Daana heard her own voice say, "He's still alive?"

"The real Willem Foss is living his best life somewhere outside of the territories, free of the Division of Divination."

Somehow that helped lift the weight in her chest. She hadn't known the real Willem, but the fact that he had gotten out made her feel better. At least someone had.

The pain in her fingertips was searing. Daana eased one eye open and saw that her hands pulsed with the same blue light of the opal. She had reached the final step of the process. The one, consequently, that was the biggest pain in the ass. Well, not necessarily in that region exactly, but "pain in the hands" simply didn't have the same ring to it.

Daana channeled her full concentration into her hands. The blistering, biting heat built until her burning fingertips began to spasm beyond her control. *Not yet,* she commanded herself. She clamped her teeth together until the familiar metallic taste of iron pooled across her tongue. *Not yet. Not yet. Not yet.*

Whisper's scaled hands felt cool against her own. Daana's flesh sizzled and popped, sparking blue with the surge of magic that pulled at her like an unruly dog on a leash. It wanted her to let go. To be set free. To return to its rightful owner and restore the balance. A few seconds more. That was all that was needed. The powerstone had to be completely empty, or Whisper would still be tied to it and, consequently, whoever held it.

That person could be you.

The unexpected thought caused Daana to falter. Her hands sputtered and the magic began to creep back up her arms.

Whisper's gaze lifted until they were eye-to-eye. "That is a dangerous thought, young Lazuli."

Daana's breaths slowed as the edge of her surroundings melded into a muddled blur. Power, real power. All her life she had been powerless. Desperate to be a somebody, something more than just another useless seeker, she'd found a way to harness the magic of others. She toiled for years, perfecting her craft in secret. She'd kept her abilities hidden until the right time, knowing she would get only one chance to impress the council. And she did. She, Daana Lazuli, was the first magic-sensitive person ever accepted into the division's magical program.

And still, the witches turned their noses up at her.

They thought themselves better than her. Her entire career, Daana had faced rejection and ridicule at the hands of those born with natural talent. But she could show them. All of them. She had the means now. The magic coursing through her veins was more powerful than that of her tormentors combined. She could take the stone and return to Sunstorn and bring the Division of Divination to its knees.

The division had used her like a hapless pawn at their disposal. As had Uncle Geralt. And Whisper. Pay—she could make them all pay for their misdeeds. For the years of mistreatment and lies. For treating her like a nothing. A nobody. For casting her out into the wilderness to die. Still clasping Whisper's hands, the magic began to pull in the opposite direction.

Whisper's melodic voice wavered as they struggled against her grip. "Daana Lazuli, release me!"

A name held power. Spoken on the tongue of a powerful witch, a single order could stop the bearer's heart. But a name was a fickle thing. In order for the spell to work, the name had to belong to you. Ellisar's voice broke through the torrent raging behind Daana's eyes. *You're not even Lazuli blood.*

There was terror in Whisper's wide eyes as realization swept over them. "Faun!"

The rune circle flared to life around them in a ring of dancing blue flames, preventing Faris from intervening. *Not even a Lazuli. Just one more thing you've been lied to about for your entire life.*

"Child, please. I feel the anger that rages within you. This is not the way."

Rage? Whisper knew nothing of rage. Daana had been overlooked for too long. Even the dark entity that was ravaging the mountainside had passed her up for the likes of Captain Monk. But, finally, for the first time, Daana saw an alternative path. All she had to do was siphon the rest of the ghost's power. With the drain already in motion, Whisper would be too weak to stop her. Armed with their magic, Daana could defeat the dark entity herself and take care of anyone who dared stand in her way. Maybe while she was at it, she would drain the entity, too. And then all the powers of the realm combined would be helpless against her.

Amid her overlapping thoughts all screaming over one another to be heard, the voice of her sixth sense rippled across her mind. *Don't give in. This isn't you. You aren't a witch.*

But she could be. She could be the best there ever was. The power to unlock her potential was at her fingertips. All she had to do was reach out and take it.

Daana lurched forward and tightened her grasp with all the strength in her hands. Cold scales writhed against her fingers, but she held strong. Magic arced between them in a spray of sapphire sparks. The surrounding ring flared higher until blue flames lapped at the ceiling like tongues of fire.

CHAPTER FORTY-THREE

What Would Rasp Do?

The lower barricade had fallen. It hadn't been much, a series of ancient stone blockades fitted with sharpened sticks, intended to hinder any would-be intruders from reaching the Stoneclaw stronghold in a timely manner. Snag had added a few finishing touches to the existing structure as well, including unspooling his collection of razor wire and dousing the wooden stakes in oil. Judging from dark plumes of smoke rising up from below, Oralia's soldiers had lit the barricade aflame moments before abandoning it and fleeing to higher ground.

Snag and the realm soldier, Zev, sprinted past the line of trees and through the slippery puddles that had rendered the dirt courtyard to sludge. Unlike the human soldier, who ran with his back straight and head bent to the wind, Snag had dropped to all fours and zigzagged at an impossible speed across the sparse landscape. A rolling swell of churning darkness spilled into the courtyard behind them. Its tendrils reached out like snaking vines of billowing smoke, consuming all in its path.

The telltale shape of a man materialized from the edge of the rolling darkness.

Oralia's hand cut through the air above her head. On her signal, arrows from three different vantage points rained down on Captain Monk. A surging black cloud erupted from the captain's hazy body, scattering the oncoming projectiles like matchsticks in the wind.

"Dammit." The very top of Rali's head peeked over the stone wall that encircled the lot. She and Oralia were crouched together, utilizing the upper barricade as cover. "I was really hoping that would work and we could avoid the whole fight to the death thing."

Oralia watched, flinching as one of the scattered arrows caught Zev in the leg. He slowed but didn't stop, dragging his injured limb behind him as he limped through the treacherous mud. The lump in her gut grew heavier. Oralia searched the surrounding haze, realizing she'd lost sight of Snaglebrag. Around them, black coils of roiling magic coated the plateau in a heavy blanket of fog. Despite the pale gray sky above, the cliffside had grown as dark as a moonless night.

Ralizak gestured wildly with her hands. "I mean, it's a little cliché, isn't it? Why can't we have a battle that's easy for once? We've been doing this for years, you'd think we'd be a lot better at it by now!"

Captain Monk moved toward Zev with unnatural calmness. Wisps of dark magic wafted from his body as smoke from flame. Through the shifting darkness, a third shape appeared. Mul moved with a grace uncanny for his bulky size. He sprang from the darkness, both battle axes swinging, and landed a decent blow before he was thrown back in a swell of crackling magic. Mul's strike would have dropped an ordinary human. Captain Monk lurched, gripping his arm, but did not fall. The magic pouring from his body wrapped tighter around him like a funeral shroud.

"Well that's disheartening," Rali said.

"He was supposed to wait for the signal!" The ground forces were not to move in until after Snag and Zev lured Captain Monk into the awaiting trap. Stifling a roar, Oralia leapt over the wall and charged. She raised her fist and signaled for the archers to release at will. Arrows zipped overhead and disappeared into the shifting dark.

Behind her, Rali clambered over the stone fortification and dropped unceremoniously to the ground with a squelchy *splat*. Unbothered by the undignified landing, Rali picked herself up and raced to catch Oralia. "So, uh," she managed between puffs of ragged breath, "your plan is to join Mul then, is that it? Couldn't we just wait for the captain to kill him and then resume the original strategy?"

Oralia's vision adjusted to the murkiness. Ahead of them, Mul was back on his feet and testing Captain Monk's defenses. Despite the Stoneclaw's tenacity, a wave of dark power swept him back every time he broke through the captain's magical barrier. With Captain Monk focused on ending his bothersome opponent, Zev started to rise. Beryl darted in from the side and quickened his escape. The pair of soldiers disappeared into the haze unnoticed by their former captain.

"Our bait is gone," Oralia grunted. "We will have to make do ourselves."

"Right," Rali said with a sharp nod of her head. "Why us, though? Isn't that what we have underlings for?"

The wet ground squished and squelched beneath her feet. Oralia frowned at her lieutenant. *Former* lieutenant. Gods, this was going to take some getting used to. "Have I ever let someone else do my work for me? I see no reason to start now."

She could have run the military from behind a desk at Sunstorn, like the other figureheads did. But Oralia preferred to be in the midst of it. If she didn't experience it firsthand, then how was she supposed to have any idea what was truly going on? Perhaps she'd been doing it wrong all these years, after all. Oh well. If anything, she could at least end her career on a consistent note.

"Additionally," Oralia began, taking in a fast gulp of air as she and Rali sprinted through the mazework of shifting darkness. While she'd expected the vaporous shadow to be difficult to navigate, she hadn't anticipated it to be on account of the smell. The stench was rancid—as if someone had mixed rotten egg with fermented garbage juice and left the unholy concoction to fester in the full heat of a summer day. It stung the insides of her nostrils and mouth as she ran. Talking only made it worse but, alas, was necessary if she intended to sway Rali into reconsidering joining her as bait. "I did not ask you to come with me. You could have stayed behind the wall."

"Well, excuse me for not realizing that was an option!"

A surge of putrid magic rolled across the plateau in front of them. In its wake, the slick ground broke into great shards of splintered rock. With a deafening crack, a chasm split open paces from their fast-moving feet. Oralia seized Rali by the back of her chainmail and leapt sideways. They hit the ground with a wet splatter and slid safely away from the gaping rock ledge.

Rali rolled over onto her back and stared at the churning sky, panting. "Well, charging the magical person head-on was a well thought out plan. What else you got?"

"Still working on that, thank you."

Oralia crawled behind a pile of broken rubble and peeked her head around it in order to get their bearings. They were ten yards out from Monk now. The captain had his back to them. He was too preoccupied with keeping Mul pinned down against the cliffside to notice their position. Dark clouds of magic swirled around the captain in great plumes of shifting smoke. The mountain trembled beneath him, dislodging loose sheets of stone that tumbled downward in an unholy rain of deadly debris.

"The magic is acting as a barrier," Oralia spoke her thoughts out loud, as if this would somehow make them clearer. If nothing else, at least it helped distract her from the film that made the inside of her mouth taste like warm sewage. "The moment we lose the element of surprise, he will throw us back out of range."

Rali slid forward on her belly until she was alongside Oralia. "So if we can't hit him with long range weapons, and hand-to-hand is suddenly out of the question, how the fuck are we supposed to kill him?"

Skill and strength were useless if you couldn't get close enough to your opponent to land a deadly blow. Drawing Captain Monk away, Oralia realized, was going to take a skillset she'd never used before—taunting. She'd seen Rasp utilize this tactic more times than she cared to remember. He used it to his advantage well, too. By tormenting his attacker, the boy would simultaneously work them into a rage while luring them into doing exactly what he wanted them to.

For the first time in her life, Oralia had the misfortune of considering: *What would Rasp do?*

"Whisper was going to use Faris to draw Rasp out, remember? Meaning that the spirit may not have full control. The vessel's personality is still in there somewhere. We are going to have to do the same for Captain Monk."

"Oh, I get it. We lure it out with the vessel's weakness. Great thinking. I'll go get Daana."

Oralia caught Rali's shoulder, fixing her in place. "Captain Monk craved power over others. Particularly those he felt were beneath him."

"To be fair, I was always beneath him. I just didn't treat him like it." Rali's thick eyebrows lowered as her expression soured. "Which, come to think, is probably why you're lumping me in the same category as you."

"We will have to split up for this to work." Oralia's gaze shifted to the loose pile of rubble collected at their feet. She selected a fist-sized stone and rolled it between her palms, testing its weight in her hands. "I will strike first, drawing him away from Mul and toward the stronghold. If I get pinned down, I will need you to move him along."

"Me?"

"Since when have you ever turned down the chance to torment an authority figure?"

"I mean, there's a first time for everything, isn't there?"

Oralia gazed deep into her friend's brown eyes. A pang of regret blossomed within her chest as she realized whatever words she said next would likely be their last. Might as well make it fucking count. "I understand." A fleeting smile pulled at her lips. "Say no more, my friend. I will ask Ellisar instead."

"Like fuck you will!" Rali snapped a rock from the ground and shook it at her. "For the record, I still think we should tie Daana to a stake first. Wouldn't hurt to at least try."

A sideways glare from Oralia sent the lieutenant scuttling off in the right direction. Not without the final say, of course. "Alright, fine! No maiden sacrifices. We'll do it your way." Rali hollered over her shoulder as her squat form disappeared into the swirl of darkness, "But only because I'm your favorite!"

CHAPTER FORTY-FOUR

Shield!

Oralia's fingers clenched around the fist-sized stone in her hand as she watched Rali duck out of sight. With the dwarf in position, Oralia's attention shifted back to Captain Monk. She took only a moment to consider the distance and wind direction before hurtling the stone in his direction. The cloud of magic responded. Serving as a living shield, it wrapped tighter around the captain's body and shattered the projectile a split second before impact. It didn't matter. Oralia only needed it to get his attention. By the time Monk turned to face her, she was already pounding across the open plateau, barely keeping ahead of the torrent of crackling magic that nipped at her heels.

Unable to outrun the black, rancid smoke, Oralia dropped behind another pile of upturned rubble. "You caught me by surprise, Alin," she shouted over her shoulder, her voice echoing against the surrounding cliff-side. "I was expecting to fight Rasp. Not you."

Oralia peeked around her makeshift cover, confirming that Captain Monk had lost interest in Mul and was now moving in her direction. He was halfway to her when a second projectile bounced off of his magical barrier in a burst of sulfuric magic and shattered stone.

"Yeah, we were expecting a real fight!" Rali's thunderous voice boomed as she drew Captain Monk into another fruitless chase.

Oralia slid from her position with a second rock already in hand. She scanned the lot for additional cover, spying a wedge of fallen cliffside several yards out. With the right speed and a little luck, she could make it before the magic caught her. Across the hazy courtyard, she saw Rali's fast-moving form ducking out of the way in time to avoid a blast of stone shrapnel that sprang up from the ground ahead of her.

Oralia bit back an agonized sigh at the realization that it was time, yet again, to willfully throw herself back into the fray. She was already mid-sprint when the stone left her hand at a lethal speed. The captain's magic anticipated her this time. It sprang up in a wave of crackling dark energy and erupted the projectile into a thousand tiny shards of jagged rock only feet from Oralia. The force from the blast knocked her sideways and she slid helplessly across the upturned dirt.

The captain walked as if he were in a dream. His movements were clunky and disjointed, like an entertainer wearing a poorly fitted costume. The familiar honey-brown color of his eyes was gone. In its stead was a deep, dark, swirling black. Tendrils of magic undulated through the shifting smoke toward Oralia. The putrid stench of rot and festering waste clogged her airways as the darkness closed in around her.

A sudden light flared as bright as the sun as it cut through the inky darkness. The fire-tipped arrow thudded into the mud at the captain's feet. A second and third arrow zipped through the roiling air toward them. The darkness rose up to intercept them. Dark clashed with light as the arrows continued to rain down. The dark magic wrapped tighter, like a protective cloth, shielding Captain Monk's dark form until he was lost from sight altogether.

Seizing the momentary distraction, Oralia tried to stand, but her legs were unresponsive. With a pained groan, she attempted again but got only halfway. A strong arm wrapped around her midsection and lifted her up. Too far, in fact, as Sascha decided against putting her down and simply threw her over his shoulder as he pounded across the debris-littered yard toward the entrance of the stronghold.

Where in the seven realms had he come from? Like Captain Monk, Oralia had been too distracted by the fire arrows to notice Sascha's unexpected arrival. In the grand scheme of things, it didn't matter. Unlike escaping. That mattered. And being put back on the ground—which was absolute priority number one given how ridiculous this looked.

Oralia gritted her teeth as every heavy step sent jolts of agony up her bandaged leg. "If I am going to die, I would much prefer to do so on my own two feet!"

"Is that so? Then why did it look like you were trying to take a dirt nap back there?"

The jostling rid her limbs of their previous numbness. This also meant her legs now felt like they were being pricked by a thousand invisible needles.

In that moment, with fear and panic racing across her muddled mind, a human phrase bubbled to the surface: Desperate times call for desperate measures. Oralia took a fast gulp of air before blurting out, "If I confess my love to you, will you put me down?"

Sascha carried her, unbothered by her weight, as though Oralia was nothing more than a belligerent sack of potatoes and not a full-sized orc in battle armor. The hammer and shield taken from the Stoneclaw armory were still with him as well. The latter was thrown over his opposite shoulder while the former was gripped in the hand not currently trapping Oralia's flailing legs against his body.

Sascha scoffed. "You wanted to use my skull as a chamber pot only mere hours ago."

Oralia lifted her head in order to get a better view of the captain. The light of the fire-tipped arrows was being overtaken by the dark. Captain Monk emerged from the churning chaos toward them. Waves of magic rippled from his body and shot forward in a shockwave of destruction as he took chase.

Sascha was fast, but not nearly fast enough. With her heart pounding in her ears, Oralia threw her chin back and yelled, "Sascha, my own sister betrayed me! After everything she put me through, the first thing I did was to try to set her free again. One of my closest friends is a pirate who, on numerous occasions, has tried to kill me. She still tries sometimes, just to keep me on my toes! My sworn enemy sent his own blood on this mission. And even though I had ample opportunity to kill her and make him hurt as much as he hurt me, I cannot bring myself to do it. My point being, that when it comes to holding grudges, I am horribly incompetent!"

"That explains so much." Sascha tilted his head in order to glance out of the corner of his eye at her. "The part about Rali being a pirate, I mean."

Oralia let out a sudden gasp as Sascha jumped, leaping across a chasm that splintered open underneath his feet, and landed hard on the other side. He picked up the pace again, still not slowing to let her down. From across the fractured yard, Oralia could see Captain Monk's dark shape gaining ground. It was either now or never. Whether she convinced Sascha or not, at least she could die having said it aloud. "Ellisar is the pirate, not Rali, but it does not matter. What does matter is that my feelings for you are real. And I am sorry that it ended this way. I cannot change the past. But I can try to do better."

"Do you actually mean that?"

His words might have been sharp, but his tone had changed. Softer, somehow. Fuck. Vulnerability was working. It was unfortunate that it felt so horribly wrong, but the situation demanded she do whatever it took to survive, including admitting what she had been holding back for far too long. "Yes! And I would like to keep loving you, if you are willing to forgive me and move past this, that is." She added sheepishly, "And maybe put me down while you are at it?"

"Is that your attempt at an apology?" Reluctantly, slowing only enough to drop her feet onto solid dirt without either of them tripping in the process, Sascha set her down.

Oralia pressed her leaden legs into a run alongside him. She dodged and weaved a path across the undulating ground as broken shards of cliff-side rained down overhead. "Sascha, I am sorry for deceiving you," she said. "But I really think you would appreciate my groveling more if we did this another time. One, preferably, that does not involve running desperately for our lives?"

Sascha stayed hot on her heels, breaking apart only to avoid an oncoming projectile before returning to her side once more. The splintered ground shook and trembled, threatening to break open beneath them. "You know, it shouldn't take a near-death experience to make you finally admit these things. If we're going to make this work, you're going to have to start vocalizing this stuff before something is trying to kill us."

Such change, luckily, required surviving their current circumstances first. A feat that looked bleaker and bleaker by the passing second. Mumbling her agreement, Oralia focused her sights on the pair of open iron doors that loomed ominously through the gloom ahead of them. She and Sascha were close now. They only had to duck and weave the crumbling cliffside a few yards more and they would reach the steps to the entrance. How in the seven realms they were supposed to lure Captain Monk inside and get out again was yet to be determined.

They were only paces from the start of the stone entryway when a wave of crackling power slammed into them, sending the pair sprawling across the slippery courtyard. Captain Monk materialized from the swirling darkness before them. He stepped closer, his black eyes fixed on Oralia. For the first time since she could remember, his booming volume was appropriate for the situation at hand. "You!"

What would Rasp do? What would Rasp do? What would Rasp do? "What was that, Captain?" she screamed back. "Could you speak up? I am having trouble hearing you!"

Sascha rolled over, groaning softly, "Seven realms, Oralia. Really?"

"Be ready with the shield," she whispered low enough so that only he would hear.

Captain Monk raised his singed hand into the air, his fingers black and twisted from the burn of the fire arrows. "In all my years, you never once took me seriously." He took another stiff step closer. "You, and the speaker, and all the others. None of you had an inkling of true power. But I hold it now. And I can finally prove to you what I've known all along. You are nothing. You have always been nothing."

Movement from the mouth of the stronghold caught Oralia's attention. Gritting her teeth, she eased upright and fixed her steely gaze back onto Captain Monk. She had never been one for talking, but now seemed like an excellent opportunity to try. "Alin, Alin, Alin." She wondered, briefly, if it would suffice to simply repeat his name until he dropped dead of boredom. Probably not. "Do you really think this spirit wants you, Alin? You, a simple seeker? And not even a good one. I heard the division could not find a use for you and that is why they hid you in the military, where no one would notice. I certainly did not."

The outrage that curled across Captain Monk's face was downright lethal. Oralia saw the start of the oncoming blast and threw herself against Sascha, screaming, "Shield!"

CHAPTER FORTY-FIVE

Don't Hesitate

Sascha heaved the heavy shield from his back and slammed it in front of them, bracing against it with Oralia caught in between. They pressed together, feeling every shake and shudder as shrapnel pelted the thick steel from the other side. The shield didn't cover all of them, especially not Sascha, but it was sufficient in sheltering the more important bits.

"You've got him good and pissed off now," Sascha said, his voice straining from the exertion of keeping the shield fixed firmly in place. "Tell me there's more to this plan than just insulting him."

"Yes, keep him distracted for as long as possible."

"So, no actual plan then. Got it."

Her former self would have kept mum. It was a semi-decent strategy, and there was no need for her to waste her breath sharing the specifics. Considering that was a big part of how she'd gotten into this mess, Oralia supposed now was as good of a time as any to demonstrate she was capable of change. Even if revealing her inner thoughts meant Sascha would be fully aware that they were nothing more than bait, and about to die a gruesome death.

"Monk nearly got taken out by an arrow because he was distracted. If I can work him into a blind rage, then his magic will be focused on me, leaving him susceptible to an outside attack."

The noise Sascha made roughly translated to "I wish you'd told me that *before* I saved your ass."

There was no time to reassure him that this had indeed been a terrible decision on his part. Oralia switched back to her Rasp-inspired tactics instead and yelled, "Is that all you've got, Alin?"

Writhing black clouds surged past overhead. The thundering magic hammered against the shield with such force she and Sascha started to slide backward. Oralia dug her heels into the soft dirt for traction as she raised her voice to be heard over the din. "You were the spirit's second choice! But I suppose that is nothing new for you, is it? You are not strong enough to hold it for long. Once your body is spent, it will leave you to die."

That seemed to do the trick. With a deep, resonating rumble, the plateau tore open behind them. The ground buckled and cracked as chunks of earth broke away and plummeted into the rift. Oralia did not know how deep the chasm went and did not desire to get any closer to find out. She threw her shoulder into the shield with fresh vigor in a desperate bid to regain ground before the magic pushed her and Sascha over the edge.

"Swallowed by the earth, Alin?" she shouted at the top of her lungs. "Are you so weak you could not kill me yourself?"

"Dear gods, woman," Sascha groaned. "It's like you want us to die!"

Oralia found herself caught between two unrelenting forces. The magic surged against the shield from the front and Sascha heaved from the back, doing everything in his power to keep them from being propelled into the abyss. She would forever be indebted to him for his loyalty, she knew that. At the moment, however, it was difficult to appreciate his efforts when all the air was being forcibly squeezed from her lungs.

"Death would be a good distraction," she rasped.

In lieu of an intelligible reply, Sascha only made a soft whimpering sound. It was quite pitiful. The sort of noise one would expect from a small puppy kicked to the curb, and not the gargantuan-sized orc currently using his body to keep them from slipping and tumbling to their deaths.

Gods, you are going to owe him so much more than a flimsy apology when this is over.

Oralia opened her mouth to volley another round of insults at Captain Monk when a blood-curdling screech erupted from the other side of the shield. The onslaught of swirling magic overhead dropped. The pressure eased and the pair lurched forward as a result. Tentatively, Oralia peeked around the edge of the shield to see the reason for the disruption. Her heart leapt into her throat at the sight.

Snag was wrapped around the captain's shoulders, clinging on for dear life as his thin knife darted in and out of the man's chest in a blurry flash of steel. Black smoke oozed from the captain's wounds. For a split second, time stood still. Snag locked eyes with her and shouted something. And then time picked up again, moving at double the speed, as if to make up for the momentary lapse. Snap leapt back in a shower of writhing magic and raced up the stone steps with the captain at his heels.

Oralia watched the pair disappear into the mouth of the stronghold as Snag's final words hit her: "Don't hesitate."

"Ellisar, now!" Oralia cast the shield aside and raced for the entrance. Sascha lurched ahead of her and had one iron door shut by the time she reached the uttermost step. Together, they heaved the second one into position. The heavy iron door groaned in protest.

Ellisar appeared from her hiding place along the top of the doorway. She moved sure-footedly and without fear, bounding across the lip of carved rock that jutted out above the entrance. It took three strikes of her flint and steel before the fuse to Snag's contraption ignited. With the starter lit, Ellisar scrambled to climb down. She abandoned her efforts partway and pushed off from the cliffside instead, allowing gravity to take her the rest of the way.

Her voice cut through the clamor. "Incoming!"

Oralia turned and caught the plummeting elf. With Ellisar cradled in her arms like the precious newborn nobody in their right mind would have wanted, Oralia broke into a desperate sprint across the demolished courtyard, clearing the rift that had previously threatened to swallow them in a single bound. There wasn't time to reach the outer wall. They had to find shelter elsewhere, and fast. Oralia threw herself behind a fallen chunk of cliffside, with Ellisar held tight to her chest like a struggling feral cat. Sascha slid into position behind them with only seconds to spare. A horrendous *boom* lit the air behind them. It rumbled as loud as thunder and rocked the entire mountainside until Oralia was certain the ground would open up and swallow them whole.

Ellisar squirmed free of Oralia's grasp and clambered over the top of Sascha, using his bent shoulders as a lookout post. Her long, flaxen hair whipped behind her as loose ash and debris sailed on the breeze. "It actually worked. Snag's powder brought the entrance down!" She glanced down her nose at Oralia, her pale face flickering from the distant flames burning near what had formerly been the entrance of the Stoneclaw stronghold. A wolfish smile pulled at Ellisar's thin lips. "Let's do the palace next."

Oralia made no reply, and the smirk soon disappeared from Ellisar's mouth. "Why do you look like someone shat in your sandwich? We got him, Oralia. It's over. We won."

She closed her eyes and rested her head in her hands. The words "don't hesitate" echoed through her mind as a sudden numbness spread from the depths of her chest to her throat. "Snag went in, too."

"He did what?" Ellisar's feet hit the slick ground with a wet splatter, sending a spray of mud around her. "That little fuck! What was he thinking?"

Oralia peered through her dirtied fingers, watching as the elf started back toward the entrance. Ellisar wouldn't get far. Mad or not, even she wouldn't attempt to rush into a collapsed cave just to berate the dead. "He did what any of us would have done."

"No! It's what *you* would have done, or Rali, maybe. But he was supposed to be smarter than that! That bastard, he . . ." Ellisar's stomping steps slowed to a halt. Oralia could only see the back of her, but from the way her head dropped, even outrage couldn't keep the grief at bay for long.

Oralia rose onto stiff, protesting legs. She passed Sascha, who was hunched over his knees, content to remain that way until told otherwise. She placed her arm over Ellisar's quaking shoulders as her own teary gaze swept across the destruction. The front of the stronghold was unrecognizable, with the stone steps buried under a landslide of rubble and loose scree. Everything else—the great iron doors, the intricately carved doorway, the very face of the cliff itself—was gone, reduced to nothing more than a pile of splintered rock.

Ellisar rummaged through the inside of her jerkin and produced a cylindrical object. It took a moment for Oralia to realize it was a wooden pipe. "You should have it," Ellisar sniffed. "His playing annoyed you the most."

She took it in her hand as the pressure in her chest built behind her eyes. The pipe was crafted from lacquered silverwood and adorned with undulating waves and several ornately carved sea monsters. Snag's finest work, by far. A masterpiece in comparison to the crude reed instruments she used to burn without ever considering what sort of effort had gone into their making.

"Did you know he could actually play? I caught him once, when he thought nobody was around. Little fucker just liked to torture us for his own amusement." Ellisar wiped under her eyes with the back of her torn sleeve. "I'd never met anybody who was almost as twisted as me before."

Movement drew Oralia's attention back to the collapsed entryway. Her eyes grew wide and she pulled Ellisar behind the shelter with her. "Get down!"

Behind them, a second blast erupted even stronger than the first. In a shower of black, writhing smoke, the fractured cliffside erupted across the plateau. Giant pieces of ruptured rock sailed through the air and struck the open courtyard, leveling everything in their paths. Oralia, Sascha, and Ellisar huddled together, shuddering each time a boulder slammed down too close for comfort. After several agonizing seconds, the onslaught subsided and an eerie quiet settled over the ridge.

Oralia crept to the edge of their makeshift barrier, gritting her teeth as loose stone shifted precariously underfoot. Peering around the corner, she saw rolling plumes of dark cloud waft from the gaping hole in the cliffside where the entrance once stood. Amid the gloom, the telltale shape of a man staggered clear from the destruction.

CHAPTER FORTY-SIX

Collapse

Briony pulled Rasp to the top of another winding staircase as the last weak rumble of a quake died down beneath their feet. He had lost track of how many flights of trembling stairs they'd conquered so far. If the deep ache in his leaden legs was to be trusted, the number was somewhere in the thousands, possibly higher. The dark, endless expanse within the mountain distorted Rasp's sense of time. Although it felt like they had been climbing for days, the logical portion of his brain insisted it hadn't been more than an hour or so.

Every other part of his body sorely disagreed.

"Years," his feet said. "Decades," his legs insisted. "Time is an illusion," some rarely visited corner of his mind declared. "It is the mortal who passes, not time. He is but a blink, a blip, to the endless sprawl of an otherwise uncaring universe. Destined to spend his years toiling in futile . . ."

Rasp stopped listening to that particular voice and settled on forever. He and Briony had been climbing forever without an end in sight. Nay, it was worse than that. It wasn't forever, because he was already dead. Yes, that made sense. He'd died earlier that day and this was his penance. Sentenced to spend the rest of eternity climbing steadily upward, desperate to stop the evil that he had started, destined to never reach it. Cruel, cruel irony!

Briony's breathy voice broke Rasp from his internal damnation. "Please tell me we're getting close."

Croak, croak, croak! Father's harsh call echoed ahead of them.

Unwilling to talk while running, Rasp stopped and sagged against the nearest wall as he translated the raven's reply. "We're on the main level now," he panted, sweat dripping down his forehead. Everything felt like it was on fire. His face, his feet, his lungs, that tender spot on the inside of his thighs where the seam of his pants kept rubbing against his skin. He'd be damned if this wasn't one of the levels of chaos. Probably not the worst one, but certainly in the lower three.

The seventh level of chaos would probably have him doing this in full armor. Or a chicken suit. A dress, maybe? No. That would have been preferable, actually. Not only would a dress offer decent airflow, but it would eliminate all of the horrible chafing too. Maybe he could ask Briony to swap clothes. That wouldn't be weird, right?

"Rasp!" Once more, his reluctant companion dragged Rasp's wandering attention kicking and screaming from his inner thoughts. "I can only handle so much more croaking. Tell me what the blasted bird is saying before I ditch the both of you."

Rasp tilted his head and listened to more of Father's obnoxious sounds. He didn't have the mental wherewithal to catch everything, but he got the gist of it. Hopefully. "He says to follow this passage and it'll lead us out the front doors."

"Finally! We're getting somewhere," Briony sighed, sounding not happy but grateful that her leg of the journey would soon be over. She could deliver Rasp to his doom, turn back, run, and only ever have to revisit this nightmare in her dreams. Lucky duck. "Alright," she said, peeling Rasp away from the cool rock like a stubborn starfish, "enough of that. These quakes are getting stronger and I would like to be outside of the mountain when it inevitably comes down."

Rasp bit back his protest and willed his legs into a sluggish run. The familiar smells of spiced spruce and damp stone filled his nose and lungs as his aching feet slapped against the ground in order to keep pace. With his body operating well enough on its own, his mind was let loose to wander at will. Naturally, it took three steps before he fell face-first down a wild rabbit hole of thought.

He'd spent nearly his whole life in this stronghold. He knew every nook and cranny and which dark corners provided the best hiding places. There should have been a sense of familiarity and yet, he felt nothing. This wasn't home. It was just a stupid, cold, uncaring mountain cave that he'd happened to grow up in.

In a way, he was grateful he was about to die. At least then no one expected him to stay and take care of the place. Destined to lead, ha! What had fate been thinking? When he died, he'd be sure to give whoever was in charge a stern talking to. It was downright cruel awarding both power and potential to someone with no aspiration to wield either. In fact—

Rasp broke from his thoughts at the realization that the floor was trembling again. He might have ignored it and gone back to his inner monologuing had it not been for one unnerving distinction. The shaking wasn't coming from below. It felt much, much closer. Before he could get the words from his mouth, a thunderous rumble tore through the empty cavern and shook them like fireflies in a jar. Father landed on his shoulder in a flurry of beating wings. The raven's frantic croaks were drowned out by the deafening din. Briony was shouting something too, but Rasp couldn't decipher the words coming from either of them.

Do something, do something, do something! With his heartbeat drumming in his ears, he swung Briony against the wall and threw his body over her. Rasp planted his feet shoulder-width apart and slammed the flat of his hands against the shuddering stone. He willed his magic into existence the only way he knew how. "Work this time, gods dammit!"

The yellow buzz in his fingertips burned bright for a split second before fizzling out. Well, so much for that. Desperate times called for measures and whatnot. ". . . Please?"

The shaking turned more violent, buckling and heaving beneath them. Briony's torch dropped from her grasp and its soft light went black. Rasp felt the wall shudder as the ceiling gave away with a deafening crash further down the main passage. Like a ripple across still water, the cavernous hallway collapsed in their direction. Heavy slabs of stone fell from the ceiling and shattered across the floor. And then, just as the clamor grew close enough to crush them, the rumbling stilled until the only noise Rasp could hear was the gritty shift of rubble sliding into its final resting place. A blurry, yellow light pulsed around him, shielding the passage around them from the cave-in.

That worked? Being nice to himself actually worked? Since when? There was a lesson here, Rasp was sure, but he didn't have the desire to dive into it. After all, just because he'd sheltered them from the cave-in didn't mean squat if he and Briony were now trapped underground. He doubted there would be anyone left to dig him out this time.

The burning tingle left Rasp's fingertips as his magic slowly withdrew back into his body. "Briony?"

"Still alive," she murmured. "Gods, that was close. Thanks, I guess?"

Rasp stiffened at her words. "You guess?"

"Well, that really depends on what sort of state we're in. I should know shortly. Hold that light a little longer, will you? The torch went out somewhere around here." Briony's hazy shape shifted, dropping to her knees beside him. Her hands slid over the top of Rasp's boot as she felt along the broken floor for the extinguished torch. He assumed she must have found it, because he heard the strike of steel against flint next. After several tries, a spark flared. Briony coaxed the flame to life with her breath and soon a soft, flickering glow illuminated the suffocating gloom.

Rasp gazed across the cavern, seeing nothing more than darkness beyond the limited light of Briony's torch. Dust clouded the air, irritating his eyes and throat. He pulled his damp shirt over his mouth and nose to keep from breathing in the particles. "Is it bad?"

Briony moved cautiously ahead of him, lifting the torch higher as she surveyed the damage. "Looks like you were able to keep our portion of the hallway intact, but the main entrance is buried." There was a sort of nervous laugh in her voice. "I don't suppose this place has a back door, does it?"

Croak.

"Stable entrance," Rasp translated, reaching up to stroke the fluffy head that bobbed near his ear. His father rewarded his need for reassurance with a harsh peck to the finger. "Gods! You want me to cook you on a spit over Briony's torch? Keep it up, old man, and I'll be picking you from my teeth."

Father flapped his wings angrily. *Croak! Croak! Croak!*

"Name-calling at a time like this? Really? Grow up."

"Hey, idiots, be quiet," Briony hissed. Rasp and the raven obediently fell silent. Rasp strained to catch what she was listening for, but heard only the occasional shift of rubble in the distance. Briony seized him by the elbow and pulled his reluctant steps back in the direction of the collapsed doorway. "This way, come on. I think I hear something."

"So your plan is to go toward it? I thought you were the smart one."

Briony's response was commendable in that she chose silence rather than settling for a nice kick between Rasp's legs. Meaning of course that, despite her efforts to remain distant, he was steadily growing on her. As they moved along the broken, upturned ground, navigating the larger chunks of fallen ceiling, Rasp finally heard what Briony's sensitive ears had picked up from farther away. It was a soft, rasping rattle. Not quite a death groan, but disturbingly close. The something was a *someone.*

"I'm coming, hold on!" Briony released Rasp's hand and darted forward without him. He heard her hooves scrape against the stone floor as she dropped lower. Briony propped the torch against the fallen rubble and heaved her full weight forward, attempting to shift an object that Rasp couldn't make out. She cursed, yelling over her shoulder at him, "Rasp, get over here! I need you for this. He's pinned."

Rasp followed the flicker of her torch light, grimacing as he slammed his knee against an unseen obstacle. He felt his way to her, sliding his feet against the pebbled ground with his hands held outstretched in front of him. Briony grasped his wrist and dragged him the rest of the way. "Here." She placed his hands at the bottom lip of the jagged slab. "You lift and I'll pull him out, okay? Hurry."

A weak whine emitted from somewhere near their feet.

Rasp's heart lurched against his battered chest like a canary trying to escape its cage. "Snag?"

CHAPTER FORTY-SEVEN

The Missing Piece

Like a hot needle, pain pierced into the center of Rasp's sternum and spread. His magic responded unsummoned. It crackled down his arms, twisting as shimmering vines of yellow and gold in the summer sun. Power sparked from his fingertips and engulfed the broken slab until it glowed the same, hazy yellow as his magic. A low growl started at the base of his throat and worked upward as he focused on the rock, feverishly hoping that, unlike the last time he attempted this, he would manipulate just one stone and not all of them.

Fortunately, he and his magic appeared to be on the same page for once. The glowing slab lifted and Briony's muddled shape darted forward and dragged Snag free. "I've got him! You can—"

Rasp was a half-step ahead of her and severed his magic, consequently dropping the stone from higher than he should have. It struck the ground and split in half. The resounding slam echoed in his ears as it ricocheted off the buckled walls, growing fainter with each repetition. Aside from the few pieces of loose ceiling that fell free and clattered across the debris-littered floor, the rest of the cavern stayed put.

"—put it down gently," Briony finished with an irritated snort.

He ignored the myriad of snotty replies that danced across his tongue and focused on being a contributing member of the team instead—which basically meant not being the guy who brought the rest of the ceiling down on top of them in a fit of misplaced anger. Rasp cautiously edged one foot closer, and then the other. Unfortunately, it didn't matter how near he got. He'd have to be on top of them before he got a proper sense for what was going on. Something wasn't right, though. This was Snag. There should have been a lot more complaining. Bizarre, poorly worded threats, at the very least.

An invisible vise seized him around the throat. Rasp struggled to get the words out. "Is he . . . ?"

There was a vicious snarl followed by the sounds of a struggle. "Snag, it's alright! It's me, Briony." Briony's next words were directed at Rasp. "You'll have to hold him. He's coming out of this fighting."

With Briony's direction, Rasp pressed the goblin to the ground. Snag twisted and snarled below him. For such a little fucker, he certainly was strong. Rasp struggled to pin him, nearly jumping out of his skin when a set of needled teeth grazed his arm. "You fucking bite me and I'll bite you back!" he shouted. "You hear me, pet? And I guarantee you're going to catch something nasty if you do. Limbs rotting off, teeth falling out, the works!"

Snag's struggle faded and his little body went limp against the floor.

Rasp would have thought him dead if it were not for the sounds of soft crying. "Shit, I'm sorry." Oh gods. This was worse. So much worse. He would have happily taken a bite over emotional duress any day. "I didn't mean it. I was just trying to—"

The goblin's ragged voice was barely a whisper. "Don't."

The guilt pressing behind his eyes spread to his tongue and Rasp found the words spilling from his open mouth, unchecked. "You know I don't think you're a pet, right? You're actually a really nice person and even though you act mean, I'm starting to think it's all a bluff. You haven't poisoned a single person this whole trip."

"Don't." Snag's pained words came between pitiful, wheezy breaths. "Save. Me."

The heaviness in Rasp's throat sank to his stomach. "What?"

"I don't want it!" He lurched upright, twisting and writhing to get free of Rasp's grasp. "Just fucking leave me. It's over. I'm done."

"You've got a handful of broken ribs and a mangled leg." Briony dutifully reported from slightly further down. Rasp heard the sound of cloth ripping as she continued her work. "You're not done. You're being dramatic."

"He's gone, maggot," Snag said, softly, as he sank back against the cracked floor. "He's gone and I don't have anything left."

"He, who?"

"Curly." There was a tremble in Snag's limbs that hadn't been there before. "Every time I find something worth living for, someone comes along and yanks it out from under me. This was the last one, I swore it. I don't have it in me to try anymore."

Rasp released Snag's limp wrists and sank onto the cold ground next to him, ignoring the protests from Briony. He didn't know what else to do. There weren't words for this kind of thing. Rasp searched until he found Snag's clawed hand and held it tight as silent tears began to leak from the corner of his eyes.

Snag's voice had an edge to it now. "What are you doing?"

"Faris squeezes me until I can't breathe when I feel like I'm on the edge and might just jump the rest of the way over. I didn't think you'd appreciate the hug, given the broken ribs and all. You're going to have to settle for uncomfortable hand holding."

"I want to go home."

"I know, but I can't let you yet. There are people out there who still need you."

"They already think I'm gone. Just let me go."

"I'll tell you what." Rasp gripped his hand tighter. "We'll go together, okay? We'll both just sit here and die a slow, agonizing death. And then Faris, and Oralia, and Rali, and Ellisar, and everyone else we've ever cared about, can die pointlessly, too. And then the darkness will spread freely across the land and take out all the good people who didn't do anything to deserve it. Remember all the babies you used to play with at Lonebrook? It gets them, too. But it won't matter, because we'll already be dead. We won't have to feel guilty about it. How's that sound?"

Snag pulled his hand away from him with a snarl. "Why are you such a little shit? You didn't have to say it like that!"

"I know what you're feeling." Rasp stared upward at nothing as a familiar hurt flooded so deep, it made his bones ache. "I lost a kid, too. Mine wasn't like yours, though. I didn't get to see him grow. No first steps, or words, or catching him with a girl for the first time. He slept, he ate, and he shat, almost exclusively. And I loved that little baby like I'd never loved anything before. Losing them is a pain you never forget. It hits so hard and fast, you never want to get up again."

Snag's voice was small. "Does it go away?"

"No." Rasp shook his head. "And the hole inside of you never grows smaller, either. But, with time, years and years sometimes, you find the missing piece is still the same size, but the rest of you is a bit bigger than before. And the pain that felt like it was going to eat you from the inside out doesn't hurt as much as it used to."

Rasp felt Briony's hand on his shoulder. Her voice was low and concerned. "I got the leg stabilized. He's fit to travel now. We need to move."

"Oh, sorry. You didn't hear? We've given up. Snugglebum doesn't have the fight to save anyone else. I told him I'd stay here and make sure his death is both pointless and miserable."

Snag produced a guttural knocking sound from within his bony chest. "You are the worst, you know that? Fine! Take me with you. I'll just die later when you're not around to bugger it up!"

Rasp helped ease him into a sitting position. "One last horsey ride? Or would you prefer I carry you like you're the bride and it's our wedding night? You're about to be very surprised when I take my trousers off."

"The real surprise is that you're wearing any at all."

Some of the heaviness in his soul lifted as Rasp moved into position. Forget emotional vulnerability, being a little shit was where he truly shone. And if that was what got Snag out of this stupid mountain alive, then he was prepared to be the biggest little shit the goblin had ever seen. "You shameless harlot! You weren't supposed to look. No white nighty for you, apparently."

"Oh my gods." With a whimpered groan, Snag crawled onto Rasp's back and slung his arms around his neck. "Get moving so I can die with dignity somewhere else."

"What? You don't want to go while riding me, Snag? That's every pretty goblin's dream." A sudden thwack to the side of his head almost cost him his balance. Rasp clenched and unclenched his jaw in a futile attempt to alleviate the buzzing mosquito sounds ringing within his right ear as he steadied his footing. "So much for being on death's doorstep. That slap had some life to it."

"Don't know what you're talking about. Must have been a wayward bat."

With Briony's help, Rasp heaved to his feet and adjusted his stance to account for the added weight. He hooked each arm under Snag's legs and flinched when the goblin howled with pain inches from the one ear that, until this point, had still been working.

"Watch the fucking leg!"

"Sorry." Rasp winced.

Snag's snarls grew weaker until he could only manage pained whimpers. With his lower jaw locked tight, Rasp followed the light from Briony's torch as she led them back down the crumbled hallway. Father fluttered ahead of the slow-moving pair, calling out directions that echoed in such a way, it sounded like multiple ravens chattering loudly over the top of one another.

"To your right, Briony," Rasp said. "There's a door tucked into the wall."

His heart leapt when he heard the iron latch click. After a few failed attempts to swing it open, Briony propped her torch against the wall and took several calculated steps backward. "It's jammed. Stay back until I tell you otherwise."

"Snag, what's she doing?"

The goblin lifted his cheek from Rasp's shoulders for a better look. "Using her head."

Slam! With a deafening bang, the door shuddered from the sudden impact. Briony charged it twice more before the aged wood gave away in a shower of splinters. With a gargled scream, the faun kicked it violently from its hinges for added measure. Amid the musty smell of straw and animal dung that hung thick in the air, a strange blue light wafted in through the open doorway. The familiar prickle of magic washed over Rasp's skin. It left the taste of sulfur and ash in his gaping mouth.

"Whisper?" He pushed past Briony and staggered toward the dancing waves of light.

"There's a step! Mind the step!" Snag shouted too late. Rasp missed it and tripped, stumbling face-first into a pile of musty hay. Snag detangled himself from Rasp's shoulders, moaning, "That's it. I'm selling you to the mincemeat shop."

A moth to flame, Rasp pushed to his feet and limped toward the pulsing blue light. Every instinct screamed at him to turn and run, but the magic humming in his ears beckoned him closer. The melody was sweet and soft. And, like the hapless sailor, Rasp drifted closer, aware he'd been caught by a siren song but unwilling to break from its enchantment. The flames licked higher as the taste of burnt matches pooled under his tongue.

"What is wrong with you?" A pair of burly arms seized him, preventing Rasp from touching the blaze. "Did Briony kick you in the head on the way in? Your first thought shouldn't be to wander toward the mysterious wall of burning magic!"

"Dingle?" Rasp's breath caught in his throat with a sudden gasp as the enchantment broke. A swell of emotions broke over him and he didn't know whether to hug Faris, bite his ear off, or merely scream until his lungs gave out. Alas, there wasn't time for heartfelt reunions. Rasp wriggled free of Faris's grip. "That's Whisper's magic, isn't it? I can feel them. What's going on?"

"I—I'm not sure," Faris stammered. "Daana was supposed to transfer their power from the stone back to them, but something went wrong."

"Faris." Briony's hushed voice was suddenly beside them. "That's not just any magic in there, that's *fae* magic."

"I know." Faris added in a tone that was more miserable than helpful, "A wind shifter, specifically."

"If Daana gets the power of a wind shifter, then we're all fucked."

"I *know*."

CHAPTER FORTY-EIGHT

No More Bright Ideas

The shimmering blue light hummed like a swarm of angry wasps. Magic filled her ears with a low, buzzing vibration as it slowly wormed deeper. The mother of all migraines pounded against the inside of her skull, causing brilliant bursts of color to warp her vision, flashing in time to the hammer of the drum. Daana snapped her eyes shut. While this measure helped ease the barrage of dancing light, it didn't stop the hammering. Nor the smell. A thick, caustic odor burned its way up her nasal passages—oddly reminiscent of the time the potions laboratory caught fire back at the academy.

She recalled peeking inside of the incinerated laboratory after the building had been cleared. No one had bothered to alert her of the danger and thus, she'd found the source of the evacuation simply by stumbling across it. Story of her life, really—left behind, forgotten, not even an afterthought. The laboratory had been unnaturally hot, filled with great plumes of smoke and char, with small portions of the structure still smoldering. That's how her head felt now. Except instead of smoke, it was runaway thoughts that crowded the space between her ears. Her mind rippled and roiled with activity, as if the conscious stream of every person on the mountain had been jammed inside her skull and set aflame.

There was screaming. So much screaming. Each voice howled to be heard over the others until the noise melded together in a single, thundering screech. Amid the raging torrent, a strange ripple caught her attention. This sound was unlike the others. It did not yell or thunder, it skimmed over the din, as soft and light as birdsong carried on the wind. Daana latched onto it, allowing the whisper to pull her above the storm of raging thoughts.

It was only then, free of the noise, that she discovered the soft voice was one she recognized. **Little bird,** it cried, branching across her mind in a desperate search for an outside source. **Little bird, can you hear me?**

To her disbelief, a second voice answered. It was muffled, like someone trying to speak from the other side of a wall around a mouthful of dry scone. Daana channeled her concentration and the outside words became clearer. **Whisper?** This, she realized, was Rasp. She didn't know how Whisper had reached him, she only knew that his voice added to the relentless clanging inside her skull with the magnitude of a sledgehammer. **Whisper, what the fuck is going on? How do I get you out?**

You have to break her concentration. But whatever you do, do not use—

Too much, too much, too much! Daana's fingers dug into the sides of her temples as the pressure inside her head swelled to nearly bursting. *Stop shouting and get out of my thoughts!*

Whisper—Rasp's voice amplified the ballooning pressure—**who's that? Don't use your magic!**

I said get out! A pulse of light surged across Daana's mind and drowned out the interference. Relief washed over her as the rampant pounding within her skull dulled to a throb. While severing Whisper's telepathic connection silenced the foreign voices in her head, it did nothing to quiet the ones gathered outside of the glowing rune circle. To be fair, given the volume at which they were shouting, she was certain the entire mountainside could probably hear them.

"What are you holding me back for?" The strain in Rasp's voice was indicative of a struggle. "Let me break them apart already!"

"Great idea, Dinglehead. Go and get trapped alongside Whisper! Is that what you want? She'd leech you dry in an instant."

". . . Why are you saying that like it's a bad thing?"

"Can we have one conversation that does not immediately get dragged into the gutter?"

"Faris is right, Rasp." While remarkably less hostile, the third voice put Daana on edge far more than the first two. The reason, she realized, was because it belonged to Briony. The one person potentially equipped with the knowledge to stop her. Channeling her focus, Daana strained in order to catch the rest of the faun's hushed warning. "If you breach the rune barrier, Daana will be able to drain your magic, too."

"Even if I'm not using my magic? Like, you know, just barge in? Fists a'swinging?"

"Any witch who steps foot into that circle is not coming out again."

"Hold up! Are you saying I could have used the emissary to get rid of my magic this whole time? And none of you thought to tell me?" There was a sudden yelp from Rasp, followed by a snarl. "Gods, Faris! Do you have to be so rough? I was only kidding."

"No you weren't."

"You're right, I wasn't. But that does give me a terrible idea. Daana!" Rasp called, magnifying his voice in a way that resonated against the solid stone walls with a rattle. "Forget Whisper, take my power instead! Free of charge. No take-backsies!"

Did he take her for a fool? He wouldn't give up his power that easily. The very idea was downright ridiculous. It was even more ridiculous that Rasp thought such a blatantly obvious plan would work. He was trying to trick her, just like everyone else. For the first time in her life, Daana finally had something others wanted. And she would be damned if she gave it away so easily!

Daana opened her eyes, squinting at the wall of magic that shimmered in a ring around her, blanketing the inside of the symbol in pale blue light. Whisper was kneeling in front of her, frozen in place, unable to tear free from her grasp. While the fae could not move, Daana felt them beneath the surface, fighting her control. Her gaze flickered to the shimmering symbol painted across the floor, wondering what spell would seal it, allowing her the privacy needed to successfully harness Whisper's magic as her own.

"Great work, Dinglehead," Faris's voice rang out from beyond the rune symbol. "All you did was make the wall of fire more fiery."

"Well I don't see you coming up with any bright ideas!"

"How about we save the bright ideas for the bright minds, yeah?"

"You never let me do anything."

Faris's tone shifted from annoyed to just shy of pleading. "Briony, you're the expert here. How do we break Whisper and Daana apart without killing ourselves in the process?"

"We have to disrupt her concentration. Draw her out. If we can reach her, then there's a chance we can sever the bond."

Heat broke out across Daana's clammy forehead and spread to her throat, pulling her airway tight with rage. She knew it! The bastards wanted the power for themselves. No, she'd worked too hard for this. The magic was hers and hers alone. She'd be damned before she let someone else strip her of the one thing that could make her whole.

She seized the strange magic surging through her veins and willed it to the edges of the glowing ring, building the protective barrier stronger, higher, ensuring no one would reach her in time. This would be the last they saw of the sniveling, weak elfling they all turned their noses up at. When she reemerged, they would finally see what she was supposed to have been all along. And then they would pay. The entire world would pay for the way it treated her.

The magic whipped and whirled around her, blustering Daana's hair against her face as the torrent grew stronger. With the gale howling in her ears, she didn't notice the staticky pop and crackle as something passed through the barrier seconds before she sealed it shut, cutting off all access from the outside.

The tightness in her throat eased. With Whisper silenced and the others prevented from interfering, she was left to fulfill her destiny in peace. She adjusted her grip on Whisper's wrists, taking a breath as she prepared to draw the last of their magic into her core. The familiar burn traveled through her fingertips, up her arms, and gathered in her chest like a molten pool of liquid iron. Daana gritted her teeth against the pain, ignoring the way her flesh sizzled and popped.

She was nearly to her breaking point when a cold hand touched her shoulder, sending shoots of ice jolting down her arm. "This isn't the way, Tadpole."

Her eyes snapped open but a veil of darkness clouded her vision, blanketing Daana's surroundings in endless black. Her breath hitched, eyes darting uselessly across the void as the ice trickled into her chest, quelling the molten rage. "No!" she screamed. "You can't take this from me, it's mine! Get back!"

Little by little, tiny pinpricks of light illuminated against the dark like stars caught in the night sky. The fuzzy voice that accompanied them felt as distant as a dream. "This isn't what you want."

What she wanted? How could they possibly know what she wanted? How could anyone know? Everyone had been so busy telling her what her purpose was, no one had ever bothered to ask! Her whole life amounted to other people telling her what she wanted! She may not have known the answer herself but, in that moment, she knew what she needed. Silence.

She gritted her teeth and willed the magic to obey, chanting within her thoughts, *Be quiet, be quiet, be quiet.*

Beyond the inky blackness, Daana felt the heat of the blue ring rise in temperature. The swirling air smelled of smoke and ash as the caustic odor returned. The wind whipped faster. Magic lashed out in sporadic bursts, nipping and biting at her tender skin as the inside of the rune circle transformed into a raging torrent.

"Daana, you're losing control," the disembodied voice said. "Calm down."

Calm down? *Calm down?* How many times had she heard those same words before? Calm down, Daana. You're making a disturbance, Daana. Stop being so emotional, Daana. Get a hold of yourself! Why can't you be more like the other ladies of the court? They know their place. They don't play the game. They don't seek adventure or power. They're content to be arranged on the board like every other empty-headed political pawn. So calm down, Daana. Just accept your place. Stop making a scene. Be what we want you to be. Quiet and compliant. Seen, not heard. Nothing.

Calm down. *Calm down.* CALM DOWN.

"No!" she screamed. "Never again! It is you who will be silent!"

The darkness pulled back from her vision in a shriveling, writhing cloak as the blue flames turned stark white. The magic glowed brighter, brighter, brighter, as the wind whipped and the fire crackled, lifting Daana from the floor. For a split second, her feet hovered in the air, before the final pulse flared from the stones on her arms. Blistering magic arced across her skin before the light was snuffed out completely.

Inky blackness closed in, enveloping her as she drifted into the void, vaguely aware of the old lullaby that hummed silently on her lips.

CHAPTER FORTY-NINE

Happy Place

Light as bright and brilliant as the rising sun flared across the darkness and chased it into the shadows. The air stilled and a strange calm settled over Daana. The crackling hum of magic was gone, replaced by the soft warbles and trills of birdsong in the distance. She no longer smelled the caustic burn of smoke, either. In its stead, she was welcomed by the familiar scent of leather book bindings and musty parchment. Daana searched the space around her with her hand, unwilling to open her eyes and lose her newfound peace.

The floor was cold and hard. It produced a solid thud when she rapped her knuckles lightly against it. Hardwood planks, she concluded. Curious. Something told her that this particular type of building material was not one used by the Stoneclaw clan. Meaning she was somewhere else. More curious.

No, terrifying. That was the word she was looking for. Definitely more terrifying. Or at least it should have been. For some reason, the old fears weren't bubbling up and scalding the inside of her throat like they normally did. Left with no other choice, Daana eased her reluctant eyelids open.

She wasn't in the middle of the glowing rune circle anymore. The painted symbol was gone, as was Whisper, and the stables themselves. The ground beneath her had transformed from compacted dirt and straw to dark, polished rosewood planks. Daylight streamed in from a stained glass window behind her, leaving a rainbow pattern on the floor where she knelt. Heat radiated from the dark wood beneath her knees and burrowed into her weary bones, banishing any lingering chill. Daana craned her head upward, studying the towering shelves of books that stretched nearly all the way to the ceiling.

The fact that she was not where she was supposed to be should have been met with more skepticism. Or at least some manner of frenzied panicking. But the sunlight on her shoulders felt good, as if it was slowly seeping all of the aches and pains from her body. She would have to search for answers eventually. But answers could wait a little while longer. For now, all she wanted was to sit and be still. Daana closed her eyes as a contented smile formed on her lips. Forget power, maybe all she had ever really wanted was peace.

Her troubles melted away as she sank deeper into the calm. In the distance, birds tweeted, grasshoppers chirped, and claws clicked lightly against the hardwood floor. Beautiful, serene sounds that melded together in—wait, claws? She started to stir from her tranquility, but her thoughts dismissed the abnormality with a gentle hush. *No, no, it's probably nothing. Rats or a cat or something. Not your concern. Ignore it. Return to your peace.*

"A library?" A voice rang out, its scratchy timbre bouncing along the shelves of meticulously arranged volumes and books. The frantic skittering of clawed feet doubled as the owner started to pace back and forth. "No, no, no, no! You got it all wrong. I'm not supposed to be here!"

Daana's eyes shot open. Definitely not a cat. She opened her mouth but the words caught in her throat, preventing anything other than a hoarse whisper from rolling off her useless tongue.

The frantic *click-click-click* of claws scraping against hardwood grew fainter as the speaker moved further away, their voice trailing after them in a high-pitched wail. "I'm supposed to be in a cottage that smells like onions and the snow's piled so high outside I can't see out the windows! There's a treetop with little paper thingies, and apples, and presents, and . . . and he's supposed to be here."

Daana scrambled to her feet. There was a disturbing lack of pain in her ribs, but there wasn't time to consider why that was so wrong. She darted down row after row of musty books before the floor opened up to an expanse of equally dusty tables. Beyond the tables was a tall, ornate mahogany desk, and beyond that, a set of imposing double doors. A small figure was braced against the right door, pulling on the brass handle with all his might.

"No, no, no." He repeatedly struck the door with his fist as he sank to the floor in a puddle of defeat, each knock growing miserably softer. "You got it wrong. I'm not supposed to be here."

Daana swallowed the lump in her throat as she inched closer. "Snag?"

Snag whipped his head in her direction. His eyes were so wide his pupils looked like tiny islands swimming in a vast sea of yellow. "Daana?"

"What are you doing here?"

He wrinkled his nose at her as if it was the most obvious thing in the world. "I'm dead. Except," his voice wavered as he lifted his chin and gazed miserably up at the towering shelves of books, "I think there's been a mix-up. I got sent to the wrong place."

"You're not dead."

"No, I definitely am. I walked into the wall of burning magic, you see. After a few sizzles and pops everything went dark and, the next thing I knew, I was in this place. Figures that you'd get sent to a tomb lined with books."

"It's not a tomb, it's a library," Daana explained.

"Well, there you have it." Snag's eyes widened as he took in the ornate ceiling with its iron chandelier and myriad of flickering wax candles. "Ain't been in one of those either. All signs still point to dead."

"You're not dead, because this is a memory. My memory." She wasn't sure how she knew that. She just did. It was as if the information had been there all along and the only thing she lacked was the ability to see it. The room in question was the Division of Divination Library—the only place she had ever felt truly safe.

Snag tilted his head at her and frowned. "How can I be in someone else's memory?"

Daana padded across the polished rosewood and settled onto the floor beside him, leaning her shoulders against the sealed door. "If it's alright with you, I'm just going to chalk it up to magic and leave it at that."

"Huh." He didn't seem to believe it but, for the sake of preserving his sanity, Snag opted to go along with her flimsy logic. "Alright. Why are we in your memory then?"

"This was my happy place." A faint smile pulled at her lips before it faded. It was starting to feel a lot less peaceful with someone else here to remind her of what she was supposed to be working through. "I used to come to the library when everything else got to be too much. I guess things aren't going too well for me out there, so the magic brought me here. Needed a quiet place to think."

"Think about what?"

Daana lifted her hands and a dazzling blue light pulsed between her palms. "This, I imagine."

Stray shimmers of ghostly light reflected against Snag's eyes as they grew even wider. "That's not yours."

"It's not. But it's what I've always wanted. At least," Daana said as her voice softened to a whisper, "I thought it was."

Snag didn't have anything to say to that, for which she was grateful, actually. The silence made it easier to process why she couldn't just reach out and seize the power burning inside of her. It should have been easy, but something was holding her back, keeping her from being everything she'd ever wanted. Weakness, probably.

"I thought it was going to make me feel something. I don't know, whole, more powerful, a little less like me, maybe?" Daana tossed the ball of light between her hands as if it were a toy. "Wishful thinking, I guess. Still me. Still miserable as ever."

"Daana, you've got to give it back. This isn't your answer. It's not going to fix anything."

Her hand formed into a fist and the magic dissipated. "Do you know how hard I've worked for this? My entire life has been leading up to this moment. And you want me to let it go? Just like that?"

"You said so yourself, it doesn't belong to you! It's not going to make you happy. Why keep it?"

The sting of ice flooded her veins. The pitch of her voice changed too. It bubbled with power straining to be released. "Because they need to pay, Snag."

"Who?"

"Everyone who's ever hurt me."

"Why?"

What was so difficult about this? Surely Snag, more than anyone else, understood what it was like to suffer at the hands of others. Revenge seemed obvious, and yet, he was acting like she was the crazy one! "Why? What do you mean why? Because they deserve it! It's time they got stepped on for a change."

"Oh."

She narrowed her eyes at him. "Oh?"

"Just doesn't sound like you, is all."

"What do you know? You don't know me."

"Obviously not." He clasped his hands together and arranged them neatly in his lap. "I thought you were a nice person."

For such a simple answer, it packed an unexpected punch. Daana opened and closed her mouth like a gaping fish, attempting to place why something so trivial stung so deep. Why did she even care what he thought? What good was being nice, anyway? She didn't want to be nice. She wanted to be powerful. Powerful people didn't have to play by the same rules as everyone else.

"Is that really what you want?" Snag asked.

"Of course it is!" Her voice sent a ripple of magic all the way to the ceiling. For a split second, the illusion broke, allowing a shimmer of blue light to peek through a hairline crack in the plaster. It was gone as quickly as it had come, neatly smoothed over until the spot looked identical to the rest of the ceiling.

"Alright then. Prove it." Snag stood and held his arms away from his body. He clamped his eyes shut with his head twisted off to the side, bracing himself for the worst. "Go on. Do it."

"I don't want to do it to *you*!"

He whipped his head back in her direction with such force, his earrings snapped in the air. Anger danced freely across his gnarled face. "Why not? I'm worthy, aren't I? I'm just as much of a shit as everyone else out there. I fought, stole, and lied my way to get where I am. I deserve to be smote as much as the next guy!"

Daana's answer blurted out of her mouth before she had a chance to consider it. "Because I like you!"

"Well, you shouldn't!" He managed a single step forward, lower jaw trembling with outrage. "I'm mean, Daana. I'm nasty. I've done shit that'd keep you up at night. I stole you, remember? And then sold you back to the same baddie that'd kept you prisoner. I knew this mission was a bad idea. At any point I could have said something, maybe turned it around, at least tried.

"But I was greedy, so I didn't. And now my best friend's dead and the only other people I care about are about to go join him. And the one thing that can save them, save everyone, is in your hands and no matter how hard I try, I can't get you to see reason. So if you're not going to do the right thing, at least spare me the runaround and kill me. I'd rather be with my family than here."

She avoided his stare, glaring at her feet so she wouldn't have to see the disappointment on his face. "I can't."

"You can't?"

"No."

"Being a killer suddenly ain't so easy, is it?" He dropped back down beside her, bony arms wrapped over his chest. "You really want to know how to make the world pay? By moving on. Live your best life in spite of what they put you through. It drives 'em mad, I guarantee it."

Daana cupped her hands together, watching the swirl of magic that pooled within her palms like liquid light. She finally had everything she ever wanted, and it was simultaneously too much and not enough. Maybe that was the true nature of power. That the more you got, the more you craved. It certainly explained a few things about Uncle Geralt. He was one of the three most influential figureheads in the entire realm and yet, he drove himself mad with an unquenchable thirst for more. Power was the only thing that ever pleased him. Somewhere along the way she must have gotten the idea that if she earned some of her own, then he would be pleased with her too.

But what was the point if it never fulfilled you? Uncle wasn't loved. He was hated, loathed, feared—by Daana herself sometimes. Is that what she wanted? For people to cower in her presence, to inflict pain on the innocent, the constant worry of knowing that someone, somewhere, was secretly plotting her demise?

"Shit." Daana stared, mesmerized by the magic within her hands. "I think I wasted my life chasing the wrong thing."

Snag snorted his disagreement. "That's a good realization to have while you're young. Means you've got time to change."

Changing meant having to admit she was wrong. About her purpose, the way she thought the world worked, about *this*. That was an uncomfortable truth to swallow.

With a forlorn sigh, Daana tilted her left hand until the magic pooled in the palm of her right. She stared at her wide-eyed reflection a few seconds more before spreading her fingers, allowing the liquid light to slide to the floor. The magic took the form of an iridescent puddle as the center gradually started to spin. It was only a ripple at first, but the more Daana concentrated on the center, the faster it whipped and whirled.

She jutted her hand in Snag's direction. "Come on."

He stared at it as if expecting her fingers to bite him. "You ain't gonna steal my soul, are you? No offense, but I saw what happened to the last person who touched you."

"I only steal deserving souls. Yours is too clean for my taste."

"You watch that smart mouth of yours, girl." Warily, Snag accepted her help. His leathery skin felt clammy against hers as Daana pulled him to his feet. He may have been scared out of his wits, but the goblin was still as dramatic as ever. "I'll have you know my soul is as scummy as the rest of me!"

She cast one final look around her, silently mourning the loss of what would never be. She wasn't Daana Lazuli any more than she was a witch. But with that pain came a small sliver of freedom. There was so much less pressure being a nobody. She probably wouldn't have long to live once she gave the power back but, for once, the future seemed more expansive than ever.

"Have you ever been a pirate, Snag?"

"Nah. Hate traveling by water. Wet, miserable stuff."

"Good point. In that case, how do you feel about land pirates?"

"Ain't that just bandits?"

Snag's grip tightened against her own the moment the illusion started to fray along the edges. Around them, the towering bookshelves caved in on themselves, joining the swirl of glowing color that lapped along the floor. "Bandits," Daana repeated, enjoying the way the word rolled off her tongue. The puddle flared white as the rosewood planking disappeared from beneath their feet. "Yes, that sounds good. I think maybe I'm going to try that next."

"How's that tie in with not hurting people?"

"Easy. I'll have a code. Steal from the rich. Feast with the poor. That sort of thing."

She couldn't be certain, but she swore she saw some of the light return to his eyes. "Now *that* might be worth sticking around to watch."

"Good. Because I'm going to need someone to teach me all the lingo."

"Like the word 'bandit'?"

With one final shimmer, the library walls vanished, leaving them in a blinding expanse of shifting white. The smell of ink and musty parchment transformed to sulfur and ash. In the distance, Daana heard the flicker of flame and faint voices calling from beyond. She took one last moment to savor the magic flowing through her veins before she stepped into the light, leading Snag by the hand as they crossed over together. "Are you sure I can't sell you on land pirates? It has so much more flair."

CHAPTER FIFTY

Tippy Top

What do you mean 'he just walked into the wall of fire'?" Rasp's voice was reaching levels of shrillness even he didn't know existed. The small stable was swelteringly hot and bursting with the stench of burnt ash and warm animal dung. The ghoulish glow of the rune circle shimmered across from him, bathing the otherwise dark enclosure in an eerie shade of bluish-gray. "Snag couldn't even hobble a few minutes ago! I had to carry him. I made jokes, some of us laughed, it was a whole thing!"

"Look, I don't know how he did it. I was preoccupied, okay?" Faris's blurry shape paced up and down the strip of dirt by the doors, adding a nice layer of dust to the already difficult-to-breathe atmosphere. "Of all the people I had to worry about walking into a burning wall of magic, Snag never crossed my mind as one of them."

"But, to be clear," Rasp said, "I was on that list?"

"Considering I had to keep you from touching the fire, yeah, you were on that list. The very tippy top, actually."

Unlike Faris and Briony, Rasp didn't actually see the moment Snag slunk inside the rune symbol. Rasp did notice the way the magic changed immediately afterward, however. A staticky *pop, pop, pop* filled the space, ricocheting from one stone wall to the next as the ring flared noticeably brighter. The obnoxious flashing lasted several seconds before the magic died back down to its original intensity.

And that was it. Snag went in, the magic went *look at me, look at me, I'm about to do something impressive*, and then nothing. Absolutely fucking nothing. Rasp found himself wishing *something* would happen. For better or worse, at least then he wouldn't have to be caught in this bizarre state of limbo, unsure of whether the invisible hand of doom would crush him now or wait 'til later.

Which, come to think of it, was probably the reason he was suddenly so dead set on picking a fight with Faris. It felt like the only thing he could do. "Keep using that tone, good sir, and you will never have the pleasure of seeing my tippy top ever again."

"That's not even a threat. That's something I would enjoy!"

"See? Even you admit it. It brings you joy."

"Oh my gods!" The holy trifecta of a simultaneous snort, hoof stomp, and ear flap permeated the still stable air. "Is this really how you want to die, Rasp? Stop twisting my words and help me find a solution!"

"How? Thanks to my stupid magic, I can't go anywhere near that thing." Briony, Rasp noted, was being unusually nonvocal. Which either meant she'd gone catatonic with fear or was in the midst of hatching a plan. For their sakes, he feverishly hoped it was the latter. "Come on, Hermit. You've got something, right? You're like the smartest person I know. Tell me our goose isn't cooked yet."

Evidently Rasp wasn't the only one feeling petty because Faris couldn't help but mutter under his breath, "I thought I was the smartest person you knew."

"Lists suddenly aren't so fun now, Dingle, are they?"

Briony spoke over them with an eerie, commanding calmness. "We wait."

"That's a terrible plan," Faris said.

"Horrible," Rasp agreed. "Looks like you're back on the tippy top of the smart list, Faris. Congratulations."

"Thank you?"

"Waiting is all we can do," Briony explained. "Daana sealed the barrier. Our only hope now is that Snag gets through to her."

"We're counting on the guy who wanted to be left inside the mountain to die? That's who's going to save us?" Oh, they were so screwed. So, so very screwed. Rasp gave the side of Faris's scruffy face a placating pat as he shuffled past, utilizing the hairline crack beneath the doorway as a guiding light. "Well, it was nice knowing you both. Take care of this one for me, Briony. Give him a little kick every now and then to remember me by, yeah?"

Faris seized him by the back of his cloak. "And where the muck do you think you're going?"

"I'm of no use here. I might as well try and go help with things outside." Rasp shrugged free of the garment, slipping away with practiced ease. Faris should have known better, really. You didn't grab an escapee by something removable. That was practically begging for a naked chase. Oh well, he'd done his best to school Faris in the ways of the unpredictable. The rest would be up to fate now.

"Come on, Dad." On command, Father descended onto Rasp's shoulder in a flurry of battering wings and sharp talons. Rasp refrained from giving him a pat too, but only because he wanted to keep his fingers. "Let's go blow the top off your mountain."

Croak.

"Gross! I didn't mean it like that, ya sicko." On the bright side, at least Rasp could die finally knowing from which parent he'd gotten his perverse sense of humor.

"Rasp, wait!"

"Sorry, Dingle. Can't talk me out of it."

"Something's happening, you idiot. Get out of the way!"

The musty air stirred as Rasp turned back to face the center of the stable. Bits of straw and dirt lifted on the current that started in slow, ambling circles near the edge of the glowing rune symbol. The loose debris pelted his skin as it wafted past. Little by little, the wind picked up speed until it churned the air with the intensity of a miniature cyclone. The magic flared, sending a torrent of hot air that slammed into him, sending him hurtling backward. Rasp's shoulders struck the wall, knocking the breath from his lungs.

Father flailed like a wild animal caught in a snare, unable to break away from where the wind pinned him and Rasp to the stone. *Croak, croak, croak!*

The raven's frantic words went unheard. Rasp's own fight-or-flight instincts were clanging like alarm bells within his head. He couldn't shake the feeling that there was suddenly something in the room that hadn't been there before. He wanted to run, to hide, to do anything other than be rooted to the spot like fear-struck prey, but no matter how he struggled, he remained pinned.

A blinding flash lit the center of the whirlwind. With a final, howling gust, the wind barreled the battered double doors wide open. The pulsing blue of the rune symbol faded to a flicker. Without the blaze to aid his limited vision, the musty stables grew dark around him. Rasp saw only two shimmering pinpoints of silver light. They lifted into the air and, with a hissing roar, ripped through the stables and out into the courtyard beyond, disappearing in a cloud of dust and loose straw.

At last, the magic pinning him in place receded and Rasp staggered free from the wall, coughing the musty debris from his lungs. "What the fuck was that?"

Father's head bobbed and dipped as he provided the answer with a series of throaty clicks.

"Don't mess with me, old man. I might be blind, but there's no way that was a dragon."

"It—it really was a dragon," Faris's wavering voice called out from among the suffocating gloom.

Figures, something awesome like a dragon appearing out of nowhere happened and he missed it. Rasp worked the tip of his pinky finger into his ear, trying to dislodge some of the loose bits of dirt and straw. "How's that possible?"

Fortunately, Faris kept his stunned answer relatively short and simple. "Daana gave back the magic. Whisper turned into a dragon."

"Oh." Too simple, it turned out, because Rasp now had a laundry list of follow-up questions. Regretfully, there wouldn't be time for anything but, "You got this from here, Briony?"

"I've got Daana and Snag," she replied. "You go do your thing."

"And you remembered what I said about Faris?"

"Yes, yes. I'll give him a kick every now and then for you."

"Remember to mix it up sometimes. He operates best in a constant state of paranoia." From beyond the battered doors, Rasp could hear the sounds of the battle raging outside. He set one foot in front of the other as he navigated the straw-littered floor. Guided by the light spilling in from outdoors, Rasp reached the open doorway and ducked through it. The air was clearer on the outside. Not by much, granted, but at least it didn't smell like donkey shit.

Faris's hooves thudded against the compacted dirt behind him. "Seriously, what do you think you're doing?"

Rasp shielded his eyes against the harsh light. The transition from unrelenting dark to the shifting hues of overcast gray was not one he was prepared for. "What I do best."

Through his muddled vision, he saw Faris's hazy shape dart in front of him. The faun's hands slammed against Rasp's chest, forcing him several steps backward. "Complaining?" Faris's voice rang out. "Getting in the way? Almost getting killed? Those are the things you're good at! Not whatever hairbrained scheme this is! You can't see, Rasp. And you barely know how to use your magic. If you go out there, you'll—"

Rasp smothered Faris's mouth with the inside of his hand. "Well aware, thank you. If you could just point me in the right direction, I'll be on my way."

And then Faris did the unthinkable. He bit down, his blunt teeth plunging into the soft flesh of Rasp's hand. "Hey!" Rasp reeled backward, clutching his wrist as a different kind of pain swelled within his rapidly beating chest. At least he could blame the water welling around his eyes on the bite. "That's my move, not yours. Stop stealing my dirty tricks."

Faris's hoof smacked against the ground, narrowly missing Rasp's foot. "You're not going and I won't let you!"

"Oh, Dingle. It's okay, you can say it. You love me."

"You are confusing love with strangulation."

Rasp said nothing, allowing a suggestive waggle of his eyebrows to do all the talking necessary.

Faris lunged at him a second time, managing to land a punch before Rasp had time to duck out of the way. "Will you stop that? Stop being you for one mucking second and think this through!"

"I have thought this through. Believe me, I had to climb a fucking mountain to get here. It would have been much easier to turn back and run. I didn't do it then. I'm not doing it now."

"So that's it then? You're just going to throw your life away?"

"Yep."

In lieu of an intelligible reply, Faris let out a gargled scream as he turned and sprinted back into the stables to go cry into his pillow or something.

"Fine! I didn't want a goodbye kiss either!" Rasp called after him as he started back in the direction of the commotion. The swelling pain within his chest had turned solid, weighing him down and rendering each step damn near impossible. *Please work*, he willed his thoughts into the empty universe, hoping something might hear his pleas and take pity on the little, insignificant speck. *Please, please, please, make this work.*

He got only a few yards out before Faris's thundering footsteps returned. The faun caught back up to him and wrapped something coarse around Rasp's waist, cinching it tight. "There." Faris gave the rope a final tug, ensuring Rasp did not have the slack necessary to wriggle it past his hips. "If you die, then we die together. Let that weigh on your conscience."

The weight in his chest burst like ooze from a lacerated boil. It was selfish to feel such immediate relief, Rasp knew, but selfish was the only way this was going to work. He threw his head back with a grateful sigh. "Oh thank gods you're such a sap."

"Wait . . ." Realization dawned upon Faris relatively quickly. By now he probably already regretted how firmly he'd secured the rope currently tethering them together. "Was all that just a ploy to get me to help you?"

A smile spread across his lips as Rasp broke into a clumsy run, pulling Faris in his wake. "Who's the idiot now?"

Faris seized the lead and corrected their path with a firm tug, shouting at the top of his lungs, "The person currently running toward the cliff edge, that's who!"

CHAPTER FIFTY-ONE

The Long Fall

Veins of black cloud wafted across the upturned ruins. The former court-yard was buried beneath fractured pieces of broken cliffside, with rifts in the ground branching like rivers around a smattering of small fires. The combination of dark magic and smoke from the explosion was aiding Oralia's current game of cat-and-mouse as much as it was hindering it. One moment visibility would be decently clear and, in the next, her surroundings would be shrouded in pitch darkness, rendering it difficult to see more than a few yards from her face.

Regrettably, she was the mouse in this particular game. Captain Monk's mangled form moved freely among the gloom, attempting to flush his prey from hiding. The only way to avoid him was to keep one step ahead, which was growing increasingly more difficult thanks to the overall lack of cover. Oralia was forced to rely on the drifting banks of smoke and ash in order to disguise her movements. Ellisar and Sascha were still with her. She couldn't pinpoint any of the others, but every now and then a familiar scent or sound carried on the breeze, informing her that the rest of her team was likely doing the same.

"Do you have a plan yet?" Ellisar hissed under her breath. She and Oralia were huddled together against a fallen boulder, willing their bodies smaller as yet another rumble tore through the mountain. A sheet of cliffside gave away somewhere behind them. The ground thundered like a stampede of elephants as loose rock and scree slammed across the open plateau, missing Oralia's position by a distance that was far too small for comfort.

"Frankly, I fail to see the point anymore," Oralia admitted. "None of the previous plans worked."

"Knock that off! I'm the morose one, not you."

Oralia didn't have the heart to argue. Surviving a few minutes more was about all she had left in her. She lifted her head and gazed out across the hazy plateau as the rumbling beneath their feet settled to an eerie calm. She'd lost track of Sascha during their last mad scramble for cover. Thanks to the gloom, she couldn't see the big lug, but her nose told her that he wasn't far.

Sascha was keeping sensibly quiet. Unlike Ellisar, who carried on in a ragged whisper beside her. "You make the plan, Rali nitpicks it to death, and I pull it off. That's how we work. Now hold up your end so I can go gut this bilge sucker."

A ragged scream cut through the eerie quiet, preventing Oralia from asking what in the world a 'bilge sucker' was. She staggered to her feet, eyes searching the shifting darkness for the source of the noise. She found it too late. The gloom cleared as a tendril of magic lifted a struggling form skyward.

Fear lanced through her as Oralia yanked Ellisar into a standing position beside her. "Who is that?"

"A dwarf," the elf said, shielding her eyes as she squinted upward. She yelped when Oralia's knee-jerk reaction was to grip her arm tighter. "Not Rali, the other one! I don't know names."

Oralia watched, horror-stricken, as the magic lifted the struggling soldier high above their heads. There wasn't time to react, to plan, to throw together a last-ditch effort to save her. Oralia couldn't even get Beryl's name out before the magic released her and the dwarf plummeted back toward the ground as a dark, fast-moving blur. Beryl's body struck the wet dirt and then went still as the last echo of her dying screams faded in the distance.

Behind Beryl's broken body, Captain Monk materialized from the churning dark. His eyes were black and he was smiling. It was a knowing, taunting smile, silently daring them to break cover and do something about it. Oralia knew better. As much as it pained her to do nothing, it was obviously a trap. Ellisar knew this as well, but evidently not well enough to care, as she was already on the move.

Oralia caught Ellisar just as she was about to dart out from behind the boulder. With both arms locked tight around the struggling elf, preventing Ellisar from breaking into a run, Oralia heaved her back out of sight. "What are you doing? Stay down!"

Ellisar tried to bite, but her teeth scraped ineffectively against Oralia's leather bracer instead, rendering the attempt not only shortsighted, but useless as well. With violence out of the equation, the elf was left with no other option but to use her big girl words—which were surprisingly less volatile than Oralia expected. "Use your eyes, idiot, and look up!" She squirmed futilely in Oralia's iron grasp. "He's about to do Rali next!"

The weight in Oralia's chest dropped all the way to her knees, nearly taking her down with it. Ellisar took advantage of Oralia's momentary stupor and struggled free. Oralia didn't attempt to stop her this time. In fact, with panic swiftly overriding logic, she found herself following Ellisar's hot-headed example and racing after her.

"Oralia, don't!" Sascha leapt from his hiding spot as she tore past. "This is what he wants!"

It didn't matter. She'd already lost Curly and Snag. She couldn't lose one more. Oralia evaded Sascha's grasping hands and forced her aching legs into a full out, desperate run. Broken ground shifted beneath her tattered boots as she charged. Oralia kept her line of sight skyward on the small shape that lifted higher and higher above her.

Ellisar sprinted just ahead of her. A wall of black, writhing cloud surged in their direction, churning the air with broken shards of rock and stone. The stench of rotten egg invaded her nostrils, spurring the bile from the back of her throat to fill her mouth as the magic drew nearer.

Lingon saw Ellisar and Oralia charge and mistook their break from sanity for the signal to advance. He ditched his cover, clearing entire stretches of stony ground in a rapid zigzag pattern as he worked his way toward Captain Monk from the other side. Focused on her and Ellisar, the captain did not appear to notice the advancing Stoneclaw warrior yet. That was something, right? Oralia was about to die, most certainly, but at least her death would not be in vain. Her sacrifice could at least afford someone else the opportunity to cleave Captain Monk's head from his shoulders.

Evidently Ellisar did not share Oralia's feelings about being the sacrificial lamb. She shouted, her ragged voice barely discernible over the roar of the approaching magic, "Up and over!"

Instinct kicked in and Oralia cupped her hands together before she had time to consider what was about to happen. Ellisar jumped and Oralia caught the elf's foot in the cradle of her hands. With a bellowing roar, Oralia heaved, catapulting the elf skyward and allowing her to sail above the wall of approaching magic. The dark wave crested over the top of Oralia a split second later, slamming her backward as hot energy crackled across her body. Debris clouded the air, lacerating her exposed skin as it whipped past, but Oralia barely felt it as fresh rage pumped hot through her veins.

Stubbornly, one foot in front of the other, Oralia pushed through to the other side. In the distance, she saw Ellisar and Lingon had reached Captain Monk. The pair danced, slashed, and weaved around him, doing everything in their power to land a blow before being thrown back by a ripple of magic.

With his full concentration set on keeping his attackers at bay, the captain could no longer focus his magic on Rali, who was now but a tiny blot against the darkening sky. The magic holding her aloft dissipated and Rali's scream grew louder as she dropped. Seized by terror, Oralia didn't register the thunderous noise behind her. She didn't feel the unnatural current that stirred the ash-laden air or the crackling blue static that buzzed overhead. What Oralia did notice was the blue-and-white dragon that surged over the top of her and spiraled upward, catching Rali in its outstretched talons.

The dragon swooped low in a rush of glittering scales and deposited Rali near the ground at Oralia's feet. She caught the dwarf on the second bounce and altered course for a section of the stone wall yet untouched by the destruction. A quick glance over her shoulder confirmed that Ellisar and Lingon had followed suit. The pair scattered for cover as the dragon dropped into a nosedive.

Oralia cleared the wall in a single bound and placed Rali gingerly onto the ground, ignoring the impulse to shake her until she answered. "Ralizak? Are you alive? Say something!"

Rali eased open one brown eye wide enough to deliver a withering glare. "That's it! My mind's made up. I'm turning to a life at sea. No more underground tunnels, or dragons, or—"

The rest of Rali's biting words were muffled by Oralia's crushing embrace.

The sounds of swiftly approaching feet drew Oralia's attention from the squirming dwarf. Ellisar and Lingon crept close to the ground with their backs bent to avoid being seen over the top of the wall. Lingon massaged the side of his face as he shot daggers at the back of Ellisar's head with his eyes. "Was it necessary to punch me?"

"You tripped me."

"Correction, I *tried* to trip you."

"Then you understand why the punch was necessary."

"Look, I saw a dragon and I reacted. It was a force of habit! I said I was sorry." The mountain man dropped down beside Oralia and pressed his back to the wall. His dirty fingertips explored the tender flesh beneath his left eye. He noticed her watching and countered her befuddled look with a question while gesturing to Ellisar with his thumb. "Are you sure that one's not part mountain folk? I thought elves were supposed to be peaceful. You know, above the pettiness of mankind and whatnot?"

"Bucko, that one is the birth mother of pettiness." Rali wriggled free of Oralia's grip and set about checking to be sure she had all of her extremities. "What does it look like out there, El? It was hard to tell while plummeting to my death."

"Whisper's got the captain on the defense for now," Ellisar replied.

Oralia forced her aching body into a crouch and watched the battle unfold from over the top of the stone barricade. Whisper rose above the clifftop and circled back, rushing Captain Monk's position. A wave of energy leapt up to meet the dragon. Black sparked against blue as Whisper disappeared into a cloud of smoke and materialized out the other end with Captain Monk in their claws. They rose high into the air, pursued by the billowing darkness that shot skyward like snaking vines in the beast's wake.

Ellisar's fingertips drummed against the stone as she cast a nervous glance at the others. "Has one of you formulated an actual plan yet?"

Lingon lifted his finger into the air and said, "I vote we let the dragon take care of it."

"Whisper can't hold the spirit on their own." Ellisar indicated an area of patchy ground coated in thick, black blood. Her words were directed at Oralia, not Lingon, as she seemed to have no desire to explain what everyone else already knew. "Your little blue devil went into the fight already injured. And the iron isn't doing them any favors. If we don't get back in there, they will soon be overpowered."

As she spoke, a burst of rock ruptured from the mountainside and shot upward in a spray of deadly stone. Whisper's silvery wings beat the air as they soared higher, forced to drop the captain in order to escape the shrapnel.

"Fuck!" The gathering grew strangely silent as every eye looked in Oralia's direction. She gritted her teeth as she worked the soreness from her fist, realizing too late that taking her anger out on the wall had been shortsighted of her. Painful, too. "The spirit is an old one, yes? A species that feeds on magic? If Whisper falls, then we have not only failed to defeat it, we will have made it twice as strong."

CHAPTER FIFTY-TWO

Thou Art Forgiven

A blood-curdling shriek erupted across the mountaintop. All heads turned as the ground split open and a second spray of iron-rich rock hurtled skyward. The shrapnel found its target and the dragon fell from the air, their glistening scales disappearing in a cloud of blue vapor as Whisper shifted forms. The fae's tiny frame broke from the clouds, hit the ground, and skidded across the wrecked courtyard.

Ellisar cursed the goddess above as she cleared the wall in a single bound.

Oralia tore after her, unsure of what, if anything, they could do. Captain Monk was closer, nearly halfway to Whisper's writhing form. He would reach the fae before either her or Ellisar. Oralia's heart drummed in her ears as she pressed her legs harder. Over. It was already over. This wasn't a last stand, it was a feeding frenzy, and she'd unwittingly provided the main course.

An eerie stillness settled over the plateau. Black and gray clouds rolled in overhead as thick as wool. And then she saw it. Barely at first, as the black-and-white bird was nearly indiscernible from the bleak sky. The raven cut through the plumes of shifting magic over Captain Monk. Its croak rang out, amplified by the stone cliffside. A surge of lightning broke from the thunderhead and struck the captain.

A voice accompanied the flash, resonating with such power it created a small mountain tremble of its own. "That's for being an insufferable dick!"

Oralia's steps ground to a halt as she stopped and turned her head, following the sound to its source. Two familiar shapes stood out against the broken horizon on the other side of the demolished courtyard. Faris, the ever-logical one, seemed to be trying to keep his partner from announcing their location to the entire mountaintop. Rasp, naturally, did it anyway.

The small man held his arms stiffly at his sides, yelling, "We haven't even got to the good part yet. I owe you for Mother, too!"

Captain Monk's body rose from the flickering flames and ash. He moved more slowly than before, his chest heaving in and out with exertion.

Oralia's panicked gaze shifted from him to where Whisper's crumpled body had been only moments before. Having taken advantage of Rasp's distraction, the fae had slipped away unnoticed. With his victim gone, Captain Monk lumbered in the direction of Rasp and Faris. He raised his hand and brought it back down, throwing a wave of rock their way.

Faris tugged the tether connecting him to Rasp. Whatever frantic words passed between them were swallowed by the distance. Rasp performed a dramatic twirl, nearly tripping over the cord that bound him to Faris, and threw up his hands in response, sending his own shockwave of dirt and stone. The two forces met in a cataclysmic slam of energy and sparks as falling rubble rained down across the battlefield.

Ellisar grabbed Oralia by the wrist and dragged her in the direction of whatever cover they could find. When the last of the debris had fallen, Oralia lifted her head from her hands and peered around their makeshift barrier. Amid the shifting clouds of dust and smoke, Monk now stood alone and bewildered. The captain looked this way and that, as if unsure where his quarry had gone.

The thunderheads parted above him, and Whisper dropped from the sky in a spiral of blue mist. The small fae whipped magic into the air, summoning a gust of wind that thundered across the plateau. The windstorm blustered Monk's mangled body closer to the edge of the cliffside. A wave of stone rose up in retaliation, but Whisper had already disappeared once more, their escape concealed by a second bolt of lightning that lanced across the dark sky like a white spear.

Oralia's sharp eyes searched the gloom, finding, at last, what she sought. Faris and Rasp had changed positions again, this time ducking behind the outer stone wall that encircled the front of the stronghold. "This way." She pulled Ellisar with her toward the nearest break in the wall.

"We've finally got a plan, then?" Ellisar panted as she raced alongside her. "Been waiting for one of you to give some fucking direction. My usual make-it-up-as-I-go strategy hasn't panned out so far."

"Rasp's magic did more damage to the captain in a single blow than all of our attacks combined, including dropping a mountain on him." Oralia followed the curve of the stone wall, ensuring she moved low enough not to be seen from over the top of it. "We find Rasp and stay by his side, protecting him at all costs."

There was no need for Oralia to voice her trepidations regarding the merits of her, admittedly, terrible plan as Ellisar graciously aired them on her behalf. "Your strategy is to stand closer to the guy actively trying to get killed? Goddess, Oralia! What's with you and incessant need to be a bloody sacrifice all of the sudden?"

"Tell me, how has stabbing the captain to death worked for you so far?"

Oralia nearly stepped on Lingon as she rounded the bend at a swift trot. He and Rali, having not moved their position since their last encounter, grudgingly formed rank. Lingon took the lead, not so much by choice, but as an alternative to being trampled underfoot. Preoccupied with keeping ahead of Oralia's thundering feet, he nearly collided headfirst into Faris, who came hurtling around the curve of the wall with Rasp in tow.

Lingon skidded to a halt. The stolac curse died on his tongue as his wide-eyed stare darted past Faris and settled on the small, filthy man desperately sucking air into his lungs behind him. Lingon's bravado failed him. He whipped around, legs springing into action beneath him. Sadly, he failed to check where he was going and, instead of taking flight, slammed into the front of Oralia, knocking himself to the ground.

Oralia barely flinched, noting the impact was akin to being body-slammed by a straw scarecrow. Not for Lingon, unfortunately, who was now curled on the ground clutching his face. "Gods dammit," he howled. "How are you still standing?"

"Lingon?" Rasp's head perked upward at the voice. He stepped closer, placing one hand on Faris's shoulder for support, as he picked his way across the swampy ground toward the source of the commotion. "Brother, is that you?"

"Uh, no?"

An unnerving smile split across Rasp's soot-caked face. "Hello, Lingon. I'm so happy we could do this before I die."

Croak! With a horrendous screech, the white-tailed raven landed between the brothers. The bird flapped its wings, hopping from puddle to puddle, as it whipped its head back and forth, berating each Stoneclaw equally.

Lingon sat up with a start, blinking the disbelief from his eyes. "Is that . . . Dad?"

Chicken Liver dipped its head all the way to the ground.

"This is where you've been this whole fucking time?" Lingon staggered to his feet, gesturing at Rasp with a wide sweep of his hand, throwing droplets of mud flying as he did so. "With him? The same fucker who killed you? We needed you here, with us. And this whole time you've been gallivanting off with our no-good—"

Croak! Chicken Liver screeched back.

Lingon's mouth curled into a snarl. Fire danced within his pale emerald eyes as he looked to Rasp and sighed. "What's he saying?"

"He says you're a sniveling coward and I have every right to wipe you from existence where you stand!"

"That's not what he said!"

"How would you know, shit stain?" Rasp challenged. "Suddenly speak bird, do you?"

"No, because I'm not a witch!"

Chicken Liver hopped between them, more frenzied than before, croaking up a storm. Oralia winced at the sound and glanced over the top of the wall at the dark cloud of shifting magic. Whisper was back up and in action, keeping Captain Monk focused elsewhere, but it would only be a matter of time before Rasp and Lingon's ruckus drew unwanted attention. Before Oralia could give the order to keep their blasted voices down, the raven quieted on its own. Its dark, beady eyes roved between the boys as it waited for its message to sink in.

The rage bled from Rasp's pinched expression. "Do I really have to say all that?"

It was not a croak that issued from the raven's tightly clenched beak, but a growl. A terrifying sound that, by all rights, should have not been possible from such a wee creature.

Rasp rolled his head back with a groan, reciting the words as though he was reading from a script. "Dad says we need to put our bad blood aside. We've all been stupid assholes to each other and all of us had a part in this mess. He says that if I was able to forgive him for what he did, and him of me, then we should stop being babies and make up, too."

Lingon appeared unconvinced. He surveyed the area around him as he spoke, as if confirming the location of the nearest escape route in the event their attempt at amends went horribly wrong. "He really said all that?"

"Does that sound like something I would come up with on my own?"

"I suppose not," Lingon admitted, reluctantly. Steadying his breath, the thin man drew himself to his full height. "Look, Dingle, about the whole leaving you for dead thing, I just want to say I was wrong and—"

Guided by Lingon's voice, Rasp bridged the gap between them and slammed his knee into his brother's groin. Lingon collapsed against him, gasping for breath. Rasp held his brother in a manner that appeared entirely too tight for either of their comfort. "There, there, ding-a-ling," Rasp said, with a few hearty thumps to Lingon's back. "Thou art forgiven. After a few hundred more of those, of course."

"Once was enough, thank you," Lingon whimpered between short breaths.

Croak!

"Calm your tits, old man. We all process our forgiveness differently, is all." Rasp released Lingon with a shove, either unaware or uncaring that his older sibling dropped helplessly into the mud for a second time. Rasp slammed his fist into his open palm with an eager smile. "Now, if Lingon's cowardly ass is here, that means those other two dingleberries are somewhere nearby. I've got so much more forgiveness to dole out."

The surprise Stoneclaw reunion had given Oralia time to reconsider parts of her current strategy. Not any of the parts involving sacrifice, regrettably. She turned to Ellisar to deliver a new set of instructions. "Gather Mul and Sascha. The three of you stick close to Whisper and keep the captain from getting too close. Rali, Lingon, and I will handle Rasp and Faris. We have a better chance of wearing the captain down for a fatal blow if we alternate strikes."

"That's not fair! I want Ellisar on my side," Rasp protested. "I've seen Lingon with a bow. He couldn't hit the broadside of a mountain."

"You want to see me hit the broadside of your face with my fist?" Lingon called from the ground with his knees still pulled to his chest.

Rasp crossed his arms and rocked back on his heels with a scoff. "And how do you propose you do that, Dingle? Are you going to restore my eyesight first?"

"Oh my gods." Faris looked to Oralia, his ears twitching as his face grew ashen. "I thought one was bad, but now you've given us two of them. Why's our side have to have two? Two, Oralia! They have a better chance of killing each other than they do Monk."

Rasp rested his elbow on Faris's shoulder in a gesture that was entirely too casual given the circumstances. "For the record, I could totally kill Lingon with my eyes closed. Right here. Right now."

"You're blind!" Faris said. "Whether your eyes are open or closed is irrelevant."

"Exactly. I'm that good. But I'm not going to, because I'm a reformed person and all that other shit you taught me."

Oralia watched Ellisar slip away as soundless as a shadow, wondering if perhaps she had made an error in judgment after all. Behind her, Rali's baritone voice stifled the argument that had broken out between the Stoneclaw brothers. "Alright, that's enough lip from you two swabbies. You can kiss and make up later. For now, get your blasted heads in the game. Faris, you just keep doing what you do best and keep bucko alive out there. We've got your back. The moment Monk gets too close for comfort, we'll jump in and draw him away. Now, Dingleberry Number Two, you got any more of those nifty fire arrows?"

Lingon gathered his feet beneath him, mindful to place Rali between him and Rasp, and stood. He took a quick inventory of his quiver before delivering his grim answer. "Well I *had* five, until some sticky-fingered elf helped themselves to my stash. I hope this plan of yours works just as well with two, because that's what we've got."

"We'll have to ration them then. One arrow per strike. The good news is you won't have to worry about hitting the target so much. Just so long as you get the flame near him. Our fire elemental here can take care of the rest."

"Hear that, Lingon?" Rasp grinned. "You don't even have to be accurate. Finally a job that fits your skillset."

Rali slammed a sturdy hand to Lingon's chest before he rose to what was undoubtedly a challenge. The impact nearly floored the poor man a third time. "I feel like this shouldn't need mentioning, but given the complicated history between you two, I am saying it anyway. *Do not* shoot bucko. No matter how much you think he might deserve it. Clear?"

Lingon muttered his reluctant agreement.

"Righty-ho then! Now that we've got that settled, time to set sail, my hearties. Time's a wastin'! We can't let Whisper do all the work here. Team Breakfast, break!"

"We get breakfast?" Rasp looked oddly hopeful for someone who had clearly already accepted his grim fate.

"No."

He trudged after Rali, grumbling, "A break, then?"

"That was your break."

"How about a nap?"

"When you're dead, bucko. When you're dead."

"Can I use you as a pillow?"

"I see no reason why not. I should be dead, too, by then."

"It's settled, then. Faris, you get to be my blanket."

"I don't want to be your dead blanket. I want to be on the other team. And alive, preferably."

Rasp reached out and patted his friend's shoulder as they followed the curve of the outer wall. "You don't get what you want."

"I know. I never do."

"Except me. You can have all of me."

"I can barely handle the amount of you I have now."

Rasp carried on as if he hadn't heard, throwing his arms wide. "All the way from my tippy top to my bitty bottoms."

"I take back everything nice I ever said about you."

CHAPTER FIFTY-THREE

Bottom of the Well

Her unfocused stare drifted along the edges of the dark, musty chamber. The thick blanket of fog that hung heavy over her mind filtered out most of what was going on. Occasionally, she felt the ground tremble or heard a muffled boom from beyond the pitted, gray stone walls, but these were nothing more than background noise. She felt a warm pair of calloused hands grip either side of her face.

"Daana?" The voice sounded distant, as if it were coming from the bottom of a well, calling upward. Or perhaps it was *she* who was at the bottom. That would at least explain the impossible darkness and the unrelenting pain that coursed through her leaden bones.

The hands let go and her head sagged to the side. There was another form beside her, she realized. Their poor, ragged shape looked as pitiful as she felt. Her thoughts transformed into slow, slurred words that slipped from her tongue like molasses. "Did you fall down the well, too?"

His sad, yellow eyes shifted in her direction. "Not far enough."

"I don't remember getting here."

"Probably better that way."

"Are you Daana?" she asked. "I keep hearing that name. I think someone up top is looking for you."

"That's your name."

She scrunched her nose at the thought. "No, I don't think so."

"Oh?" he said. "Then what is it?"

She searched her mind before settling on the obvious answer. "Tadpole."

He produced a sort of sharp, barking laugh. The effort must have been painful because his weary face flinched immediately after, and went pale. He saw her notice and tried to smile around the pain. His mouth cracked open, revealing a set of needled teeth. "Alright, Tadpole. I think it's time to come out of the well. Are you ready?"

"No," she said, feeling a sudden drop in her stomach. "It's not very nice out there. The world is big and cruel. Your whole life everyone tells you to be something great. To rise above any challenge and make something of yourself. I tried. And you know what I learned? I'm not great. I barely pass for ordinary. Nobody warns you how hard it is to be ordinary."

That other voice was back, the soft one. It called from above so lightly, she barely heard it. The voice said, "Tilt your head back, Tadpole. You have to drink this for it to work."

Her companion in the well was watching something above them, beyond the muddled dark. "You're not ordinary," he said.

"Yes, I am. I had the chance to be something magical." She leaned her head back against the cold stone siding. She could just make out a blurred shape as it grew steadily closer. "I have been chasing that dream for so long, that when I finally got it, I realized it wasn't what I wanted. Not really. It's what other people wanted for me. They pushed it so much that I thought if I made them happy, I'd be happy too."

Something pressed against her lips and a foul syrup trickled over her tongue. It tasted like burnt tea leaves and shoe polish. She swallowed, gagging, as it burned like liquid fire on its way down. The tonic hit her stomach and spread like raging wildfire to the rest of her extremities. Daana's drooped eyelids snapped open as the fog hanging over her thoughts burned away in the heat.

Briony knelt before her. The edges of her eyes lifted with relief. "Welcome back, Tadpole."

Daana found Snag propped against the wall beside her. His leg was heavily bandaged and the exposed skin on his face and arms had a sooty, singed look to it. He raised his hand meekly, gesturing to the leather satchel resting near Briony. "She's out of the well. I'll take that back now."

The faun flicked her ear at him as she maneuvered the bag further out of reach. "I think it's best if I hold onto it for the meantime."

Daana rubbed the soreness from her face, which succeeded only in spreading the pain like warm butter on dry toast. "I'm afraid to ask what happened."

"According to Faris, you were attempting to channel the magic from a powerstone back to the wind shifter it belonged to." Briony dutifully filled in the blanks. "And then somewhere along the way, you thought about keeping it for yourself."

Daana's heart lurched. She glanced down. A pale opal hung from a chain around her neck, empty.

"You gave it back," Briony continued, glancing across at Snag. "With a little help."

He stared upward, purposely avoiding eye contact. Snag's voice was as empty and brittle as a dried husk. "I want my bag."

"Oh, I heard you." With a snort, Briony slung his leather satchel over her shoulder and stood. "And if you ask again, I'll call your warrior sisters in here and tell them what you're trying to do. Would you like that?"

His frown deepened around the edges, but Snag, wisely, said nothing.

"Good. Now if you'll excuse me, I want to see for myself how truly fucked we are." Briony's hooves thudded against the dirt floor as she strode to the entrance and eased open one side of the battered double doors. She poked her head around the corner, allowing a heavy plume of smoke and ash to drift in from the outside.

Daana placed her hand on Snag's tattered shoulder. "Thank you."

He lifted his hand and rested it over hers, continuing to stare at the cracked ceiling without speaking.

"I'm going to join Briony," Daana said. "If you need anything, just ask."

His voice was small and pitiful, like a moth with a broken wing floundering mere inches from the flame it so desperately wished to reach. "She took my knife, too."

Daana rose on stiff legs, offering him a sympathetic smile. While she might have told him to ask, she had the sense not to promise to fulfill his request. "Between the three of us, it's probably best that she has it. I saw her threaten someone with a weed once. It was as confusing as it was terrifying."

Limping, Daana joined Briony at the door, and together they gazed out across the hazy, ash-riddled courtyard. Tiny fires dotted the open plateau, weaving in and out between the scattered piles of broken cliffside. Distant flashes of light broke through the gloom on the other side where the battle still waged.

"Can you sense anything?" Briony asked.

Her sixth sense was still raw. Daana winced as she held her trembling hand upward and closed her eyes, feeling for the familiar vibrations of magic. The darkness hit her like a punch to the gut. Daana stumbled backward, gasping. "It's too strong."

"Who is? Monk? But it's one against," Briony paused, furiously counting on her fingers before giving up. "I don't know how many, but at least two of those are magical!"

Daana closed her eyes again, processing what her instincts were picking up. Two additional energy signatures thrummed within her mind. The blue aura was concentrated in a single area, its edges ragged and fading. The second source of magic, a vaporous cloud of yellow, was stronger but stretched too far and too thin, like translucent paper. "Whisper's magic is faint. And Rasp's power isn't focused. It's too spread out. Even together, it won't be enough."

Briony paced back and forth along the straw-littered ground. She mumbled and muttered as she worked through what appeared to be several scenarios in her head at once. Daana remained stationed between the stable's double doors, mindful not to get in the faun's way. Briony was speaking far too quickly for Daana to catch any of what was said. Not that it would matter, anyway. Her sluggish thoughts were still playing catch-up with everything going on.

"The spell!" Briony said with a snap of her fingers. She produced a tiny green notebook from the inside of her vest and furiously flipped through the brittle pages at rapid speed. Finding what she sought, Briony approached with the open notebook in hand, tapping the inked symbol she intended to use. "This one."

Daana was more focused on the book itself than she was the symbol. "Why do you have my spellbook?"

There wasn't time to hear Briony's answer. An icy chill lanced up Daana's arm, warning her of oncoming magic. She turned to see a building wave of lethal shrapnel hurtling in their direction. With only seconds to spare, Daana slammed the double doors shut. The debris struck from the outside, sending shockwaves shuddering through the tiny stable's stone walls. Wave after wave pounded from the outside, each surge thankfully less powerful than the one that preceded it.

"Considering the lot of you left me high and dry after the whole mutiny thing, you should be happy I had the forethought to loot through your stuff!" Briony had jumped into position beside Daana after the first wave hit. Her cloven hooves bore deep trenches into the compact dirt as she fought to keep the doorway shut, shouting over the din, "Which you're welcome for, by the way!"

Several shakes and trembles later, the protesting double doors fell still once more. Briony turned and slumped against the aged wood, panting, "Just look at the damn book already and tell me if it'll work."

Daana took the spellbook from her, studying the page. Her answer, alas, was not the breakthrough Briony was hoping for. "A seer's trap only works on lesser witches. It would hold the captain for a few minutes, at best."

"Long enough for you to drain him?" Briony ventured. Her amber gaze lowered to the pendant hanging around Daana's neck. "We've got an empty powerstone."

Dread settled into the pit of her stomach. Freeing Whisper had taken its toll. Attempting a second extraction would come at a hefty price. "Theoretically, yes, I could. But how would we get him into the trap?"

Snag's harsh voice cackled from the other side of the stable. "You need bait."

He started to rise, but a forceful stomp from Briony's hoof discouraged him. "No! You, stay where you are. We have this handled, thank you." She turned back in Daana's direction, murmuring, "He's right. How do you feel about standing in the center and batting your eyes at Monk?"

"I can't sense the captain anymore. The dark entity is in control, not him. We need what the spirit wants."

"Which is?"

"Magic."

"Alright then. Let's get ourselves some magic." Briony edged one of the doors open and cupped her hands to her mouth. "Faris, in here! We need you!"

From the outside, Daana saw a flash of blinding light, followed by a thunderous boom. Two dark shapes, backlit by a raging blaze of orange and red fire, bounded in through the doors. Faris immediately sought the wall, his barrel chest heaving with exertion. "Please tell me one of you is ready to switch off. Monk seems to have it out for us."

"You're not the one he's aiming for." Like Faris, Rasp's body was coated in a thick layer of dark gray soot. If Daana hadn't known any better, it would have looked as if the pair had gone into the chimney sweep business. Given their bleak expressions, they probably would have preferred it.

"Yes, Dinglehead," Faris said, tugging the tether that connected them. "But whatever hits you is hitting me, too!"

Briony grabbed Whisper's water pail and a fistful of straw and then, first checking to be sure the area was clear, bounded out into the open courtyard. Red liquid sloshed against the wooden sides of the bucket with each jostle and bounce. "I'll draw the symbol," she called over her shoulder to Daana. "Be ready for my signal."

"Where are you going? Briony! Briony, wait!" Faris whipped his head in Daana's direction, horror etched across his smoky features. The faun's nostrils flared with each wheezing breath. "Signal for what?"

"So, we have a plan." Daana couldn't hold Faris's unrelenting stare for long. She dropped her gaze to her trembling hands, clasping one over the other as she outlined the gist of the idea. "But it involves using you, Rasp, as bait. You'll probably die. Or, at the very best, get hurt really badly, but—"

"Sounds lovely. What do I do?"

Daana never knew quite what to expect from Rasp as far as reactions went, but it certainly wasn't outright acceptance. His willingness should have come as a relief, and yet, the queasiness raging inside of her somehow worsened. "We're making a seer's trap. All you have to do is lure the captain into the circle. Once he's stuck, I'll drain him of the spirit's power."

Faris flicked his ears at her with a snort. "Won't that get Rasp stuck, too?"

The words came from her mouth automatically, as if she wasn't the one speaking them. Shock, she realized, had a funny way of protecting the mind that way. If one didn't fully grasp the reality of the situation, then perhaps the inevitable wouldn't hurt nearly as much. "I mentioned the dying part, didn't I? I'm not going to sugarcoat this. It will most likely kill you. Me too, probably." She lifted her eyes to Rasp's grim face. "But nothing else has worked and at the very least, maybe we can weaken it."

He stared somewhere above her head. Not necessarily in deep thought, but some sort of state of mind that kept him from shouting "Pass!" at the top of his lungs. Rasp's answer was remarkably soft. "Okay."

"Okay? What do you mean, okay?" Faris's response was, in contrast, not soft. It hit hard and loud, threatening to bully the both of them into reconsideration. "No, not okay! I've been running my ass ragged keeping you alive out there. You think I'm just going to stand back and let you sacrifice yourself for a plan that might not even work?"

In what Daana suspected was supposed to be an act of compassion, Rasp reached for Faris's shoulder but missed terribly.

"What is with you and touching my face?"

A wry grin pulled at the corner of Rasp's mouth. "Hush. This is the part where I promise tender sweet things to you. None of which I mean, of course. Because I'm about to die and don't have any obligation to fulfill them."

With an infuriated grunt, Faris slapped the hand away and barreled into him. It was not an attempt to throw Rasp to the ground, as Daana first thought, but a rather violent-looking hug. Faris buried his face into Rasp's shoulder and mumbled something she could not hear.

She turned away, allowing them to say their farewells in semi-private. Daana returned to her post and peeked through the crack in the double doors. Briony was forty yards out, scuttling close to the ground as she dragged a handful of straw behind her in fast, slashing strokes. She would duck, occasionally, as a blast of magic flung various debris—rocks, tree branches, a cursing dwarf—from the other side of the battlefield.

Behind her, Daana heard Rasp say, "You're still naming the dog after me, right?"

Faris's voice came out muffled. "You'll be lucky if it's a goldfish. Raspberry the mucking goldfish!"

". . . Figured it out, did you?"

"Your brothers are Lingon, Mul, and Bil. You call each other a shortened version of Dingleberry. It really wasn't that hard to piece together."

From the outside, Briony stood and waved the painted straw frantically overhead. Daana passed her a nod of acknowledgment before turning to Rasp and Faris. "That's our signal," she said. "You two ready?"

"No. How could we possibly—for muck's sake!" Faris shoved Rasp away in disgust, furiously wiping his face with the back of his torn sleeve. The action succeeded only in smearing the dark soot across his pale face. "Did you just lick my eyeball? What is wrong with you?"

"For good luck." Rasp pulled Faris by the tether as he picked his way toward Daana. "Alright, Dingle. Get me to the trap and then you run, got it? I want you halfway down this mountain by the time the captain reaches me. And, Daana?"

"Lick me and I'm smacking you."

"Stand back. If we're going to die, then we're doing it in style."

The air stirred around her ankles, picking up bits of hay in its wake. Daana ducked out of the entryway as Rasp threw his hands out in front of him. The double doors ripped from their iron hinges with a deafening screech and tumbled across the open yard as effortlessly as dry leaves in the wind.

"That's just not fair," she grumbled.

"What the fuck are you lot doing? You realize you just announced your location to the whole bloody mountain, don't you?" A willowy figure materialized from the surrounding smoke, hurtling toward them at an unfathomable speed.

"Hello, El!" Rasp greeted cheerfully. "Sorry, can't talk now. Daana's sending me to my untimely death. Punch the others real hard for me, won't you? You know, as a goodbye and all that? Anyways, gotta go!" Without further explanation, Faris broke into a fast run, tugging Rasp by the rope lead behind him.

When Ellisar's bewildered stare shifted in her direction, Daana merely gestured over her shoulder into the stable. "Snag can fill you in."

Ellisar's dull eyes grew wide. Wordlessly, she ducked around Daana and disappeared into the space where the double doors had previously stood. Snag's harsh voice rang out seconds later, caught somewhere between a whimper and a scream. "Oh dear gods, let go! You're not supposed to be the affectionate one. It's unnatural!"

CHAPTER FIFTY-FOUR

Brace Yourself

Daana watched Rasp and Faris from the doorway. The pair raced across the open lot with a sort of practiced precision that suggested running for their lives had become an everyday occurrence. To Faris's apparent horror, Rasp wasn't finished making his presence known. He placed his fingers between his teeth and let out a blasting whistle, followed by a shout in the stolac tongue. A black-and-white raven swooped from the surrounding cliff and shot overhead toward the far end of the lot, where the battle still raged. Daana could pick out Oralia's hulking shape among the others. The protector seemed to realize what was about to take place because she threw the nearest warrior over her shoulder and scrambled for cover.

The raven passed over the top of Captain Monk and let out a harsh *croak!*

Rasp raised his hands over his head and brought them down in the direction of the raven. A crack of lightning broke from the thunderheads above and struck the area where Monk stood. The blinding flash subsided and the battered captain emerged from the smoldering ash at a headlong charge. Faris wrangled Rasp into position only steps from the edge of the seer's trap. The faun unfastened the lead and, with a final dismayed glance over his shoulder, bolted for the distant tree line beyond what remained of the crumbling curtain wall.

There was something to be said for silence. The quiet transcended spoken word. Daana had read many a legend that told of a single hero who stood alone, in the face of evil, quiet and accepting of their fate. The silence was stoic. Respectable. A concept completely foreign to Rasp, who taunted the oncoming entity with a slew of colorful epithets. "You want me? Then you better come fucking get me, you bastard!"

Dark coils of magic streamed from Monk's mangled form as he pounded across the battle-torn yard. Rasp lowered his shoulders in anticipation. Yellow magic pooled at his feet as he gathered his strength for the impact. Whatever attack Captain Monk was expecting, it was not the lack of one. He slammed into Rasp, and their magic flared in great swirling clouds around them. Through the churning debris, Daana saw Rasp wrap his arms around Monk's body. He pulled tight, forcing the captain's feet to lift from the ground, and then stepped back. The seer's trap flared around them as great shafts of light and dark shot skyward.

Daana raced across the slippery ground, clutching the empty powerstone to her chest in one hand with the other extended before her. She burst through the wall of dancing light, screaming as the waves of magic rolled over her. The skin on her arms burned as if it were touched by flame. She dropped to her knees and wrapped both arms around Monk's leg and hugged it to her chest.

"*Exhaurire!*"

Dark magic surged through her hands and up her arms in a torrent of blistering heat. It ripped through her flesh, running rampant through her veins in its search for a hold. The poison pooled in her chest and, for a split second, she thought her heart would burst. And then the stone reacted. The heaviness in her chest eased and she gasped, pulling cool air into her lungs as dark magic arced across her skin. With Daana's body serving as a conductor, the powerstone pulled the dark entity into itself.

Captain Monk struggled against Rasp's grasp as waves of dark energy poured from his body. The magic whipped the air like a whirlwind, testing the invisible walls of the spell that caged it. From the corner of her eye, Daana saw the light of the seer's trap begin to flicker and fade. The dark entity was too strong. Already, the symbol was beginning to chip away at the edges.

Whisper materialized outside of the deteriorating ring from a cloud of blue smoke. The mahogany cloak clasped around their shoulders shifted to black as they staggered closer. Dark blood speckled the ground with each pained step. Whisper's silvery eyes took in the scene in a single, worrying glance.

"The symbol!" Daana shouted over the raging din. "It won't hold."

"Daana, I don't know who you're talking to, but somebody do something, please!" Rasp screamed. "I can't hold him much longer."

"It's panicking." Whisper locked eyes with her. "When the trap fails, the spirit will abandon the vessel and seep back into the mountain. It will go dormant again. Is that not what you wish, child?"

"Fuck no!" Rasp said. "We're finishing it right here. Once and for all."

Whisper pulled a thin knife from their cloak and drew it across their wrist. Their dark blood fell faster, spattering the dirt in a continuous circle as they limped the length of the symbol. With the ring complete, the fae dropped to their knees and marked the ground. Whisper's fingers moved to place the final strokes, but hesitated. "This is a blood spell. It will be enough to hold, but it comes at a price. Whatever enters the ring cannot leave until my spilt blood has been repaid tenfold."

Daana glared at them. "That spell wasn't in the notebook!"

A half smirk pulled at the fae's mouth. "And give you the means to trap me? My dear, I am not an idiot."

"We're not getting out alive. We get it. Just do it!" Rasp managed between gritted teeth.

Whisper pressed their scaled hands to the ground. Gradually, one painted stroke at a time, the seer's trap flared blue. Daana, mesmerized by the shifting spell, did not see the oncoming rush of magic until it was too late. A wave of dark power crashed into her, forcing her toward the edge of the circle. She dug the tips of her boots into the slick dirt for traction, still clinging to Monk's leg with all the strength in her hands.

"It's pushing me out!" The magic hurtled her toward the section of the seer's trap yet untouched by Whisper's spell. "Seal it! Whisper, hurry! It'll lock me—"

Monk slipped from her grasp. In a swell of crackling energy, the darkness rose before her and slammed Daana backward. She slid across the upturned ground, fingertips bleeding as she clawed at the soil for a handhold. Something solid caught her from behind, preventing her from crossing the painted symbol. A pair of crushing arms hoisted her upright and with a single, agonizing step, propelled her forward. The swell of dark magic engulfed them, whipping at Daana's unprotected face as it tried to force them into retreat. Stubborn, her rescuer edged another step closer into the circle, and then another.

"Brace yourself," Oralia's ragged voice rumbled in Daana's ear. "When the next wave subsides, we rush the center together."

Daana braced her legs against the onslaught. Her knees trembled, threatening to give out beneath her. Her skin felt raw and blistered, and the heaviness in her chest weighed her down. As the last of the swell thundered past, Daana, at last, caught her breath. A roar rippled through Oralia's chest as she hooked her arms under Daana's shoulders and charged. Behind them, the final piece of the seer's trap flared blue. The circle glowed, channeling skyward in a great beacon of shimmering light.

"Keep a hold on it, boy. We're almost there," Oralia roared as she closed the final stretch of ground.

"Not helpful!" Rasp stood with his back arched and sweat pouring down his dirtied face as he strained to contain the struggling captain. "And where the fuck have you been anyway? Enjoying a nice break while I do all the heavy lifting, is that it?"

"Stopped for tea, actually."

"Well you'd better have brought me a scone! One of the good ones. With honey and lemon, none of that raisin crap."

"If I ever come across pastries made of fruit excrement, I vow to purchase you all of them."

"No, see, that's what I *don't* want you to do!" There was the briefest of pauses before the fury on Rasp's tightly clenched brow lessened. "Oh my gods, that was your attempt at a joke, wasn't it? I swear, it is so hard to tell with you."

Daana bridged the last step on her own. She leapt onto Monk's back, locking her arms and legs around him like a spider. Her fingertips dug into his writhing flesh as the familiar crackle of magic jolted through her aching bones. The entity tried to slam Daana backward, but Oralia braced against her. The orc threw her arms wide, locking the four of them together in a crushing embrace. Oralia and Rasp shouted nonsensical things about breakfast back and forth to one another as the hum of magic grew louder in Daana's ears.

She clamped her eyes shut and channeled her concentration on draining every last ounce of magic from Monk's withering flesh. He was losing strength, she could feel it. With every strand of energy she siphoned from his body, he grew weaker. The connection didn't hurt as much this time. Whether this was a testament to an increase in her pain tolerance or if her body had simply given up on deciphering new pain from old, she wasn't sure. She could feel the weight of the powerstone grow heavy around her neck. It pulled at her like an anchor, weighing her down.

"Rasp?" Oralia's gruff voice rumbled deep in her chest. Wedged firmly between Monk and Oralia, Daana could feel the protector's words rattle against her cramping shoulders.

"Unless the next words out of your mouth are 'you're doing a fabulous job, I'm rethinking that statue,' I don't want to hear it!"

The protector's steady voice did not match the rapid drum of her heartbeat. "Tell me that is you lifting us from the ground."

Daana's eyes shot open. She tilted her head in order to look down as dread dropped into the pit of her stomach like a stone. True to Oralia's word, they were now hovering several yards above the glowing seer's trap. While Whisper's spell kept them from breaching the circle, it did not limit how far they could go above it. Billowing clouds of dark smoke wafted below them, propelling them nauseatingly higher.

Rasp's foot searched the area around him for solid ground. "Ah, fuck."

"Steal any more of my power, little elf, and there will be nothing to hold you." The voice that came from Captain Monk's mouth was not his own. It was like ice down Daana's spine.

"Daana," Oralia said through gritted teeth. Daana could feel the orc's arms shake from exertion. "Do not stop."

The voice was in Daana's head now. **Your heart races, child. But it is not from fear. You desire a power of your own. I can give you everything you wish and more. You only have to say yes.**

A pang of remorse flickered in the back of her mind. Despite her efforts to snuff it out, the idea wrapped like creeping vines around her inner thoughts. Not again. She'd already turned down unfathomable power once this day. Was it necessary to go through the heartache a second time? "I'm not a witch," Daana whispered, her own voice foreign to her.

I can make you one.

A future flashed before her eyes. Daana walked the streets of Sunstorn with her head held high. The crowd jostled for a chance to see her. She was loved. She was revered. She was everything she ever wanted. Everything that her parents had been denied. Daana Lazuli, Director of the Division of Divination. She did not have to die alone as a nobody on a forgotten mountain. She could live on, remembered forever as the most powerful witch the realm had ever seen.

Everything you have ever wanted.

"I'm not a witch!" she screamed. "I will never be a witch. I don't want to be a witch! Because a witch can't do what I can do, and what I can do scares you. And if I can scare you, then I'm something better!" She gripped Monk tighter, willing the stone to drain faster. The spirit ripped and clawed at the air, spiraling in great gusts as it attempted to scatter. The air dropped out from under them. They plummeted toward the ground as the last of the spirit seeped into the powerstone.

Her excitement turned to ash on her tongue as Daana glanced down, realizing the rapidly approaching ground was still a very, very far ways down. "Rasp, do something!"

Rasp threw his head back, chanting, "I hate the ground, I hate the ground, I hate the ground!"

As far as spells went, it was probably the most nonsensical one Daana had ever heard. What was even more nonsensical was that it worked. Below them, yellow magic sprang from the ground like shafts of sunlight peeking through the clouds. The soil split open into great, stony chasms. Centuries of dirt and rock shifted away as slabs of buried stone lifted into the air. The largest rose up to meet them faster than anticipated. Daana gritted her teeth as her feet struck the boulder and shockwaves of pain rocketed up her legs.

Oralia recovered first. Heaving to her feet, she tucked both Daana and Rasp under each arm and took a running start. She sailed through the air and landed on the next closest boulder, rocking back on her heels in order to stay balanced. The rock trembled beneath their collective weight. Above them, the top stone listed downward. Oralia jumped an instant before it collided with the second.

Before Daana could register the landing, they were plummeting through the air to the next platform. Chunks of broken stone rained down above them. A rock struck Oralia's shoulder and knocked her off balance. She fell, still holding them. Oralia slammed into the lower boulder on her back. Their weight tipped the stone and in the next moment, all three of them slid over the lip into a free fall. Daana hit the upturned ground and bounced, landing on top of Rasp, who cushioned her fall in the same way a birdcage might catch a sack of potatoes.

She eased her heavy eyelids open and screamed. With the spell broken, the airborne boulders were hurtling down toward them.

Rasp shoved her off of him and threw his hands into the air. His magic flared once and then sputtered out. "Fuck, fuck, fuck!" he shouted. "Come on, not now! Not when I need you."

A buzz of yellow arced between his hands as the closest stone struck the ground beside them with a squelchy thump. It bored a hole into the upturned dirt nearly a foot deep. Cursing, Rasp threw his hands high over his head. Power sprang from his palms in the shape of a dome and shielded the three of them from the falling boulders. The heavy stones rained down on top of them.

Boom! Boom! Boom! Each thunderous strike caused Daana's heart to jump out of rhythm. The waves of magic pouring from Rasp's hands began to flicker and fade. Around them, the shield shrank. It grew smaller, smaller, smaller, as the giant slabs of stone shifted precariously closer.

Rasp's voice was weak, like a whimper. "I can't hold it."

CHAPTER FIFTY-FIVE

Heartfelt Jealousy

The magical barrier steadily closed in around them. Oralia squeezed Daana to her side, huddling against Rasp as the space inside shrank smaller and smaller. Rasp held his shaky arms aloft, struggling to keep the dome above their heads. One by one, the yellow sparks raining from his hands fizzled and popped until the individual lights dimmed into empty nothingness. With a groan, the heavy boulders shifted a few inches closer.

They would be crushed the moment Rasp's magic subsided. Judging from the violent tremble overtaking his body, it would not be long. The question in Oralia's mind was no longer "What would Rasp do?" but rather "What would Faris do?" Unfortunately, despite her best efforts, Oralia was still not entirely sure what it was Faris actually did.

"Rasp." Oralia's grave voice echoed softly against the dome of fading magic. "Do you remember when we were trapped in the cave? And how Rali made us tell our version of the afterlife?"

"That's the last thing on my mind right now!"

"If we are to die, then it is only fair that someone tell you. You poked fun at Faris's version of the afterlife, but you misunderstood. It was never about dinner. It was about being with family."

"You've met my family, Oralia. They're horrible. An afterlife with them would be worse than the seventh realm of chaos." The yellow dome grew tight around them. Its shimmering walls waned in brightness. Rasp braced against it, his arms trembling. "I know you think this is supposed to be encouraging, but it's not. Get to your point!"

And they called *her* dense. "He meant you, boy! Family is not forged by blood, it is whom you choose."

Perhaps it was false hope, but the magic appeared to burn a little brighter than before. Oralia continued, attempting to mask the panicked desperation that flooded her insides. "He could have picked any family supper. He picked the one with you." It was a good start, but she needed her point to hit harder for this to work. "The fact is, even now, in the face of certain death, he still picked you. I reached the circle only steps before Faris did."

Rasp's dirtied face was bathed in flickering, warm light. Some of the tension in his gritted jaw lessened. "I told that fucker to run."

There it was—the last, small glimmer of hope. Oralia seized it, knowing that even if she was grasping at straws, at least she would go out having tried. "Faris is waiting for you on the other side as we speak. If you want to see your family again, then get us out of here!"

Rasp's voice was small. "I don't know how."

"How you have always done it. You make a choice. Are you just going to sit here and die? Or are you going to fight for what you want?"

He rose to his knees as the light from his hands crackled and popped before it died back down to a simmer. Rasp's rigid shoulders drooped. "I meant how do I not fuck it up again? Like the last one? Everything I've ever wanted has gone to shit."

The stones shifted lower as Oralia considered her answer. She, more than most, understood what it was like to sabotage her deepest desires. Friends, family, the stupidly handsome fuckmate who should have given up on her years ago—quitting before she had a chance to ruin everything a second time was, admittedly, the easy way out. The true challenge came from picking up the pieces and attempting to make something whole from the mess she'd made.

The answer she gave Rasp was as much his as it was her own. "It will never be easy, but the most any of us can do is try."

She waited, breath drawn, watching as the dwindling magic faded more and more. Tears filled her eyes at the realization that it simply had not been enough. She'd tried. She'd fought tooth and nail to earn her second chance. To restart. Do things right this time. Gods, she hoped they would know that and, in time, forgive her for falling short one final time.

Daana had been silent throughout the exchange. From the hollow look in her weary eyes, she appeared to have come to terms with her fate. With a forlorn sigh, the elf rested her hand on Rasp's knee and whispered, "It's okay if you can't manage this, Rasp. Really. Just remember, Faris will always have Briony."

Rasp flinched at her words. "What?"

Oralia tilted her head back, caught in a swell of absolute awe as the dome pulsed with new light. This was what Rasp responded to? Not heartfelt encouragement but sheer jealousy? Oralia prided herself on rooting out one's inner motivations, but it was clear now that she'd been working Rasp from the wrong angle. "A true friend," she agreed, awarding Daana a look of commendation. "I think I saw them holding hands."

"No, you didn't! You're just saying that to make me mad. And even if it was true, I wouldn't care, because whatever makes him happy makes me happy! Which, by default, means I'm Faris's best friend, and that's something Briony will never have the privilege of being!"

Shimmering gold and yellow light reflected against the stony ground with twice the intensity as before. Oralia offered a shrug, realizing too late the effort was wasted upon Rasp as he had no way of seeing it. "In that case, I suppose there is no harm in describing the way they were gazing into one another's eyes with heartfelt longing."

"If you're going to go that far, then you might as well tell him about the kiss," Daana added. "Absolutely stunning. I've never seen such unbridled passion before. I think I overheard Faris whisper something about finally having someone else to share his bed with."

"They were not doing any of that! And don't think I don't know what you two are doing!" Rasp staggered upright, snarling, "And, no, before either of you say anything, it's not working, either. My magic is back because it's my choice. Just like I'm *choosing* to save your asses right now. Not because you're manipulating me into being jealous of Briony—who is not in a relationship with Faris, by the way!"

Magic pooled at his feet as Rasp raised his quaking arms high over his head and braced his shoulders for the final push. He paused, rasping, "Not jealous. My choice. Everyone got that?"

"Yes!" Oralia and Daana said as one.

"Because I am a good person who is in touch with his stupid feelings!" Rasp threw his head back with a scream as a wave of magic surged from beneath him. Like the glowing power pouring from his flesh, his words too, erupted from his mouth unhindered. "Except the ones about magic, because they still confuse me! And I don't know how to admit this, but I think maybe I like being a witch. But if I say it out loud, it means I've been wrong this whole time and I'm not sure my ego can handle that. And I don't know why I'm saying all of this right now, but neither of you are going to tell a soul!"

A channel of blinding magic shot above their heads. With a thunderous crack, it struck the boulders and disintegrated the stone to dust. Rasp stood tall in the center of the blaze of shimmering light. The crackling buzz was deafening. Daana huddled closer against Oralia as they waited for the onslaught to subside. When the magic faded, Rasp collapsed over the top of them. His chest heaved in and out with each labored breath.

"You did it!" Daana sat upright and squeezed him.

Rasp planted his palm against Daana's face and searched for Oralia with the other. His voice was ragged and came between wheezing gasps of breath. "I'm serious, though. Not a word to anyone."

With her chin tilted upward, Oralia watched in awe as the surrounding blue ring grew noticeably dimmer. The thick clouds of dust shifted direction on the breeze and began to settle outside of the circle in great sheets of brown-red sediment.

"The blood spell is broken," Daana remarked as she gazed around them with wide, brown eyes. "I don't understand. Surely there hasn't been enough blood spilt between the three of us to fulfill the atonement."

Rasp provided the answer, his voice somewhat muffled considering Daana was still holding him uncomfortably tight. "Whisper never said it had to be our blood."

"Oralia." Daana's gaze shifted from the sky to the ground. A layer of powdered rock coated the inner circle, obscuring the shapes beneath. She found her answer regardless, half buried under a shattered slab of bloodied stone several yards away. "Did you drop Captain Monk while we were airborne?"

"Kicked, actually. As hard as I could after that first stone broke our fall." Oralia eased onto her back and stared upward at the churning sky, wearily. She had considered shouting something about avenging Curly, or all of those that had suffered at the captain's hand, but, in the end, all Monk truly deserved was to die as he had lived—completely unnoticed by those around him.

"Oh my gods, you used him as a blood sacrifice!" Rasp wriggled free of Daana's grasp and lunged for Oralia. He squished the orc's face between his hands like very unamused putty. "I like you so much more this way."

She clicked her tusks at him. "Release my face."

"You're right. I really should be doing this to Faris." With a final, patronizing pat to her cheek, Rasp rolled away. He attempted to jump to his feet, lost his balance, and then staggered a few steps before righting himself and starting off in whatever direction he happened to be facing. "Dingle!" he called as his small form was swallowed by the billowing clouds of dust and ash. "Where in the realm are you? That ugly face of yours isn't going to smoosh itself, you know!"

From the corner of her eye, Oralia saw Daana collapse into the rubble on her back, too weary to move to a more suitable location. The elf reached for the powerstone hanging from her neck and held it over her face. The gem was black as ink and moved with a life of its own. Daana's lips parted, but the words were replaced with a sudden, harsh gasp. Her hand spasmed, dropping the stone on her chest as her fingers curled into a trembling fist.

Every muscle in her back screamed as Oralia pushed herself into a sitting position. "Daana?"

The elf's eyes were wide and unfocused. What had started as a small tremble quickly transitioned to full-body shakes. "My arms," were the only words she was able to get out before her eyes rolled upward.

Black, branching lines snaked up Daana's arms from her wrists to her inner elbows. Oralia's stomach lurched, nearly upending itself, as she peered closer, realizing the dark veins were wriggling like leeches beneath the elf's skin. "Help!" she shouted at the top of her lungs, afraid to tear her gaze from Daana for even a second. "We need help!"

Footsteps pounded against the buckled ground behind her, nearly drowned out by the sounds of several voices shouting at once. She swore one sounded like Faris, screaming something at Rasp, but the words simply weren't clear enough to hear. Oralia gripped Daana's shoulders, offering soft words of encouragement as the commotion around her muddled to a single, humming drone.

The wind picked up, blustering the lingering smoke and ash from the plateau. It cooled some of the heat radiating from her sweat-soaked forehead. A shaft of sunlight broke through the cloud coverage just as help reached her. Someone grabbed her arm and tugged in a misguided attempt at aid. Oralia, whirled around, snarling at them to leave her be and assist Daana instead.

She found herself face-to-face with Rali. The dwarf's mouth was open wide and she was gesturing wildly, but the hum in Oralia's ears was making it impossible to understand what Rali was so worked up about.

"I need Whisper," Oralia said. "Find me Whisper!"

At last, Rali's booming voice broke through the static in her ears. "That's what I've been trying to tell you. Look up, dammit!"

A dragon with shimmering blue and white scales swooped low overhead. It dove so close, Oralia was forced to duck to keep from being swept up in its powerful draft. The dragon glided over the demolished courtyard and snatched Rasp in its outstretched talons before spiraling high into the sky above her. A glimpse of sunlight caught the beast's scales, casting a prism of rainbows across the land, before Whisper disappeared into the clouds.

Ahhhhhh!

"A hhhhhhhhhhh!"
Little bird.

"Ahhhh!"

Little bird!

Rasp wasn't even conscious of the screaming. It was simply a part of him now. A function that operated independent of his control, much like breathing or blinking. Although both of those were growing more difficult at the moment, considering how far Rasp assumed he and Whisper were from the ground. He regretted telling the ground he hated it now. As it turned out, the air was far, far worse.

It was impossible to determine how high up they were. He squirmed in Whisper's grasp as he twisted his head from side to side, trying to make out something other than the unrelenting grayish-white light around him.

Little bird, stop thrashing. I am weary. Were you to drop, I fear I would not be able to catch you before the ground broke your fall.

Rasp complied, not out of obedience but because the air was suffocatingly thin and his head was getting woozy. Not wanting Whisper to mistake him for the cooperative type, he switched from struggling back to shouting. "Why are you doing this? Put me down!" was what he meant to say. In reality, it came out sounding more akin to the brays of an inebriated donkey.

Whisper seemed to understand the overall sentiment despite its lack of coherency. **In case you have forgotten, you and I struck a deal. While recent events may have caused a temporary disruption in your training, you are still my apprentice. And you will accompany me wherever I go until you have reached your potential.**

"Then take me home. You can train me there!"

Your home is in ruins.

"Not that one! The real one. With Faris and his family." The whole dragon-plucking-him-from-the-ground thing had really thrown a wrench in his plans. He and Faris would return to Lonebrook and spend the next few weeks in a drunken haze as they tried to forget everything they'd been put through. Afterward, Rasp would swear off the drink forever and go back to working on being a better person. Maybe even a better witch, if he felt so inclined.

He'd planned a whole dramatic speech and everything! Unfortunately Whisper had reached him before Faris did. The next thing he knew, he was swept up into the frosty air, being dangled over the passing landscape by a set of massive dragon claws.

"Take me to Lonebrook." Rasp felt the slow trickle of exhaustion working its way through his battered body. His eyelids grew heavy as his leaden arms sagged lower and lower. It was only once his limbs had ceased their futile struggling that he became partially aware of the strange squiggly sensation taking place around his neck. It felt like something was alive and moving beneath the skin.

Gritting his teeth, he chalked the sensation up to delirium and persisted. "Take me back and I will learn everything you want to teach me there, I swear."

Is it your wish to endanger your family?

"Oh come on! I'm not that bad with magic."

That is the first place the realm will go looking for you, little bird.

Oh. He hadn't thought of that. Still, it would have been nice to have at least been consulted before being whisked away into the sky without warning. "You could have at least let me say goodbye!"

You said your goodbyes *several* times.

"Yeah, but those were before I survived all the stuff that was supposed to kill me." It was a losing argument and Rasp knew it. As much as he wanted to continue debating with Whisper until he was blue in the face, there wasn't any point. His consciousness was slipping. More and more, the need for sleep pulled at him, dragging him kicking and screaming into a restless slumber.

Just as his weary eyes closed and the dark embraced him, a panicked croak erupted near his ear. Rasp's eyes fluttered open, barely conscious of the sounds of furiously beating wings as a raven struggled to keep pace alongside him. "Find Faris," he said. "Tell him to go home and stay there."

Croak?

"And when he refuses, help him find me."

About the Author

Anna Orr is the author of the Silver Curse series, which she originally released on Royal Road because she had a passion for writing but no idea what she was doing, neither of which has changed. A resident of the state of Alaska, Orr spends her free time shoveling snow, baking, drawing, and catching more fish than her husband.

DISCOVER
STORIES UNBOUND

PodiumAudio.com